The Invisible Reich

Kenneth Allan Pazder

DISCLAIMER:

This is a work of fiction. Resemblance to reality, including but without limiting the generality of the foregoing, real people, places or events is entirely coincidental. This is a story to promote awareness of a hidden, but ubiquitous war taking place against millions of non-human creatures on the planet every day – nothing more, nothing less.

978-1-7753309-2-9

Published by: Tarot and Chi Publishing Inc.,
1460 – 800 W. Pender St.,
Vancouver, BC,
V6C 2V6

2018 first edition

This book is dedicated to animals everywhere –who make the world a far richer place than Midas ever could.

The greatness of a society and its moral progress can be judged by the way it treats its animals. —**Mahatma Gandhi**

CHAPTER 1

Declaration of War

Death comes in many forms.
    None are good.

This one was a tall, black clad soldier who looked like he stepped out of a Call of Duty video game. Lithe and muscular, he moved like a great cat, with no wasted movement and little sound. The university laboratory's security would present no problem. He had easily disabled the archaic alarm system, which was installed when the George Regis University Dental Lab was built in the early fifties.

The night was particularly dark, ink black even, with no clouds or moon to be seen. Only a few distant stars would bear witness to these unfolding events. The dental lab was located on the northwest section of the campus tucked in among some mature dogwood trees and a stand of overgrown Virginia creepers. At this late hour it was deserted, or should be.

Behind drawn shutter blinds, ugly florescent lights burned on the third floor. On the ground, shadows moved across the backdrop.

The black-clad figure deftly picked the lock on the building's back door and entered the dark hallway. Inside, there was no sound. Only the faint red glow of an exit sign provided an outline of a staircase leading to the higher floors. The soldier reached into his knapsack for his night vision goggles, which he pulled on, then carefully began exploring the ground floor. He stopped dead still every few seconds, listening for the slightest noise.

His crepe-soled combat boots made no sound as he moved, and he had methodically wiped them on the mat before entering, so no footprints would be left behind. No one would ever know he was in the building unless he wanted them to. On the second floor, he searched the hallway end-to-end to ensure that no cleaning staff or security guards were present. He painstakingly repeated this sweep on the third floor until he was positive that the only people in the laboratory were himself and the people he was searching for.

The soldier had re-conned the building for several days before this night and was certain that no one but he and his target would be present. Still, after tours of duty in Afghanistan and Iraq he had learned that death can come quickly when even the smallest things are left to chance. In the business of war, no surprise was ever a good surprise.

The soldier clicked the mike button on the ear buds connected to his Blackberry Z30 and whispered, "Anything?"

"All clear in the neighborhood," came the reply.

"Roger that."

The lab's old wooden door was locked. He had expected it would be. Its slightly cracked glass pane was covered on the inside by a blind pulled almost all to the bottom of the frame. Almost—but not quite. He removed the goggles and leaned down for a look. There was enough light in the lab for him to see what was happening. His blood froze. His eyes narrowed to dark slits and his breathing slowed almost to a stop. However, his resting heart rate of fifty-five beats per minute did not change. He had seen all kinds of shit before, but it usually involved people.

His trained eye took in the whole gruesome scene in a quick panoramic sweep. There were three operating tables, with a surgeon standing near them. She was clad in standard green operating scrubs, masked and gloved, holding a bloodied scalpel in her left hand. Strapped onto her forehead was an ocular device with a bright LED light attached. A machine resembling a miter saw stood nearby on a cart. On either side, two O.R. nurses, one male and one female, both similarly attired, waited. The soldier guessed the surgeon to be early forties and the nurses maybe a decade younger.

On each operating table lay a dog. The first was a jet black German shepherd who had been placed flat on its back. The soldier knew enough about the breed to note that pure black was a highly unusual color for this formidable canine. Its jaws were pried wide open with a vice-like contraption and it appeared that several of its teeth lay in a tray off to the side of the operating table. The second dog was most likely a Wheaton/Cavalier mix and was positioned similarly to the German shepherd. Unlike the shepherd, however, a new set of implanted teeth had been set into its jaw. On the third table lay a Bassett hound. The soldier felt certain the Bassett was dead.

Blood spattered into the metal pans beneath each operating table.

The dogs' tongues hung grotesquely out the sides of their mouths, but the shepherd's eyes were open. The Wheaton had a huge gash cut out of the side of its throat. The soldier knew that would allow the surgeon to cut into its jaw to extract a bone sample for analysis at another lab. The surgeon had apparently not gotten to this stage with the shepherd. When the procedure was completed, the dogs would be killed and dumped into the bio-waste disposal chambers for incineration—the soldier had little doubt about that.

Between the noise of the ventilators and the outdated air conditioning units in the windows, the soldier picked the lock to the laboratory without being heard. He slipped on a black silk balaclava, drew his silenced, Glock 20 automatic and calmly stepped into the room.

CHAPTER 2

Last Mission

"Shoot them, Master Sergeant! That's an order!" shouted the team leader.

"What?" Pearce shouted back. "Are you kidding me?"

Lieutenant William James Kellen, a hardass combat veteran of twenty years, leaned his face into Pearce's. "No, I'm not fucking kidding, soldier. I said shoot them—take them out!"

Pearce looked at the three civilians cowering in the makeshift hut of scrub and conifer branches—a terrified Afghani mother, maybe twenty years old, and her two kids, a boy and a girl. A pathetic trio caught in the crossfire between competing forces in the rugged mountainous terrain.

"Look." Kellen still shouting. "It's them or us! In maybe twenty minutes a gang of Al Qaeda fighters will be all over us and they will make these *Hajis* talk and then kill them anyway." He looked toward the trio in disgust. "Either way they're dead!" He wondered if he was getting through. "If we kill them and hide the bodies, we've got a chance that the Al Qaeda outfit won't twig to us and maybe, just maybe we get out of here in one piece."

Pearce glanced at the small family. "There's got to be a better way Sir," he said. "They're civilians. How about we tie them up and maybe hide them…"

Boom! A couple of mortar rounds went off in the distance. Boom!

"Tie them up with what? Half our gear is back *there*." Kellen pointed in the direction of the explosions. "Again. Even if we found something to tie them up with *and* hid them, either Al Qaeda finds them, makes them talk and kills them or *nobody finds them* and they end up starving." He wasn't backing down. "Like I said. Either way, they're dead."

"All due respect, sir," Pearce answered, "I'm not killing three non-coms!"

"Well then…" Kellen reached for Pearce's Kalashnikov, but Pearce was quicker than he was.

"And neither are you!"

Kellen violently pulled his arm away. "Get your hands off me, soldier, and I mean NOW!" He was eyeball to eyeball with Pearce. "Don't you *ever* fucking put your hands on me or you'll be looking at a court martial or a bullet up your ass!"

Pearce released his grip, but his right hand was poised to draw the Glock.

The two warriors glared at each other, both ready to kill each other, despite being on the same side.

A few tense seconds crawled by. It seemed like an eternity. Neither man dared to blink. The small Afghani boy started to cry, his terrified mom trying desperately to hush him. She prayed that two foreign devils didn't kill them all. The boy's cries were enough of a distraction to break the stalemate.

Pearce took the initiative. "Look, Lieutenant, we each grab a kid. Their mother can run on her own. She'll slow us down some, but she's young. She looks like she can keep up."

Kellen looked at him as if he was crazy. "I've been in the field twenty-two years, on tours all over hell and back and I'm damned if I am dying for a few worthless *hajis*." He sneered at the civilians.

"Nobody's going to die," said Pearce forcefully, "if we can just get the fuck going!"

"Ah, shit." Kellen looked skyward, thoroughly exasperated. He reached for the girl, a four-year-old with jet black hair and big, green eyes, but she recoiled and clung to her mother. "What the…"

Pearce held up his hand. "I know a bit of Farsi, I hope she understands *for her sake*." His Farsi was indeed minimal and halting, but he gave it a shot. "Look, you … ah, come with us now. No… hurt you, but … Al Qaeda… coming, kill you." Pearce said slowly. He was struggling with the language and hoping like hell he wasn't too far off. More mortar rounds went off in the distance. It was like the enemy was randomly shelling the area just behind them, but they were closer now, than before.

The mom, Anoosheh, covered her eyes with the palms of her hands like she was trying to block out the whole world. Her husband was dead. Two soldiers were holding their lives by a thread. What was the right choice? The soldiers had been arguing, and still were. The one who had tried to speak her language, his eyes were so cold. She looked for a sign, any sign. Then she noticed that the soldier with the eyes of ice wore a small, Kunzite pendent set in silver around his neck. It was an Afghani talisman of good luck and purity from ancient times. Her name, Anoosheh, also meant good luck. Just like the pendent. It just *had* to be an omen! She pushed herself. "Decide now, or die."

Speaking slowly enough in Farsi, she hoped the soldier would understand her. She communicated that she and her children would come along with the soldier. "Please don't hurt us," she added.

She got through. Pearce nodded, reassuringly as possible, given the circumstances.

Kellen had spotted something in the far distance with his binoculars. A dozen Al Qaeda fighters appeared on a rocky ridge, maybe a mile due south below them. Shit! They were way closer than either man had thought. They needed to buy some time and fast. He told Pearce what he'd seen.

Pearce signaled Anoosheh to take her kids *over there* and put his hands over his ears to show them to do the same. He grabbed the M107 sniper rifle from its dirt and watertight carrying case and started pulling pieces out—lightweight bolt carrier, rear grip, monopod socket, scope rings, rear sight, muzzle brake... "A hand, sir?" he asked Kellen, who quickly turned and pulled the detachable bipod and spiked feet from the case and handed them to Pearce. The Lieutenant snapped the ten-shot magazine into the rifle. The fifty-caliber, high-velocity, armor-piercing shells could penetrate damn near anything short of double-reinforced tank armor.

Pearce attached the bipod and feet to the rifle, gently settling it on a tree stump for stability. Taking a small brush from the case, he meticulously cleared every twig and piece of dirt from the stump. Ever the perfectionist, he produced a soft microfiber cloth from the drag bag cleaning kit and rubbed it over the scope lens with great care. Time was short and it would be a tough shot at the best of times— almost a mile, but he had actually made tougher ones on occasion.

"Wind?" he called.

"Not much, maybe three clicks eastward," replied Kellen, grabbing the azimuth chart.

"Distance?"

The range finder binoculars precisely indicated 1,655 yards. Kellen called out that number.

Pearce adjusted the Leupuld scope to correct for a roughly

2.2-second drop and about a half-meter side swerve. Traveling at 850 meters per second—far faster than the thundering sound which would follow soon after, the M33 high-velocity ball cartridges would take just under two seconds to reach their targets. Pearce clamped a set of noise protectors that looked like headphones over his ears and adjusted the recoil pad. The Long Range Sniper Rifle, called the "LRSR," was a monster by any calculation—no ear protection, you go deaf. No recoil pad and correct positioning, you get a broken collarbone from the recoil generated by 55,000 pounds per square inch of pressure in the chamber.

The late afternoon light was still sufficient. Sky was clear. He motioned Kellen to put on his ear protectors and raise his binoculars.

The first target appeared in his scope—a rangy, bearded fighter, maybe in his fifties and brandishing a rifle, appeared to order the others about. A second target about two meters to his right was operating a portable radio. A third man behind the first two had a couple of rocket-propelled grenades slung over his neck. Pearce sighted a half a dozen more fighters, all carrying Kalashnikov's.

Although the magazine was preloaded with eight shells, Pearce estimated he could get off three or four rounds max, before the noise caught up with the destruction and everyone hit the dirt. He would pump out a few more for good measure, but wasn't likely to hit anyone. With any luck he thought, touching his Kunzite pendent, the armor-piercing bullets would blast right through the targets and hit some of the others in the rear. He re-sighted on the first target and took a slow, deep breath. The enemy had stopped to ascertain the most likely path the intruders had taken, so for the moment they were not advancing.

Per standard procedure, Kellen would call the numbers and Pearce would fire, then swivel the long gun on the bi-pod for the next shot.

"Ready?" Kellen asked, raising his binoculars.

"Ready," replied Pearce as his index finger caressed the sensitive trigger. He flicked the safety off and lay flat on his stomach, barely breathing now, heart rate steady at fifty-five. The air was dead still. Anoosheh, her little boy, Daryoush and her daughter, Ronak were ten meters back, hands over their ears.

"Fire one!" commanded Kellen.

KA-BOOM! The first slug tore through the muzzle at lightning speed. Recoil was fierce, but Pearce fought it. Red hot gases blew out from the muzzle brake on the barrel opposite Kellen.

Fire two! Fire three! All three sizzling projectiles were off and running. In five or six seconds the terrifying thunder would reach the fighters. No more time to sight properly. Pearce squeezed off three more rounds BOOM, BOOM, BOOM. That's all the time he would get. Quickly he disengaged and pulled back the rifle for dismantling. Kellen would report on the damage. Pearce's job was to get the gun apart fast.

When a bullet is traveling almost a mile, even the slightest miscalculation can cause a miss or a near miss. The first was a near miss. The armor-piercing slug failed to hit the target chest but got him in the shoulder, spinning him like a rag doll and removing most of his shoulder in the process. His disconnected left arm went flying into the bushes. He would be dead from shock in minutes.

Target two fared even worse, if that was possible. The shell hit him directly, blowing a gigantic hole in his chest, hurtling him backwards as if he had been hit by a speeding Mac truck. Target three had moved a bit. The bullet took off his right hand at the wrist, hitting one of the RPGs in the process and setting it off. The rocket-propelled grenade hurtled into a nearby stand of fir trees and exploded into a huge fire ball, knocking down most of the remaining fighters who clutched at their ears to block out the deafening blast—but it was too late for that. Yet the gods of war had smiled upon them, because the severe jolt from the grenade blast had saved at least three fighters from rounds four, five and six from the LRSR which harmlessly slammed into the ground where they had been standing.

The carnage was massive. No sooner had the men noticed that their leader's shoulder was blown clean off, when the radio man went somersaulting backwards as if by magic. A split-second later the combatant holding the RPG lost his hand and only *then* the deafening booms of the heavy gun resounded, alerting the men that they were under attack. The RPG then tore into the conifers and pine trees, breaking all hell loose. Flames and smoke swooshed into the sky. Then three more thunderous booms were heard. At nearly a mile away, no muzzle flash could be seen. The sound of gunfire at that distance was of no help to the fighters in trying to determine its origin.

The remaining eight fighters had grabbed their weapons and were firing blindly in all directions. Kapow, kapow, kapow! Rat-a-tat-tat-tat-tat-tat...an Uzi was emptied in the general direction of Pearce and the others, but the bullets fell far short. One fighter even fired an RPG into the mountainside, but his aim was far from Pearce's location. This added to the confusion. Pearce, Kellen and the family took off a mile and some, up the gorge.

Pearce hoisted four-year-old Ronak on his back. She was serious as a judge. Her forty pounds, together with the LRSR at thirty pounds and his own gear totaled close to a hundred-pound load. Ronak was a gem though. She didn't wiggle or even cry.

Kellen had three-year-old Daryoush, whom he carried on his chest, the boy's arms wrapped around Kellen's neck and feet tucked into his bandolier. With weapons and the rest of his gear, he was also lugging some ninety-five additional pounds. No problem however. Their grueling physical training at Dwyer Hill allowed these guys to travel all day and night with the extra weight if need be.

Anoosheh however, was not holding up as well. Her thin sandals were soon tattered and a strap broke, forcing her to run barefoot over the stones and rough terrain. Her feet were now bleeding and bruised and she slowed measurably. Darkness was almost upon them now, but they could not stop. It was at least another ten miles before they could get to a safe rendezvous point in Jalalabad and that seemed like ten thousand miles at the snail's pace they were now traveling. At this rate, they would be caught within an hour by the rest of the Al Qaeda fighters, whom they had to assume, were still tailing them.

No way could they survive a fire fight with these three in tow. Finally, they stopped near a gorge overlooking a large black lake, the full moon reflecting itself languidly in the centre as darkness had fallen. Both Pearce and Kellen were dripping with sweat and each gingerly plunked a kid on the ground. Pearce handed Anoosheh three protein bars from his pack and walked Kellen a few meters away out of earshot, even though no one in the family likely understand more than a word or two of English.

"Not good," grumbled Kellen. "Those bastards are going to catch us." He examined his Kalashnikov AK-47 assault rifle and counted the number of magazines of ammo he had left. Although the team had access to the latest, most sophisticated weapons in existence, in jungles and other inhospitable terrain they usually opted for the basic Russian military rifle invented by the late Russian Army General Mikhail Kalashnikov, for whom it was named. Perhaps not as quite accurate as the top end military rifles, its reliability was legendary among soldiers the world over. It was practically jam-proof. Clog it with dirt, sand, mud, drop it in water—it didn't matter. It worked anyway. In a fire fight, a soldier armed with a high-end M-16 assault

15

rifle that wouldn't shoot died sooner than planned when facing off with an AK-47.

"You're right," replied Pearce, looking Kellen straight in the eyes. His withering stone-cold gaze had returned, causing even Kellen to involuntarily shudder. "Keep going with the family to the rendez-vous point and I'll meet you there. I think that the kids can walk the rest of the way, but you'll have to carry Anoosheh at least some of the distance." Pearce's voice was dead calm, as if he were commenting on the weather.

"Shit," said Kellen. "Why the hell I let you talk your CO into this in the first place is a goddamned mystery—for a fuckin *haji* family no less!"

"Should I go with the family and you meet us at the rendezvous point sir?" Pearce was blatantly rhetorical.

"Don't be a smart ass, Master Sergeant," the lieutenant said. "You're the best goddamned mop-up guy I've ever commanded."

Pearce went back to Anoosheh and tried in his best Farsi to explain that Kellen would take them to safety and he would meet up with them later. He took his knapsack, two extra mags for the Glock, a silencer, Ka-Bar 1255 black combat knife and a couple of ninja throwing stars, something he always took ribbing for from the team, but he'd be damned if they didn't come in handy on occasion.

The LRSR was too heavy to carry further–and not particularly useful at night, so he buried the $16,000 rifle, minus the firing pin, which he threw away. No sense in arming the enemy if they happened to find it.

Anoosheh gingerly climbed on Kellen's back putting her slender arms around his powerful neck. Daryoush and Ronak were each given a knapsack to carry. Then Kellen grunted and waved for the kids to follow him. When he turned around Pearce had already vanished into the night.

One lone JTF2 ranger against maybe a half a dozen heavily armed, seasoned Al Qaeda operatives––and in their own goddamned back yard no less. What the hell were the odds of Pearce surviving *that* Kellen wondered. He contemplated it for a minute or two. "Fifty-fifty" he decided, knowing Pearce. He was one dangerous son of a bitch.

CHAPTER 3

You Can Take the Boy Out of Alberta, But You Can't Take Alberta Out of the Boy

University of Alberta Law School was more than a full-time job for Kenneth Joseph Ares Pearce (or "KJ" as he was dubbed on the courts). Although he was a bright and hardworking student, like most twenty-something males, his time was often occupied by sports (he played second string point guard for the U of A Golden Bears), drinking (while watching sports with his buddies) and of course there was the sport of pursuing female students (like Kiara, his uber gorgeous classmate who had no interest whatsoever in sports or jocks).

When he wasn't on court practicing so he could make first string or watching Monday night football or Hockey Night in Canada with the guys, he taught a self-defense class on campus to help pay for his tuition and books.

There had been a wave of sexual assaults on the sprawling U of A campus over the last fifteen months and no arrests had been made thus far. The rapes naturally caused the female students and professors to feel insecure. A carry permit for a concealed handgun was almost impossible for a civilian to obtain in Canada—even in Alberta, a province well known for hunting, so a solid alternative was a good self-defense course. Pearce was a natural-born teacher. His roster of a dozen students was invariably booked up.

His grandfather, Captain Joseph Ares Pearce, had spent many years in post-war Japan as an Army translator for the U.S. Marines. While in Japan he became friends with Daiki Tanaka, a sixth Dan Aikido master who, in an extraordinary gesture of comradeship had agreed to train his *gaijin* student in this deadly art. KJ's dad, Lieutenant Leonard Joseph Ares Pearce, in turn, had been Joseph's first and only pupil for almost twenty years. It was inevitable, then, that from an early age, KJ began playing at Aikido with his dad, Leonard, and took to it like a duck to water. Normal father-son roughhousing

17

was soon replaced with wrist locks, throws and leg sweeps which often went from dawn to dusk.

There was no mom to balance things out—not that she would have tried to anyway. Leonard's bride, Corporal First Class Andrea Pearce (nee Demicchina), was a black belt in karate and would have encouraged her son every step of the way and then some. Tragically however, Andrea would never get to see KJ grow up. She was killed by an IDE road side bomb while on patrol in Afghanistan with the U.S. third infantry. KJ was only two at the time.

Shortly after the death of his wife, Leonard, a dual U.S.-Canadian citizen, returned to Canada where he was stationed at Griesbaugh Barracks, an army base in Edmonton. By age ten, KJ had entered local martial arts tournaments in Alberta, aided and abetted by his father. In his teens KJ was winning provincial contests, and by eighteen he was fighting on the U of A martial arts team and kicking ass for Canada in competitions all over the continent. He was often described as the "ultimate competitor" by teammates and opponents alike. He was seemingly unfazed by bad calls, biased refereeing, injuries, cheating opponents, hostile crowds and pretty much anything else.

In typical Canadian fashion, KJ flat-out nixed that characterization. "I just don't want to let the team down," he said, unknowingly quoting, almost verbatim, Lynne Jones, the gold medal Canadian Olympian.

CHAPTER 4

Hunting Al Qaeda

Moving like a wraith, Pearce left Kellen and the Afghani family. He disappeared into the Afghan dusk without a trace, which was doable because he felt completely at home in the wilderness—any kind of wilderness. In his teens, he had spent many a season with his dad in the numerous climes of Alberta, Canada—harsh, sub-zero winters in the Rocky Mountains, hot summers in the Badlands, windy, bright springs in the prairies and picturesque falls in the endless spruce forests. He learned to track deer and cougar, a painstaking process requiring the patience of Job. He had to learn to invisibly blend into any kind of scenery night or day.

One summer night he spent almost five hours in complete stillness, channeling his *chi* to become one with the bushes in which he was hidden. He was patient like a cat and did not move, while remaining calm and alert hour upon hour—all this to spot a magnificent male cougar on the prowl that he had been tracking for several days. Suddenly the big cat appeared as if out of thin air. KJ carefully raised his hunting rifle, sighted for the cougar's right shoulder…ever so softly caressing the trigger. Sensing him, him the cougar stopped in its tracks and began sniffing the air. Its dark, feral eyes turned directly toward Pearce, who was perhaps a hundred and fifty yards away and completely invisible to the naked eye, human or cat, even in the bright moonlight.

The cat may not have been able to see him but surely knew he was there. In this muted light, Pearce could sense as much as see the great cat's *presence*. His martial arts training had included the study of *chi*, sometimes called life force—the ethereal, omnipresent energy which connected everything and everyone in the delicate and intricate web of life. Being able to sense *chi* in certain circumstances was a significant advantage, particularly when the other was outside of one's normal sensory range.

He inched the barrel to sight on the cat's head. The cougar remained still as stone—as if waiting, daring him even.

"Gottcha," whispered Pearce. He pretended to pull the trigger.

The impressive male cougar shook his head from side to side as if to dismiss the amateur marksman, and then disappeared into the forest. The cat would live to hunt another day. The Al Qaeda eight would not be so lucky. They had spread out twenty to thirty yards apart, covering a breadth of nearly two football fields. By employing this tactic, the wily operatives could cover a wide swath while avoiding being gunned down at once by a surprise machine gun attack or an RPG strike.

On the other hand, a well-hidden adversary could be overlooked in the space of twenty or thirty yards, especially if he could literally dissolve into the surroundings. The terrain of northeastern Afghanistan heading toward Jalalabad was mountainous and rocky, with no shortage of boulders, caves, ledges and craters. Pearce had dug himself into a rock formation of three huge boulders near the opening of a small cave. The cave mouth was just big enough for one man to squeeze in so he reckoned that should the nearest adversary pass by he would check out the cave but just walk by the boulders.

Pearce was right. The stocky fighter passed him not more than two feet away, peering into the darkness of the cavern. K-bar in hand, Pearce moved swiftly, plunging the blade into the man's neck as he clamped a gloved hand over his mouth to muffle any scream. The K-bar sunk in four inches. The man bit hard on his gloved hand once, then went limp. Pearce pulled out the knife, turned the fighter over and slit his throat. When found, the corpse would let the other fighters know a similarly gruesome fate would befall any of them foolish enough to continue on with the pursuit. Pearce tossed the Kalashnikov and slunk back into the shadows. The others would take a few minutes to notice that their comrade was not communicating and that would offer another opening.

As darkness was almost upon them, he slipped on his night vision goggles and screwed the silencer on the Glock, then settled back into the small boulder formation and waited. Five or six minutes later, two fighters warily approached, softly calling, in Farsi, "Faisal, Faisal, are you here? Faisal..."

Phut! Phut! From his hidden vantage Pearce shot them both. Two head shots, two dead. After each man collapsed to the dirt, Pearce waited patiently for a trailer. Thirty seconds, sixty seconds, two minutes... Then he heard it, a combat boot softly crunching the coarse sand. No voice, no calling card. The man stepped cautiously, but with purpose, his Kalashnikov held at shoulder level, finger on the hair trigger, sweeping the barrel from side to side.

Pearce would have to kill him instantly, before he got off a burst and the others came running. He had to think fast. Grabbing one of the dead soldiers he had stuffed under some bushes, he dragged the body into the open face down and placed the K-bar into the man's right hand, squeezing his fingers around it. Pearce then laid down, pulling the corpse over himself, and positioning the knife to make it appear that the combatant had stabbed Pearce but also had been killed in the process.

He focused his *chi* on stillness, breathing steady—heart rate at 55 bpm. He slowly withdrew a ninja throwing star from his belt and waited. The seconds crawled by like hours. A breeze rustled the bushes and a scorpion approached, its stinging tail swaying side to side. Pearce tried to will the arachnid to move on. Finally, as if warned by a sixth sense the stinging creature changed direction and scuttled away from the danger zone, just as the Al Qaeda warrior saw Pearce and his victim.

Rather than checking his comrade-in-arms for signs of life, he kept the barrel of his Kalashnikov trained on the bodies and waited a full sixty seconds, before deciding that both were dead. He inched the barrel of the AK-47 tucked in his comrade's armpit and slowly lifted it in order to roll him off the enemy beneath. As his comrade rolled sideways, the dead man's fingers released the K-bar. It fell to the ground. It took just a split second to register that the knife was not actually buried in the enemy's chest. This was the last thing he ever saw. Before he could swing back the gun barrel, Pearce flicked the throwing star in a lightning-fast backhand sweep, imbedding it in the enemy's throat. The man dropped his rifle as he clutched at his windpipe.

In a flash, Pearce grabbed the K-bar and drove it into the man's solar plexus, turning it upward with all his might. The man was dead before he hit the ground. Four down, four to go.

CHAPTER 5

JTF2

Joint Task Force Two, shortened to JTF2, is a highly secret covert ops group run by the Canadian government. One might be tempted to ask, with considerable skepticism, whether the Canadian government even has a Special Forces unit, given that it's the government that sends peacekeepers rather than combat troops and generally opts for a diplomatic solution rather than a military intervention. As a result, the country of Canada has a sterling reputation as a law-abiding and peaceful nation. Alas, all may not be as it seems in the *true North, strong and free*, as the national anthem goes.

JTF2 was established in 1993 to replace the Royal Canadian Mounted Police's Special Emergency Response Team ("SERT") amidst public clamor that the police were being trained to use lethal force against the civilian population of Canada. Since then, JTF2 operations had taken place in Bosnia, Haiti, Iraq and Afghanistan. Technically a part of the Canadian Armed Services ("CAS"), the unit is the responsibility of the Commander Special Operations Forces Command which is accountable to the Chief of the Defense Staff. The Chief of the Defense Staff is accountable to the Minister of National Defense who, as a Minister of the Crown, is directly responsible to the Prime Minister of Canada.

JTF2 recruits from all branches of the CAS. Its teams are without doubt, the best of the best. They regularly train with and often out-compete their counterparts in the U.S. and Britain. However, unlike other special forces outfits, JTF2 is virtually invisible to the Canadian public. Most information about this elite unit—self-described as a "precise and accurate tool that can be applied to any threat"—is classified secret and not publicly commented on by the government of Canada. In fact, most Canadians have never heard of JTF2. Despite its comparatively small size, JTF2 has been referred to in its own covert circles as the ultimate special forces unit–effective, indefatigable and with a never-back-down-no-matter-what attitude. On more than one occasion, its commander, Major Connell, pooh-poohed such praise stating that "JTF2 simply can't let Canada down, period. It's our job. Like the Nike slogan, we *just do it*."

That approach fit Pearce like a glove. After second-year law school was finished, KJ got the call from his dad, Leonard, indicating that there was an opening for tactical support in this highly sought-after unit. Although KJ was no longer in the military, his five-year off-the-charts service record in the CAS merited this highly unusual invitation. In its twenty-two-year history, no civilian, ex-military or not, had ever been asked to join JTF2. It was an honor he could not pass up, even though he had only a year to go to finish his law degree. Serving his country at this elite, special forces level was the highest possible calling and not, in Pearce's opinion, remotely comparable with defending DUI's or helping clients flip condos for a quick buck. His answer was an emphatic yes.

Pearce's two best friends, Kiara Davies and Rafa Matus, from law school, weren't completely surprised he was taking a leave, but they would miss him. All three were brilliant students who cheered each other on. Bidding them goodbye, and promising to stay in touch, Pearce was off on a Hercules transport to the Dwyer Hill operations center near Ottawa, the nation's capital. He would not, however, last long on the tactical support team. Within a month of starting, he was training at Fort Bragg, North Carolina with U.S. Airborne, Navy Seals, Green Berets and British SAS elite commando teams in counter-terrorist operations using the most advanced weaponry and technology in existence.

KJ took to that regime like Wayne Gretzky to a hockey rink, spending every waking minute of his four-month stint at the biggest military base in the world immersed in every aspect of warfare. There was sniper school, bomb and explosives making, surveillance, wilderness survival, communications, basic computer hacking and of course, hand-to-hand combat—at which he excelled.

By design, his training at Fort Bragg ended with the final hand-to-hand combat tournament. In fact, it was an elimination contest which started the week that he arrived. After eight military MMA-type matches with the toughest, meanest soldiers on the planet, Pearce was thus far undefeated. The finale was a big event, the highlight of the whole four-month exercise for a bunch of outstanding soldiers fueled by an overabundance of testosterone and machismo. His final contest was one he would not soon forget. With his eight-match winning streak on the line, and the *Fort Bragging Rights* front and centre, Pearce drew a particularly odious opponent, a British Special Air Service ("SAS") commando also with an 8-0 record who had hospitalized most of his previous opponents with serious injuries.

A Delta Force soldier Pearce had bested a few weeks earlier tipped him off that his opponent, a hulking bruiser named Wallopin' Andy Walton, was going to "cripple the snot-nosed Canadian with the fancy martial arts moves"—and damned the consequences if he got disqualified. This bloody well wasn't Sunday school.

No, it certainly wasn't.

The hand-to-hand combat training centre at Fort Bragg used an octagon-shaped ring, like the popular UFC mixed-martial arts tournaments in the private sector. The rules were similar–no eye gouging, biting, punches to the throat or elbows to the back of the neck, but pretty much anything else was allowed. In fact, the rules were interpreted so loosely that no one had ever been disqualified since the tournament began, over a decade past. Full contact meant just that. The only equipment allowed in the ring was fingerless fighting gloves and mouth guards. No shoes, no boots, no bracelets, chains or other paraphernalia that could be used as weapons were permitted, although more than once in the tournament, prohibited items were confiscated by the ref in his pre-fight inspections.

The arena was packed. To KJ it seemed like every damned one of the 55,000 military personnel and 11,000 civilians connected with Fort Bragg had weaseled their way into the huge arena. Needless to say, the crowd was raucous, with soldiers pulling for each man. Some U.S. marines and Airborne soldiers hollered for Pearce. "Kill the fucking Limey!" British troops supporting Walton were so loud the atmosphere resembled a World Cup soccer match.

The referee was a veteran Green Beret commander with an attitude. He topped off his explanation of the rules saying, "When I say break you break, understand?"

Pearce nodded.

Walton remained motionless staring holes into Pearce.

"Hey Walton, are you deaf?" yelled the ref stepping in between the fighters to confront the hulking fighter. "What did I just ask you?"

"I heard you ref," snarled the Walloper. "But the only thing that's going to break is this tosser's neck," he declared in his cockney accent, while leaning forward and shifting side to side on his feet, as if being restrained by an invisible leash." At 6'3" and nearly 265 pounds, the Walloper was built like a Sherman tank. Nineteen-inch neck, twenty-inch biceps and legs like tree trunks. Andy was carrying some excess fat to be sure, but there was no shortage of rock hard muscle underneath it. In his trademark, sleeveless tank top with "Love to Kill" under a Union Jack emblazoned across the front he looked strong enough to pick up a small truck. Being an experienced brawler with half decent fighting skills didn't hurt either.

Pearce, at just a hair under 6'2" and tipping the Toledos at a shade over 200 pounds definitely didn't want to get into a grappling match with this guy.

Unlike traditional boxing or martial arts matches, Fort Bragg-style MMA had no weight restrictions. The theory was that the enemy you might run into in the trenches or jungle or where ever else would not necessarily be in your weight division and hence you had to be willing and able to take on all comers. While that definitely favored the bigger, heavier combatants, it was the law of the jungle and that was the law prevailed in this venue. As a combatant, you simply fought the guy opposite you and if you won you kept on fighting until you either lost a match or ended up winning the tournament. Matches were nine minutes, consisting of three three-minute rounds. Winning was by knockout, submission or tap out (hopefully just *before* the other guy broke your arm or your neck).

KJ wore a black karate gi cinched at the waist with a black cloth belt. It was a classic match-up—massive brawler against highly skilled martial artist. The local handicappers were favoring Walton two to one. Pearce had thus far approached each fight as a challenge to overcome without necessarily ending his opponent's life or career. After all, these guys were all on the same side. This one was different however. He could *sense* the malicious nature of his final opponent long before Walton had even uttered a word.

The Walloper would try to maim or cripple him before the ref could do anything about it -of that he was certain. This could really be a fight to the death. He hoped not.

The bell rang and the ref stepped back, dropping his hand between the fighters to signal the start of the first round of combat. The crowd was boisterous and excited sensing an explosion right off the bat. They didn't have to wait for long. The Walloper came at KJ like an attack dog, lunging forward seeking to grab a hold of the front of his cotton gi and throw Pearce to the canvas. There he would employ the *ground and pound* style which had won him every match so far. His enormous strength and massive weight would pin Pearce to the floor while fists and elbow strikes would pummel him into unconsciousness.

Rather than try to retreat or dodge the onslaught, however, Pearce unexpectedly stepped forward allowing Walton's hands to grasp his gi at chest height. KJ immediately snapped his forehead down, head butting Walton on the bridge of his nose, shattering bone with a *cra-a-a-a-ck* that sounded like a hockey stick breaking on a slap shot attempt. The Walloper instinctively pulled his hands toward his bloodied face, but KJ deftly slid his right arm beneath Walton's bent right arm. Grabbing Walton's wrist with both hands and using his own shoulder as a fulcrum, Pearce yanked down hard, pulling the other man's arm up and backwards.

The move dislocated Walton's shoulder. He bellowed like wounded bull, his right arm hanging uselessly from its shoulder socket. KJ continued the attack, sweeping Walton's leg, knocking him to the canvass. Before the ref could step in KJ grabbed Walton's right wrist with both hands, deftly separating his index and middle fingers from the ring and small fingers, then yanked them apart, dislocating all four fingers. Walton screamed as if he had been knifed in the kidneys. But rather than letting go of the wrist, Pearce applied massive pressure backwards snapping it in several places. This time, the Walloper passed out.

The crowd went nuts, despite the fact that the whole match lasted under 60 seconds. Score one for JTF2.

CHAPTER 6

Diet for a New America

When you grow up in Alberta, Canada you eat meat, meat and more meat. Breakfast is usually sausages and hash browns or *Canadian*-back bacon and eggs. Cold cut sandwiches are a lunch staple and pork chops, steaks or hamburgers round out the dinner menu. Of course, there is a pot roast for Sunday dinner, a turkey for Thanksgiving and Christmas days and a ham for Easter Sunday. Like most Albertans (and in fact most everyone else for that matter), KJ did not think much about where his meals came from. With a busy schedule that included going to law school, teaching martial arts classes, playing basketball, drinking with the guys and watching sports while trying to squeeze in a social life—worrying about how the hamburger got onto the supermarket shelves had never even crossed his mind.

That is until one fateful day when he happened to wander into Audrey's Bookstore on Jasper Avenue in Edmonton. He had lent out his textbook, Waters' *Law of Trusts* (but he couldn't remember to who) and now he needed a replacement. Sold out at the university bookstore, he figured Audrey's might just have a copy of this perennial classic for law students needing to learn about the legal fiction whereby one person could be the registered title holder of something which was really owned by someone else.

He crossed several aisles glancing at the general topics as he went—cooking, self-help, gardening, sports, entertainment and business. Law couldn't be far behind. As he moved past the business books section he weaved in the narrow aisle to avoid a junior-high-school-aged girl sitting cross-legged on the floor in the *Social Justice* section. In doing so he accidentally bumped the floor-to-almost ceiling shelving. As if by magic or perhaps fate, *Diet for a New America, 25th Anniversary Edition* slipped from a high shelf falling towards the girl's head. KJ snatched the book out of mid-air causing the girl to raise her eyebrows. He smiled back and cocked his head, as if it was a fluke that he caught the book.

The book's distinctive red, white and blue cover caught his attention. It *had* flown into his hands. He flopped down into a big easy chair at the end of the aisle. He would just skim a few pages, pick up his textbook and then be on his way. While he was not exactly into diets, he thought that there might be something in there to maybe give him an edge by boosting his performance on the courts. However, two and a half hours later he sat still as a stone, utterly mesmerized by this stinging indictment of the eating habits of the people of the richest, most powerful country in the history of the world—and how those habits were devastating the planet and many millions of creatures on it.

Being in many ways a clone of its southern super-power neighbor, Canada's dietary preferences and practices pretty much lined up in lock-step with America's—so the book's message hit Pearce like a linebacker at full stride. Incredibly, the book was published a quarter of a century ago and until now, he was completely unaware of this travesty. Had he been asleep the whole time?

"What the hell…" he thought as he read on about the commercial production of veal. As the socially responsible, at least in the minds of consumers, including KJ, dairy industry has no use for male calves they are forcefully separated from their mothers at a month's age and caged in 4'X 4' wooden crates. The calves typically have their heads chained to the front end of the crates, thus making it impossible for them to turn around or comfortably lie down. The neck-chaining means that they develop almost no muscle and consequentially fall prey to serious medical problems.

That was no big deal however—painkillers and antibiotics to the rescue! Normally clean animals, these creatures have nowhere to defecate, so they live confined in their own excrement.

To make matters worse, they are forced to stand on wire mesh which is not suitable for hoofed animals. Thus development of serious foot sores and infections is routine. The baby calves are fed an iron deficient diet purposely to make them anemic apparently so that their meat is tastier dining. After twenty weeks of this pure hell, the calves are violently slaughtered for their meat, which is fed to restaurant patrons as a delicacy—*baby veal chops*.

"Holy shit!" Pearce said out loud, literally sick to his stomach. He had eaten veal on many occasions. Never in his wildest dreams did he think that creatures had endured such unspeakable torture. There is no way that this could be true! Like non-farm folk everywhere, Pearce sort of *knew* that cows and pigs and chickens were eventually, somehow (presumably humanely) killed after living out their lives on a farm or acreage.

After all, that's where the food has always come from—the local farm. Agri-business however, in its relentless pursuit of profits, introduced the concept of *factory farming* to agriculture.

"Sorry sir, we're closing now," the store clerk reminded him, jolting him out of the confines of the book.

"Damn, I lost track of time," Pearce said glancing at his watch. Almost nine o'clock. "I would like to buy the book—and I'll need two extra copies." Kiara and Rafa had to read this. They would be devastated.

CHAPTER 7

Mission Accomplished

Kellen and the three Afghanis could just make out the dim lights of Jalalabad in the distance. Grunting and swearing, he let Anoosheh slide off of his back—which ached after carrying her close to eight miles with few stops in between. More than once he considered dumping the lot of them and making his way to safety, but he would have a hell of a time coming up with an explanation that would placate Pearce and the inevitable inquiry which would follow from JTF2 command. No, he was fucking stuck with them for better or worse.

The kids, Daryoush and Ronak, had not been half bad, keeping complaints and grumbling to a minimum. Each carried a fairly heavy (for a kid) satchel of food and ordnance. Since Kellen could not speak a word of Farsi, he had relied on hand signals and gestures to communicate with the trio. He put a vertical finger to his lips to signal quiet and took the night vision binoculars from the satchel Daryoush was carrying.

As he was scanning the southern edge of the city, a vague feeling of unease came over him. Biologist Rupert Sheldrake has postulated in his book, *The Sense of Being Stared At*, that people have a *sixth sense* which can alert them when they are being watched or observed even from quite a distance. This is what Kellen was feeling, but he didn't wait to think about it. He motioned Anoosheh to go *down now* with the kids while he ducked into a thicket grabbing one of the satchels.

"It damned well better be the right one," Kellen thought to himself. It was.

He pulled out the Uzi submachine gun, screwed on the silencer and jammed in a magazine. It was his last one. Maybe Pearce hadn't gotten all of them after all. In Farsi, Daryoush asked, "Mom, where did the man go? Are we lost now?"

"Shhuuush," replied Anoosheh.

"No talking!"

That was enough to alert the two Al Qaeda fighters on their tail. They both broke into the thicket at the same time, rifles raised and spotted the trio.

The kids screamed. The three of them were almost shot to death on the spot. Anoosheh threw herself in front of her children and was rewarded with a rifle butt in the face which cracked her cheekbone, knocking her unconscious and sending her sprawling in the dirt. Both kids lost it. Their screams intensified as only children's can.

"Shut up you motherless ..." said one of the fighters, as he started to raise his rifle. It was the perfect distraction. Suddenly one fighter's head snapped backwards while his shoulder appeared to be pulled upwards. At the same time his stomach caved inwards. He spun sideways violently crashing into the bushes. The second fared no better. He dropped his Kalashnikov clutching at his left arm as if it had been stung by a swarm of wasps that wouldn't stop stinging. His other arm, his side and then his neck all took hits. That dropped him in his tracks.

The Uzi's barrel was smoking. Kellen had emptied the whole mag into the enemy. Seeing Kellen, the kids calmed down somewhat and both jumped on their mother's unconscious form trying to wake her up. Kellen fished out a mini-maglite from his utility belt and gruffly shoved the kids aside to have a better look at Anoosheh. Her heart rate was steady, but her breathing was fairly shallow.

"She'll live," he figured, realizing that she was actually quite pretty in an *A-rab* sort of way, but goddamned if she wasn't going to need some major surgery. The left side of her face was black and blue and swelling up like a balloon. "Oh well, that's somebody else's problem," Kellen thought as he picked up the slight, young Afghani woman and slung her over his right shoulder, motioning to the kids to grab the sacks and fall in behind him.

"Better get the hell out of here before anyone else shows up—unless of course, it's Pearce," Kellen said, unconcerned that the kids didn't understand. He re-balanced Anoosheh on his shoulder while snapping a clip into his .45 caliber hand gun.

"But since these two assholes got through," surmised Kellen, "he's probably dead." A twinge of sorrow touched his heart, but only for a moment. Everybody's got to go sometime.

CHAPTER 8

Once You Know

There are seminal moments in every person's life. For a kid that might be learning that there is no Santa Claus. For a fan, it might be witnessing the fall of a once seemingly invincible sports hero. Maybe it's learning that the *good guys* aren't always what they are cracked up to be. For Pearce, it was discovering that there was a war going on right under his nose. A war that was institutionalized, planetary and ubiquitous.

Jesus Murphy, the casualties on the non-human side exceeded ten billion, that's with a "B"—every year! Cruelty, torture, medical experimentation, captivity and enslavement were standard ops. In fact, the regime carrying out this war — this **INVISIBLE REICH** — made Hitler's *Deutsches Reich* look like a picnic, as callous as that might sound. Pearce was something of a student of the history of war and he was quite familiar with the atrocities of the infamous Third Reich. However as unspeakable as they were, they absolutely *paled* in comparison to the war against animals of every species which was taking place today—every day in point of fact.

"Did you know about any of this Kiara?" KJ asked his former classmate, now an environmental lawyer with Sierra Legal Defense Fund.

She stirred her café latte slowly and shifted forward in the spacious faux leather armchair at the ever-busy Starbucks on Robson Street. Her long, silky blonde hair glistened in the late afternoon sunlight framing her high cheekbones and sky blue eyes. She doubtless could have been a runway model but wasn't particularly comfortable being the center of attention. Judging by the interest of the other male patrons in the restaurant, if she wasn't at the center, she was pretty damned close.

"Well, certainly not in the way Robbins describes it," Kiara replied, sipping her latte. Like Pearce she had read the book cover to cover in one sitting. "I mean," she continued, "ever since animals were domesticated—what, maybe 12,000 years ago, there has been a sort of social contract with them."

"I'm listening," Pearce replied.

"People have fed and housed animals on farms and acreages and at some point had to kill them for food." She looked KJ in the eyes and said, "Everyone kind of knows that although I doubt that most people are aware of or even want to know the details." She slowly twirled her hair around her index finger and then un-twirled it. "I guess I was just as guilty as the next person for not bothering to find out what was really going on," she admitted quietly.

KJ pounced. "That's just it, the details are hidden behind the myth that this so-called *social contract* that you mentioned still exists. Clearly, it does not!" He was uncharacteristically animated. Something in that book had really hit home for him. He continued, ignoring his cooling latte.

"Every first-year law student learns that there has to be *consideration* for a contract to be binding," he said picking up a packet of sugar from the holder. "You promise to do something for me," he said, "and I have to either promise something back or give you something in return, like this packet of sugar." He handed it to Kiara. "To legally seal the deal so to speak."

"You're right. Even a *social* contract implies that both sides get *something of value.*"

"Factory farming, agribusiness and the blind pursuit of profit have taken everything of value to animals off the table," he said, "only— the average consumer doesn't know it." He went on, "In point of fact, many of these farm creatures never see the light of day, have no freedom to even turn around in their crates and suffer unbelievable torture throughout their brief lives." Pearce's expression went pensive for a brief instant.

"..... unless of course, Robbins is making this all up," KJ remarked.

"And clearly," Kiara added, "agribusiness wants to keep this situation off the public's radar, with food disparagement laws—remember Oprah and the hamburger law suit, *ag-gag laws[1]* and *SLAPP*

---

1   **Agricultural gag ("Ag-gag")** laws are passed by agribusiness through puppet politicians to prevent anyone from criticizing their food production practices or products for any reason, scientific or otherwise.

suits[2] a plenty, at least in the U.S."

The line at the counter kept the baristas going nonstop as their generally young, hip customers departed with lattes, o'laits and espressos at four bucks a pop.

"Kiara." Pearce leaned in. "I've been on both sides of the border lots and Canada is not exactly what I would call a *safe haven* for animals."

"You're right."

"Look at this!" He picked up a complimentary copy of the New York Times with a front page story about a horse racing scandal in New York. The article stated that there was a law in the U.S. prohibiting the slaughter of horses (race horses for the purposes of the article, but all horses were included), but when the horses were spent, local race horse owners just shipped them north to Canada, or south to Mexico, where they were killed for animal and *human* consumption. "Who on earth eats horse meat?" Pearce wondered out loud.

The article went on to explain that the racehorses had been shot up with many growth hormones and pain killers to keep them racing when they shouldn't be, and that those substances entered the animal and human food chain when the horses were slaughtered in Canada. The owners of a renowned race track, several racehorse owners and a high-profile trainer were all being investigated by the New York Attorney General's office and could be facing felony charges.

"Score another one for PETA," exhorted Kiara.

Pearce squinted. "What's PETA?"

"You've never heard of PETA?"

"No." He gathered he should have. "I haven't."

"People for the Ethical Treatment of Animals," she answered, confirming that it was video coverage from their undercover operative that had been the basis for the story in the *Times*. She explained that PETA was formed in 1980 by Alex Pacheco and Ingrid Newkirk,

---

2   **Strategic lawsuit against public participation ("SLAPP")** is a lawsuit that is intended to silence critics by saddling them with the enormous cost of a law suit until they cease and desist. Such lawsuits have been made illegal in many jurisdictions on the grounds that they impede freedom of speech. Normally an American phenomenon, in 2016 the Vancouver Aquarium in British Columbia launched such a suit, framing it as copyright infringement against a local filmmaker for exposing is mistreatment of dolphins and beluga whales at its facility.

although Pacheco resigned many years ago over PETA's *in your face* style of public awareness campaigns.

PETA had grown to become a worldwide champion of the rights of all kinds of animals, from the exotics like tigers and jaguars to domestic farm animals—and every kind of species in between, including even the lowly lab animals, millions of whom are routinely tortured and killed for causes ranging from cancer research to lipstick testing.

PETA's mantra was clear: "Animals are not ours to eat, wear, experiment on, use for entertainment or abuse in any other way."

"They are not exactly top of JTF2's required reading list—or, if you recall, even mentioned in a single course in law school for that matter," he stated, without being defensive.

"Well," she continued, smiling, "they do get publicity, most of it negative, from time to time in the mainstream media for public demonstrations against cruelty to animals. She downed the balance of her latte and then delicately polished off the remains of her biscotti.

"1980," Pearce said.

"What?"

"1980 is over 35 years ago and what has PETA actually accomplished since then?"

"Well, at least a few things," she replied. "The article in the *Times* lists a few of the milestones they have achieved. She handed Pearce the article:

" ….. over the years the PETA organization has been credited for:

Undercover investigations of pig-breeding factory farms in North Carolina and Oklahoma revealed horrific conditions and daily abuse of pigs, including the fact that one pig was skinned alive, leading to the first-ever felony indictments of farm workers.

PETA's undercover investigation of a Florida exotic-animal "training school" revealed that big cats were being beaten with ax handles, and encouraged the U.S. Department of Agriculture to develop new regulations governing animal-training methods. Further, PETA persuaded Mobil, Texaco, Pennzoil, Shell, and other oil companies to cover their exhaust stacks after showing how millions of birds and bats had become trapped in the shafts and been burned to death.

A California furrier was charged with cruelty to animals after a PETA investigator filmed him electrocuting chinchillas by clipping wires to the animals' genitals, which caused the animals to experience the pain of a heart attack while they were still conscious.

In another undercover exposé, PETA caught a fur rancher on videotape causing minks to die in agony by injecting them with weed killer. Both farms agreed to stop these cruel killing methods.

After two years of negotiations with—and more than 400 demonstrations against—the company worldwide, McDonald's became the first fast-food chain to agree to make basic welfare improvements for farmed animals. Burger King and Wendy's followed suit within a year's time, and within two years, Safeway, Kroger, and Albertsons had also agreed to adopt stricter guidelines in order to improve the lives of billions of animals who are slaughtered for food.

Thanks to PETA's lengthy campaign to push PETCO to take more responsibility for the animals in its stores, the company agreed to stop selling large birds and to make provisions for the millions of rats and mice in its care."

"Well, I suppose that's something," Pearce said.

"Something?" Kiara interrupted him. "It's a lot."

He nodded. "You're right. Considering that no one else seemed to be taking a stand or holding the perpetrators accountable for any wrong doing. But," he paused, his eyes going stone cold, causing an involuntary shudder through Kiara's frame, "there is also something missing."

"What do you mean?" she tossed her long golden hair to one side as she looked up from her empty cup at Pearce. She felt a little apprehensive.

"Well." He snatched the paper from the table, "Let's re-cap what the article said." He read: "Some lowly farm workers get charged, a big farming operation agrees to stop poisoning minks with weed killer, an exotic animal business is persuaded to discontinue beating big cats with axe handles ..." He stopped reading to challenge his friend. "Come on Kiara, think! What's missing?"

She paused for a minute. "Consequences!" she stated triumphantly.

"Aha!" said Pearce.

The pupil and her ad hoc teacher were learning together.

CHAPTER 9

Pat on the Back

"Step forward, Lieutenant Kellen," directed general Thomas Mansville, the head of Department of National Defense ("DND").

Kellen snapped to attention and briskly walked across the gleaming wood floor to the podium. His look was *spit and polish* in his formal uniform. The large auditorium in the Dwyer Hill facility was packed with wide variety of Canadian military brass. Except for those deployed abroad, all members of the JTF2 force were present, along with several hundred CAF soldiers.

Kellen smartly saluted the general as he reached the podium. The general returned the salute and shook Kellen's hand. The audience was dead silent. "Congratulations Lieutenant Kellen," said the general. "Take a seat *there*," he ordered, motioning to his left.

Kellen sat and the general took the podium to address the assembly.

"Honorable Minister of Defense, Colonel Jefferies, Colonel Markham," as he started listing the various dignitaries in attendance. The general had been a career soldier since age eighteen and his father had been served in the Second World War. His grandfather had been a brigadier general in WW I. *Military* was encoded in his DNA.

"I am proud to say that Joint Task Force Two has pulled off another successful mission in Afghanistan, having destroyed Al Qaeda's largest stockpile of weapons and explosives in a hidden encampment about twenty-five miles south of Jalalabad." Applause followed and stopped immediately as the general continued.

"Under the command of Lieutenant Kellen, a half a dozen JTF2 soldiers accomplished this feat in under ten days, suffering zero casualties but," he shifted his reading glasses higher on the bridge of his nose for effect, "leaving an estimated thirty dead Al Qaeda terrorists to rot in whatever hell they believe in." More applause and cheers ensued. Again, immediate silence as the general resumed.

"Although separated after the mission, all of the JTF2 members eventually re-united at Jalalabad to rendezvous with our U.S. allies." He scanned the room. "And," he continued with a look of satisfaction, "I tip my hat to Commander Davidson of the U.S. Special Forces in attendance to my right." He motioned toward the Commander who nodded almost imperceptibly in acknowledgement. The U.S. was not exactly bowled over by Canadian military ops and Davidson had to be literally dragged to this ceremony. That fact seemed to be lost on the general as he continued.

"JTF2 forces were welcomed by our allies in Jalalabad and provided with safe haven until our CAF Hercules transport could return them here to Dwyer Hill the following day." He droned on to his captive audience. "In the process Lieutenant Kellen's team acquired valuable documents outlining the whereabouts of a number of other hidden Al Qaeda bases and as a result he was relentlessly pursued by a band of these thugs over some twenty odd miles, all the while dodging mortar fire and the occasional booby-trap."

Kellen looked straight ahead, motionless, not blinking.

"What is unusual is that while being pursued, the Lieutenant made a command decision--at some peril to himself and his sergeant, to save an Afghani family of three—a mother and her two small children," the general stated. "It is likely that these non-combatants would have been interrogated, tortured and possibly killed by the Al Qaeda pursuers, having witnessed the Canadian soldiers pass by. So Lieutenant Kellen took it upon himself to assume responsibility for their protection and safety and indeed, he carried the injured mother on his back for the last ten miles or so to Jalalabad." All eyes shifted to the lieutenant.

"Please stand, Lieutenant Kellen."

He rose and stood at rock-solid attention as the general pinned a purple heart on his chest—a high honor for exceptional bravery. He looked every inch the Canadian hero--tall of frame, rugged of feature and loyal to the core.

"This is what we expect of the Canadian military," stated the general, "extraordinary skill, outstanding bravery and compassion for the civilians who are invariably caught in the crossfire of military operations. Lieutenant, you may briefly address the assembly," directed the General.

Not used to public speaking, Kellen tried to keep it short and to the point. He had rehearsed this speech into the ground.

"I am very proud as a Canadian soldier to receive this high honor on behalf of my special ops team," said Kellen in a firm and deep voice. "Honorable Minister, General Mansville, Colonel Jefferies, Lieutenant Colonel Markam, Commander Davidson and all the brave soldiers in attendance," he went on. "In a nutshell JTF2 is the iron fist in Canada's velvet glove." He lifted his left hand and motioned as if he were donning a gauntlet with his right hand.

"We are absolutely dedicated to succeeding in every mission *and...*" he paused to emphasize his meaning, "If we are lucky enough to be able to rescue an innocent non-com or two in the process without compromising the mission we will do so every time. This time we did," he advised the audience, to a few claps.

"And I am pleased to say that the small Afghani family we rescued has been returned safely to their village after the mother, Anoosheh received emergency surgery at our U.S. host's army medical center to repair her smashed-in face. This was an injury she sustained while distracting two Al Qaeda fighters who were on the verge of killing us."

While that was not exactly true, Kellen had put that spin on it when he was debriefed by his superior and the U.S. base commander in Jalalabad. It had helped persuade the base commander to authorize emergency surgery to repair her face at the U.S. temporary medical facility, where they had excellent surgical support for a field operation.

"That was enough to allow me to kill them both and get the family safely to Jalalabad," Kellen concluded. The crowd started to slap but waited, as the general rose.

"Thank you, Lieutenant," said the General. "You and your entire unit have acquitted yourselves admirably." He again saluted Kellen and he in turn saluted the general and the audience, snapped his heels together and briskly sat down.

The audience stood and saluted Kellen in return—including Pearce, who had not received a word of mention. Had he not deepsixed the remaining Al Qaeda operatives on their tail there would be no ceremony today. Had he not stopped Kellen from terminating the family at the outset there would be no one to take credit for rescuing. Hell, he had even found the documents outlining the additional Al Qaeda bases after they had broken into the compound and terminated everyone on the premises with extreme prejudice.

A hard slap on his shoulder jolted him out of his musing.

"Damned good job soldier," said a beaming Kellen, the purple heart front and center on his upper left jacket pocket.

Pearce immediately stood and saluted his CO. "Thank you sir," Pearce replied in a firm, but neutral tone of voice. "It was an honor to be part of the mission, sir."

Both men knew the real score but they both followed military protocol and said nothing more about it. The top dog gets the bone and the others wait their turn. Just like the Octagon at Fort Bragg, it wasn't fair, but it was the way it was. JTF2 was no exception.

CHAPTER 10

First You Know and Then You Do

Pearce's two-year commitment to JTF2 was coming to an end in a couple of months. For him, it was a dream come true to be serving his country in an elite, special forces role at the highest level. *Diet for a New America* aside, he would have signed on for another two years in a heartbeat, but now he was having second thoughts. Canada needed him to be sure, but JTF2 had many other exceptional soldiers at its command.

However, animals in Canada and the world over had no soldiers anywhere fighting for them, not even one. The massive question was staring him in the face. "Was he *the one*?" To be sure, he was an extremely capable soldier, tactician, martial artist and having two years of law school under his belt, he was not bad at reasoning and analysis. He could read and understand a prospectus, a complicated contract or a purposely opaque piece of legislation, not to mention complex military logistics and field operations manuals.

Long gone were the days when soldiers, particularly special forces operatives were just mindless weapons. Now they had to be thinking, calculating–even semi-autonomous weapons. Assuming that he actually took up the cause, he preferred to frame it as "the challenge of protecting a vulnerable population," it would be a Herculean task for one man to make even the smallest dent in the massive economic machine which currently ground up and spat out ten *billion* animal souls a year for profit.

"A hell of a challenge for an army, much less one lone soldier," Pearce thought. Shit, what the hell was he thinking? This was sheer lunacy to even consider. After all, he had a sky's-the-limit career in JTF2 if he wanted it. He could finish his law degree and move up in the military ranks or go into private practice—maybe even with Kiara at Sierra Legal Defense. He stood up and paced back and forth in his compact, perfectly arranged quarters at Dwyer Hill.

He looked out the small window into a clear black sky surrounding a brilliant full moon which reflected light from a sun some ninety-three million miles away. It took a little over eight minutes for the light to get to the moon and then another second and a half or so to reach his eyes. This night it literally took his breath away. He stopped pacing and stared intently at the ancient moon which had witnessed every action of mankind–good and bad for the last three million or so years since the first near-human, *Australopithecus* emerged upright from the African savannah.

If, and that was a really big if, he chose to get involved on the side of non-homo sapiens he might well have the whole world against him. On the other hand, JTF2 never backed away from a mission because of bad odds—hell the force thrived on bad odds, particularly if the stakes for Canada were high. The stakes were enormous for the animal world. They were being killed by the millions every day. In fact, Pearce had recently read a report by the World Wildlife Fund which estimated that *half* of the world's wildlife had been wiped out over the past four decades. What should he do? How could he stand by and do nothing? But could he reasonably throw away everything he had worked for his whole life on a million-to-one long shot?

As his martial arts training dictated, he had to quiet his agitated mind to reach the right conclusion. Ultimately, he would decide at the very deepest level—that of complete and utter stillness. He pulled a large sitting pillow from the sofa and dropped to his knees on it, then sank into a full lotus position. His back was straight, he sat crossed-legged, his eyes were closed and his breathing was slowing, slowing, slowing. Heart rate dropped from 55 to 53 to 50. It stabilized at 45 BPM. Gradually his thoughts began to fade into a black, quiet stillness which the seers of old referred to as *the Void*. This was a *no-state* state of being. It is said that from this void of absolute nothingness comes everything–every form, every substance, every thought and idea, even Life itself. That is where his answer would be found.

CHAPTER 11

I Am from Missouri

When KJ was born his mom had bought a life insurance policy. At that time she was only twenty-years-old and not yet in the military. She married Corporal Leonard Pearce who, being three years her senior had already been enlisted in the CAS for four years. Andrea Pearce would keep that policy in place until she died. KJ had been the principal beneficiary of the policy, a tidy $75,000, non-taxable sum.

On the advice of his dad, the entire amount had remained sitting in a mutual fund consisting entirely of major Canadian bank stocks—Royal Bank of Canada, Toronto Dominion Bank, Canadian Imperial Bank of Commerce and Bank of Montreal—*the big five*, as they were known in Canuck land. As any savvy investor knows, Canadian bank stocks are essentially bulletproof, as the Canadian banking system is a highly regulated, very conservative oligopoly, the members of which have routinely recorded ROI's of 15% to 18% for as long as anyone can remember. After the Wall Street-precipitated financial meltdown of 2008, world praise was showered on the Canadian banking system, which remained completely stable and solvent throughout.

Now that Pearce had just turned twenty-nine, the fund's last quarterly statement showed that it had topped the $350,000 mark, a tidy 466% gain over twenty-eight years—of course falling precisely within the banks' historical ROI range. His martial arts self defense classes had enabled KJ to attend law school without dipping into the fund and of course his pay at JTF2 had not only covered his expenditures while in the military, it enabled him to buy a car—a mint, retro-styled red 2003 Thunderbird which the local Ocean Park Ford dealer had acquired for him on a buying junket in California. Leonard had also been something of a car buff, owning a restored 67' Corvette and a 70' Dodge Challenger project which was still in the works.

He decided that he was not going back to law school, at least not yet, nor was he returning to JTF2. KJ would sparingly use the fund to live off of while he investigated the assertions he had read in *Diet for a New America.* While the author was credible and highly respected by his peers, KJ would see for himself first hand. He was hoping, more than expecting, that the claims made in the book were wildly exaggerated and that the plight of animals on the planet was not nearly as bad as portrayed. And so he decided he'd visit locations in Canada and the U.S. Having dual citizenship, he could move freely across the border and stay as long in either country as he wished. KJ's training in law school and the CAF had taught him to patiently and methodically investigate first, plan second and then execute the plan with surgical precision third.

He was now ready to start phase one.

CHAPTER 12

Seek and Ye Shall Find

The top was down on the Thunderbird on this gorgeous summer day as KJ pulled into the sprawling Nebraska chicken farm which was a principal supplier to some of the biggest fast food restaurants in the U.S. He had made an appointment to see the CFO to discuss investment in the operation—a cool ten million dollars to make the farm more efficient—at least that was the story.

The farm, Natural Chicken Haven, had run an ad in the trade rag, *The Chicken Reports Journal*, seeking investors to partner in a venture to modernize industrial scale chicken production. Pearce answered the ad claiming to represent a group of Asian investors who wanted to make at least 25% per year on their investment, with a view to eventually licensing the improved production technology to agribusiness in China.

Pearce wore a double-breasted navy linen suit and Serengeti Aviator shades. He looked the part of a savvy investment broker to a tee. Part of his training at Fort Bragg had involved a practice called *role camouflage*. It's based on the psychological premise that people don't usually see what *is*, rather they see what they *expect* to see. This is the basis of all hustles and confidence schemes. The crook must appear to "fit the bill" as a credible and trustworthy character. The biggest individual hustler in history, Bernie Madoff was able to bilk almost fifty billion dollars from in investors by appearing to be the paragon of trustworthiness and honesty in the financial services world.

Pearce met Irving Cohen in a modern single-story wood frame building about one hundred fifty yards from the first of over a dozen gigantic barns. The man was forty-ish, with wire rimmed glasses with circular lenses and wearing an expensive Brooks Brothers suit which was rumpled but serviceable. Pearce thought to himself that if he had been wearing a green visor Cohen could have worked at

Gringotts.

"Sit please Mr. Allan," he said in a nasally voice.

Pearce dropped himself easily into the black leather chair, slipping the Aviators into his breast pocket. "Call me Scott. All my business associates do." Before Cohen could respond Pearce jumped in. "Look, let me get right to the point. I've got a group of five Asian investors who are prepared to put up two million dollars each into modernizing your operations," he stated matter-of-factly.

"That buys them a ten-per cent equity position in your company and an exclusive license to market the new improved technology in Asia." Pearce raised his eyebrows slightly, now awaiting a response.

Cohen replied that he wasn't looking for equity partners, only investors.

"My guys won't look at anything less than twenty-five percent per year, with collateral security on the operation," Pearce countered. "And of course, the exclusive Asian license."

"What kind of security?" Cohen was showing a bit more interest.

"A second mortgage or better—with least thirty-five percent equity remaining," replied Allan, "and of course, title insured by First American or Stewarts."

Rubbing his chin Cohen explained that the rate and security were doable but he wasn't sure about the net equity position after adding the new loan. "The loan to value could be less than the thirty-five percent requested," Cohen speculated.

"Less equity, higher rate," replied Pearce. "That's the way it works."

"Yes." Cohen nodded. "I know. I'll have to check on the first mortgage balance and take a look at the bank's last appraisal. That'll take at least a couple of days."

"No problem," Pearce said, "my guys won't melt."

"Call me when you have the numbers."

"Will do, Scott."

Pearce aka Scott Allan handed over a business card showing that he was employed as a "Private Equity Consultant" by a company headquartered in the Cayman Islands. He firmly shook Cohen's hand and turned to leave, then stopped abruptly and turned back. "Hey, Irv," said Pearce, assuming that they were now on a first-name basis. "Since I'm here anyway, how about we take a quick look at the operations and you can give me the skinny on the new tech proposal?"

Irv glanced at his watch. "You got thirty minutes to spare?"

"Sure do."
He was in.

CHAPTER 13

The Guts of Natural Chicken Haven Farm

The barns, all fifteen of them were more or less identical. Each wooden structure was about two-hundred-fifty-feet long by about eighty-five-feet wide, standing two stories high. Irv instructed one of the Mexican workers to slide the barn door open and to turn the lights on. Two tiers rose up on each side of the barn with each tier containing some twenty odd layers of wire mesh. On every level of the mesh were hundreds of chickens.

The tops of the wire mesh layers were also wire mesh, standing about a foot or so high— just enough room for the chickens to stand upright. The floors were also wire mesh. Each tier contained an opening which permitted farmhands to stuff the chickens into the mesh enclosures.

"Voila," said Irv, extending his bony left hand in a sweeping gesture, as if they were entering the Taj Mahal. On right his hand was a blue sapphire ring to match the Rolex Oyster Perpetual on his wrist.

The noise was almost deafening and the stench of chicken excrement was palpable. Pearce's trained military eye took in a lot in a couple of quick glances. The chickens were in obvious distress, due to severe overcrowding. Many of them were trying to peck at each other, unsuccessfully it seemed.

"Quick rundown for you," Irv said. He was almost jovial. "Each barn's got twenty-thousand chickens give or take. The racket is due to the fact that the chickens want more space," he explained. "Because of that their natural instinct is to peck at each other, which for us is bad news since they can seriously injure or even kill each other with those sharp beaks."

Pearce appeared noncommittal.

"Here, have a look at our de-beaker." Irv maneuvered Pearce towards the edge of the barn and motioned to a Salvadoran farmhand named Pedro to grab an incoming chicken and show Scott how the device worked. As he had done thousands of times before, Pedro grabbed a live chicken clasping his left hand around the chicken's legs and scooping it up in the air so that it was upside down. The chicken, already frightened and disoriented from its rough transportation was squawking at the top of its lungs. In a fluid motion Pedro spun the bird upwards with his left hand still holding its feet together and grabbed it around his neck with his right hand such that it was horizontal. He moved the bird rapidly toward the "de-beaker," which was a device which worked much like a cigar clipper. The bird's beak was pushed through a small opening and a red-hot metal blade seared off its beak.

With no anesthetic, the bird might go into shock or blindly hop around in excruciating agony. Pearce imagined his reaction if someone seared off his nose—not that he'd let that happen.

Oblivious to the chicken's condition, Pedro deftly stuffed it through the opening and into the mesh enclosure. He quickly grabbed another chicken and started to repeat the process, which he would do over 500 times a day. One time Pedro had paused to examine a bird in such a state that it seemed to be going into respiratory arrest, thus interrupting the debeaking process for over a full four-minute period. His supervisor noticed and immediately strode over to reprimand Pedro, then grabbed the convulsing chicken and broke its neck, throwing on the dirt floor as if it were garbage.

"I'm docking you an hour's pay motherfucker *and the cost of that chicken!"* shouted the angry foreman.

"B...bb..but senor… *el pollo*, the chicken, how you say *moribundo*, already dying," protested Pedro.

In a swift, unexpected motion the burly foreman grabbed Pedro by the straps of his coveralls and slammed him against the wall of the barn. "What are you, spic, a fuckin' vet or something?" he growled, waving his finger in Pedro's face. "Your goddamned job is to chop the beak and chuck the bird into the cage—that's it! Comprende, moron?

"Si senor, yo comprendo senor." Pedro could not afford to lose this prized job. He was an illegal and could not work anywhere else in the country. One word from his boss and Homeland Security would put him on a plane or boat back to El Salvador. The meager few hundred dollars a month that he sent his family would vanish.

"God damned good thing you do, asshole," cussed the exasperated foreman. "And let's make that two hours pay for good measure!"

Pedro would finish that ten-hour workday for a mere eight dollars. He would never forget this costly lesson.

Cohen continued without missing a beat. "As I was saying, once the beak is gone the chickens can't do a lot of damage to each other. Trouble is about seven percent of them die of shock."

Pearce rolled his eyes and said, "Irv, that's gotta be fixed. Seven percent is way too high of an impact on the bottom line."

"I know," answered Irv, "that's why you're here, right?"

"What else needs upgrading?"

Cohen looked truly apologetic as he explained that the overcrowding, coupled with the occasional dead, rotting chicken in the mesh enclosures ("hey we can't spot this all the time"), and the chicken excrement which rained down on each level of chickens from the level or levels above ("that way they don't have to leave their cages to poop") required massive doses of antibiotics to be added to the already way too-expensive chicken feed.

"Otherwise the whole bunch dies of infection or disease," explained Cohen.

"What's the hit on that Irv?" queried Pearce, in a somewhat accusatory tone.

"I hate to even say it." Irv winced. "It's close to eighteen percent."

"That's atrocious!" The money man's outrage was feigned. He put his hand on Irv's shoulder. "Now, let's hear about this new technology which is going to stem the gusher of red ink."

CHAPTER 14

The Legal Status of Chickens

In his first year of law school, KJ learned that chickens, like all animals, are considered at law as *chattels*. A chattel is personal property. An automobile, bicycle or home appliance is a chattel. These are of course, inanimate objects.

Chickens on the other hand are animated, sentient creatures which have complex social structures and communication protocols. To lump them—and all other animals—in with toasters and jewelry borders on the absurd, but as Pearce had observed in his law school classes, the law is often an ass. Classifying animals as personal property pretty much eliminates any rights or freedoms which these living beings might otherwise enjoy.

But rights or no rights, it is undeniable that man's treatment of animals on a daily basis is nothing short of egregious. Notwithstanding that, the human race's ingenuity for rationalizing its awful behavior towards other beings on the planet knows no bounds. The divine justification for subjugating animal kind to mankind's whims is often said to be found in the Bible: And God said, "Let us make man in our image, after our likeness: and let them have dominion over the fish of the sea, and over the fowl of the air, and over the cattle, and over all the earth, and over every creeping thing that creepeth upon the earth." (Genesis, King James Bible version)

The word *dominion* is conveniently given its most expansive definition to include torture, experimentation, captivity, enslavement, amusement and of course, death. One has dominion over one's children, but none of the above would be considered remotely reasonable behavior towards them. But naturally, one's children are *homo sapiens*, not animals, birds, fish or reptiles. Interestingly, mankind, at least in its modern incarnation, has a particular quirk when it comes to atrocious behavior. It is not permissible to admit or acknowledge it publicly.

Hence, there are no school tours or field trips to the slaughter houses or factory farms. The media is also generally kept as far away from these operations as possible. Ag-gag laws in many U.S. states keep whistleblowers and concerned citizens quiet by making it an offense to report animal abuse in factory farming operations, which are, by the way, mostly exempt from animal cruelty laws, anyway.

And lastly, the factory farming industry and its partners in crime, the fast food industry, have teamed up to engage in a massive and on-going public relations and advertising campaign. The goal is to convince the public that the millions of cows, pigs and chickens which are inhumanely raised and slaughtered for the sake of Whoppers, McNuggets and Papa Burgers are just pleased as punch to be helping out their human benefactors by providing a tasty meal.

Politicians, who heavily rely on campaign contributions to get elected and re-elected, have no stomach to take on these powerful lobby groups. So it is an uphill battle for anyone with a scintilla of conscience to make a dent, legally, in the multi-billion dollar food machine. For those reasons, Pearce was convinced that the Animal Bill of Rights was not coming to a theatre near you anytime soon.

CHAPTER 15

See for Yourself

Pearce repeated his investigations several more times, first posing as a health inspector at a dairy farm in North Dakota, after which he stopped drinking milk immediately. His second stop was a pig farm in Arkansas. This time he claimed to be conducting a survey for the *Pig Review*, the industry-sponsored trade rag. In his short time there he learned that the local town folks were embroiled in a battle with the multi-national farm operators. Pearce wasn't surprised to hear they were said to be polluting the ground water supply with manure generated by 50,000 pigs kept only a half mile from the town limits.

It was jobs however, that were at the forefront of the debate in this not-so-prosperous state. The governor was on a first-name basis with the CEO of the biggest meat processing company in the U.S. Needless to say, it just so happened to be the parent company of the one involved in the controversy. The company's CEO assured the governor that clean drinking water was no longer a live issue and the governor chose to believe him. And then there were the industry experts who conducted their own private investigations, after which they proclaimed the town's drinking water safe for human consumption. Interestingly, the company itself continued to have bottled drinking water trucked in from a city over 50 miles upstream—purely as a precautionary measure, of course.

To Pearce, it seemed that the scenario was the same everywhere, only the names of the players and the locations changed. A large business or corporate entity would set up shop on an industrial scale having either bought out or forced out the local competition, often with subsidies from the state or county authorities no less. This was accomplished with the usual empty promises of local jobs and spin-off business, such as farm equipment, feed and other supplies. Coupled with the huge anticipated tax revenues which, ironically, got whittled down to a pittance with tax loopholes negotiated by the same agribusiness entities, the deal was virtually irresistible to any local or state politicians.

Grease the wheels with generous campaign contributions, and any requisite business or environmental permits were a virtual *gimme*. The negative impact on the local environment and often the health of the citizens living in the area was generally pooh-poohed if not outright ignored, leaving the locals two choices—put up with it or move out. And the disastrous effects agribusiness had on the farm animals were so far down the list they were pretty much invisible. This pattern was repeated again and again seemingly everywhere that large-scale farming operations took place. The sixty-four-thousand-dollar question was how to disrupt the pattern?

He paid cash when checking out of the quaint Robinwynd B&B on Arch Street in Little Rock, Arkansas. The young woman at the front reception desk gave KJ an approving glance as she rung up his receipt. Pearce swung the T-Bird north on I-55 where he would pass though West Memphis and Blytheville, eventually hitting the Missouri state border. As he drove he considered his options for a plan of attack. He would continue north through Missouri, Illinois, Wisconsin and into Ontario, Canada where he would return to Dywer Hill to advise his CO that he would not be returning for another tour of duty with JTF2, much as he would miss that.

This mission could take a while.

CHAPTER 16

Tactical Support

Pearce left his CO at Dwyer Hill fuming at losing such a capable soldier *and to what?*

"KJ, if it's law school, we'll pay for your last year's expenses if you'll agree to work for us when you are done," offered Major Connell, a powerfully built man in his late fifties, formerly an active member of JTF2, now stuck at a desk. "You want to stay in the field a few more years, no problem," he added without prompting. "Or if you want to go into the legal arm of JTF2, the door's open." He was direct, no-nonsense and always dead serious.

"Major Connell." KJ matched his CO's directness. "I really appreciate the offer, but I'm not going back to law school just yet. And much as I love being a part of JTF2 something else has come up, Sir. I need to attend to it."

Connell swiveled in his high-backed chair to face Pearce squarely. He removed his glasses and clasped his hands on his desk. "And what might that be, Master Sergeant Pearce?" Clearly, he pulled no punches.

"Sorry, Sir, I am not at liberty to say," replied Pearce staring directly at Connell.

"Private sector or government?"

No immediate reply was forthcoming as Pearce considered his response. Connell waited a few seconds and then grimaced. "Oh no, not those assholes at Canadian Security Intelligence Services for Chrissake?"

Pearce was as blunt as Connell. "No, it's private. I can't say more at this time."

"Goddamn it, KJ, you're a superb soldier, one of the best we have ever had--and that says a LOT, so I hate to lose you to … to who—or what? How can I top their offer if you can't tell me what it is?" Connell closed his eyes and rubbed his temples in exasperation.

KJ sat still, but said nothing.

"Is it the money?"

"No."

"Better venue? I mean Dwyer Hill isn't exactly L.A. or even Vancouver, but hell, a JTF2 mission can take you anywhere on the globe."

"No, it's not a better location."

"Job security?"

"No."

"A girlfriend who wants you to get out?"

"No."

"Then what the hell is it?"

"I wish I could say sir, but that's not possible," Pearce responded. "Major Connell, it's been an honor to serve Canada by being a part of JTF2, but I can't stay on and there is nothing you can say or do to change that." Pearce was matter-of-fact and left no doubt that his mind was made up.

"Dammit soldier, I hope that you know what you are doing." There was no mistaking the aggravation in Connell's voice. "And not just throwing away a brilliant career in the most elite military unit in the country—hell one of the best in the world—for nothing."

"I sincerely hope not," replied Pearce, as he rose to his feet. He saluted his commanding officer. "Sir."

Connell returned the salute. "Good luck, soldier."

"Thank you, sir." He would need it in spades.

He signed his final release papers at the JTF2 legal department on the third floor of the Dwyer Hill headquarters, already starting to miss the place and he had not yet left the building. He'd had a great team of first-rate soldiers to work with from the get-go. As everyone who has ever played a team sport knows, any player on the team—including the star quarterback, point guard or pitcher—is only as good as his team enables him or her to be. Every player is integral to the ultimate success of the team, even if only a few get to bask in the limelight.

Pearce had ultimate respect for everyone on the JTF2 team—Robbie, the best demolition man he had ever seen, Cosmo, the ultimate sniper, Sharel, a communications genius who could find a link or line when no one else could, Reb, the master armorer who could disassemble and reassemble any weapon blindfolded, not to mention fixing them in his sleep, Margo, a field strategist extraordinaire—the list went on and on. Now he had to set about assembling a new team.

The imron-red Thunderbird slowly rolled through the heavy metal gates at the front guardhouse of the Dwyer Hill compound for the last time. Pearce was heading west on the Trans-Canada Highway toward Vancouver, British Columbia, where he would recruit key allies to provide tactical and logistical support for his campaign. It would be a long haul, but it would give him plenty of time to plan, and planning was critical if this mission was going in his dossier under the "accomplished" folder.

To start, his team would be as small as possible, a few personal friends whom he could trust with his life, if need be. Kiara was his first choice. The no-holds barred litigator had scored major victories against B.C.'s biggest foresters for their illegal clear-cutting; multi-national miners for contaminating local watersheds; and most recently in a joint lawsuit with the B.C. SPCA, for trying to cover up several cases of deadly avian flu in its national factory farm near Abbotsford. If Pearce could sic the courts on some of the bad guys, that would help, but even a modicum of research on WestLaw revealed a dearth of animal protection laws in Canada and the U.S. Still, Kiara could publicly ask tough questions and dig for answers without raising suspicion about her motives or contacts.

His next choice would be Rafa Matus, a quintessential computer guy— hacker, programmer, researcher. If it had anything to do with computers he could do it. A master of *slow,* he took what appeared to others to be his own sweet time to solve a problem–but as far as Pearce knew, he never failed to get it done. In his own defense, the somewhat introspective, twenty-eight-year-old Nicaraguan would tell you, "if it was a job worth doing, it was worth doing *well."* He had never studied mindfulness or read Jon Kabat-Zinn's insightful book, *Where Ever You Go There You Are,* but like a cat, Rafa was innately mindful. When he got his teeth into a problem like neutralizing a computer virus, finding a software bug or knocking down a firewall, he was relentless, single-minded and focused. Time had no meaning nor was he even aware of it.

He had never in his two-year call to the Bar, been reported to the Law Society of British Columbia for disciplinary action, incompetence or anything else that lawyers might fear, but he was paranoid about keeping secrets and always flying under the proverbial radar. His one-man firm specialized exclusively in computer law, and Rafa insisted on dotting the I's and crossing the T's, particularly when it came to compliance with the thousands of rules and regulations imposed by the British Columbia Law Society to protect the public from cutthroat, money-grubbing lawyers.

That did not mean, however, that Rafa was a pussy when it came to pushing the legal envelope. He just made sure that he was either just onside legal ground and that no one short of Edward Snowden could trace his digital tracks.

When he reached Vancouver, Pearce would meet up with his two good friends to discuss plans and see if he could enlist their invaluable assistance.

CHAPTER 17

Where to Start

Tactically speaking, when trying to solve a gigantic problem it is best to break it down into small pieces. As Lao Tzu said, "the journey of a thousand miles starts with a single step." Pearce's military training would dictate the application of force to obtain a solution, but the question was what kind of force and where to apply it. Fortunately, the tools for this type of endeavor were still at Pearce's disposal. One of his contacts at Fort Bragg was able to procure pretty much any military ordnance in existence from RPG's to automatic assault rifles and everything in between. The almost trillion-dollar-a-year U.S. defense budget enabled all of its army bases to offload anything less than state-of-the-art surplus weapons and equipment to Homeland Security. That department in turn provided the surplus to cash-starved police forces across the country *gratis*. Some would argue this process was unnecessarily militarizing the American police forces but that is an issue for another day.

Slipping through the cracks, a small portion of such weaponry leaked out to private contractors and mercs for near fire sale prices. Pearce didn't want to risk transporting such hardware across the border, so he relied on his contacts at JTF2 to obtain ordnance in Canada when needed. He had his own personal war chest to finance this campaign, although he was hoping not to fully deplete it. However, he would use up every penny and ten times more if that is what it took to get the mission accomplished. Sir Isaac Newton's first law of motion states that an object either remains at rest or continues to move at a constant velocity *unless acted upon by an external force.* Peace would be that force.

His base of operations would be South Surrey, British Columbia. He took out a one-year lease on a small farm on 24th Avenue just shy of the Langley border. On each side of his property—in fact all the way from 24th to 160th Streets were similar acreages, used for raising chickens, boarding dogs and horses, growing specialty crops and general hobby farming. The small farms were mostly fenced and densely treed with spruce and fir, which provided a good deal of privacy for all concerned. Neighbors knew each other to say hello, but most farm folk, even on hobby farms, are pretty self-sufficient and don't disturb their neighbors' privacy unless it's important. That was just fine with Pearce.

The four and-a-half-acre spread had a barn and outbuildings, including a large workshop, complete with a wood and a metal lathe and gardening tools. To top it off, a ride-on John Deere mower in what appeared to be questionable condition was stored in one of the small barns. He christened the four-and-a-half-acre-spread "*Animal Farm*" and promptly set about acquiring a few sheep, two llamas and of course, a couple of hounds (which he could get on loan from his dad) to guard the place when he wasn't there.

A huge, old double garage would accommodate the T-Bird, and a two-year-old black, customized Dodge Durango 4X4 would nicely fit into the neighborhood. Privacy or not, he had to maintain the appearance of being at least a dilettante hobby farmer as he did not want to draw any unnecessary attention to his base of operations.

CHAPTER 18

New Recruits

"So, what's this new venture you're into, KJ?" Kiara Davies didn't beat around the bush. Perched on a barstool, elbows on the countertop, she wore a black silk blouse open at the neck and a white kerchief around her neck. Add to that her Calvin Klein jeans and Pearce thought she looked close to perfection. A couple of PETA pendants dangled from her silver bracelet.

Kiara's apartment was southwest-facing over False Creek on the Yaletown side of the Burrard Inlet, a stone's throw from Vancouver's downtown financial district. From the 28th floor the view of the inlet with its marinas and the popular Granville Island Market could not have been more magnificent. Sleek Chris Crafts, Sea Rays and virtually every variety of dinghy, sail boat and yacht were nestled in their berths abutting the famous market that was ranked by travel journals as "one of the coolest open air markets in North America to visit."

Rafa sat in a lotus position, looking curious as a cat on the 12-foot black microfiber sofa. Neither he nor Kiara had seen their friend since he left for his training in Dwyer Hill operations center near Ottawa, and then Fort Bragg, but had they kept in touch by email and the occasional Facebook post. However, KJ's posts and messages were always oblique and vague for security reasons. Now out of the blue he was out of JTF2 and back in Vancouver, with something up his sleeve.

"Okay, KJ, you've got us hanging," Kiara said. "What's up? Spill it!"

KJ stood next to the floor to ceiling windows of Kiara's apartment, sunlight streaming in behind him—the Canuck version of Marvel's Captain America, ready to take on the bad guys and right any wrong, anywhere. "Well." He started slowly. "You remember that book I gave you guys…"

"*Diet for a New America 25th Anniversary Edition* I believe," chimed in Rafa. Clearly, he remembered.

"That was mind-boggling," Kiara said, recollecting her conversation with Pearce about the travesty befalling the animal kingdom on a daily basis at the hands of people everywhere.

"Yes! It's been bothering me ever since I read it," KJ said, pacing like a puma.

"Yeah, I kind of figured that."

"Even though it seemed pretty credible when I read it, I bet it was exaggerated," Rafa said. "You know, to sell copies."

Pearce nodded. "That crossed my mind so I went to see for myself." He paused, remembering the conditions he'd witnessed. "And, if anything the book doesn't do the reality justice."

Rafa and Kira exchanged glances. "How so?" Rafa asked.

"It's far worse."

Kiara left the barstool, dropped herself into a huge arm chair and asked Pearce how he had discovered this.

"First, I visited a place called "Chicken Haven Farm" in Nebraska and got a bird's eye, pardon the pun, of the plight of about a 160,000 chickens packed into a dozen or so barns—ready to be turned into Chicken McNuggets.

"How'd you get in there," asked Rafa, incredulous. "I mean they don't usually give guided tours of those kinds of places, do they?"

He laughed a little. "No, they don't. So I answered an ad the owner had placed in a trade rag called *The Chicken Review*. He was looking for an investment proposal to modernize his operation. I told Irv Cohen, the chief investment officer there, that I had a half a dozen Asian investors who would put in up to two million bucks each for a piece of the action, and in the process, I got the full tour."

"Lemme get this straight," said Rafa, always the doubting Thomas. "You just waltzed in with what, a fake business card and some aviator shades, bamboozled the CIO with some bullshit about foreign investors and he just walked you through the whole operation?"

"Yeah, that's pretty much it," KJ replied. "But I had on a nice, dark blue Armani suit too."

"Wow, you have come a ways since first year law school." Kiara smiled.

KJ pushed on. "Then, while I was in the U.S., I got a look at a dairy farm in North Dakota. Conditions were so bad there I ditched milk and cream immediately after visiting it."

"You pretended to be the sheriff I suppose, checking on local ordinances?" chided Rafa.

"Close. I printed a state health inspector's card created from a website and that got me in."

Kiara rolled her eyes. "That was probably illegal, you know, posing as a state official and all."

"Well, Kiara, I might just have done the odd thing that could have conceivably been illegal on the many JTF2 ops that I was part of," Pearce responded, adding "if you want to get technical about it." He was feeling slightly defensive.

"Yeah, but those were sanctioned by the Canadian government, correct?" Rafa asked.

Pearce was silent for a few seconds then said, "Right. Our actions were legal under Canadian law, but if we got captured by Al Qaeda or ISIS we would still have been interrogated, tortured and likely killed—legal or not."

"Good point." Rafa knew that lawyers always tend to overemphasize the importance of lawfulness.

"Anyway," Pearce continued, "in the last case I impersonated a pollster taking a survey for a trade journal called the *Pig Review.* This was in Arkansas and I almost couldn't finish the tour, the conditions were so gross. I had a half a mind to spring the fifty thousand or so pigs and burn the place to the ground ..." His voice trailed off and his eyes and for the briefest instant his eyes were pure ice.

Both Kiara and Rafa experienced an involuntary shudder. Their ex-soldier friend wasn't kidding. Pearce was a soldier first and a potential lawyer a far distant second, so the legality or lack thereof of his campaign was not an insurmountable roadblock in his mind. As they knew from law school discussions, in Pearce's view when man-made law was patently unjust, unfair or immoral it was to be considered subordinate to natural law. His preliminary legal research had showed him that powerful lobby groups in the U.S. and Canada pretty much wrote the laws they wanted when it came to the animal world, so his recourse to the courts, through Kiara, would be both limited and sporadic.

Needless to say, he did not plan to be apprehended or even identified by any law enforcement organization or security agency and hence, Rafa's superb technical prowess with computers and communications would be invaluable, not to mention his obsessive compulsion to cover his digital tracks at all times. Three and a half hours later Pearce was heading back to his operations base in South Surrey, with two necessary allies firmly on side.

CHAPTER 19

Hunting the Hunters

The Vancouver Sun had just announced that the annual B.C. Grizzly Bear Hunt was back—bigger and better than ever, boasting a larger territory and higher kill quotas. The birthplace of Greenpeace and many other environmental activist organizations, British Columbia was literally a backwater jurisdiction when it came to protecting these magnificent creatures. The annual hunt was ostensibly justified by three factors. First, it generated government revenue by way of license fees. Second, guides and outfitters were hired by the hunters. Add to that lodging, transportation and supplies—all supported the local rural economies of the province, which it seemed were perpetually in dire need of economic stimulus. The going rate for a guided grizzly bear hunt was about $15,000—$20,000 for foreign visitors, with license fees, travel and accommodation included.

The third factor was the ironclad guarantee of the Ministry of Forests, Lands and Natural Resource Operations ("FLNRO") to the good people of B.C. that grizzlies were not in short supply in the province. Government estimates put the grizzly bear population at about 16,000 at last count, so in their view, the hunt was benign—except of course for the several hundred bears which would be killed.

Pearce was keenly aware that even the best military logistics were just an educated guess. Barely twenty years ago some *15,000* full-time, well-paid civil servants working for the Canadian Department of Fish and Wildlife repeatedly assured the Canadian public that there were plenty of fish on both coasts of Canada. The public sadly watched as the Atlantic cod and West Coast sockeye salmon stocks virtually disappeared under their collective noses. Thus, he took the government's claim regarding the size of the grizzly bear population in B.C.—which was based on hair-snagging, DNA-based inventories, mark-recapture and a refined multiple regression model—with a grain of salt.

Grizzly bears, which are technically a sub-species of *ursus arctos*, the brown bear, can be fiercely intimidating creatures, with mature males reaching over a thousand pounds and standing upwards of nine feet tall on their hind legs. And despite their huge size, they are very speedy and can easily outrun any person. Very powerful omnivores, they devour massive amounts of meat or fish, particularly when they are preparing for winter hibernation.

However, it is one thing to have a bear show up in the backyard of your residential neighborhood in Deep Cove, North Vancouver, and quite another thing to go looking for one in the wilderness, like the massive Great Bear Rainforest. Although Pearce grew up hunting and fishing in the forests and mountains of Alberta, he always had a problem with killing the animals he had so expertly learned to track. However, he had no such compunctions when it came to killing people on JTF2 missions, but that was a different entity.

Since he was a kid, it had seemed to him that wild animals already had a lot to deal with just to survive—like finding food and shelter, avoiding predators, negotiating extreme weather conditions and caring for their young without having to deal with hunters who killed them for sport, rather than as a necessity for survival.

"Pull the trigger, KJ," his dad would say after an arduous day spent tracking a mountain lion or big horn sheep high in the Rockies.

"Can't dad," he would invariably reply. "Got him in my crosshairs--that's good enough."

Leonard would try to explain to his son that hunting was a manly sport practiced by warriors throughout the ages, and bagging a puma's head as a trophy for your den or living room wall was akin to receiving a badge of honor.

"Son," he would say, sighting his rifle on the prey. "It's that big cat's time because he is in our crosshairs at this time and place."

"No can do," KJ would counter, and emphatically so, gently lowering the barrel of his dad's Weatherby. "And he's in *my* crosshairs, not yours. His karma is to live to fight another day."

Leonard had grown up hunting, having gotten his first hunting license at age ten. To him tracking and killing a wild beast was a feat of skill and perseverance. In fact, it was as natural as breathing. However, he had nearly infinite patience with his one and only son and he always ended up capitulating. "We might as well be carrying cameras instead of rifles," he chided KJ more than once. Not too long after those comments sunk in KJ began lugging his dad's Canon

35mm SLR with a huge telephoto lens on these father-and-son expeditions. Pictures of would-be kills piled up--some of them worthy of a spread in *National Geographic*. On one of their last hunting trips, KJ had a magnificent big horn sheep in his sights at 300 yards near the peak of a rugged plateau in the Rockies. The morning sun was rising behind the mountain, turning the sky a golden, orange hue, and the imposing male big horn was slowly and methodically ascending the peak.

"That would be an absolutely perfect specimen to mount on the wall, KJ. Are you *ever* going to fire your rifle?" asked Leonard.

"When they start shooting back is the time I pull the trigger dad."

American and European trophy hunters who were willing to pay twenty grand to bag a B.C. grizzly had no qualms about going home with a bear's head in tow. Soon a couple of hundred of them would descend on the Great Bear Rainforest with their retinues of trackers, guides and outfitters to risk their very lives in this dangerous endeavor. The fact was that in the history of the hunt, no hunter had ever been killed by a bear--not even close; however, one or two had been accidentally shot by other less than *skilled* hunters who apparently could not distinguish a bear from a human.

Pearce decided that it was time to throw in a little more risk into the equation. Through the technical wizardry of Rafa, an anonymous message was superimposed on the homepage of the B.C Ministry of Forests, Lands and Natural Resources Operations' website. The message appeared in large bold printing:

"To All Hunters— (the smoking barrel of a hunting rifle graphic appeared here)

2015 marks the start of a new twist to B.C.'s Annual Grizzly Bear Hunt. You cannot only legally kill more bears and hunt over a much larger territory than ever before, but you will now enjoy the thrill and excitement of potentially BEING HUNTED yourselves!

I have been commissioned by the Association of B.C. Bears to "level the playing field," so to speak. I will be in the Great Bear Rainforest during hunting season AND I WILL BE HUNTING YOU.

I might look like just any other hunter (or

maybe not).

I feel it only fair to warn you that I will be ARMED and DANGEROUS.

The Rainforest is over 12,000 square miles (about 32,000 square kilometers for our Canadian and European friends who prefer metric), so your chances of missing me are quite good.

However, if you are unlucky enough to run into me the only way you will be leaving the Rainforest is in a body bag.

Best of luck."

Within minutes the message was spotted by a U.S. hunting enthusiast who re-posted it on the American Outfitter and Guide Association website. It went viral immediately, setting off a virtual firestorm of controversy. Little did the hunters know their troubles were just beginning.

CHAPTER 20

Laying out the Strategy

KJ, Rafa and Kiara, had met at Rafa's this time. His apartment number was a lucky one – 777. The building was on 653 West Hastings St. in the up and coming area called Gastown. A trendy loft boasting a 20-foot ceiling in the living room, it was Rafa's pride and joy, as well as a good location to strategize in.

KJ was the first to speak. "How in the world did you do that?" He was amazed and very pleased with Rafa's message to hunters.

"What, the message post or the GIF?" Rafa looked over to his old friend.

"Both."

"Oh, a little bit of this and that," Rafa explained, modestly. He went over to his Dell Alienware 17 laptop and gestured like he was tossing a digital salad. A gamers' delight, the Alien had massive computing power and blazing speed, a combination also ideal for hackers. "Just start with some dummy internet accounts, half a dozen anonymous proxy servers, a touch of *TOR*, a bit of creative programming, a hack or two, pre-paid (in cash) credit cards and voila!" he explained, as if everyone knew how to do that.

"After a month or two of intensive investigation, if they get that far, the trail will finally end at an internet café in Amsterdam." He shrugged, obviously a bit pleased in spite of his modesty. "By the way, did you like the smoking gun GIF?"

"Hey, that was absolutely first rate! A very nice touch. It definitely added to the impact."

"Kiara plunked herself into Rafa's gigantic, orange beanbag chair. "And now if you two boys are through congratulating each other, I would like to know what the next step is. I mean, KJ, you're not going to actually carry through on that warning and start killing off the hunters?"

No one spoke.

"Are you?"

Deftly parrying her question, KJ explained. "The hunt is scheduled to commence in six weeks. As you can see..." He motioned to Rafa who typed in some keystrokes on the Alien and then turned its big 17-inch plus screen towards Kiara. "The message went viral within minutes of Rafa posting it and just a couple of days later, it's got over twelve million hits –that's *million*, even though Rafa confirmed that the government took it down almost right away."

"Not only that," Rafa added, his words coming fast as his excitement, "but it's *everywhere* on the conventional mass media—all the major networks are carrying news reports on it—CBS, NBC, ABC, CNN, FOX in the U.S. and CBC and CTV in Canada and dozens of smaller players. The late night shows have gotten in on the act, along with all the hunting and outfitter groups. Hell, even the NRA has weighed in on it."

"Wow, you couldn't buy that kind of exposure," Kiara said. "Good job, amigo."

"Fortunately, we don't have to," Pearce said, "since we don't have nearly the budget for it. The good news is, the media has an insatiable need for stories—the more sensational or outrageous the better."

Pointing to the Alien's screen, he continued. "Groups like ISIS and Boko Haram have made use of this fact to garner worldwide publicity for beheadings and burnings of hostages –and the media has fallen for it like sap from a tree."

"That's for sure," observed Kiara. "It seems like they're in bed together. While the media purports to decry the violence, they report it on the front page every time because it generates site hits and sells copy to the dwindling few who still read the printed page."

"*If it bleeds, it leads*, is still the mantra of the news media," Rafa said. "That's always sounded a little crazy to me, but it seems to bear out." He hit the remote and his 60-inch big screen LED TV came to life in full 1080 HD and Dolby sound, no less. He switched to a FOX broadcast.

"In case you've just joined us we are speaking with Brody Walsh, a counterterrorist expert from the Brookings Institute in his office in Washington, D.C. Good evening, Brody," said Greta Van Susteren, the celebrity FOX news anchor.

"Good evening to you Greta," said Walsh gruffly, a fifty-something, no-nonsense Irishman.

"We've reproduced the anti-hunting message which was posted

on the government of British Columbia website a few days ago, including the smoking gun graphic," Greta said, pointing to the TV monitor where the message, GIF and all, was in plain view for everyone to see.

"Mentioned again! I love it!" exclaimed Rafa, spinning around and giving KJ a high five.

Greta was just warming up. "Brody, what do you make of it? Is it just a prank?"

Behind his huge wooden desk stacked with important, no doubt confidential papers and reports, glasses down on the bridge of his nose, jacket off with the sleeves of his crisp, white cotton shirt rolled up, Brody Walsh looked exactly like any respectable, desk-bound, counter-terrorist expert should. "In my professional opinion, it's definitely not a prank Greta," he said emphatically.

"First off, it took some considerable prowess to hack the B.C. government's website." He leaned against the back of his chair with his hands clasped together for emphasis. "I've personally talked to their technical people and they have a pretty robust security system in place."

"Okay, Brody, but there are hacker groups like *Anonymous* who have the technical know-how to hack into any government's system," Greta said. "As you most likely recall, SONY has been hacked. In the past year even the CIA and the Pentagon have suffered major cyber-security breaches, as well."

"All too true," Walsh responded. "But as far as anyone can tell, the origin of this breach is virtually untraceable. Most hackers leave digital trails which can be analyzed to provide clues as to where they originated from." He paused to let that comment settle in. "So far this one is a complete dead end!"

"ALL RIGHT!" Rafa pumped his fist, just like his tennis player namesake Rafa Nadal would do after scoring a big point.

Brody grabbed a file from his desk and held it so the cover wasn't visible to television viewers. "Greta, we've also analyzed the message itself and it does not seem to be the work of a prankster."

"How so, Brody?" She appeared to be earnest.

"Firstly," he said, "the message is calm and factual. It is not written with false bravado or rancor. There is also a bit of humor there about the author being 'commissioned by the B.C. bear population to level the playing field' which would tend to appeal to the animal activists who oppose hunting on principal."

For once, KJ was grateful for Fox's large audience.

"Go on," Van Susteren said, appearing on the split screen as serious and interested, as she always does.

Brody leaned forward again, looking into the camera and continued. "The author goes on to say that he—and we are assuming that this is a male—might look just like any other hunter or maybe not." He dropped the folder on his desk for effect. "Now that's down right insidious," he stated. "No hunter who shows up for the 2015 hunt can safely assume that any other hunter in the forest is not there to kill him. Talk about putting everyone on edge—and remember, all the hunters will be carrying high-powered rifles!"

The colorful host of *On the Record* interjected, "That's of course assuming that this guy, if he is a guy, actually shows up, right?"

"That's just it Greta. He doesn't even have to show up," said Walsh. "Who in their right mind is going to risk getting killed, if not by the terrorist who posted the message, then by one of the 150 or 200 odd hunters who may get spooked and shoot first and ask questions later?"

"Hey, guys." Kiara looked at her comrades. "Where does he get off calling us terrorists? How about the morons running around with guns terrorizing the bears?" she added.

"Is there anything else the message tells us?" Greta knew she was running out of scheduled interview time.

Brody's reply was instantaneous. "Yes. It tells us that the author is probably American with a military or ex-military background. I would guess that he probably served in Afghanistan or Iraq."

Van Susteren raised her perfectly sculpted eyebrows, looking for an explanation.

"He uses *miles* to describe the size of the Great Bear Rainforest and then he converts that into kilometers for "the metric users," being the Canadians and Europeans," Walsh said. "Only military personnel, particularly if they have served in an active combat theatre would refer to anyone leaving the rainforest in a body bag."

Pearce mentally punched himself for making that reference. He would have to be much more careful with his public messages in the future.

"So our suspect is likely an American male, twenty five to thirty, probably ex-military," concluded Van Susteren. "And he's serious?"

"Dead serious, in my opinion," replied Walsh.

"And your expert advice to viewers who might be thinking of

going bear hunting in British Columbia this spring would be what?"

Brody, looking stern as a fundamentalist minister, replied. "Skip it or you may very well get shot—if not by the guy who posted the message, then by one of the hunters."

"Works for me," said Pearce feeling triumphant.

Rafa flipped the channel to CNN, where Colleen Page, an F.B.I. psychologist and profiler from Quantico was also weighing in on the veracity of the message.

"No doubt in my mind that the message is for real," she stated emphatically, clear blue eyes looking straight into the camera. She was a knockout and frequently sought after for her opinions on profiling yet-to-be-caught criminals. The ratings always went up when she was interviewed. "The guy," she stated, "and it's definitely a guy who posted this message, is about twenty-five to thirty, ex-military, I would guess even ex-special ops and obviously an animal rights sympathizer."

"Why would you think ex-special ops, Colleen," asked the interviewer.

"He's obviously very confident of his ability to confront an armed hunter and his similarly armed guide and/or outfitter and still send the hunter home in a body bag. He's likely been trained in a variety of wilderness settings, possibly at Fort Bragg so he feels very much at home in the wilderness.

"Holy shit," said Pearce. "What the hell, is she clairvoyant?"

"Ah, she's just blowing smoke." Rafa looked unimpressed. "What soldier in the U.S. *hasn't* been trained at Fort Bragg?" He paused for effect. "And lots of soldiers in the States have got some kind of *special status* like the S.E.A.L.s, the Delta Force, the Green Berets, the Rangers, the Marines, Airborne—it's all a shell game to get these guys to risk their lives. Call them *special* and they will do anything, risk anything for you."

Pearce had never thought about it quite that way.

FOX's *Hardball with Clay Kennedy* was next on Rafa's channel surfing expedition. They caught the president of the NRA. "Every American not only has the God-given right to bear arms which, I might add, is supported in law by the Second Amendment to the U.S. Constitution of December 15, 1791, but to hunt with said arms where hunting is legally permitted—and that means British Columbia, Canada during grizzly bear season, so hunters, I urge you to go out there and shoot some damned bears!"

No surprises there.

Dianne Sawyer put a totally different spin on it by advising her *Face the Nation* viewers to, "Pass on the hunt and save some human lives. I mean," she said earnestly, "you might accidentally kill another hunter, thinking he's the terrorist or vice versa." Her closing remark was stern. "Let me be clear. That is not giving in to the wacko who posted the message, it's just plain common sense."

The ancient and venerable Canadian news anchor, Peter Mansbridge, often noted for his in-depth reporting, opined on the CBC National that, "This guy can't be Canadian, because that's not the way we settle our differences of opinion in this great country of ours."

"Oh yeah, that's true," said Pearce. "We would discuss them ad nauseam, have a Royal Commission, a couple of Senate committee studies, a parliamentary debate and by then everyone on both sides would have died of old age. Speaking of dying, *talk radio*, an industry on its way out, got a big boost, as urban dwellers on both sides of the border took aim at the, in their view, barbaric and senseless killing of bears which, far removed from civilization, posed no danger whatsoever to humans. Farmers, trappers, guides and outfitters and the hunting population fired back with both barrels berating the radio hosts for letting so many left-wing, namby-pamby city slickers litter up the airwaves with their animal rights bullshit.

Hunting was after all, a time-honored tradition in both countries throughout much their respective histories.

"So was child labor," thought Pearce. "But times change. Time to get with the program people."

Hunting news stories spread like wildfire.

In Des Moines, Iowa the local S.W.A.T. team had to be called to a local elementary school when a six-year old boy brought his dad's loaded .45 Sig Sauer to *show and tell*, explaining how he had seen his father "drop a moose" with the powerful handgun. He accidentally shot out the classroom windows, sending the teacher and other students scurrying.

In Winnipeg, Manitoba a high school class discussion about hunting got out of hand when the teacher, an avid bear and moose hunter himself, suggested that the students were equally culpable as any hunter because, "if you check your lunch box you will find that your mom probably made you ham or roast beef sandwiches. Where do you think that comes from if not from dead animals? Farmed or hunted down, it makes no difference," argued the teacher.

"Dead is dead!" he stated categorically.

The kids didn't see it that way and slashed his 4X4's tires and spray-painted "Bear Murderer" on the hood.

Phone lines at the Ministry of Forests, Lands and Natural Resource Operations in Victoria, B.C. were burning up and twice in the same day their website had crashed due to being bombarded with one-hundred-fifty-five-thousand hits—more than it had ever received in its fourteen-year history.

The first volley had definitely found its mark.

CHAPTER 21

Turning up the Heat

Never one to lose the initiative, Pearce began planning the next maneuver immediately. This one would be in the U.S.A.

His training at JTF2 had taught him to hit the enemy hard with multiple strikes from different directions, thus keeping them off balance and preventing them from re-grouping and retaliating. This initiative would definitely get the fur flying.

The fur trade was one of the first industries in North America, playing a vital role in the development and colonization of the U.S. and Canada for more than three hundred years. It began in the 1500's when European explorers sailed across the Atlantic searching for gold and silver. Such were not to be found at that time, but upon encountering Native Indians the explorers began trading tools and weapons for fur, particularly beaver fur.

By the later part of the century a great demand had developed from Europe for fur from overseas. Many fashionable European gentlemen had taken to wearing hats made of beaver fur. Later such furs as fox, marten, mink and otter also were also traded.

On the Canadian side, the French explorer, Samuel de Champlain established a major trading site in what is now the city of Quebec. The French later expanded their trading activities along the St. Lawrence River and all around the Great Lakes. On the U.S. side, English settlers developed a fur trade with the Iroquois Indians in what are now New England and Virginia, eventually expanding to Maine and down the Atlantic coast to Georgia. Large companies like the Hudson's Bay Company, the Northwest Company and later the Russian-American Company were established in the 1600's and 1700's to further promote and profit from the booming trade in North American furs.

So from a historical perspective, the fur trade is as American as apple pie and as Canadian as maple syrup. Although not what it once was, the North American fur industry still generates about two billion dollars in sales per year. Virtually all of the early fur trade involved the trapping and hunting of wild animals, but that has practice been largely replaced in modern times by *fur farming*. Pearce was soon to discover that fur farms looked a hell of a lot like factory chicken farms and cattle ranches.

Minks by Minx Ltd., the biggest U.S. mink farm operation had just showed up on Pearce's radar. While the majority of mink farms were small family operations often passed down from generation to generation, MBM, as it was known in the trade, had U.S. operations in Montana, Utah, Idaho, New England, Missouri, Oregon, Colorado and Wisconsin, as well as several farms in Manitoba and Ontario, Canada. All told, MBM was running twenty-seven mink farms which produced close to 550,000 mink pelts annually. At an average price of $60 U.S. per pelt, that generated gross revenues of some $35,000,000 per year.

Their biggest operation south of the border was located about sixty-five minutes south of Denver on a large spread seemingly in the middle of nowhere. Oddly, no adjacent farms were present and no towns or villages were within miles. The farm consisted of multiple barns, each equipped with hundreds of two-foot wire mesh cages stacked on top of one and other. Each small cage would house a mink for most or all of its short and entirely miserable life.

A quick bit of research had shown Pearce that minks, which are semi-aquatic members of the weasel family, normally occupy a territory approximately the same size of the entire farm—some fifty acres. Often locating near rivers or streams, a typical mink would spend a good deal of its lifetime in the water, where its oily, waterproof fur would serve it infinitely better than it would on the back of a well-to-do female fashionista.

Depriving a far-ranging, partially aquatic mammal of both space and water would certainly drive it to distraction, clearly constituting *torture* if it involved homo sapiens.

However, the thinking in the fur industry went something like this. What difference would it ultimately make if the farmer provided a better standard of living for the captive minks—since they were all destined to be killed anyway? It would just end up eroding the bottom line on the balance sheet and that is a definite no-no in a capitalist system which strives to ensure that profit is maximized at all times—regardless at whose expense.

And speaking of killing, on most U.S. fur farms, including all of MBM's, one of the most frequently used methods of killing animals is electrocution. The farmhand puts a metal clamp in an animal's mouth and a metal rod in its anus. Then a high-voltage current is sent surging through the animal's body. Sometimes the power surge forces the rod out of the anus, so the procedure must be repeated several times to kill the animal.

Other commonly-employed techniques include homemade gas chambers, such as a box hooked up to a tractor exhaust pipe, lethal injection of various chemicals that kill through paralysis, which can result in immobilized animals being skinned alive and when all else fails, neck breaking. None of this particularly surprised Pearce, although it definitely freaked out Rafa and Kiara who were both horrified and disgusted.

Secret prisons in Syria, Egypt and other Middle East countries were used by the U.S. and its allies (indirectly including Canada) to hold and interrogate political prisoners and suspected terrorists. Once so detained, these prisoners were not subject to U.S. or international law including habeas corpus, the right to counsel, the right to remain silent, the right to face one's accusers and the right to a trial within a reasonable period of time. The torture routinely inflicted on such prisoners was remarkably similar to that suffered by factory farmed animals.

Obvious to any soldier in the field is the fact that people are every bit as cruel to each other they are to animals. However, that is another story and not germane to this mission.

MBM had a long and highly antagonistic history with animal rights activists across the U.S. for egregious treatment of its mink. Not surprisingly, no charges had ever been laid, to Pearce's knowledge, since the farm and agricultural industries were pretty much exempt from any anti-cruelty laws. MBM had made it clear repeatedly in its press releases and on its corporate website that it considered animal rights groups and anti-fur campaigners as troublemakers and malcontents who were hell bent on destroying "the very industry which helped found America."

To obtain eagle eye imagery of the MBM Colorado mink farm, Rafa hacked into one of the fifty or so new, private nano-satellites now circling the globe. Crystal clear digital images revealed that the farm was flanked by Box Elder Creek on one side and Cherry Creek on the other. Further south, a small tributary of the Arkansas River ended several hundred meters short of the farm's southernmost boundary. The Burlington Northern Railway had a spur line which snaked southward from Denver passing within a few miles of the farm.

The MBM minkery was 49.3 acres, fully fenced, which was somewhat unusual for a farm of that size, especially since the animals were all held in pens, and contained thirty-two small metal barns which appeared to be on stilts or poles of some three to two feet in length.

The barns would hold the population of the farm, which Rafa estimated to be about 4,000 mink.

Several regular sized barns were present, presumably to store equipment, supplies and food for the mink.

At least a dozen vehicles were parked here and there—three or four pick-up trucks, a back-hoe, small grader, dump truck, a sixteen-wheeler with semi-trailer attached, an old motor home, an SUV and several cars. There was a huge, modern, wood frame, two-story house with a five-car attached garage and what appeared to be a guest house and a couple of single story motel-type buildings which likely housed the workers.

Thermal imaging detected a few ponds about fifteen hundred meters from the barns but also a couple of structures, possibly partially buried or partially hidden near the middle of the farm. It also indicated twenty-two people present on the minkery at the time the satellite image was taken.

All the people would have to be removed for Pearce to complete this mission, namely to release all of the mink into the wild, destroy everything on the compound while inflicting no civilian casualties and making damned sure that there was no insurance coverage in place to offset MBM's loss.

CHAPTER 22

Preparation

"Victorious warriors win first and then go to war, while defeated warriors go to war first and then seek to win"
—*Sun Tzu, The Art of War*

KJ had just finished a grueling workout at the Steve Nash Fitness Club in the Morgan Heights complex in South Surrey, not far from his operations base. The workout was a combination of a half hour on the state-of-the art weight machines, which ingeniously mimicked every manner of exercise you could do with free weights, a half hour of stretching, a half hour on the treadmill and finally some serious sparring with one of the personal trainers who happened to have a black belt in karate.

"Holy shit, KJ," said Gus Woodward, the most senior personal trainer on staff. "Where the hell did you get that from?" KJ had just put Gus down flat on his back and stopped an elbow strike just short of his right temple.

"Just got lucky I guess," replied KJ, panting heavily.

Sweat had soaked through his black cotton gi.

"Lucky, my ass," said Gus sarcastically. "Fifteen years in martial arts, I've seen maybe three people who could do that."

KJ helped him off the mat and they bowed to each other in a ritual manner of mutual respect. "How about I buy you a beer?"

"No way," replied Gus, "but I'll take a protein shake at the Jugo Juice bar."

"You're on."

But before they could leave the gym, a half a dozen of Gus' students swarmed them, full of questions. They had never seen anyone put Gus on his behind that easily. After answering numerous questions ("It's called Aikido," "My dad learned it in Japan from his dad who learned from a sixth Dan sensei there," "Yeah, just like Steven

Segal,") and promising to maybe come and teach a class with Gus, KJ hit the showers and jumped in the black Durango, to head back to his South Surrey base.

He would have to cross the U.S. border and start assembling some military ordnance near Denver. First stop was his R.B.C. bank machine to withdraw twenty-five grand in Canadian money. Next trip would be to a currency company, Vancouver Bullion & Currency Exchange, which would convert the cash to U.S.D. at the most favorable exchange rate, which was far better than his bank would, thereby stretching the dollars as far as possible. He didn't have unlimited funds after all.

Furthermore, no questions would be asked as the currency exchange company routinely converted hundreds of thousands of dollars back and forth between currencies every day for travelers, business men, lawyers, accountants, realtors and anyone else who walked in the door.

All purchases in the U.S. would of course, be cash only. Pearce would bring some fake ID and a few prepaid VISA cards with name "customer" printed on them. Whatever he had to buy or rent with a credit card would thus be totally anonymous also.

If this mission was to go anywhere, he had to remain completely unknown to the enemy and of course, to the authorities on both sides of the border. As Sun Tzu had opined, many hundreds of years ago, extraordinary planning and preparation were essential to being victorious long before any fighting ever began.

KJ settled into his South Surrey base and pulled up the satellite images which Rafa had obtained. He started planning the mission. He would cross the border at the Peace Arch crossing near White Rock, British Columbia in the Dodge Durango. KJ would explain to a bored U.S. border services agent that he would be doing some sightseeing near Seattle for a few days.

Once over the border he would head along I-5 to Seattle and then veer eastward on I-90 past Yakima, through Oregon and stop in Boise, Idaho for a bite to eat. From there it would be smooth sailing south along Interstate 84 through Utah and then east on I-80 through the cowboy state of Wyoming. Finally, the last stretch would take him south into Colorado.

A detour to the west on I-25 south would place him in Boulder, Colorado where he would meet up with Jake Watts, an old buddy from JTF2 days who had relocated to the U.S. after serving in both the Canadian and U.S. military for nearly fifteen years. He was honorably discharged from the U.S. Marines in 2012 and started a gun shop in Boulder, where he carried everything from target pistols to assault rifles. And for those in the know (and whom he trusted), he could procure any discarded U.S. military ordnance on the black market—which was pretty much anything one could ever want.

Pearce would pick up his handgun of choice, a Glock 20, a Kalashnikov AK—an AK-47 assault rifle, some night vision goggles, half a dozen concussion grenades, a long-range listening device, some detonators and enough C-4 explosives to level the entire mink farm. While Jake could certainly procure other types of industrial explosives, like TNT, Pearce wanted investigators to know that this was a military strike—he wanted maximum exposure in the mainstream media which doubtless would be all over this like a dirty shirt.

Once the hardware was securely stowed in the Durango, he would take highway 36 south passing through Denver and eventually to Englewood, where he would rent a motel for a week and carry out a detailed reconnaissance of the mink farm each night until he knew the place like the back of his hand. He would locate every road in and out of the farm from every direction and identify the closest fire and police stations and military base.

He had to assume that a fairly rapid response would ensue after he left his calling card. But by then, he would be long gone.

CHAPTER 23

To Hunt or Not to Hunt? That Is the Question

"I'll be damned if some nut bar is going to screw me out of a full season's income," declared Abraham LaFlamme, proprietor of HuntPro B.C., a longtime guide and outfitting company operating out of scenic town of Nelson, British Columbia. Around the solid oak table were an assortment of his guides, suppliers and business associates, all looking grim and anxious. Abe had built up a nice little family business over the last twenty odd years guiding U.S. and European hunters throughout the interior and northern wilderness of B.C. during the scheduled hunting seasons.

B.C. law requires all non-resident, big game hunters to be accompanied by a licensed B.C. guide and to obtain the appropriate hunting and species licenses. No more than two hunters to one guide were permitted. During peak times, Abe had up to eight employees, not including his wife, Molly who it was widely rumored, served up the best grub in town for the guests. That made him one of the town of Nelson's biggest employers. All of his guides were registered with the Ministry of the Environment, Fish and Wildlife Branch and each and every one of them knew both the terrain and the animals inside and out.

The Annual Grizzly Bear Hunt was a real draw, since more and more jurisdictions around the world were either banning or severely curtailing bear hunting, as the worldwide population of these magnificent creatures was dwindling. Although in fairness to HuntPro B.C., licensed, seasonal hunting was not the main threat to the bear population. As with most species, it was the continued erosion of their natural habitat by incessant human development. However, that would not be stopping anytime soon.

Fortunately for Abe, the B.C. government was, as usual, at least a decade behind every other jurisdiction in the world when it came to identifying leading trends. This left an opening for now. The ass clown who somehow posted a ridiculous challenge on for god's sake, the Ministry's own website, had drawn a shit storm of publicity from all around the world.

And worse, it was all negative!

"Bear Killers!"

"Why is hunting still legal?"

"Save the Grizzlies!"

Out of nowhere, goddamned activist groups like PETA and Mercy for Animals showed up. Not too far behind was the Animal Legal Defense Fund—some pain-in-the-ass American outfit that routinely used the U.S. court system to harass legitimate businessmen like cattle ranchers, furriers and rodeo operators just trying to make an honest buck. They all had jumped on the bandwagon to put B.C. guides and outfitters out of business. His bookings, normally a dozen to eighteen hunting parties per grizzly season, were down to two; and one of those was a definite maybe.

"What the hell was wrong with these guys," Abe asked. "I mean, it's not like they're gonna be unarmed themselves."

"Well," responded Don Longshadow, his longtime Métis guide and good friend. "Hunters are used to shooting, but not being shot at."

"And especially by an ex-special forces guy," added Charlie Longshadow, Don's nineteen-year-old son and apprentice guide.

"Who the hell said the guy is special forces, for chrissake?" Abe shot back. "And that's even if the guy really exists!"

"Oh, no, Abe, he's real," Pete Connors said, a warning tone in his voice. "Don't kid yourself." A stocky blacksmith, Pete would be sure that any horses used on Abe's hunting expeditions were properly shod. "All the commentators on TV have said so, and the fella on Diane Sawyer's show figures he's probably got a team," he continued. "Maybe ex-black ops or mercs are backing him up–else how could he cover even a thousandth of the forest himself."

Abe grimaced.

"Yeah, that's all you need," added Colin Cromwell, owner of Shoot Straight Small Arms, "the fucking Delta Force coming down on you like a ton of bricks while you're just minding your own damned business engaging in a lawful activity like bear hunting." Colin supplied the ammo and hunting rifles on the excursions. It was very difficult to lawfully bring weapons into Canada—for any reason.

"Delta Force, my ass," said Slim Jenkins, chewing on a wooden toothpick. "This guy could be a Green Beret or even a Navy SEAL. Those guys are trained killers."

"Are you guys completely retarded?" Abe shook his head in disbelief. "This guy has not even fired a shot and all of a sudden he's fucking Rambo reincarnated and everybody is pissing their pants!"

"But all the experts have said …"

"Fuck the experts!" Abe slammed his fist on the table. The coffee mugs rattled. "Those stupid talking heads couldn't find their own dicks with a flashlight."

"Maybe so," said forty-nine-year old Tony Proudfoot, probably the best tracker Abe had ever met in his life. "But they got guys worried. That's why we don't have the bookings."

As usual *Mr. Fucking Know-It-All* was right—thought Abe. "All right, all right" he said, raising his voice to a shout. "We've got to fight fire with fire!"

Everybody stopped talking and looked at him.

"Molly." "Ring up your nephew, you know, what's his face, the nerdy web kid—Elroy or Elton…?"

"Elmer," answered Molly, his wife of twenty-two years. She could still turn a head or two. "Elmer Herzog."

"Yeah, thanks, that's it. Ring up Elmer and tell him to post a message on our website that as of this minute, we will start providing armed, trained security, Canadian Armed Forces or better for every hunting party–at no extra cost!"

Approving looks greeted Abe around the table.

"Hey, that's not a bad idea," Don said, "not bad at all."

"I like it." Tony nodded in agreement. "I feel safer already. And I bet the hunters will too, once they hear about it," he proclaimed with confidence.

"And, Molly…" Abe's voice was gruff, but his wife was used to that. "Tell Elmer to get ahold of all of those dipshit media outlets and let them know, too. And don't forget to ask the kid to stick it on our Twitter and Facebook pages." He was hoping it just might go viral. "We're not going to take this shit lying down."

CHAPTER 24

Ready, Aim, Fire

K iara had done her legal homework on the U.S. insurance industry. Not unlike Canada's insurance laws, virtually every state in the Union exempted coverage for "acts of war, insurrection or domestic terrorism…" All of the pro forma policies that she had examined on the Colorado Insurance Commission's website were in lockstep with that view. Pearce would make damned sure that his visit to MBM's minkery would fall into one of those categories. No sense in making a point if the enemy's insurance policy mopped up all of the losses. This one would hit MMB in the pocketbook–and hard.

It was a bonus for KJ, not having to use his Fort Bragg connection and drag all the hardware across the country. By a pure fluke, he had run across Jake Watts' gun shop in Boulder on a Google search while researching the lay of the land in Colorado. Watts Guns & Ammo had advertised on its website that it carried "anything and everything you need to protect yourself and your property." On scanning the site, Pearce's reaction was an unconditional "Wow!" The list of brands in stock was very impressive–Glock, Sig Arms, Smith & Wesson, Springfield, Remington, Sako, Winchester, Heckler & Koch, Browning, Colt, Beretta, Mossberg, Savage, Kimber and FN. There were handguns, hunting rifles, assault rifles, and sniper rifles and accessories galore and this didn't even include the off the grid ordnance.

Watts had been a master armorer in the service. He could build and repair virtually any kind of gun and it was said that he could field strip an M-16 blindfolded and put it back together perfectly inside of a minute. Now he and his wife, Marcy, and their two eighteen-year-old sons, Nick and Billy Ray ran WGA. Due to the incredible selection of guns and Watts' seemingly limitless knowledge of them, he had rapidly become the go-to supplier for the local police department, the nearest Army base, the Boulder Gun Club and a few local motorcycle gangs.

After a scrumptious homemade dinner with Jake and the family (vegetarian at KJ's request), the two men climbed the stairs down from the top level of the two-story building, that housed WGA. Jake had taken his military pension in a lump sum when he left the service. This enabled him to purchase the small, brick commercial building on the corner of Folsom Street and Iris Avenue, just over from the Wells Fargo bank.

He applied to re-zone the top level to residential, and with a small mortgage loan from WFB he turned the empty space into a decent, three bedroom and den living quarters for the family. It was tight for four, but as the boys got older they were gone more and more of the time, so it didn't really feel like it. For Jake, the commute to work was just one flight of stairs.

After catching up on old times and swapping some combat stories, Jake began helping KJ load the ordnance into the Durango which was parked at the back of the building in a dark area. When it was done, KJ pulled out a wad of Ben Franklins, two hundred and fifty in total, and handed it over to Jake, who quickly stuffed it into his windbreaker without counting the money. That would be considered an insult between comrades-in-arms.

"Thanks, my friend," said KJ shaking Watts' callused hand.

"These munitions will be put to good use–and on the right side for once."

Although a breach of protocol, Watts just had to ask, "So where's the war, KJ?"

KJ smiled and shook his head. "You don't want to know, Jake."

As the black Durango slowly pulled out of the parking lot behind WGA, its V8 hemi burbling a low rumble, ex-master armorer Jake Watts saluted his former comrade. "Kick some ass, guy!"

CHAPTER 25

Looks Can Be Deceiving

The brouhaha over the Grizzly Bear Hunt had only increased since KJ's challenge was posted on the B.C. government's website. Surveys showed that almost ninety percent of British Columbians were opposed to the bear hunt. However, the B.C. Guide and Outfitters Association had contributed over eight hundred thousand dollars to the current liberal government's election coffers over the past decade. If there is one promise that politicians on both sides of the border always keep, it is to pay back their major campaign contributors. This was no exception. The hunt would stay -come hell or high water.

However, with "the challenge" still occupying the air waves on a daily basis, the number of hunters who had actually applied for 2015 licenses through registered B.C. guides was only twenty-two. This number was well down from the usual 150 or so applications that would have been received by this point in the year.

"It looks like KJ's strategy is working," Rafa said, as he pulled the latest stats from the government's website.

"It has indeed." Kiara agreed. "A ninety percent drop in licenses applications is not exactly small potatoes."

Rafa adjusted the screen resolution on the Alien so he could get a better look at her via the secure-link webcam they were using to communicate with. Even a seventeen-inch, super-high-resolution screen didn't do her justice. She was a looker by any measure.

However, Kiara didn't exactly see it that way. As a child, she was significantly overweight and invariably teased about that and her corresponding lack of physical skills. She was always the last one to be picked for a team in gym class, but surely the first one to be picked on in the school yard.

"Hey tubs, you think you can play left field for us?" she could still recall that smart ass Steve Laird asking her in grade six. He was the hotshot of the class—new BMX bike, always going skiing on the holidays and it seemed that all of the girls wanted to be his friend.

"I doubt that anybody will hit the ball out there, but we need someone to block out the sun," quipped Steve which drew a big laugh from the group. Although the now-overused term, bullying, is finally being recognized as a serious problem for both kids and adults alike, back in the day it was just about sucking it up and not being a cry baby. Kids in the playground have always been the absolute masters of bullying and in Kiara's case, the torment was almost nonstop.

Fatty Arbuckle, heifer, chunky soup, blimpo and cheese dog were just a few of nicknames she endured throughout elementary and secondary school from both girls and boys alike. In fact, sometimes she felt that the most hurtful comments actually came from her female classmates.

"You're never gonna get a boyfriend with a lard-ass like that," Candace Brinsmead, the class deb of the ninth grade constantly reminded her.

School proms were such a nightmare, she just skipped them invariably claiming illness as an excuse.

Only her supportive parents and Xuxa ("shoe sha"), the family dog, kept her going. Every weekday she couldn't wait for school to be over so she could go home. Any dog owner knows that there is a reason why canines are called man's best friend. They are there to greet you when you get home and they don't care if you are overweight, ugly, not cool or anything else. The fact that you have arrived home is always enough for your dog.

That characterized "the Xu" (as he was affectionately referred to) to a tee. And the fact that he was a stunning, brindle Afghan hound who looked pretty much like a rock star himself, definitely didn't hurt either. Although he had passed away years ago, she would never forget the unconditional love and acceptance from that incredible canine to her dying day.

It had seemed like an eternity, but finally in her senior year in high school, things began to change for Kiara. Firstly, seemingly out of the blue she got taller, a lot taller. A local martial arts studio was having an open house during Christmas break so her math teacher suggested that she take advantage their free two-week promotional pass. Inexplicably to her overjoyed parents, when she tried karate, it stuck like crazy glue.

Over the year, Kiara shed almost thirty pounds of unwanted fat and transformed another ten or so into pure, rock-hard muscle. Five days a week after school she was in the dojo training until she was literally ready to drop. She had her brown belt before the end of her senior year.

With her mom's prompting ("Hey sweetie, this one is your last chance") and wearing the belt under her dress for extra confidence, she decided that she would attend her very first high school prom. The jet black, Christian Siriano evening dress Kiara had picked out with her mom was surprisingly low cut and sported a lower-body slit, which, when she moved, revealed a gorgeous pair of long, highly toned legs. This caused a plethora of objections from her dad. But since this would be their daughter's one and only prom night mom had put her foot down and forced him to zip it.

"Besides, she can take care of herself," Mom reminded him.

On prom night, her anxious dad dropped her off at the school in the striking dress. It proved to be a memorable night indeed. Despite a couple of last-minute offers from guys who had never given her the time of day before, Kiara had decided to go to the prom without a date. Naturally, the Big Man on Campus immediately spotted her coming in through the door of the school gymnasium alone.

"Hey, what happened to the Goodyear blimp?" Steve Laird joked to a couple of his pals. "She actually doesn't look half bad!"

His buddies, Neal Strauss and Joey Henley studiously ogled her and decided that she now rated a two thumbs-up.

"I just gotta check this out," Steve boasted as he started moving towards Kiara.

"Hey Steve, your chick, Rebecca is gonna be pissed and she's right over there watching us," one of the boys warned him, pointing.

Cocky as ever, the Lairdian One flashed a big, white toothy grin told them he was just going to "give her a treat" and would be back in two shakes. For the benefit of his pals, Steve made a big production of swooping in from behind Kiara and firmly grabbing both of her breasts.

"Holy shit, no bra!" was his last thought before Kiara's reflex elbow strike broke his nose and sent him crashing to the floor. He was out cold. And the boys were right, Rebecca was not amused.

Even though that somewhat satisfying incident occurred over ten years ago, Kiara still bore the psychological scars of years of torment at the hands of her classmates. Despite now being six-feet tall, as drop-dead gorgeous as any model in *Sports Illustrated*'s Swim Suit

Edition and very athletic (the brown belt had long since become second degree black), Kiara still found it pretty hard to look at herself in the mirror without seeing her former self superimposed over her reflection.

She had plowed right into university straight from high school and obtained her undergraduate degree in commerce. She quickly followed that up with a top ten finish in her final year of law school at UBC. Now a litigator at Sierra Legal Defense, despite being only a two-year call to the Bar, she was not someone the other side was ever happy to see in the courtroom.

"Hellcat," "fucking bitch," and "aggressive harpy," were some of epithets losing, male counsel had taken to calling her—behind her back of course.

As litigation counsel, she could live with those. They sure as hell beat chunky soup.

"Hey Kiara, did you get the U.S. insurance info that KJ needed?" Her image was clear as crystal on the Alien screen now.

"I did, Rafa," she replied. "It's pretty much the same as here. Any damage caused by an act of war or a terrorist or civil insurrection will not be covered by any commercial policy."

"Great," replied Rafa appearing on her MacBook retina display screen. "I've almost worked out how to bring down internet and cell phone coverage for about a fifty-mile radius around the mink farm—that is after I let them know that there is a massive, toxic gas leak coming their way in a hurry."

CHAPTER 26

He Who Hesitates is Lost

KJ sat still in the driver's seat of the idling Durango. The full moon shone brightly in the middle of an otherwise black canvass that was Big Sky Country. A dozen tall spruce trees kept the SUV in the shadows of the Starlight Motel parking lot. The black-tinted windows and a dark tarp would keep the ordnance safe from prying eyes and a state-of-the art alarm system would alert KJ if anyone tried to tamper with the vehicle. He would not risk being seen carting in a bunch of military grade ordnance into his room, and wouldn't do so until much later in the night. Then he would field-strip it and examine every component in excruciating detail.

In the meantime, he had time to think–too much perhaps. Was this even the right play? Once the war got underway, he knew that there was no going back. Should he be taking the law into his own hands? After all, this mission was not sanctioned by the Canadian or U.S. governments, so there was no safe harbor to retreat to if he was pursued on either side of the border.

What if some farm workers, cops or military personnel got killed in the process?

What if he couldn't pull it off?

What if he got caught? If he did, there was not a hope in hell that he would surrender.

Hence, it was a lead pipe cinch that more than a few bodies would pile up if he got cornered somewhere before he bit the dust. What if? What if?

He grabbed his Contigo thermos and gingerly took a sip of steaming coffee. Best damned coffee mug on the market and at sixteen bucks for a pair of them at Costco. It was truly a bargain. The hemi continued its low, methodical rumble. He instinctively flipped the CD switch on the Durango's console, which locked a CD into place playing "OM meditation chant @ 432 hertz."

It was said by wise men and sages of old that the OM sound is the heartbeat of the Universe. For KJ it never failed to put him in to a state of utter stillness. And with stillness always came an answer –in his mind, invariably the right answer.

AHHHUUUUMMMMMM… AHHUUUUUMMMMM… AH-HUUUUMMMMMMMM.

Just like the low rumble of the engine, the relentless, gentle rhythm continued. This particular track had temple bells and the sounds of birds interspersed with the chant. Five minutes, ten minutes, fifteen minutes. The chant would last an hour and thirty minutes, but Pearce seldom needed more than fifteen or twenty minutes to find a solution hiding in that universal mantra. The CD was pre-set to pause at the twenty-minute mark and it did.

Abruptly KJ's eyes snapped open. His answer was crystal clear, leaving no uncertainty in his mind whatsoever. He'd read the play for a course in English Lit in high school. Its message hit him square between the eyes.

"Our doubts are traitors,
And make us lose the good we oft
Might win
By fearing to attempt."
William Shakespeare, Measure for Measure, Act 1, Scene 4

"Fuck the doubts, I've got a mission to fulfill!" he reprimanded himself. Not wasting a second more, Pearce speed dialed Rafa on his Blackberry Z30 Smartphone, its securely encrypted line safe from the NSA's or anyone else's prying ears.

"Hey KJ, are you there yet?" asked Rafa from his apartment in Vancouver.

"Yeah, I'm here and I've picked up the packages," revealed KJ, taking another sip of coffee. "How's the sat imagery coming?"

"Great, I'll email it to you tonight. It's super clear and the software I have will give you both distances and 3D topography."

KJ nodded, although Rafa couldn't see him. "You got the skinny on the nearest police station and military bases in the area?"

"Roger that. Nearest police station is forty-four miles due north in Denver," explained Rafa. "And the closest military base is Fort Taylor, a hundred twenty miles due east of the farm."

"Perfect," replied KJ. "That means even their best response time will be way too late."

"I think that I should also be able to monitor the police bands in the area for roving patrol cars, just in case one happens to be in the vicinity when the dominos start to fall," offered Rafa.

"You just read my mind," said Pearce. "Ask K to call me when she can about the insurance angle would you?"

"You got it."

CHAPTER 27

The Price of Security

"Hey, Molly, we got any takers for the security gig?" Abe asked his wife, staring at the kitchen clock as if it could answer his question.

She was cleaning the dishes after a hearty breakfast served up for Abe and a few of his crew. Flapjacks with butter and maple syrup, Canadian back bacon and hash browns were the day's fare—at least two thousand cals per serving, not that any of the men were exactly counting.

He watched her efficiently clean up. She still looked damned fine, even in an apron and blue jeans.

"Guy answered the ad is pulling into the driveway now," she said. A 1986 dark blue Chrysler LeBaron convertible came to a stop in front of the HuntPro Lodge.

"Jeeze, now that's a relic from a bygone era." Abe peeked out the window.

And speaking of relics, Jesse Spooner stepped out of the vehicle, accompanied by his son, Tanner. Jesse stood maybe six-four and looked to be about two-forty. Mid-sixties would be giving him the benefit of the doubt, Abe figured. Jesse's son, probably half that age, was close to the same height but looked to be under two hundred. Both had short hair, were clean shaven and carried .38 caliber service revolvers at the hip.

Abe met them at the front door of the lodge before they could knock.

Jesse extended his hand and said they had come about the security ad on "the Face Book." Abe grabbed his hand encountering a strong, firm grip (always a good sign).

"Glad you could make it. You guys are the first ones to answer the ad." Abe figured it likely the kid had spotted the online ad, as the dad obviously wasn't a computer guy. The Face Book? Everybody knew *the Napster* had convinced Mark Zuckerberg to drop *"the"* out of the name long before the initial IPO, a little piece of advice that netted him a cool three hundred mil. Inviting them into his office, Abe motioned that they sit across from the big oak desk.

"We're interested in the security positions with your company." Jesse was the first to speak. "For the hunting season," he added, earnestly.

"What's your background?" inquired Abe as he pulled out a large white pad to jot down some notes. These types of job seekers weren't likely to bring in a professional resume.

Jesse moved forward in his chair and rested his large, callused hands on the desk. He told Abe they both liked hunting and fishing and were completely opposed to anybody meddling with the Grizzly Bear Hunt in B.C. That included both the government and the crazy vigilante who posted the challenge.

In answer to Abe's next question, no, they were not overly worried about their own personal safety. "Me, I served twenty-five years in the Canadian Armed Forces and retired at fifty-nine in 2011," Jesse said. "My son, Tanner, he is currently a U.S. deputy sheriff and he, ... well you tell him, son."

"Mr. LaFlamme, I'm a deputy sheriff in Whatcom county in Washington state just south of the border of your fine province. "And I served a six-month tour in Afghanistan comin' up on five years ago this month."

"How can you work for me if you're a sheriff in the States?" Abe challenged.

"Fact is that the department is short on cash, so they are askin' us deputies to take some time off where possible. I'm the most junior so the pressure is on me to find some alternatives." Tanner shifted in his seat and continued. "So the three-month hunting season, would suit me and the sheriff's department just fine."

"Hmmm." Abe was thinking that a retired vet and an underemployed sheriff with some combat experience weren't the worst possible candidates on the planet. "Any problems working in Canada?"

"None I can think of," said Tanner.

"Dad's talked to a friend of his in DND and he pulled a few strings with Immigration Canada and they sort of like, pre-approved a short-term security contract, if one is offered."

"It's kinda like a reciprocal deal," explained Jesse, "since Canada and the U.S. both had troops on the ground in Kandahar for so long on the same mission. Both countries have a real good working relationship on the security side," he proudly stated.

Tanner nodded in agreement.

Abe pulled out a pack of Camels from his vest pocket and offered one to each man. Tanner took one and said thanks. Jesse said he quit about ten years ago and if he had a smoke now he would be back to a pack a day by next week.

"So what are you boys figuring to make, cash-wise?" Abe was direct.

"I dunno. What's on the table?" Jesse asked, not wanting to come in too low, but definitely wanting the job.

"Well, if we get busier with you guys on board, I could offer you each five grand a month for the next three months." There was silence while pair thought it over. "It would be a contract position, so of course, there's no source deductions off the top," added Abe.

Another pause.

To sweeten the pot, he offered to include room and board since they would be travelling with the expeditions anyway. What's another meal or two? And ammo. Just in case they needed to shoot anyone. After what seemed like an eternity, Jesse said that since he lived in Canada he could live with the five K, but Tanner would need at least sixty-five hundred a month—"to even out the shitty exchange rate."

After a much shorter deliberation, Abe said he could live with that. "Subject to running a background check on you guys, I think we've got ourselves a deal!" He shook hands with both guys, who were now beaming.

Expeditions generally ran a week, at fifteen to twenty thou a pop, so if the additional security could garner even two or three extra parties a month (as opposed to the single, confirmed booking he had now), he could save the season from financial disaster. And goddamned if he might not just bag another trophy in the process, namely one ex-military asshole who was trying to screw up his hard-earned business!

Now *that* would definitely go viral!

CHAPTER 28

Recon

In the wilderness, it is almost pitch black at midnight. There is no reflective glare from the city lights skyward to the clouds to provide even the dimmest of lighting. It is also dead quiet, since a plethora of nocturnal creatures are out hunting. Anything making any excess sound could easily wind up being something else's next meal. Pearce pulled the black Durango next to a tall thicket of wild blackberry bushes that were smothering the northern fence line of the MBM Mink Farm. About fifty feet away was a locked, metal cattle gate, behind which, a long winding road quickly disappeared into the blackness. Pearce quietly exited the Durango. He donned a pair of night vision goggles and grabbed a knapsack full of goodies.

He was wearing black combat garb and his face was smeared with charcoal. For all intents and purposes, he was invisible in the pitch-black night. His Glock 20 rested comfortably under his armpit in a custom fit shoulder holster along with a half a dozen ammo clips. A silencer was tucked into his vest for easy access. Also in easy reach were a couple of concussion grenades, throwing stars and, of course, his trusty K-bar military knife. For him this was light armament, as this would be a soft entry only.

Pearce checked the lock on the gate with his mini-maglite–an easy pick when the time was right. He squeezed between the wide-set bars and punched the speed dial icon on his Blackberry Z30, the most secure wireless phone in existence. A favorite of criminals, police, security agencies and the U.S. government, Blackberry's military-grade encryption defeated even the most ambitious snooping agencies.

"On site. You copy?" said Pearce into the tiny mike connected to the wire running from the Z30 secured in his vest pocket to his left ear bud.

"Acknowledged," Rafa replied. "You want to go due south along the road ahead of you for about a half mile."

Pearce started walking along the road, the night vision goggles creating a greenish field of vision ahead of him.

At the twenty-minute mark he spoke into the mike. "Hey, you picking up anything on my right about twenty yards off the road? It looks like a couple garages. No, wait, they are too small for that, maybe storage sheds…"

"Not much showing on sat view," Rafa replied.

"I'm going to have a look." Pearce drew the Glock and carefully screwed on the silencer.

The two sheds stood maybe eight-feet tall and appeared to be about ten by ten, so possibly a hundred-square-feet each. That's the average size of an office. Pearce pulled out the mini-maglite and began searching for trip or alarm wires. He slowly circled both sheds, checking the perimeters near the ground level and, again, around each door. In the daylight, the sheds would be concealed from the air by the tall spruce trees which encircled them. He noted no motion sensors, alarm wires nor surveillance cameras. The sheds were metal, probably half-to-three-quarter-inch thick with no windows. The doors were deadbolt…

"Ah shit," Pearce whispered into the mike.

"What's that?" Rafa responded.

Too preoccupied with checking the perimeters, Pearce hadn't noticed the keypad above the deadbolt locks which bore the label, *Schlage Sense.* "Can you look that up?"

Ten seconds later Rafa advised him that the locks were state-of-the-art, Bluetooth-enabled "Schlage" devices, which operated with Apple Home Kit technology. This meant end-to-end encryption and authentication between the Schlage Sense™ lock and the owner's iPhone, iPad or iPod touch.

"Hey, you can even use *Siri* to open the door," quipped Rafa, reading the lock maker's material online.

"Thanks for that tidbit," Pearce replied, somewhat testily.

Rafa carried on reading aloud. "The Schlage Sense™ lock provides Grade 1 security, the highest rating certified by Builders Hardware Manufacturers Association and Built-in-Alarm Technology, which issues an alert when it senses potential door attacks."

"Can you override it or disable it without triggering an alarm signal?"

"Maybe, but not in five minutes," Rafa said. "I would have to get a hold of one and take it apart then analyze the coding."

"Please do so *stat*," said Pearce. Why would someone go to the expense of putting expensive, Bluetooth-alarmed, digital locks on a couple of steel sheds in the middle of the farm? No matter, he would look into it on his next visit after Rafa figured out a way to defeat the locks. Meanwhile, he had a lot of terrain to cover and would not be done until he had inspected every structure and road on the farm to his extraordinarily high standard of satisfaction.

CHAPTER 29

Rafa Matus

Born in 1986 in Managua, Nicaragua to working class parents, Rafa Manolo Matus was likely destined to be a peasant farmer or common laborer, but for a chance encounter with the daughter of a wealthy businessman. A naturally gifted learner, Rafa had grown up in the midst of the Iran-Contra affair in Nicaragua, which saw U.S. President Ronald Reagan illegally funneling millions of dollars from arms sales to Iran to the Contra guerillas in his country. They were attempting to overthrow the leftist Sandinista government.

As a child, Rafa had quickly learned the value of secrecy and stealth. Civilians living in the midst of a guerilla war know better than to publicly express any views, pro- or anti-government, for fear of being punished by one side or the other. One sunny afternoon in 1994, on a busy thoroughfare in Managua, eight-year-old Rafa was returning from the inner city public school he attended when he saw a strange incident. A fancy white car, maybe a Cadillac, he thought (it was in fact a Maserati Quattroporte sedan), was forced to the side of the road by a jeep carrying three armed soldiers. The car jumped the curb, sending a few pedestrians scurrying, and came to an abrupt stop.

Two soldiers got out of the jeep and started shouting at the car's driver to *"salir del coche, salir!"* The driver began shouting back, indicating that he would not get out of the car and that they should be on their way now.

"No, no. Nosotros vamos pronto," the driver exclaimed. But he was roughly dragged out of his seat by his lapels and thrown to the pavement.

"Abra la puerta ahora!" one of the soldiers shouted to the man in the back seat. When the soldier yanked the rear door open, out jumped a pint-sized Pomeranian dog, immediately pursued by a young girl who was shouting.

"*Mi perro se ha escapade! Vuelves!*" She tried to run after the dog, but her dad caught her arm fearing that she would run into traffic.

Stupid girl, thought Rafa from across the street. She would never catch her dog with all the cars going by. But then he saw that she was crying hysterically, totally upset over losing the dog. Obviously, the little dog means a lot to her, he thought, although who knew why—it was just a frigging *Pom* for Pete's sake! The soldier was arguing with her dad, who, in turn, was not letting go of the girl's wrist.

Without thinking, Rafa bolted into the traffic, nearly causing a multi-car pile-up as motorists valiantly tried to avoid him. Vehicles screeched to a halt and a few loud bangs could be heard as metal bumpers crumpled in the distance.

The *Pom* was confused and disoriented by the noise. There were cars and trucks everywhere. She started barking and darting under and between the stopped vehicles. After running from lane to lane several times, Rafa spotted her and called out in his most enticing and welcoming voice, "*Vamos perro!*" On instinct, *Medi the Pomeranian* appeared from under a nearby tow truck and jumped into Rafa's waiting arms.

"*Bueno! Muy Bueno!*" shouted Rafa, elated. Preoccupied with the dog he stepped to his right, inadvertently placing himself in the bus lane where an *autobus* was hurtling along trying to stay on schedule. To do so it was skirting the ad hoc traffic jam. Drivers were docked up to a full day's pay when they were found to be running late for stops, regardless of the reason.

Diego, a veteran driver of twelve years, reckoned this was just an excuse by the bus company to save money, but ruse or not, he was not going to lose one peso this pay period. On the sidewalk, Ernesto de Velasquez and his daughter Medina looked on in horror, knowing that Rafa and her beloved *Medi* were about to be run over by the bus.

Medina couldn't watch. She shut her eyes and turned her head into her dad's body. He put his arm around her.

"*Mierda!*" Ernesto swore under his breath. He grimaced, stomach clenching at what would surely be a gruesome pedestrian-canine fatality. But unbelievably, it never happened. As if conjured out of thin air, a *mensajero moto* (bike courier) *on an estupendo rapido* (fast as possible) delivery came streaking along between the stopped vehicles and the bus lane. With a deft pull of his gloved hand, he yanked on Rafa's hoodie just enough to halt him mid-stride while the *autobus* whooshed past. Such was the rider's consummate skill that he did not have to slow down, much less stop.

Like the bus, he simply sped along towards his next destination—no big deal that he had saved a kid and his dog from being road kill. Ernesto and Medina raced across the empty bus lane. She grabbed *Medi* and her dad heartily embraced a thoroughly embarrassed Rafa. By then the three negligent soldiers and their driver were being escorted away by their commander, as they had identified the wrong car. They would be berated at the army base and then severely punished for their high-handed treatment of this wealthy *padrone* (who, it turned out, was a major supporter of President Daniel Ortega). Once through with the soldiers, Ernesto insisted on driving Rafa to his modest house where he met Maria and Henrico, Rafa's parents.

Over tea and homemade tamales prepared by Maria, Ernesto told them of Rafa's heroic behavior. Maria almost had a heart attack on hearing that her only son had stepped into traffic and, even worse, in front of a speeding bus *to save a Pom*. Ernesto, however, was most impressed with the young boy's courage and after considerable haggling with Maria and Henrico, it was settled that he would pay for Rafa's education at a private school and beyond—as far as the boy wished to go. No further objections would be permitted.

As the Quattroporte blanco drove away with the girl and the Pom, Rafa realized that his life might just have been irrevocably altered by that single act.

It was.

CHAPTER 30

Last Look

Pearce had completed his third recon of the mink farm by 4:00 a.m. on Thursday. Fortunately, no dogs patrolled the property, perhaps because they were antagonistic to the mink. By then he had memorized every road, structure and exit on site. It turned out that the metal sheds held some mighty interesting contents.

With the help of an engineering student at B.C.I.T, Rafa had disassembled a Schlage Sense lock and written a program to defeat the alarm and break the simple four-number key code. It wasn't as hard as he thought it would be–but then Apple is not exactly renowned for its outstanding phone security. Shed number one held a large number of mink coats (not pelts), all packed neatly in unlabeled, clear-topped shipping cases so the colors could be easily seen. These included cases of white, brown, gray and rare Finn Jaguar, a bright white with clearly defined black spots similar to a Dalmatian's coat. Pearce conservatively estimated maybe two hundred coats. At anywhere from ten to fifteen thousand bucks a coat, depending on the fashion designer label that got eventually sewn inside it, that represented a street value of $2,000,000 to $3,000,000. Why the coats were in unmarked cases and stored in this location was not readily evident.

The second shed was even more intriguing. Over a hundred bundles of unmarked one hundred dollar bills were stored in a small safe. The digital combination was peanuts for Rafa to crack with his de-encryption program. Again, Pearce's conservative estimate was around $2,000,000. Why all the cash? And why keep it here? No apparent answer. No matter. He had already decided what to do with the contents of the sheds. He would be back the following night to launch a strike on the MBM Mink Farm after a briefing with Rafa.

Everyone, all twenty-two inhabitants of the farm—owners, managers, cook and workers—had to be gone for the operation to proceed. When he was done, however, there would not be anything for them to return to. There would be no casualties, civilian or otherwise if Pearce could help it. Meticulous planning and smooth, seamless execution would all but guarantee that. All but, was the key phrase. In any military operation nothing was ever guaranteed, so he would do his best to be ready for any manner of surprise which the gods of war could think up. And as Pearce well knew, they could be quite inventive.

CHAPTER 31

Hanging on by a Thread

Rich Coburn of Pioneer Lodge Outfitters in Lillooet, B.C. quickly learned of his competitor's one-upmanship from Bobby Cromwell, the town big mouth, who seemed to never have a job, but always knew everybody else's business. For once, this was a good thing, since Rich wished that he had thought of the idea himself. Just like Abe's business, Pioneer Lodge was on life support for this season, with one confirmed booking and only two other inquiries.

"Hey, are there going to be cops out there to keep us safe?" one of the non-confirmed hunting parties had asked.

The other wondered if the Lodge had any insurance coverage for death or injuries to expedition members caused by armed animal rights activists.

"Hell, I don't know," the beleaguered lodge owner said. "Twenty-seven years guiding hunters like you through every part of B.C. wilderness and I never lost one so far." That didn't cut it. Neither party confirmed their booking. Desperate, Rich had called the local RCMP detachment but the sergeant in charge quickly pooh-poohed the idea of a public police force providing what was essentially private security for a local business.

"Unless there is a confirmed specific threat to life or property," said Sergeant Lucien Provost to an argumentative Rich Coburn, "we can't justify the manpower."

"Well what the hell is that posting on Ministry of Forest's website that's been plastered over the TV and radio stations for the past week—if not a direct threat!" shouted an exasperated lodge owner, at the top of his lungs. After all, his business was hanging in the balance. Like most small business owners, Rich was always struggling to make the payroll. On top of that nut to crack there was the mortgage on the house and the mortgage on the lodge, not to mention payments on the new four by four, property taxes, home and business insurance, maintenance and upkeep, advertising, food, kids' expenses and on and on it went. Fat ass cops on the other hand, just sat around picking their noses in the police station or, worse yet, chowing down on free donuts and coffee at the local Tim Hortons. No need for the dicks to bill a dollar either. No sir-ee, just sit back and collect your goddamned paycheck with your bloated benefits—medical, dental, paid sick leave, bereavement leave, maternity leave and fully indexed retirement pension, all paid for courtesy of taxpayers like Rich Coburn, who actually had to work for a living. Once in his entire adult life, he asks the cops for help dealing with some psycho lunatic ex-marine or whatever, who is single-handedly ruining his business, and all he gets is attitude.

"Hey, calm down." Sergeant Provost used his most conciliatory tone of voice. He took the phone off speaker, grabbed the handset with his right hand, and slowly swiveled in his easy chair, Tim Horton's coffee mug in his left hand. "First of all, we don't even know if this guy, this so-called, ex-special forces character, even exists," he said. "It could just be a prank pulled by some tech geeks, like maybe Anonymous, who are having a good laugh at all of us now."

"Well what the hell does it matter if the guy exists or not? He's bloody well ruining my business and from what I can tell, most other outfitters', too!" exclaimed Rich. He continued, obviously stressed big-time. "My wife, Sherry, who happens to be four months pregnant, by the way, is having to pull double shifts at the diner just to keep the bank off our ass, and with spring break coming up, we'll have the kids back from school." He was literally wringing his hands. "I'm afraid it's gonna get ugly real fast if I don't get some bookings."

Lucien leaned back in his chair, took a swig of Tim's new dark roast coffee and said, "I heard HuntPro is offering to provide security on their expeditions and that's increased their business somewhat up in Nelson."

"How'd you know about that?" Rich asked.

"You know, Bobby's been talkin it up at the White Spot," replied Provost. "He's been following this story like a hawk and I think just knowin the dirt first, kind of makes him feel important, 'specially since he's not workin and all."

"Yeah, it's funny, I heard it from him too," Coburn said. "Big man, shootin off his mouth and all, but I don't see him exactly getting off the dole and signing up for back-up security with one of the outfitters—not that I could pay him much anyway."

Provost set down his Tim Horton's mug. He'd remembered something. "You know, I got just the guys you might want to talk to if you want to try the same thing as LaFlamme."

"Ok, I'm all ears."

"Come down to the station and I'll fill you in." Lucien finished the last of the delicious dark roast *double double*.

CHAPTER 32

Liar, Liar Pants on Fire

Back in British Columbia, the Ministry of Forests, Lands and Natural Resource Operations offices were abuzz with activity. Reporters were being directed to the Ministry's Communications Director who was definitely not used to this kind of scrutiny.

In her fourteen-year stint with the Ministry, Pam Clearwater had not received more than a handful of requests to interview Ministry officials. Now it was a daily event.

"Can we interview the Minister?"

"Then who's next in line?"

"What's a deputy Minister?"

"Will they come on our show?" U.S. late night talk shows and news reporting programs alike had been besieging the Ministry for 'talking heads.'

"Well, then who *can* come?"

The Colbert Report had been merciless. Every day someone from *The Report* called requesting the Minister's presence for an on-air interview for a full half-hour. Fat chance, thought Pam. The right honorable Geoff Hinkson would be skewered on the show, a laughing stock for all to see. Doubtless Colbert's staff would dig up enough dirt to thoroughly embarrass the minister by insinuating that the many campaign contributions to the Liberal Party from the Guide and Outfitters Association had something to do with the government's steadfast position, year after year, of ignoring the overwhelming opposition to the Grizzly Bear Hunt by the general public of B.C. For sure, by the end of the interview, Hinkson's head would become a trophy on Colbert's wall of shame.

"Nope, don't hold your breath for that interview, Steven," she said, finishing the twelfth memo to her communications officer and politely turning down yet another interview request.

The Premier's Office was faring no better. Requests from U.S.

talk shows for an interview with the first female premier of B.C. were similarly at record levels. Her handlers were busily weighing the pros and cons of letting their star politician loose on a stage where they could neither control the questions nor prepare pablum answers for her as was the normal practice. Most politicians, including the President of the United States, actually read all of their material off of a teleprompter set-up outside of camera range. That kind of shit should be embarrassing for any politician, much less the president— but it isn't.

"Madame Premier, we've got requests from Conan, Jimmy Fallon, Letterman, Jimmy Kimmel and Bill Maher," said Victoria Wang, her communications officer.

"Which ones do you like?" asked the premier as she applied some last-minute concealer for a local news conference.

"Well, Letterman is far too caustic," Victoria said.

"I thought he was retired." The premier assessed herself in the mirror.

"No, he's still around for another season." Victoria was a savvy communications assistant. "Anyway, you definitely don't want to wind up on his Top Ten List, so I would steer clear."

"How about Fallon. He's cute and he seems pretty nice on camera."

Victoria envisioned Fallon's silly antics. "That is a definite maybe."

"Good, call his show back and book me on it."

"You sure?"

"Sure I'm sure," replied Premier Connors. "When else could I get on a major U.S. television show with an audience in the tens of millions?"

"But we won't get a list of his questions in advance. I already checked."

"You checked?" The premier was impressed.

"I always check," said Victoria. "I mean we can prepare the best possible answers if we know what the interviewer is going to ask, right?"

"I suppose so," said the premier. "But somehow that seems like cheating."

"Not at all, Madam Premier, it's just good politics."

CHAPTER 33

Getting Ready for Battle

Pearce was soaked in sweat. The guy he was sparring with was good, really good.

KJ had tried many of his standard "can't miss" moves—wrist lock, leg sweep, elbow strike—all to no avail. The sensei of the dojo countered his every move and had Pearce backing up as he initiated his own offensive maneuvers including multiple fist strikes, kicks and feints. Students and onlookers were mesmerized by the speed and power of these two combatants who moved like two tomcats in a turf war. Everything was a blur.

He had sought out the dojo while he was staying in Englewood, to maintain his ritual of ongoing training—even while on a mission. Hell, especially while on a mission. As all professionals know, rituals and routines are an absolute must before any big game—or in this case a big mission. Interrupting one's normal routine regardless of the reason can result in sub-par performance, which in turn can spell disaster on the football field or in Pearce's case death or capture on the battlefield. The Big Sky Academy of Okinawan Karate was the only studio of its kind in town, and a little internet research revealed that its founder was a ninth-degree black belt who had successfully competed for many years on the martial arts circuit.

Pearce had dropped in with his gear and asked if he could hire the founder of the club for a half-hour sparring session. The girl at the front desk, a pretty Japanese twenty-something who looked to be in fairly decent shape herself, looked him in the eye and said, "You are kidding, right?"

"No, I am not kidding. How much would it be for a session?" KJ dropped his duffle bag to the floor and reached for his wallet.

"Master Ishikawa, no longer entertains private sparring sessions," she said with a tinge of sarcasm. "No one has lasted more than two minutes with him in years."

111

Pearce looked directly into her luminous eyes. "Okay, I can respect that, but I really need the workout. What would he charge for a half hour if he was still offering that option?"

"$150," she said, figuring that this would end the discussion. The sensei was her father. She'd virtually grown up in the dojo.

Never one to back away from a challenge—and he definitely needed the workout—Pearce countered, "Okay, $150 it is, and if I can't last the full half hour with him, tell him that we'll double it."

The young woman rolled her eyes. "Okay, I'll ask him. But it's your funeral," she added, a glint in her eye as she turned away from the front counter. KJ could not help but notice that she moved with grace and balance. Perhaps a martial artist herself, he thought. And not a half bad rear end either. She glided out of the room, fully aware of the scrutiny.

Ishikawa listened to his daughter Akira present the man's proposal, then studied Pearce through the slats in his office blinds. He immediately intuited that this guy at the front desk was a serious martial artist, noting Pearce had a calmness about him and radiated subtle confidence. His chi was strong and balanced. This could prove to be interesting, the master thought. He could not have cared less about the money.

And so the sparring session began. Because of Ishikawa's involvement, dojo regulars were interested enough to stop what they were doing and watch. Both the sensei and Pearce exerted maximum effort and neither got the better of the other. Although close to fifty, Ishikawa seemed indefatigable. Ten minutes, fifteen, twenty and the back and forth strikes and counter strikes continued. Almost breathless with anticipation, the spectators sensed that something had to give.

It did.

Pearce tried an arm lock. As he anticipated Ishikawa about to counter, he pulled back ever so slightly as if abandoning the move. Ishikawa instantly pulled back himself, only to have KJ immediately grasp his wrist and bend it backward and with a rotating motion, flipping the master on his back. A fight-ending elbow strike to his exposed Adam's apple would stop a half-inch short of killing him. The session was over after twenty-eight minutes. Students and other onlookers clapped in earnest appreciation of a martial arts match worthy of primetime MMA.

Both men rose and bowed deeply to each other. Master Ishikawa smiled, but Akira Ishikawa was speechless. No one had ever bested her father—ever, in her twenty-two years on the planet. And a gaijin (if he was in Japan, that is) to boot! The pretty woman started to rush to her father, but he held up his hand.

As if by halted by an invisible force field she stopped short of the mat.

"This one is a worthy competitor," said the sensei to his daughter. "Will you do me the honor of joining me for a sake?" he asked Pearce.

"It would be my great honor, sensei," replied Pearce with a second, respectful bow, holding his clenched fist against his other open palm.

"Akira, please ready my office for our guest," the master asked his daughter, who dutifully complied with her father's request. Others returned to their training, stunned at the turn of events and even more awed by the sensei's sense of equanimity.

CHAPTER 34

MBM—Employee Relations

Don Burdenny was fifty-three and looked his age. He was five-eight and about two-twenty. Balding, but he couldn't bring himself to shave his whole head like so many follicly challenged guys do these days. Maybe a hair transplant, some day. He was a director of MBM Inc. and the principal shareholder of the local farming operation, MBM (Colorado) Inc., which had its registered office in Denver at the offices of Seamor, Hobbs LLP, a respectable, litigation firm of twenty-eight lawyers. His wife Ruby, forty-seven, did the books and his twenty-nine-year-old son, Dominic, ran the day-to-day operations of the mink farm. Don and Dom (the "dreaded D's," as the staff referred to them behind their backs) were both, to put the best possible spin on it, total assholes.

Don was an absolute miser and paid the mostly Mexican immigrant workers on the farm next to nothing. "Those fuckin wetbacks are eating us out of house and home," he would constantly remind his family and Caucasian staff. In fact, he fed them mostly generic porridge with skim milk, day-old tortillas which his wife picked up in town by the crate from the local Taco Time and often, overcooked refried beans which they bought in bulk from Costco.

"You know." Don would launch into one of his harangues. "There's hardly enough food left to feed the mink. These guys are like pigs at a trough!"

Dom, the other half of the "D's," was rumored to have been a distant relative of Simon Legree. He drove the staff relentlessly from six a.m. to eight p.m. No overtime was ever credited for fourteen-hour days. Dom constantly reminded the peons that they were lucky to have a job and that could easily change with one call to U.S. Customs and Immigration or Homeland Security.

Each of the sixteen illegal migrant workers was paid $25 per day, minus a $5 "administration charge" and given room and board.

The "room" consisted of a large open space with eight double bunk beds, a few dressers, a wall mirror, a twenty-inch analog TV which could receive only two channels and a single adjacent bathroom with a shower. The migrant workers were expected to work five days a week and if necessary, six or seven still at their normal wage.

Today, on the front veranda of the large house lived in by the Burdenny family, Jose Jiminez was almost in tears, pleading for his son's job and swearing "on my mother's grave" that "nothing like that would ever happen again."

Eighteen-year-old Emilio Jiminez had been spotted talking to Inaara, Don Burdenny's sixteen-year-old daughter. It was entirely innocent. Inaara had been riding one of the family's horses. The horse was spooked by an errant mink which had somehow escaped from its cage. Emilio, who had a little bit of experience with horses back in Mexico, ran over and blocked the horse's path, which was actually kind of stupid since he could have been run over and seriously injured. However, his ill-advised maneuver distracted the five-year-old Appaloosa and coupled with Inaara's firm pull on her halter, the horse came to a complete stop and began to calm down.

She whinnied as Emilio patted her head. Inaara thanked him and asked his name, thinking that she could maybe put in a good word for him with her dad. However, one foreman who saw only the tail end of this interaction reported it to Don and then the proverbial shit hit the fan.

"That fuckin spic kid did what?" screamed Burdenny. Johnny the foreman explained again what he saw.

"…tryin to hit on my daughter! Jesus fuckin Christ if I can get him locked up in Guantanamo I am going to bloody well do it!" He turned to Johnny. "Get that kid's fucking ass over here NOW!—and his dad's too!"

Shaking, Jose explained to the Dreaded D's what had happened. "Por favor, you can ask your daughter. She will say this is true," pleaded Jose.

Don Burdenny back handed Jose across the face sending him staggering toward his son, Emilio, who grabbed his dad, stopping him from stumbling off the porch. "Like I give a shit if it's true or not!" shouted Burdenny. He moved forward toward Jose. Pointing to Emilio, he snarled, "Spic junior here keeps it in his pants and he never talks to my daughter, you understand never?"

"Yes sir, I understand never. Nunca senor."

"He never even looks in my daughter's direction, much less says a word to her! No mirar, got it?"

"Si Senor."

"But I didn't mean anything by it…" protested Emilio, benignly moving toward Dom. His father grabbed his arm.

Dom took offence at this intrusion into his personal space and took the liberty of punching Emilio in the face, knocking him clean off the porch. Dazed, but defiant, Emilio got up and rushed the porch but Dom kicked him in the balls and then landed an upper cut as Emilio bent over to grab his privates. Jose tried to stop the fight, but Johnny grabbed him and put him into a full nelson, a wrestling hold he had learned watching WWE on television.

Jose was effectively incapacitated.

Dom was almost eleven years older than Emilio and had a good fifty pounds on him.

It was no match, but Dom didn't care. He pummeled Emilio mercilessly with punches and kicks until his opponent was bloodied and down on his knees. Don watched impassively, but with some satisfaction. The kid deserved a beating and he was getting it pretty good. On his knees, Emilio held up his hand to signal that he was done, but Dom, who had a mean streak in him, stepped forward and kneed him in the face breaking his nose in the process.

Emilio fell backwards clutching his face in agony. Don signaled to the foreman to let go of Jose, who ran frantically to his son's prone form.

"Get him cleaned up and back to work," Don snarled, "and make sure that the other wetbacks see him first." His son was smirking, as Jose helped his son to his feet. "Might as well let them know what's in for them if they step out of line," said Don.

"Happy to oblige dad," said a now smiling Dom.

Like father like son.

"Now, let's get back to real business, son. Get your mother and meet me in the office."

CHAPTER 35

Inside MBM Colorado Inc.

The parties convened in the west wing of the ten-thousand-square-foot family home, simply referred to as "the office," a modern, spacious room with a huge L-shaped desk of black tempered glass and steel with three sumptuously padded leather office chairs facing it. Behind the desk was a similar black glass credenza flanked by a huge wall safe. Along the opposite side of the room, a contemporary white leather couch was stationed and two matching arm chairs, also in white leather. Some nice, authentic local artwork adorned the walls—a few Robert Adams framed photographs, a John Carlson landscape and a Mindy Bray, picked out by Dom at a local art studio.

Don sat behind the desk, befitting his CEO status, puffing on a Cuban cigar, much to the chagrin of Ruby who had been on him for years to "get rid of those smelly things which are stinking out the house."

Alas, to no avail.

Ruby sat in one of the leather armchairs, as far away from the smoke as she could manage. Dom sat on the couch with his laptop and cell phone out, the CEO in waiting.

"Dom, grab that inventory list will you," asked Don. "No, not that one," he motioned, "the one in the safe."

"I got it," said Ruby, leaving her armchair and heading in the direction of the large wall safe. She twisted the combination dial back and forth and when the final "click" was heard, she swung the door of the heavy Brown Class M safe open. The damn thing could withstand a barrage from a fifty-caliber machine gun the salesman had assured him. Not even drilling with carbide-tipped drill bits could get through this puppy. Don had reflected that was just as well. He stored some pretty incendiary stuff in the daunting safe.

Ruby handed her son Dom the unofficial inventory, a listing which included the two hundred mink coats in the steel sheds on the farm.

"Ready when you are dad," said Dom.

"Okay, Ruby now do you want to grab the preferred client list, asked Don, "yeah, that's the one, just below the top shelf."

She reached back into the safe and pulled out a thick yellow folder containing numerous pages of twenty-pound bond, embossed paper with an impressive MBM watermark. The best clients always get the best paper. Ruby spread the list out on her desk and took out a gold Cross ball point pen to start marking off the deliveries.

"Natalia!" shouted Dom almost at the top of his lungs.

A young, diminutive Spanish woman came into the room. "Senor?"

"Grab me a java will you, pronto," said Dom.

"Yeah, me too," said the second DD.

"Might as well make it three Nat," added Ruth. "Only three sugars in mine though. I'm cutting back."

The servant departed to the kitchen, to return ten minutes later wheeling in a small cart which carried three flavorful, steaming coffees on a silver tray. A carafe of organic cream and a bowl of raw, Madhava coconut sugar from the Philippines with three sterling silver spoons and three, off-white, Supima cotton napkins completed the service. After pouring the cream and thoroughly stirring the coffees to dissolve the sugar, Natalia quietly left the room to await her next summons next time the bosses needed something.

"That's damned good Joe," said Dom, smacking his lips.

"Royal Kona, straight from Hawaii," quipped Ruby. "And Nat makes it the best."

"Yeah, that's great, but can we get down to business now," said Don placing his own coffee on the desk. "Okay, who's first on the list?"

"Which list, the money list or the coat list?" asked Ruby.

"Let's start with the coat list," replied Don. Very soon, two hundred preferred clients of MBM (Colorado) Inc. would be getting stunning mink coats, gratis.

"First one is Senator Martin Rodale," said Ruby.

"Girlfriend or wife," asked Don.

"Wife," said Dom.

"Next, is Congressman Bill Wiley, from good old Colorado."

"Girlfriend," said Dom.

"Girlfriend?" exclaimed a shocked Ruby. "We know Bill personally. He has been our dinner guest more than once," she stated emphatically.

The D's looked at her quizzically.

"I mean why the hell is June, his wife of thirty-one years not getting one of our coats?" demanded Ruby. "What is she, chopped liver or something? She has given the best damned years of her life to that old goat and now he wants to give our mink coat to some floozy intern!"

Ruby was as steamed as her coffee.

"Nope," said Dom, checking the file in his laptop.

"What?" queried Ruby.

"She is not listed as a staff member of Congressman Wiley's office."

"Then that's even worse!" shouted Ruby. "What is she an escort or something?"

"Mistress probably," said Don cautiously, not wanting to sound too knowledgeable about these sorts of things.

"What the hell do you know about mistresses, Don?" Ruby glared at him just daring him to look back at her.

He didn't.

"Nothing, I was just guessing is all," he said defensively. He wished he had kept his big mouth shut.

Thankfully Dom chimed in. "Can we just move it along now? I mean, like, if we cut out every politician, judge and businessman on our list that is cheating on his wife, we won't have a list. Am I right?"

After a brief pause, Ruby relented. "Yeah, I suppose so," she said, as if somewhat resigned to the crassness of the male species. She continued. "Number three is Harold Waxman, chairman of the Senate Ways and Means Committee. He's definitely a heavy hitter."

"Wife or girlfriend?"

"Both," said Dom.

"He gets two coats?" asked Don. "Two? That's got to be worth close to 35K."

"Yes," said Ruby, "but his support in the Senate is worth at least ten times that to us, so don't make a big deal over it."

"You are absolutely right Rube." Don was now trying to be agreeable.

"Don't call me Rube," she fired back, still agitated about Congressman Wiley.

"It reminds me of a hayseed or a bumpkin."

"You are definitely neither of those. Mea culpa," said Don, know-

119

ing very well the bedtime consequences of pissing off his wife of twenty-seven years.

On and on it went.

Police Chief Wexler, Boulder District—wife. General Donald Sexsmith, Ft. Wayne army base—personal assistant. Colorado senator Harvey Blondell—girlfriend. NSA Director, Joe Lieberschitz—wife and personal secretary. By the time the two-hundred mink coats were divvied up, the split was about fifty-fifty, with half the coats going to spouses and the other half to somewhat significant others, including girlfriends, interns, assistants, secretaries, mistresses, female companions, Girl Fridays and even a few personal trainers—who would give a mink coat to their personal trainer?

The coats would secure favorable consideration for MBM's operations on the municipal, state and federal levels of government, no hassles with by-law enforcement, zoning violations, pollution issues or, perish the thought, some idealistic politician who was trying to introduce legislation to improve the living and/or dying conditions of the mink.

Gifts to the police chief, army brass and of course, the FBI and the NSA honchos would guarantee air tight security.

The cops would come running at a moment's notice and the security agencies would pro-actively sniff out any lunatic animal rights whackos who wanted to free the mink. Before making any mischief, the miscreants would be apprehended as potential terrorists under the auspices of the U.S.A Patriot Act and the keys would be thrown away. Good fucking riddance.

"Okay, it's time to look at the money list," announced Ruby, pulling yet another list out of the Brown. The coats were one thing. But money? It always galled Don to have to do this in a so-called industrial Western democracy, but he was able to rationalize it in his own mind as simply a cost of doing business in America. The two million that would grease the political wheels would seem like a drop in the bucket if he found himself out of business due to the passage of a new unfavorable law or regulation. Still, this wasn't Mexico or Columbia so the whole process rankled from time to time.

"I mean MBM Colorado Inc. paid its fair share of taxes. Wasn't that enough for those lazy, fat cats in office and the laggard bureaucrats?" Apparently not, since MBM Inc., the national umbrella company for the whole operation, also had to do the same thing on a country-wide scale. As the senior Director, he was on the national

Preferred Clients Gratuity Committee, but they were careful not to overlap the gifts given by the state mink operations. The cash bribes would be spun as campaign contributions to the political action committees of those who didn't get a coat.

Sigh.

Another two-million-dollar cost of doing business in the best country in the world!

CHAPTER 36

The Deutsches Reich

About thirty-million animals a day currently die at the hands of the master species. This slaughter continues unabated seven days a week, three-hundred-sixty-five days a year. Animals, birds, reptiles and sea life are perceived as property of mankind, to be eaten, worn, experimented on and exhibited for amusement.

"Shit, that sounded like a PETA slogan in reverse," Pearce once remarked to Rafa. But it rang chillingly true nonetheless. Various religions and cultures around the world had concocted conveniently self-serving stories that placed mankind on a pedestal, separate and apart from all other creatures and even from nature itself. Then, of course, there is always the oldest code of conduct known to man, namely that "might makes right."

By way of clarification, Pearce found World War II Germany to be a frighteningly accurate analogy to the decimation of the animal kingdom. That monstrosity revealed, in chilling detail, the brutality and single-mindedness of the human contribution to a global death.

Hitler launched his empire with *Mein Kampf*, a book and manifesto he wrote in the mid-1920s while he was in jail. In it, he railed against Jews, Gypsies, Bolsheviks, consigning them to sub-human status. Aryans were practically super-human in his estimation. This less than stellar literary work underpinned what would become the Deutsches Reich or The Third Reich (or "the Greater German Realm"). It lasted from 1933 to 1945. During that span of time, Hitler created an absolute, totalitarian dictatorship, and he was its "Fuhrer." The Nationalsozialistisch Deutsche Arbeiterpartei ("National Socialist German Workers' Party") was known to the public, and history, as the Nazi Party.

Famously, the nightmare that was The Third Reich was characterized by ruthless brutality and complete disregard for the lives of any but the Aryan master race. Soldiers of the Reich were perpetrators of almost every crime imaginable, including mass murder, rape, enslavement, medical experimentation, torture and the so-called final solution—death camps and genocide. Estimates place the death sentences meted out by the soldiers and collaborators of the Third Reich at about eleven million.

Pearce, like most students of war, had studied the Third Reich from the perspective of military strategy and tactics. In the process, he could not help but observe the massive ancillary carnage deliberately visited on civilian populations by Hitler's soldiers. In Pearce's view, a soldier's job was to defeat enemy soldiers in battle—usually a do-or-die struggle which more often than not brought out the worst in both sides. Still, for the most part there were rules of war. The modern code of conduct of the professional soldier is meant to prevent the deliberate harming of civilians on the other side. That is not to say that civilians, enemy or otherwise, do not get killed in wars, but their deaths are supposed to be ancillary to the war (euphemistically referred to as "collateral damage" in modern parlance) as opposed to being specific targets of military operations. Hitler's troops ignored any code of conduct and were, from the viewpoint of Pearce and many other members of the allied military, unworthy of the term "soldiers."

Compounding this atrocious behavior, the law of Germany favored the Nazis even when it was clear that they violated it. In such cases, prosecutions were rare and almost never occurred unless they involved crimes against western European victims. The Third Reich's "ethos" was that inferior races did not deserve the protection of law nor consideration under any ethical or moral principles—so egregious behavior in the extreme was tolerated, even condoned in the name of the master race.

Every war, no matter what its cause, always has to have a story, if you will, to justify its existence. This story gives the war meaning for the troops who fight it and the civilians who support it. The "other side," is invariably deemed to be inferior, sub-human, evil, a threat to world security or peace, or otherwise completely undeserving of life or territory. Believing the story allows the denizens of the country initiating the war to justify their actions.

The parallel between the Third Reich and the current reign of the "master species" on the planet earth was glaringly obvious to Pearce. Clearly our *story* was that all of the non-human, and therefore inferior species were put here for the sole benefit of mankind. The behavior of this **Invisible Reich** toward every other living thing was every bit as brutal and callous as that of the Deutsches Reich, but infinitely more pervasive and long lasting.

It is politically incorrect to acknowledge the oldest code known to mankind, namely that *might makes right,* but when push comes to shove, it invariably governs all human interactions. Soldiers know that political diplomacy always ends at the barrel of a gun. They also know that when the cost of the spoils gets prohibitively high, even the most savage dictator, warlord or predator will back off in their own self-interest. Pearce was about to increase the cost—quite a bit.

CHAPTER 37

Breaching MBM

MBM Colorado Inc. was about to get a taste of the military doctrine of "shock and awe" first-hand. Harlan K. Ullman and James P. Wade wrote the doctrine, technically known as "rapid dominance," in 1996. It advocates the use of overwhelming power, dominant battle space awareness and maneuvers coupled with a massive display of force to crush the enemy's will to fight. In addressing the media, President George Walker Bush used the term in describing the America's invasion of Iraq to the media in 2003.

It was close to 7:00 p.m. on a Saturday night that shock and awe hit the minkery. Pearce pulled the black Durango into the same hedge of blackberry bushes that he had used for cover on the past four trips to the farm. Only this time a small trailer was in tow behind the SUV. It was windowless and fully enclosed with a locking double rear door. Pearce approached the metal gate, skillfully picked the lock, swung the gate open and did a brief recon and a telephone check with Rafa to ensure that no roving police cars were in the vicinity. There were none so he returned to the Durango, backed it up and pulled into the mink farm. He exited the vehicle again to close the gate and reposition the lock. If anyone drove past it would appear that all was in order.

The black Durango began slowly devouring the dirt road heading into the heart of MBM Colorado's mink ranch. Pearce had on his night vision goggles, so no need for running lights. His vehicle seamlessly blended into the black night like an invisible predator should. After about ten minutes, the Durango pulled up alongside the two metal sheds, still partially concealed by surrounding foliage. In the darkness and behind the wheel of a vehicle, no one would even notice that they were there. In fact, had Pearce not re-conned the place on foot, he would have likely missed them too.

"Rafa, can you give me the code for the first shed," he said into his tiny mike.

"13, 9, 14, 11," came back over the crystal clear digital signal via BBM Blackberry messenger mode.

"Cute," said Pearce into the mike.

"What's that?" asked Rafa.

"The combination spells *mink*," he replied. "You know, by assigning a number to each letter of the alphabet."

"How original," quipped Rafa.

Exiting the Durango, Pearce punched the combination on the Schlage Sense lock and "bingo," it clicked open easy as pie. A thorough check via mini-maglite for trip wires, sensors, cameras or any other monitoring devices revealed nothing—as it had the first time he had gotten into the shed. KJ's grandfather, a highly skilled craftsman who could make almost any weapon out of wood often told him, "Measure twice, and cut once." He knew that preparation and measuring won more battles than fighting, or cutting, so he was painstakingly careful about discovering surprises rather than dealing with them after they happened.

Pearce grabbed the first box of mink coats. It was light but cumbersome. He followed up with a second and third box and headed back to the trailer, where he commenced loading the coats, box by box. Seven trips later, Pearce had twenty-five boxes of mink coats neatly loaded.

Now for the cash grab. He gently closed the door to the first shed. The Schlage Sense lock re-activated itself, now guarding an empty space.

Rafa called out the second combination and updated Pearce on police and army presence—none for the moment.

"Roger that," said Pearce as his gloved index finger again punched the combination, 6, 1, 18, 13, which spelled *farm* in the alphabet code. The second Schlage Sense clicked open and Pearce entered the shed and again carried out the measuring with the mini-mag. When he was certain that nothing had changed since his last visit, he headed straight for the safe. Same combination, but he noticed it was a random number which did not follow the alphabet code. Obviously, the safe maker did not have the same sense of style as Burdenny did with the Schlage.

The safe door swung open, revealing the stacks of C-notes. Accessing a large, military duffle bag, Pearce began packing the bundles, each one containing about $10,000 U.S. This process was considerably quicker than the coats, and he was done in under three minutes. He closed the safe, then the door, reactivating the Schlage. The black Freetoo military tactical gloves he wore left neither a print nor a trace of DNA. These indispensable nylon, breathable gloves enabled him to do most anything including shoot, all the while warding off scratches, cuts and other wear-and-tear hazards normally encountered in rough terrain, fire fights or hand-to-hand combat.

Before leaving the sheds, Pearce pulled two half blocks of C-4 out of his satchel and stuck one on the side of each shed. A radio-controlled detonator was inserted into each block. The small blocks, which looked like two lumps of dirty white modeling clay, were malleable enough they could be molded into the corrugated walls of the sheds, just like moist clay. C-4 is a plastic explosive which is part of the family of explosives known as *composition C*. Made up of RDX (cyclotrimethylene trinitramine), diethylhexyl and polyisobutylene, it is a favorite of the military as it highly stable. In fact, it will not explode if accidentally dropped or impacted, even by a bullet, or set on fire or even subjected to microwave radiation. Explosion is only by simultaneous combination of heat and a shockwave, as produced by a detonator.

Pearce acknowledged placement of the charges to Rafa and added, "Get ready, you're up next." Rafa had the *Alien* powered up and ready to cause some mayhem in the general area of MBM ranch. Meanwhile, Pearce continued along the dirt road for another five minutes until he came to a hydro pole connecting the power and telephone lines to the house and barns. He carefully ascended the pole and cut the power lines, but spliced the phone line and placed a feeder wire and transceiver on the telephone line running off the pole. This would enable Rafa to intercept all outbound calls placed on the landlines. Someone inside was sure to be calling the power company any minute asking what happened to the electricity.

As cautiously as he ascended the pole, Pearce carefully descended and climbed into the Durango. He pulled it off the road out of the sight of anyone who might come looking with a lantern. Not two minutes later, a call was placed by Ruby to the Xcel Energy emergency services line via the landline.

"Emergency services," said Rafa. "How may I help you?"

"Hi, this is Ruby Burdenny. I'm a customer and our power just went out now."

He asked her to repeat her name and for her address.

"Ruby Burdenny. We're on a farm about 40 miles south of Denver, its …, hmm, let me find it …"

"Jesus, Ruby," called Don from the TV room. He was watching *Furious 7*, starring Vin Diesel and the Rock, on satellite when the power went out and was not happy about it. "You should know the address by *now!* 22891—Karaway Road."

"Yeah, I know that," answered Ruby who then spoke into the receiver, "228891—Karaway."

"No, you said it wrong honey, it's 22891!" an exasperated Don called out.

"That's what I said Don," she stated.

"No, you said 228891," explained her husband.

"That's too many numbers, why would I say that?"

"Shit, how would I know?" still from the other room.

"Well, you wouldn't know, because I didn't say it," answered his wife. "And don't swear at me. You know I hate it when you swear."

"I didn't swear *at* you honey, I just said *shit,*"

"If you say that one more time, that's what you will be in, Don," her tone growing more owly.

Rafa was enjoying this immensely, but he thought that he better cut in as Pearce was on a tight timeline. "It's okay," he said interrupting, "I've got you at 22891 in our system," in his most official voice.

"See Don," she called out, putting her hand over the mouth piece of the receiver "the power guy's got us at 22891."

"But that's not the address you gave him *hon*," said Don, still stubborn.

"If I gave him the wrong address, then how come he's got the right address now, Don?" her tone now downright surly. "Do you think he's maybe got *auto-correct* on the phone line?" she asked.

"No, I don't think that anyone has got that Ruby," said Don, "but I heard what I heard and you didn't give him the right number, okay?"

"Maybe you better get a hearing aid Don, you know one of those digital ones that that you can turn up so…"

Rafa cut in, this time with more authority. "Excuse me, but your power is out due to an explosion at the army base."

Ruby immediately stopped arguing with Don and started listening.

"Apparently there has been some kind of toxic gas release from a secure storage facility," explained Rafa. "It's not clear whether it is on or near the base, but we understand that it's the army's responsibility, nonetheless."

"Toxic gas?"

"Yes, it could even be nerve gas," advised Rafa, "but the army won't confirm or deny it."

"Nerve gas? Isn't that fatal or poisonous or something like that?"

"That's what I'm told," said Rafa.

"Why on earth are you talking about nerve gas, Rube?" called Don, still waiting for the power to come back on so he could see how *Furious* ended. He already knew that Paul Walker was not going to make it, but Dom and the Rock, well now that was a different story.

Ignoring being called *Rube*, she almost shouted. "The power guy says that there was an explosion at the army base and nerve gas could be headed our way!"

"What the hell are you talking about?" Jumping out of his lazy boy he hustled to the next room, barked, "Gimme that phone," and snatched the handset from Ruby's more than willing hand. Don listened, flabbergasted, as Rafa explained what had happened.

"And the Department of Homeland Security is probably going to block internet access and cell phone communication in this area of Colorado, that is until they figure out what caused the explosion—you know it could be a terrorist strike."

"Hey, Ruby, try to get on the internet on your IPhone," asked Don.

"Right now?"

"No, next week!" he shouted. "Of course, right now!"

"No signal."

"Damn! It's happened, just like the power guy said," he said.

"We are advising all of our customers to immediately leave their homes and head due south by car as quickly as possible to avoid the toxic gas leak," advised Rafa in his most calm and clinical voice—like a dispatcher sending out a squad car.

"Shit!" exclaimed Don. "We are on a ranch with over 5,000 mink in pens and they are damned well not air tight! What happens to them?"

"Well, they would likely die," advised Rafa, "as I believe Sarin gas, I think that's what my supervisor called it, will kill most everything."

"At sixty bucks a pop, that's almost $3,000,000 down the drain," Don screamed into the phone, clearly choked up about the plight of the mink.

"Well, I guess that you could release them, too," Rafa advised. "Animals have a pretty keen sense of smell and they might just head south as well to escape the gas. Maybe you could capture some of them later," he offered, "when it's safe to come back that is," leaving the bait dangling.

If Burdenny released the mink on his own, it would save Pearce the enormous amount of time of having to do so himself.

Rafa didn't want to give Burdenny too much time to think and continued. "The animals are up to you, sir, but we highly recommend that you evacuate your family right away." He let that sink in. "We are being told that about twenty-five to thirty miles due south of your area, you will likely pick up internet and cell access again, but I would get going immediately if I were you."

"At that range, any gas would have dispersed to a low-enough level to be harmless," said Rafa, as if any concentration level Sarin gas was ever harmless.

Don Burdenny slammed the phone down in its cradle, not even considering thanking the Excel Energy employee, and ordered Ruby to get ahold of Dom, right away.

"And Rube, see if he can find Johnny stat," shouted Don, "He's got to round up the wetbacks as well," thinking that if he could only leave them behind that would save him an enormous food bill.

"But then who would do the work?" he mused.

CHAPTER 38

The Hunt is On

All told, eighteen parties had signed up to try their luck at bagging a grizzly bear in supernatural British Columbia, Canada. This was, of course, on receiving the promise of military-grade protection against the spook who posted the threat on the internet. And this was advertised by the guides and outfitters "at no extra charge," so not one additional nickel (Canada doesn't use pennies any more) better show up on the twenty-thousand dollar-a-week bill.

Normally a fiercely competitive lot, the outfitters had decided to close ranks under the guidance of LaFlamme and up all of their fees to a flat $20K a week to cover the extra security.

Thus, as the security tab had already been factored in, they could all honestly say that nothing extra would be added to the bill for the additional bodies they were providing to ensure that the hunters would come back in one piece. The standard "terrorist exclusion" precluded any claims against any of the outfitters' insurance carriers should one of the hunters be killed or injured by the elite, special forces assassin waiting out there. *The guy's* reputation seemed to be growing exponentially with every mention in the media—despite the fact that he had never been seen.

At any rate, eighteen parties split up among a half dozen or so guide companies was way down from the normal one hundred to one hundred fifty or so, but it was better than nothing, and word seemed to be spreading, so there could be more coming.

Although they would never admit it in a million years, hunters were themselves much like sheep, and once one went ahead with something, others would surely follow. And that would hopefully save the 2015 season for the B.C. guides and outfitters, assuming, of course, they could all stay alive until it ended.

"You think you can keep those dumb clucks from shooting each other?" LaFlamme asked Coburn as they sat across at the breakfast

table at the HuntPro Lodge. Abe had called a meeting of B.C. outfitters to make sure that they were all on the same page, at least for
this season.

Almost all of the contingent was there and the others would be
arriving soon.

"Hey Abe, I ain't got the deep pockets to hire ex-military and
off-duty U.S. marshals like some of us do," chided Rich defensively.

LaFlamme ignored the barb and asked, "Well where in hell did
you pick up those nitwits?" He referred to the ragtop threesome of
overgrown moppets.

Somewhat sheepishly Rich replied, "Truth be told—just between
us mind you, Sergeant Provost of the Lillooet RCMP kind of loaned
them to me as a favor, seein as how I am a major employer of sorts
in the town, especially during the hunt."

LaFlamme pulled out a Camel and lit it up. He took a deep drag
and slowly exhaled a stream of smoke through his nostrils, waiting
for Coburn to continue with his story. Damned, that smelled good,
thought Rich, but he'd "swore on the bible" to his wife, Eileen that
he would not smoke while she was carrying, so he could only eye the
inviting pack Abe had graciously placed on the table between them.

"The Travis boys, Eddie, Donovan and Shane—triplets no less,
have been in trouble with the law in Lillooet since the day they were
born," explained Rich, "and they are now required to perform three
months community service at the tail end of their sentence for a
botched B & E at a Husky gas station on the outskirts of town last
summer."

"Nice," commented LaFlamme.

"Provost gave them the option of shoveling shit at the Mason's
cattle ranch or doin security work for me during the hunt," Rich said.
"It was a no-brainer. Now here they are."

LaFlamme asked Molly to pour them both a coffee.

"Make mine strong and black please," requested Rich.

Abe took another drag on the Camel. He studied his long-time
competitor and asked, "This cop, Provost, is he retarded or something?"

"Why do you ask that?"

"The three stooges are on community service for a break & enter
and they are going to be packing loaded guns on your expeditions?"
As he spoke Abe unconsciously checked his watch, wondering when
the others would be showing up. It was a rugged, all weather Ca-

sio PAW 2000 which seldom left his wrist. The damned thing was solar powered and always one-hundred percent dead on time—its multi-band atomic time keeping mechanism received radio signals six times a day to adjust the time from an atomic clock in Fort Collins Colorado. On top of that it contained an altimeter, thermometer, digital compass, barometer, world time in thirty-one zones and it was waterproof to over three-hundred feet. No respectable outfitter would ever be without one in the back country.

"Just doesn't seem too bright of an idea to me," he continued, tapping his cigarette tip on the lip of the ashtray.

"That's the genius of it Abe," Rich said coyly. "The guns will be loaded alright, but with blanks!"

"What!"

"That's right. Only me and Provost will know it," a smiling Rich offered, "and I guess, now you too."

LaFlamme was left momentarily speechless. "What the hell kind of security can you provide for your hunters if your guys are carrying guns loaded with blanks?" he finally asked.

"Come on Abe, who needs security?" Rich challenged, shifting in his chair, while still eying the pack of Camels wistfully. "Provost figures that the joker who posted the threat is probably some hacker just pulling our leg, you know like the Anonymous bunch." Rich had never heard of the online vigilantes known as Anonymous prior to talking to Provost, but he wanted to impress Abe with something maybe he didn't already know about.

"I thought that this could just be a hoax, too, although I never heard of anybody called Anonymous," said Abe, downing the last of the steaming black brew. "But what if the guy isn't just a hacker and he shows up and shoots somebody?"

Rich seemed to ponder that for a while and started scratching his ear. He asked Molly for a second cup. "Please Ma'am."

"Sure, no problem," she said as she leaned over for his mug and headed over to the stove. She was a definitely an eight or nine, thought Rich, even for an older babe. Finally, he said, worried, "Abe, I need to eke out something from this season or I'm goin under."

Molly placed the rich mug of Joe in front of him and he proceeded to load four sugars into it. He stared at it as he desperately stirred it again and again, as if he could dissolve his problems along with the sugar. "Twenty-two years in this business and all I got is always ridin on the Grizzly Bear Hunt to pull us through, year after damned year."

"Hey, we're all hurting," countered LaFlamme. "Nobody's becoming Bill Gates by running a guide and outfitters shop, you know."

"Who's Bill Gates?"

"It doesn't matter, Rich, it's just an expression."

Coburn continued. "The thing is, Abe, if—and that's a real big "if," this guy is some fancy pants Green Beret or merc or something like that, then loadin the Travis boys' guns with real bullets ain't goin to make a damned bit of difference, cause we'll all be dead anyway if we happen to run into him."

"You might have a point there." Abe wondered how much oomph his sixties something CAS war vet and his off-duty sheriff's son could come up with in a real fire fight. Just then:

BOOM! Glass from the upper deck windows of the HuntPro Lodge came raining down outside the window of the kitchen.

"Jesus H. Christ, are we under attack already?" shouted LaFlamme. He and Coburn both jumped to their feet and headed for the front door.

Abe grabbed a 12 gauge off a wall rack, cocked it and jammed two shotgun shells into the breach. As he snapped it shut, he warned Molly to stay inside and get ready to call the cops on his signal. Opening the door, they figured to run into *the guy*, but no, it was only the Travis boys, looking embarrassed as hell.

Shane Travis had accidently shot out the lodge's upper floor windows while showing off his rifle to a couple of local chicks. "Please observe, ladies, you just hold the weapon like so and put your finger on the trigger ever so gently and when Mr. fucking Rambo shows up you just … whoops … holy shit there goes the window!"

"I thought you said their guns were loaded with blanks?" said LaFlamme to Coburn.

"They were damned well supposed to be" Coburn fumed, "but who figured that they'd bring along their own ammo!"

CHAPTER 39

Exit Stage Left

Lights were ablaze around the main compound on the MBM Colorado Mink Farm within minutes of Ruby's call to Excel Energy. Men scrambled to and fro. Engines in SUVs and pickups roared to life and the distinctive xenon headlights of the family's BMW sedan blinked on as Natalia fired up the Burdenny's family car. The foreman Johnny rousted the Mexican workers from their spartan quarters. This included Emilio, who had to be helped off of his cot by his father.

"Get the hell up and get ready!" Johnny yelled to the workers, most of whom had already turned into their bunks from the sheer exhaustion of a fourteen-hour day with only a half-hour lunch break and two five-minute water breaks.

"Where are we going to, Senor Johnny?" a farmhand asked while, hopping on one foot trying to get a sock on. He was rewarded with a smack on the back of his head.

"It's none of your damned business where you are goin," replied Johnny. "I'm not gonna say it again. Just get ready hasta pronto!"

Meanwhile, the Dreaded D's were filled trepidation as they contemplated releasing some five thousand mink into the general wilderness. "Dad, you're not really seriously thinking of releasing the mink, are you?" Dom was incredulous.

"Well, what the hell choice do we have?" Don was nearly shouting at his son in frustration. "If I keep them locked up, they will die from the gas and if I let them go... If I let them go ... and assuming that they are smart enough to move south, and away from the fumes, we will probably not be able to recapture many of them."

"If you let them go, Dad, the insurance company damned well won't compensate you one penny." Dom was suddenly the legal eagle.

"Yeah," said the senior D, "but if it turns out to be come kind of terrorist incident, the insurance won't pay either, since there is a blanket exclusion for terrorist anything in our commercial policy. Your mom told me that right after 9-11 and she's the one who looks after the insurance renewals."

Dom scratched his head. Hmmm, was it his imagination or was his hair thinning a bit too. He replied, "That's weird, Dad, because your chance of being injured or killed by a terrorist in this country even after 9-11 is less than the chance of being hit by lightning."

"And your point is?"

"Well why would they exclude something from the policy that almost never happens?" Dom asked, almost rhetorically.

Exasperated that his twenty-eight-year-old son did not already know the basic principles of the scam that was known as 'insurance,' the senior D rubbed his palms over his temples, and loosened his tie. "Because they are fucking insurance companies, son! They exist solely to collect premiums, not to pay out goddamned claims—no matter how unlikely those claims may be!" He grabbed a hammer from the cupboard and slammed it down on the heavy wooden butcher block as if to pound the point home to his son. "That is why every guy ("bang!") and his dog ("bang!") hates insurance companies ("bang!") with a passion! ("bang! bang!"). Don was on a roll, and like a freight train, once he got started it was hard to stop. "Like the smooth operator on the TV says, you're in good hands with Multi-State." He mimicked the actor in the commercial by putting his hands together as if he was holding a fragile bird's egg in his palms. "Until you make a claim that is." He moved his hands apart as if letting the invisible contents drop to the ground to shatter. "Whoops, Mr. Policyholder, it looks like you fell through the cracks in the coverage," he said with mock concern.

"Okay, pops, you can put away the hammer. I got the message," Dom said. "Let's go let the mink out."

CHAPTER 40

Retreat

Pearce watched the exodus with some satisfaction through his night vision binoculars.

The silver BMW 750i sedan wheeled out of the long driveway first. It was driven by Nat. Her boss, Ruby, sat in the back seat with the two, family Chihuahuas. A couple of hastily packed suitcases had been shoved into the trunk just in case the family could not return later that night.

An ancient motor home, driven by Johnny's assistant foreman, carried the Mexicans who brought no luggage nor belongings, not that they would have had much to bring in any event.

Johnny drove his own 2014 Ford Escape which also carried the family cook, gardener and housekeeper. The rest of the staff and workers rode in two minivans, trailing the other vehicles. A black 2015 Audi SUV owned by Dom Burdenny remained parked at the house. The Dreaded D's had hoofed it over to the main barn, a silver metal shed quite similar on the outside to all of the others on the farm. This one, however, housed the operations center. In it was the Realtek computer system which controlled the lights and heating for the other twenty-two barns housing the five thousand or so mink. The actual number fluctuated from day to day, since on occasion a mink would be found dead in its pen due to any number of causes. The operations barn also contained a small bank of video monitors which allowed the foreman to view the inside of each of the barns. After five really profitable years in succession, Don had bit the bullet and installed this high-end computer monitoring and surveillance system that allowed him to open the pens of all of the mink' cages with the click of a mouse. He sure as hell didn't anticipate having to ever use it though.

Dom flipped the power switch and the monitor screen illuminated. The emblem for Realtek Security popped up with the usual user name and password combo on the right corner of the screen. "M i n k f a r m" was carefully typed in as the user name followed by "Toretto" as the password, which of course was the lead character of the *Fast & the Furious* movie franchise, played by Don's favorite action hero, Vin Diesel. He scrolled through the options—temperature, lighting, monitoring, accounts, contact us...until hitting on security.

"Open Pens" blinked off and on.

"Hit it," commanded Don.

"Are you sure?" asked the screen.

"Fucking smartass computer!" sneered Dom. "Goddamned right we're sure!" Double click. "Shit, there goes three million bucks!" His eyes widened.

"Tell me about it," said Don. "Now let's get the hell out of here before we get gassed!" The D's jogged back to the Audi Q5 TDI which Dom powered up. His lead foot got them moving in a hurry. The powerful 240 h.p. diesel's 428 ft. lbs of torque spun all four tires simultaneously, spraying dirt and gravel behind them as they roared out of the compound. In no time flat, they caught up with the van, which had a fifteen-minute headstart on them, heading due south on a side road, flanking Interstate 27. Good thing too, as the two-lane road was old and the speed limit was only 50 mph.

Satisfied the exodus was underway, Pearce dropped the binocs into his satchel. He slid back into the black Durango, backed it out of the bushes and began inching the vehicle toward the main compound, sans headlights or running lights. Even though it appeared that everyone had left the compound he was cautious, as often an enemy force leaves a straggler or lookout—even though in this case that would be unlikely as the Burdenny family seemed to have bought Rafa's ruse hook, line and sinker.

Having hacked a telecommunications satellite used by several of the local cell phone providers, Rafa had temporarily interrupted cell phone and internet coverage for close to a fifty-mile radius around the main compound but the pulsed interference signals he was able to cause were sporadic and would soon be ineffective as the Burdenny caravan was speeding south, out of the satellite's range. Once they picked up reception again a phone call or an internet search could unravel his masquerade and have the cops high tailing it over to the farm.

Pearce had debarked from the Durango with a duffle bag full of C-4.

It was a godsend that the D's had actually sprung the mink themselves, as it now seemed unlikely that he would have had time to complete that task before the jig was up and the cavalry arrived. No matter. Sometimes you get lucky on a mission. Pearce would not look this gift horse in the mouth. He just had to get in and get out post haste.

"The coast is clear," whispered Rafa into the secure BBM connection, meaning that no roving police vehicles were in the vicinity.

"Roger that," said Pearce, "have you got the detonation protocols programmed?"

"Done yesterday."

"Can you pick up any movement on the property?"

Using the satellite's thermal imaging system, Rafa indicated no, he could not pick up any heat signatures that appeared to be human, but with thousands of mink in the process of escaping he could not be entirely sure. Without that assurance, he would simply have to assume that there was still someone around and proceed with extra caution, even though that would slow him somewhat—and time was a precious commodity at the moment.

Pearce approached the house from the rear through a stand of spruce trees. Everything looked faintly green through his night vision goggles, but at least he could see. As the family had doused the lights when they left, the grounds were almost pitch black. That was fine with Pearce. From his previous reconnaissance, he knew that the home was equipped with external surveillance cameras which covered the perimeter of the house and garage about one-hundred feet outward. In addition, there was a motion sensor alarm on each door and window, should any be opened without the code being punched in.

If the alarm was triggered a loud siren would sound continuously for one-hundred-twenty seconds and a signal would be sent to a monitoring center somewhere in the U.S. The dispatcher would try to contact the Burdennys, probably first on their landline at the house and then default to a cell number for a call or text warning to a specified member of the Burdenny family. Standard alarm company protocol would dictate that if no one answered the landline or cell phone the next call would be to the nearest police station. Police get thousands of false alarm calls from monitoring companies every day across the country so the local constabulary might respond or not, depending on whether the monitoring company could provide some sort of verification that a break in, robbery or other crime was actually taking place. Also, it would depend on what sort of relationship the owner of the property had with the police or civil authorities, an important businessman or other pillar of the community like Don Burdenny often getting preferential treatment.

Pearce did not know where MBM Colorado Mink Farm Ltd. fit into that equation.

However, as Rafa had temporarily disabled internet access, and cell phone communications and landline calls from the home were being re-routed to Rafa via the phone splice that he had connected atop the power pole, it would be improbable that the monitoring company would ever receive an alarm signal. The siren would likely not attract anyone's attention since the main compound was far from the perimeter of the property. On the other hand, if there was someone left lurking about the premises, they might just come running at the sound.

Pearce did not have to get into the house to blow it up, but he wanted to be sure that no one was in before he did. He had factored zero civilian casualties into this campaign. In fact, even one innocent, and that was definitely a relative term in The Invisible Reich, civilian death, and the public could turn against him on a dime. Not that he particularly cared what the citizenry thought, but he was counting on public pressure to eventually help end the war on animals. There was no sense in giving them a human target to focus on rather than on the plight of the tens of millions of creatures being victimized every day.

"I'm going in," said Pearce into the ear bud mike on the Blackberry.

"Make it quick," replied Rafa. "You have about twenty-five minutes to get the whole job done and be on your way."

"Copy that." Pearce broke the kitchen window beside the door, reached in and flipped open the deadbolt on the door. As expected, thirty seconds later the siren started wailing at a deafening 110 decibels. Ignoring the noise, Pearce drew his Glock, dropped the satchel of C-4 in the kitchen and looked for the light panel which would illuminate the whole place. Then he proceeded to quickly walk through the rest of the house, room by room.

Rafa meanwhile continued to monitor the police and army frequencies to see if any reports were coming in. Kiara had been following the goings on with the Grizzly Bear Hunt and called in with her report. Rafa briefly switched lines and listened with interest to her intel. He would pass it along to KJ once he was off the property and en route to neutral territory.

Pearce almost sprinted through the eight bedrooms, four bathrooms and upstairs kitchen and family room. Jeez, the place was as big as South Fork and he half expected to see Miss Ellie or Bobby Ewing pop out of the woodwork any minute. Fortunately, no one came out from anywhere after his tour of the ten-thousand square foot palace. He quickly planted bricks of C-4 in the main-floor kitchen, family room and office. The detonators were radio equipped and would be triggered by a signal from Rafa at the appropriate time. Pearce was pleasantly surprised no one was in the house, but since the words *pleasant* and *surprise* did not normally go together in his world, he stopped to consider his further options.

Time was ticking, however, and he did not have the luxury of simply waiting for the trailer, if there was one, to come to him. If any person was still around he would have had to have heard the alarm, which thankfully had stopped ringing. That meant that he, the trailer, was waiting outside somewhere for Pearce to emerge. Pearce raced back to the office and flipped on the external monitoring cameras, which covered the immediate grounds around the house. He located the external floodlights and turned them on and his eyes darted across the dozen or so monitors.

Driveway—clear, side yard—clear, front—clear, other side yard—clear, back—clear... no wait a minute! He caught just the tiniest blur of movement in the monitor covering the back yard. It came from the exact spot that he'd stood in the stand of spruce.

"Damned, almost missed you!" As the detonators were securely implanted into the C-4 charges, Pearce had no further reason to stay in the house so he quickly exited through the front door. Before he left he located the lights panel which he'd guessed would be equipped with a timer. It was. He set the timer to leave the lights on, including the external flood lights, for five more minutes. No use alerting the guy that he was leaving just yet.

"Rafa, there is a man on the north side of the compound?" Pearce asked. "Can you locate him?"

"Hey, that's pretty crafty of them." Rafa's voice betrayed some begrudging admiration. "How did you know that the Burdennys would be that smart?"

"I didn't," he replied, "but its standard military ops, so if anybody on Burdenny's security staff is ex-military, that would be their m.o."

"Hmmm," muttered Rafa as he scanned the crystal clear display on the Alien... okay, I've got a bigger heat signature, about fifteen yards due north of the west corner of the house, which would be about forty yards from you at forty-five degrees. That's probably him."

Pearce left the satchel of C-4 near the front verandah and started making his way around the house, navigating a wide circle so as to come upon the guy from behind. With time running out far too fast for his liking, Pearce crept along a gardener's path in the thicket of rhododendrons which spread out from the house and garage to form a partial ring around the compound. The brilliant red rhodos were in full bloom—quite a sight to behold during the daytime. This night however, they provided Pearce pretty decent cover. There was the off-chance the other guy had night vision capability as well.

He checked the super luminous numerals on his black Cobra military watch. "Shit, only twenty-one minutes left!" Sneaking up on someone is tricky at the best of times, but when that someone is neither preoccupied nor distracted and one is in a hurry, it can be downright perilous. Using the satellite data now on his Blackberry, Pearce quickly located the man about ten yards to the east of his position. It would be easy enough to shoot him with the Glock from that range, but that was out of the question. He had to disable him, drag him out of harm's way, finish his mission and get out—all in under twenty minutes.

Something rustled in the rhodos beside him. Pearce pulled out his Glock and dropped into a crouch. Could there be a second straggler? He held his breathing steady, steady, waiting, waiting...

Out of nowhere, two mink bolted past him in a definite hurry. He exhaled and checked the Cobra again... thirty seconds until the lights went out in the house and grounds. He detoured again back along the path until he was between the man and the house, but within the confines of the flowery bushes. Ten, nine, eight, seven... At zero the house and grounds went black. The man drew his gun and lurched forward convinced that Pearce would be exiting the house any second. As he ran by, Pearce, who was virtually invisible in the bushes, stuck out his foot and tripped the man, who pitched forward losing his balance and his pistol in the process. He tried to brace himself with his arms but his torso slammed into the turf, knocking the wind out of him. His face bounced hard off of the grass.

In an instant Pearce was on him, delivering an elbow strike to

142

the back of his neck and knocking him senseless. Without losing a second, Pearce dragged the guy past the rhodos and well down the driveway, then pulled him off the road, near an old fir tree, and rolled him over onto his stomach. He took his standard army issue Sig Sauer .45, wallet, watch, car keys (although he hadn't seen any other car nearby), cell phone and slapped a pair of nylon, tie-cable hand cuffs on him.

If the guy happened to wake up before Pearce was gone, he would not be able to do much of consequence. Fortunately, for his sake, he had not seen Pearce's face. Sprinting back to the front of the house, Pearce retrieved the satchel of C-4 and headed for the barns.

CHAPTER 41

Disclaimer

Kiara's intel was interesting. Fully twenty-eight parties had now obtained licenses through local outfitters to hunt grizzly bears for the 2015 season. Although this was way below the normal number of one-hundred-fifty to two-hundred, it was still twenty-eight too many, in Kiara's view. All of the outfitters had cobbled together some sort of security to protect the hunters from KJ. The security forces consisted of an off-duty cop and war vet (Laflamme's hires), three criminals serving out community service terms (Coburn's crew), some unemployed construction workers and a few washed up amateur boxers from Nanaimo who had been unsuccessful in turning pro (Wilderness B.C.'s security team). That complement was rounded out by an assortment of twenty or so tough guys, bouncers, security guards and police and army wannabes.

The provincial government had flat out refused to provide RCMP to accompany the parties, claiming that sort of security was a normal cost of doing business and not a legitimate public expense. However, this year, due to the publicity and notoriety which Rafa's viral message had created, the Ministry of Forests, Lands and Natural Resource Operations had mandated a meeting of all of the interested or involved parties on the opening day of the event—seven days hence.

Province of British Columbia/ Hunting License Application

"The licensee does hereby for himself, his heirs, executors and assigns, fully and absolutely release the Government of British Columbia, the Ministry of Forests, Lands and Natural Resource Operations ("FLNRO") and their employees, agents, servants and assigns, of

and from any and all liability arising out of the official 2015 Grizzly Bear hunt ("the hunt"), including but without limiting the generality of the foregoing, death or injury to licensee or destruction of the property of the licensee directly or indirectly caused by the person, entity or organization who on or about April 1, 2015 posted an unauthorized, unsanctioned warning message on FLNRO's official website threatening death to any hunter who encountered said person, entity or organization on the hunt."

In addition to the legally beefed-up disclaimer of liability which the government insisted that every hunter, guide, outfitter and their security details sign as a condition to the granting of a hunting license, FLNRO officials were going to hold a public meeting on the opening day of the hunt, to ensure that all parties were unequivocally aware that they were proceeding at their own risk. Local TV stations and the press would of course be invited to this meeting and doubtless there would be considerable national and international coverage as well, given the intense debate that Rafa's message had generated north and south of the border, as well as in Europe and South America.

Doubtless many environmental and animal rights groups who opposed the hunt—PETA, Mercy for Animals, the SPCA and Humane Society, Animal Legal Defense Fund, Animal Justice and the Association for the Protection of Furbearing Animals—would show up. So would pro-hunting advocates like the NRA, Ducks Unlimited, Safari Club International, U.S. Sportsman's Alliance Foundation and Hunters Against PETA. In addition, there would, of course, be the usual contingent of trouble makers and rabble rousers, uniform and undercover police, security agencies like CSIS and the FBI, yes, even in Canada, and many onlookers who just wanted to see what was going to happen. In short, this would be one circus you wouldn't want to miss.

"The venue and specific time were still to be announced," advised Kiara. "But the smart money was betting on the main entrance gates to the Great Bear Rainforest at noon on the opening day of hunting season." Ever the relentless researcher, she would track down as much information as humanly possible as to the details of the meeting, security, media coverage and anything else she could find which might be of use.

Based on this intel KJ planned on making an appearance to leave no doubt in anyone's mind that "*the guy*" actually existed and more importantly, meant business.

CHAPTER 42

Bringing the Heat

Thirty-two barns, thirty-two half blocks of C-4 and he was down to his last detonator. "All done," Pearce said into the mike as he ran back towards the SUV.

"Detonators activated," replied Rafa after a slight pause. "We are good to blow."

Pearce had to manually open a couple of the mink' cages as the electronic unlocking mechanism had failed on a few, but for the most part it was clear sailing. The remaining mink flew out of the cages with no prodding, heading for the hills and grateful for the unexpected jail break.

Still, Pearce felt that something was off kilter, but he couldn't pin point it. With only six minutes to go, however, he did not have much time to think about it. He reached the Durango and flipped the remote, unlocking only the driver's door. The military-grade security system he had installed in the SUV when he bought it was still armed. Whenever he was engaged in extra vehicular activity, the doors automatically locked and the alarm activated itself. He had watched too many movies where the good guy jumped into his vehicle only to find some asshole with a gun or a knife waiting for him in the back seat. Nope, not a hope in hell that was going to happen in the Durango. Throwing the empty satchel, along with the night vision goggles and the Glock into the passenger's seat, he punched the mike button on his ear buds and said, "Mission complete." With the turn of a key, the powerful hemi rumbled to life. Pearce put it in gear and started pulling away from the compound.

With the farm deserted except for the occasional mink still making its way out, the Durango's powerful halogen head lights now replaced the night vision goggles. Pearce saw something. "What the f …!" he exclaimed as he hit the brakes. He immediately felt the trailer push against the back of the vehicle.

"What happened?" Rafa asked.

A teenager, maybe fifteen or sixteen years old, wearing jeans and a sweatshirt was standing in the middle of the roadway directly in front of the SUV, her arms held high shielding her eyes from the powerful quartz halogen beams.

"Shit, Rafa! There's a girl standing on the road blocking my path!"

"A girl?" queried Rafa. "Where the hell did she come from?"

"Damned if I know. No one was in the house when I searched it and I went through every room."

"Maybe she's a squatter," suggested Rafa, "or a trespasser, like you. Can you just drive around her?"

Although Rafa couldn't see him, Pearce shook his head. "No, she's two feet from the front of the vehicle." In less than five minutes the Burdennys would be back in cell and internet range and it would probably not take them long to put two and two together. By then, Pearce knew he had better be long gone. A command decision was in order. In five minutes the whole place would be blown to bits. He rolled down the power window.

"Get in."

The teenager stood still, frozen in the high beams.

"Now!" he commanded. He reached over to the passenger's side door and swung it open. She gingerly made her way around the front of the hood, placed one pink sneaker on the running board and paused, uncertain as to whether to get in or not.

"Preferably this year," said Pearce in a neutral tone, not wanting to spook her, but needing to get moving post haste. He had tossed the night vision goggles and knapsack to the back seat. She slid into the passenger seat and closed the heavy door with both hands resulting in a solid thunk.

Pearce put the vehicle into drive and accelerated into the blackness. With no one else to worry about, he hoped, Pearce could reach the perimeter of the farm in about four minutes. Rafa's calculations put Burdenny's caravan about five minutes outside of cell and internet range, so it remained a tight timeline, as he had expected.

The pair drove in silence for a minute but Pearce soon seized the initiative and asked the girl what her name was.

"Inaara," she said shyly.

"You have a last name?"

"Burdenny."

"So your dad owns this place?"

"I can only hope that he's not my real dad," she said defensively as if Don Burdenny was some kind of undesirable that one would not want to be related to. "And he's a total asshole and I hate his guts!" He could tell she was dead serious when she added, "I just wish this whole place would disappear with him in it!"

Well, he thought, he could grant at least half of that wish. "Why don't you tell me what you really think?" He was surprised by her candor. Able to pick up speed now that the road was straightening out, he flew past the two metal sheds which formerly housed the coats and the cash. Another minute and he would be at the gate.

"Why would I? I don't even know you," she said. "Who are you, anyway?"

Pearce kept his eyes on the road and his foot on the gas, making sure that the miles ticked off faster than the remaining few minutes.

"Me, I am just a..." He slammed on the brakes, suddenly, then accelerated as he swerved to avoid a half a dozen mink scurrying across the road. Whew, he thought. Gotta be careful not to roll the trailer with a sharp turn like that. It was of no use conning Burdenny into springing the mink only to run a bunch of them over himself.

Distracted, Inaara asked, "I wonder how so many of the mink got out of their pens?"

"Good question," replied Pearce. "Maybe the guy who you hope is not your real dad had a change of heart and decided to let them go free."

"Yeah, that'll happen when Justin Bieber gets back with Selena Gomez!" Pearce didn't know who those people were but he assumed that "when pigs can fly" could be substituted.

At last, he could see the gates in the distance. No flashing red and blue lights. That was a good sign.

"Don and his real son Dom, they are called the Dreaded D's for a reason," Inaara explained. "They are so cruel to the poor mink—and even to the Mexican workers. It makes me really sad, but angry too!" She teared up. "I was going to run away tonight so I hid in one of the barns after dinner; then all of a sudden, everybody packed up and left the farm."

The Durango came to an abrupt stop. Pearce asked Inaara to jump out and open the gate.

"But I don't have the key!"

"The mechanism on the outside only looks like it's locked. Just

149

twist it and it will open," he instructed.

She looked at him quizzically, but did as she was told. To her surprise, as the guy had said, the gate was not locked. It swung open when she twisted the lock and pushed. She wondered how he knew that. Now that she was out of the vehicle and far from the compound, Pearce had a half a mind to drive through the open gate and leave her behind. The cops and fire trucks would be arriving shortly. Inaara could easily flag them down and then get in touch with her family.

Okay, that's a go. He drove past her.

On the other hand, if the police asked her how she happened to be there, she would likely tell them that a guy in a black SUV hauling a trailer gave her a ride out of the compound just before it blew up. Somehow, he knew that the gate was unlocked and had her open it before he drove off without her. Yeah, he headed north on I-51. That conversation simply could not happen. The massive Brembo disc brakes brought the Durango and trailer to a dead stop thirty feet past her. The red brake lights stood out in sharp contrast to the blackness of the night. The engine quietly rumbled as the vehicle idled, waiting.

"Are you coming or what?" shouted Pearce through the driver's window.

CHAPTER 43

The Politics of Hunting

"So, Madame Premier," Jimmy said. "Or may I call you Teagan?" He raised his eyebrows.

Flustered, she responded, "Teagan is okay, I guess." She paused. "For this venue."

This venue was the *Tonight Show Starring Jimmy Fallon* from Studio 6B in Rockefeller Center. The Emmy and Grammy winning host was a favorite of the premier's and she hoped that his tens of millions of viewers would gain a favorable impression of her home province, frequently advertised to the world at large as "supernatural British Columbia."

Jimmy's previous guest was another B.C. girl, Pamela Anderson, former star of *Bay Watch*, avid animal rights activist and longtime PETA supporter.

Cheeky as ever, Jimmy arranged to interview Pam prior to the premier, to fan the flames of the controversy raging in B.C. and playing out on the internet almost the world over. This was, of course, the 2015 Grizzly Bear Hunt in the politician's fair province. Vancouver had hosted the highly successful 2010 Winter Olympics which had showcased the natural beauty of the Lower Mainland of this province and definitely put the city on the map as one of the go to places in North America.

As expected, the still gorgeous actress vehemently opposed the hunt as archaic, useless and cruel. She effortlessly rattled off statistics on the worldwide declining bear population, the overwhelming (almost 90%) opposition to the hunt by B.C. residents and the unreliability of the provincial government's bear count. Asked by Fallon what she thought about the menacing message on the government's website which had brought the hunt to the forefront of the news—and her and the premier to his show, she replied thoughtfully.

For the umpteenth time on the air, the message and smoking gun

GIF were projected onto a huge screen behind the host and his guest. Had he been watching, Rafa would have been delirious.

"Well Jimmy," she said. "I don't condone violence to get one's message across. Groups like PETA—which I wholeheartedly support, are trying to stop unnecessary violence against animals around the world." She gave her golden locks a shake and continued. "So it wouldn't make a lot of sense to replace violence against animals with violence against people—even if you don't agree with making such a threat!"

"Spoken like a true Canadian," quipped Jimmy, "even if you live in LA!"

The mostly young, hip, New York audience responded with an approving round of applause. "Bring back *Baywatch*!" a youngish male voice shouted from the back row. Pam flashed her million-dollar smile, but continued in earnest looking directly into the camera.

"If there is anything good about that warning, it's that it has focused worldwide attention on the barbaric practice of killing animals for sport."

Playing devil's advocate, Jimmy said, "Barbaric or not, Pamela, it's legal in B.C. isn't it?"

"So was slavery at one time, Jimmy, but that didn't make it right," she shot back, to a way bigger round of applause this time. The New Yorkers were urban dwellers and not hunters, for the most part, so they were on the same page as Jimmy's guest.

"Touché," said the host. "And on that cheery note, let's bring out the head honcho of the province of British Columbia, Canada to see what she has to say about her government's authorizing the cruel and senseless murder of innocent grizzly bears!"

Hearing that, even in jest, from the famous host had premier Teagan Connors' heart in her mouth and her legs feeling like jelly as Fallon's pretty assistant ushered her out of the waiting area and into the spotlight in front of some twenty million viewers. What on earth had she gotten herself into?

CHAPTER 44

Up in Smoke

As the Durango accelerated north on I-51 Pearce touched his phone mike and said, "All clear."

"Bye bye, MMB," replied Rafa as he placed the cursor over the detonate icon on the Alien's screen. The remote triggering program which came with the C-4 detonation devices was too cool for words. Its graphics and animation were world class and Rafa thoroughly enjoyed setting up and initializing the program. Almost immediately Pearce and Inaara heard massive explosions, even though they were well north of the mink farm by then.

When C-4 is detonated it rapidly decomposes to release nitrogen, carbon oxides and other gases. These gases expand at the staggering velocity of twenty-six thousand feet per second. The walls of the Burdenny home blew outward, and with no support the upper floors collapsed downwards in a massive heap of rubble. The five-car garage fared no better as its roof exploded upwards, showering the driveway with splintered roof tiles. After the initial expansion, gasses generated by the C-4 explosion rush back to the center of the blast causing a second, inward wave of energy, so if the first blast didn't finish you the ensuing one surely would.

The second blast sent shards of glass and pieces of wood, plaster and bits and pieces of furniture flying across the lawn and driveway for a hundred and fifty feet in all directions. The metal barns and sheds blew apart like egg cartons, leaving nothing standing. MMB Colorado Inc. had been completely, totally, unequivocally razed to the ground.

"What the heck was that?" asked Inaara in a nervous voice, as she glanced backwards. "That was the mink farm disappearing," answered KJ as he increased his speed to the maximum of seventy miles per hour.

"Oh my God," Inaara screamed, grabbing KJ's right arm, "Really?"

"Really."

"But what about the mink?" He could tell she was genuinely concerned.

"They were all released," Pearce reminded her.

"Oh, yeah, right."

"It was their lucky day. First, they scored a get-out-of-jail card and then the jail blew up," Pearce dryly pointed out.

Impulsively, Inaara slid over and hugged him as hard as she could, almost causing the vehicle to veer off the road. She cried with happiness.

"Jesus, don't ever do that again!" he shouted as he swerved, barely avoiding the ditch. Inaara slid back to her own side, still pleased as punch, notwithstanding his sharp rebuke. Like most people he met, she had taken an immediate liking to Pearce. No big surprise there. His vibes, even in circumstances like this, were positive, reassuring and strong.

"That is just about the best birthday present I could ever get!" She was as happy as if she had just been given front row tickets to see Taylor Swift.

"Police vehicles on route from their station in south Denver," advised Rafa, interrupting the conversation. "ETA eleven minutes."

"Give me an alternative route," requested Pearce, not wanting to pass the police vehicles, even in the opposite direction.

"Okay, take a right in fifteen hundred yards. That'll put you on the old I-51, but it will get you where you want to go."

The Durango slowed as Pearce searched for the turn. Fortunately, there was virtually no traffic on the road at this hour.

"Sixteen, if you are wondering," said Inaara.

"Hey, that's great," said Pearce, straining his eyes and flicking on the blinding intensity of the halogen high beams. "...sweet sixteen. That only happens once in your life. Now where the hell was... oh, there it is," and he swung the vehicle right onto the alternate highway.

"Where are we going?" asked Inaara, not seeming too worried, considering that she was in a vehicle with a strange guy who somehow knew in advance that the gates of the farm were going to be unlocked and that the mink had been liberated just before the whole place blew up.

"I'm going to drop you off at a friend's. His wife can fix you something to eat and you can call your parents to come and get you tomorrow," answered KJ.

"No way in hell that's going to happen," Inaara objected.

"And why is that?"

"I hate the Burdennys and I am never going back to stay with them ever again!"

"Get me a route to Watts Guns & Ammo in Boulder, KJ said into the ear bud mike.

CHAPTER 45

In the Hot Seat

The premier had been on a strict juice-only diet for the last two weeks in anticipation of being on the *Tonight Show Starring Jimmy Fallon*, as she was aware that TV adds about ten pounds to a person from the viewer's perspective. A chubby premier from the most-fit province in Canada was not going to cut it on national television. She had lost eight pounds on the juice diet so she figured that it would be a wash. Fallon has a way younger demographic than Leno, so she wore something young-ish, but not stupid. She was, after all, still the premier of British Columbia and had to maintain some sense of decorum.

On the advice of her stylish protégé, Victoria Wang, Teagan wore a silk cream-colored Armani suit, accented by a black, Egyptian cotton blouse with just enough cleavage to be of interest. Although guests are not paid to appear, in addition to the first class air ticket and digs at the uber-luxurious Chatwal hotel in Manhattan, Fallon's show sprung for a $600 to-die-for hair-do from the Sally Hershberger Salon on West 14th as a treat for the premier—scissored by Sally herself no less. Later, her Kerrisdale constituents would tell the premier that cut took ten years off her four-point-nine decades.

"Okay, Teagan it is," said Jimmy casually. "You look too young to be a premier. Am I right, audience?" Lots of cheers and applause followed.

"I'm sure it's just the Sally Hershberger haircut," she blurted out nervously, inadvertently name dropping. That comment elicited some oohs and aahs from those in the audience who were aware of the famous Manhattan stylist and her infamous prices. Sensing that this might well set off a controversy back home, Teagan looked into the camera and remarked, "Not to worry if anyone from B.C. is watching, it's on the show's dime!" Fallon jumped in and said, "Teagan, let's change the subject from haircuts to bear cuts, shall we."

Oh shit, here we go, thought Victoria, from the green room in the wings. After booking the premier on the show she tried every which way to get a list of questions Jimmy would ask her boss. "Come on, we get them all the time," she cajoled.

"Not from this show you don't," Nick Whyte had said. The guest manager, Nick had been in the talk show business for nearly quarter of a century and spoke from experience. "What's it going to hurt?" pleaded Victoria, batting her unusually hued jade green eyes at Nick. Victoria was only twenty-eight and most definitely a looker.

"It's going to hurt our credibility if it ever gets out," explained Nick.

Victoria laughed softly and rolled her eyes. "What credibility?" She looked Nick squarely in the eyes and said, "This is a celebrity guest talk show! No one expects credibility, they just want to be entertained."

Nick held his ground and explained that live meant live, not rehearsed and giving a guest the questions in advance would allow them to rehearse the answers.

"But they would be better, more thoughtful answers, don't you think, Nick?" she argued.

"Spontaneous answers can be much more entertaining and as you said, our viewers and audience want to be entertained," he countered.

Victoria gave her long, straight, jet-black hair a shake and sat back in her chair. The carefully placed highlights in her hair caught the light. Her impeccable midnight blue navy suit and pure white blouse would have been apropos in any Fortune Five-hundred boardroom. Nick White on the other hand was dressed in a pair of faded Calvin Klein jeans and a black, double-breasted Boss sport jacket (as would befit someone on a TV or movie set).

The premier's assistant was not going to take "no" for an answer. "Nick, I can't let my boss be embarrassed on national TV," she stated emphatically.

"Hey, Victoria, Jimmy is not Letterman okay? He might get a laugh or two at the Premier's expense, but it's not his style to skewer his guests." Nick's reply was earnest. "That's why they always come back. It was no different on Late Night with Jimmy Fallon a few years back."

Sensing that this particular interview might be different in light of the huge controversy over bear hunting, Victoria pressed on. "How about I give you a blow job for the questions Nick?"

"Right here and now?"

"That's right."

"Are you any good?"

"My boyfriend thinks so," she said coyly.

"Won't your boyfriend be pissed?" asked Nick.

"Not if you don't tell him—and since you don't know who he is that would be unlikely," she explained.

"You'd give me a BJ just to save your boss from being embarrassed?" asked Nick, feigning incredulity.

"Definitely."

"Well what if I accept the blow job and then just stonewall you on the answers?" he asked half-jokingly, the corners of his lips turning upwards in to a small smile.

"Then I'd beat the crap out of you," said Victoria matter-of-factly. "I have a black belt in karate and I doubt that you do."

Somewhat taken aback by her distinctly non-Canadian attitude, he replied, "Hmmm, you hit the nail on the head there Ms. Wang. Jason Statham I am not." He looked right back at her and added, "Hey, I was just messing with you—and vice versa, right"? He winked—a genuinely friendly wink this time.

She continued staring into his eyes, demanding an answer.

Following a huge sigh Nick said, "Truth be told Victoria—and I would love to accept your offer by the way, but only Jimmy knows what Jimmy is going to say. He adlibs his entire guest interviews."

"Are you serious?"

"As a judge on sentencing day." He motioned for her to follow him into the backstage bullpen to see the five thirty-something full-time literary warriors who wrote most of the jokes and gags for Jimmy. "Gary, Shupe, Connie, Morley and Caruso—meet Victoria Wang."

She said "hi" and so did they and then he moved her along to the research department.

He continued, "Our six researchers are first rate and they dig up every bit of information available on every guest—which will include your boss." As they walked he continued, "The internet is a wonderful tool if you know how to use it and our staff are flat out experts, if I do say so myself." Victoria was advised that Jimmy reviewed the researchers' guest summaries a day before the show to help him to keep the interviews moving along if they unexpectedly stalled on the main topic for which the guest was being interviewed.

"So, for example," Nick explained, "if your boss was not being forth-coming about her government's position on grizzly bear hunting in B.C., Jimmy could change tack and ask her why she preferred to be referred to as a MILF rather than a cougar."

"Where the hell did you dig up that information?" Victoria was incredulous.

"'That was an interview with your boss that aired on Jet FM December 19, 2012 in Courtney, B.C.," replied Nick, "reported in the Huff Post." Nick twirled his long mustache and said, "You know the old saying, once it's on the internet…"

"…it stays on the internet," Victoria finished the sentence for him.

"On the other hand," said Nick slyly, "if Jimmy wanted to switch the topic back to the hunt and the reason that it continues, despite the fact that eighty-six per cent of the residents of your fine province oppose it, he could ask the premiere if the $875,000 that the B.C. guides and outfitters have contributed to the liberal party's campaign funding over the previous five years has anything to do with that." After a short pause for dramatic effect he added, "As I said, he's not Letterman—but he's no push-over either."

"Double damn," she said, knowing that her boss could be in big trouble.

CHAPTER 46

New Allies

"Jake, this is Inaara Burdenny," KJ said, closing the door of the Durango after now sixteen-year-old Inaara's pink sneakers alighted on the parking lot. He'd pulled in behind Watts Guns & Ammo.

"Nice to meet you, Inaara," said Jake in a friendly voice, his firm handshake reassuring. "This is my wife, Marcy." Inaara and Marcy shook hands. "Let's go in and talk." He led them along a nicely manicured, tiny side yard abutting the two-story, brick building that housed WGA. Opening the front door, he flipped on the lights and deactivated the security alarm. There was a stairwell at the back of the store leading to the second-floor residence. It was one of the three ways to enter and exit the residence. Jake's military background dictated multiple exit options in case they ever had to leave in a hurry.

"Holy cow!" Inaara exclaimed, looking around. "I've never seen so many guns in my whole life." She walked down the aisle toward the back of the store. Even Pearce was impressed, and he had seen his share of well-stocked armories in his day. Rack upon rack of numerous makes of rifles and pistols lined the walls either encased in Plexiglas or locked in with a high tensile steel bars through the triggers. Ammunition of every type was available at WGA and in the rare instance when a particular caliber or type of commercially manufactured ammo was not in stock, Jake or either of his two sons could custom make it for a client themselves. Dozens of brands of scopes, shooting glasses, ear protectors, holsters and belts, slings, vests, magazine holders, bandoliers, speed loaders, shooting sticks, bipods and range bags were all neatly displayed—not one even an inch out of place.

Jake was a stickler for precision and it showed in his shop. He hit the remote on his key fob and the triple-bolted, steel-reinforced door unlatched, opening to the stairwell leading to his home. When they were all upstairs and seated around the kitchen table, Marcy poured an ice tea for Inaara and put on a pot of coffee for the guys.

"The thing is, Inaara needs a place to stay for a few days. Her family's home was destroyed earlier tonight," Pearce said. He didn't mention that he was the responsible party. "You'll probably read about it in the paper tomorrow."

"That's terrible," Marcy said. "Is the rest of her family okay?"

"Yeah, they are," said Inaara deciding to answer herself, "since they all left before me."

"They left?"

"That's right, my mom and dad and all the farm staff and workers piled into their cars and trucks and left the farm just before it blew up," she explained.

"The farm blew up?" Marcy was incredulous.

"It sounded like it," Inaara responded. "We were already driving away when we heard the explosions."

"That's right," Pearce cut in. "Several major explosions seemed to come from the farm where she was living. Maybe they had some fuel improperly stored on the premises and it caught fire."

Jake remained silent but Marcy wanted to know why Inaara hadn't left with her parents and the workers.

Inaara took a sip of ice tea and said, "I was running away."

"Oh."

"I hid in the barn after supper. I was going to try to catch a ride with one of the farmhands into town but out of the blue, everybody just got into their trucks and cars and the old motor home on site and raced away from the farm."

Marcy and her husband exchanged glances. "Well, wouldn't they look for you before they left?" she asked.

"You would have to ask them that," Inaara said, "as we are not exactly on speaking terms."

"How's that?"

The guys sipped their coffees, silent as statues, as Inaara confided to Marcy that her real mother, Maya Rangarajan, had been a waitress at The Longhorn in Denver. She had gotten to know Don Burdenny who often frequented the bar when he did business in town. From the first time she served him a Bud, he had taken a shine to Maya, who was friendly, outgoing and, as many cocktail waitresses, extremely easy on the eyes. She was also the only East Indian woman he had ever met. Before long, Don was stopping off at her apartment after her shift ended and one thing lead to another, ultimately resulting in the birth of Inaara. Don was hopping mad that Maya got pregnant—particularly since he was already married to Ruby and had a son, Dom. Donald Burdenny regarded himself as a family man and devout Christian so an abortion was simply out of the question. He insisted that Maya have the baby and he would send her money on the QT. This arrangement carried on just under four years. Maya drowned in a whitewater river rafting accident on the Roaring Fork river in Glenwood Springs. The coroner's office ruled out foul play.

Her death was just an unfortunate turn of events, plain and simple. Don and his attorneys cooked up a story about Maya being a distant relative of his deceased manager, Parm Dhaliwal, which enabled him to get custody of Inaara, since no other relatives came forward to claim her. As a consequence, Don's litigation lawyers were able to wrangle a decent settlement out of the rafting company's insurers on Inaara's behalf so she was something of an economic benefit to the Burdenny family—not that they particularly needed it. Ruth never totally bought the story, even after seeing the official papers his lawyers had doctored. She was always suspicious of Don's sudden benevolence.

"She needed a home and no other relative could be found. I owed that to Parm. That damned Paki worked his ass off for me!" As a consequence, Ruth never fully accepted Inaara into the family, nor did her creepy son, Dom. Besides, she wasn't white, although her mixed parentage made her much lighter skinned than her mom.

The offshoot of this was that Inaara had spent the last dozen or so years on the giant mink farm with a dad who could never admit to being her dad and a stepmother and stepbrother who resented her from day one.

"That mink farm was MBM?" Marcy's eyebrows shot up. "The place that burned down or blew up or whatever tonight?" Being the biggest mink farm in Colorado, MBM was well known to most residents.

"Yeah, that's the one," Inaara said, finishing her ice tea and asking for a second. Pearce had requested that Kiara do a bit of snap research on the legal status of a sixteen-year-old in Colorado. For most purposes in that state, an eighteen-year-old could do most anything including buy cigarettes, lottery tickets—even a handgun. She could marry without parental consent, vote in an election, sue or be sued in the courts and would be tried as an adult if she committed a criminal offence. Sixteen, on the other hand, was not as simple. Technically a sixteen-year-old in Colorado is a minor and subject to the control of her parents. There is no emancipation statute whereby a girl of this age could petition the court for an order recognizing her as a quasi-adult, with the rights and privileges of say, an eighteen-year-old. Hence, Inaara could stay with the Watts for only a day or two before they would have to notify her family.

After considerable discussion and whining by Inaara that life was unfair, it was decided she could stay for two days before Jake contacted her dad to come and get her. The story would be that she ran away from the farm and hitchhiked to Boulder, where she ran into Jake who was sympathetic to her plight, but legally bound to turn her in so to speak, to her parents. Pearce would not be mentioned in the narrative.

The next morning, Inaara watched KJ drop some supplies in the Durango as he prepared to leave. "Hey, you never told me who you really are," she said. "Your friends, Jake and Marcy call you KJ. Do you have a last name?"

"Does that really matter," he asked, tossing the last of the gear into the backseat.

"Yeah, it does if I want to call you. How can I call you if I don't even know your last name?"

"You can't, but I'll keep in touch," he said, climbing into the driver's seat and powering down the window.

"Promise?"

"Promise."

"Cross your heart and hope to die?" she entreated, crossing her own heart and putting her hands together in a praying motion.

He sighed and said, "Cross my heart, but I never hope to die, so you will just have to take my word for it," as he donned his Serengeti aviators.

"How are you going to find me?"

"You gave me your cell number and email, remember?" He didn't bother to mention that Rafa could likely track her down almost anywhere on the planet without her telephone number, email address or anything else.

"Did you really blow up the farm and let the mink go free?" she asked hopefully, grabbing his free hand. Pearce turned the key and the V8 hemi rumbled to life, its deep, powerful tone almost visceral. He took off his shades and looked directly into a pair of innocent blue eyes and said, "Let's just say that I happened to be in the neighborhood." She held his gaze, wanting more, and he obliged, "But, I am definitely glad that the guy that is maybe not your real dad saw the light and released the mink before whatever caused the explosions happened." He added, "A mink is a ferocious creature that belongs in the wild, not on the back of some rich woman who is trying to make a fashion statement."

She pressed his free hand which was resting on the open window of the driver's door—hard. "That's what I think too!" she said with as much feeling as she could muster.

"Good. We are on the same page, Inaara," he said, the aviators now back. He revved the engine—a sign that he had to get moving.

"Can I help with your campaign?" she asked, still not letting go of his hand. He raised his eyebrows, invisible to her under the shades. The kid sure wasn't stupid and her heart was definitely in the right place.

"Maybe," he said, leaving her hopeful. Jake and Marcy waived from the upper balcony as the black Durango rumbled out of the parking lot, headed toward Nebraska where the pristine mink coats would be distributed by an old army buddy to those in need. Inaara's eyes didn't leave the Durango until it finally faded into the distance in the bright morning sunlight.

CHAPTER 47

From the Frying Pan into the Fire

"Are you in favor of hunting grizzly bears for sport, Teagan?" Jimmy asked.

She unsuccessfully tried a smile and said, "Well Jimmy it's not really important whether I am in favor of it since I am just one person. However, as the premier of British Columbia I have to represent the will of the people who elected me and the members of my party which forms the government." She was happy with that answer, but it left Victoria squirming in her seat.

"Yeah, but what do you think about the Grizzly Bear Hunt yourself?" asked Jimmy, his expression serious. "Do you support it personally?"

"My government supports it."

Out of the blue Jimmy's expression changed. "You do understand English, Madame Premier?" So much for Teagan. Jimmy was getting testy–he was not used to interviewing politicians on his show.

"Since we are conversing in English, I will assume that is a rhetorical question, Mr. Fallon," the premier shot back.

The audience became dead quiet, intrigued by Fallon's dramatic change of tone *and* his guest's. "I'll ask you the question one more time then, in plain, basic English, and maybe you can answer it, as opposed to answering a different question which I did not ask." He watched her squirm in her seat. "You can do that can't you, Madame Premier?"

"Of course, I can," she said, looking much less at ease than she was trying to sound.

"Okay, let's try it again," he said, slowly and deliberately, as if he was speaking to a second grader.

"Do you (pause)… or do you not (pause)… personally support the Grizzly Bear Hunt in B.C.?" he asked, standing, spreading his arms wide apart and looking to the audience for support.

The Premier paused.

"Let's try it once more so there's no confusion. Crowd, let's ask the question again shall we?" This time Jimmy and the whole audience asked, "Do you (pause)... or do you not (pause) ... personally support the Grizzly Bear Hunt in B.C.?"

Teagan remained frozen like a proverbial deer in the headlights. Victoria willed her to say something neutral. If she said she agreed with the hunt, the city dwellers in B.C. would turn on her. If she said that she opposed the hunt, the guide and outfitters would stop contributing to her re-election campaigns. Politics is a tricky business. A good politician has to be able to answer a question without saying anything. And incredibly, despite a so-called independent press, no one is allowed to challenge that chicanery in the Western world. Back home, if a reporter was being too inquisitive (like Jimmy was being here) the premier's handlers would shut down the interview with a "sorry that's all the time we have guys," and hustle her away. That particular interviewer or reporter would never be invited back to talk to the premier. However, here on *The Tonight Show Starring Jimmy Fallon*, she had no one to shut down the interview for her.

She paused, wondering if her "made for a woman, protects like a man" underarm deodorant would hold up. She prayed with all her might for a commercial break. How about a power failure or fire alarm? Would the TV gods please smile on her? Seconds crawled by like hours. For a split second, Victoria contemplated running out on stage to do something, but that would probably make things worse. No, Madame Premier would have to get out of this one herself, she told herself.

The New York audience was getting restless, but sensed that something was coming.

"Hey Teagan, bear got your tongue," shouted an audience member.

"Are you going to *bare* it all?" added another, to a round of laughter.

"Come on now, Teagan, your stalling is becoming unbearable!" Jimmy chimed in, feeding off the crowd, a true master of his craft. Despite being made for a man, her deodorant was definitely not holding up to its billing. The premier's arm pits were soaked and she was mortified thinking that sweat patches might show through on her cream silk jacket on national TV.

"Okay, okay you got me," she confessed. "Me, personally—

speaking only for myself, not the government of British Columbia nor the liberal party of B.C., nor for the Ministry of Wildlife, I don't personally agree with the Grizzly Bear Hunt! But that's just me," she added.

A huge round of applause erupted from the audience—glad to see that she was on the right side of the debate, in their view. She actually blushed, not used to such genuine, spontaneous approval.

"Then why don't you put a stop to it since eighty-six percent of the people in your province oppose it?" asked a wide-eyed Fallon, clearly exaggerating his expression of incredulity.

Victoria almost fainted. The show cut to a commercial break—thank God!

CHAPTER 48

Back to the True North Strong and Free

Pearce had left the black trailer and remaining ordnance with Josh Norris, a buddy he served with briefly in the Sudan. Josh believed that he was a distant relative of the legendary actor and martial artist, Chuck Norris, but he had no proof of that nor had he ever met the man. He was, however, a big fan, having seen *Code of Silence* and *The Octagon* so many times he knew the lines by heart. Hence, in his mind, there was a kinship there even if it wasn't genetic. He was happy to pick up a free trailer; and the weapons, ammo and assorted accessories would go into his underground bunker. He was the quintessential survivalist and prided himself on being able to hold out for "at least a couple of years" in the event that some calamity or natural disaster rendered civilization in the U.S. unsustainable.

Josh also had a soft spot for vets who had come back injured or incapacitated from America's numerous military escapades around the globe. Many of the ex-soldiers, even special forces guys, had physical disabilities or PTSD or both, and were essentially unemployable. The coats would help to keep them warm in the cold Nebraska winters for sure, he assured Pearce.

"The guys who get these aren't the types to put the furs back up on E-Bay for a quick buck."

Pearce knew that the chances of his vehicle being searched by the border patrol at the Peace Arch crossing between South Surrey, British Columbia and Blaine, Washington went up about four-fold if he was hauling anything. For some reason, the guards felt that they had to have a look-see at almost every trailer or motor home that passed under their watchful eyes. Pearce bid his friend good bye and headed upstate toward South Dakota. At the northwest corner of the state he would turn west into the big sky country of Montana, passing briefly through Idaho and finally into Washington. While he could enter Canada from North Dakota, which would put him in Saskatchewan, or from Montana, which would place him in Alberta, he was sporting B.C. plates on his vehicle and preferred to return to B.C. That would, in his opinion, reduce the chances of his vehicle being searched to the lowest possibility.

Over Rafa's strenuous objections, he decided to bring the $2M cash back with him across the border. "KJ, anything you bring back over $10K CDN has to be reported to Customs at the border under the Proceeds of Crime—Money Laundering—and Terrorist Financing according to your legal expert, Kiara," Rafa warned.

"I hear you," Pearce responded, cruising along the I-5 towards the Canada-U.S. border. It just dawned on him that the twenty-five thousand in cash that he had brought over the border to purchase C-4 and other weapons from WGA could have been confiscated. "It's a calculated risk I am prepared to take," he said. "By the way, what are the penalties for failure to report?"

"Forfeiture of the cash and a fine of up to $5,000," Rafa advised.

"I could live with that in a worst-case scenario," Pearce responded. He was about a hundred miles south of the border and would be approaching the crossing in a little over an hour and fifteen minutes, as traffic was light.

"You know better, KJ." Rafa shrugged, though Pearce couldn't see him. "That would put you on the government's radar screen way sooner than you have to be." A Washington state patrol car pulled out onto the highway behind Pearce from an exit in Redmond. He slowed the Durango to seventy and a bit, even though most other vehicles on the road maintained speed. There was no sense in getting pulled over for speeding by a bored patrolman.

"Maybe it could even connect you to the loss of funds at MBM, you think?"

"No way." KJ was emphatic.

"Why not? The numbers would match up. The cash you have versus the loss reported by MBM would be the same."

"MBM will never report the cash as being missing in the first place," Pearce assured Rafa. "It's pay-off money, plain and simple. No legitimate business would store several million dollars in cash in a locked, alarmed shed hidden away on their farm."

"Hmmm, so you think the money is dirty?"

"Let's just say that neither the authorities nor Burdenny's insurance company is going to be looking for it," KJ said.

"Wow, that's going to be a nice war chest," said Rafa excitedly, "assuming you get it across the border, that is."

"That's the plan." In about forty-five minutes, Pearce would pull into the elegant Semiahmoo Resort, where he would have a leisurely meal at the Pierside Restaurant overlooking the bay. While Andrew Gates, the superb chef, would create a sumptuous salad of Cloud Mountain Farm Organic Honey Gem baby lettuces, cherry tomatoes and haricots verts with tarragon vinaigrette he would be fabricating a false itinerary to support his whereabouts in the U.S. for the last week.

Soldiers, cops and border guards are consistent if nothing else. When they ask you a question, they want a simple, no-bullshit answer. Red flags go up if you hesitate, smile or volunteer too much information when you reply. Josh had given KJ an operable, used fishing rod and reel, some inert bait and other fishing gear in an old tackle bag along with serviceable hip waders—not a bad trade for the guns and the trailer! An avid outdoorsman himself, he told KJ where to find the best lakes and streams to catch Jack Smelt and Blackfish and he also picked up a three-day non-resident fishing permit from Nebraska Game & Parks, for $27.00 U.S., assuming KJ would be needing it. A used pup tent, sleeping bag and some utensils completed the ad hoc camping gear.

By the time he finished his meal, KJ would have memorized his fake itinerary so he could answer all of the usual questions which the Canadian Border Services guards would ask any citizen returning from a weeklong fishing and hiking trip in the U.S. His used gear, if the guards checked, would appear to be appropriate for his trip. No, he had eaten the fish he caught while he was there. Outstanding smelt and blackfish by the way! With tools provided by Jake Watts he had taken apart the inside door panel, put the cash into several cavities located between the door braces and, in his opinion, did a pretty fair job of putting back the door panel exactly as it had been. Ever the stickler for detail, he washed and hosed down the inside of the door panel, making sure that there was no random finger print or hair to connect him to the location of the money. After drying the inside with a blow dryer, he donned the Freetoo tactical gloves and stuffed the cash securely in between the metal door braces.

This subterfuge would withstand casual scrutiny (a level one search), but if Canadian Border Services decided to pull the vehicle apart it was a lead pipe cinch that they would find the dough. He would, of course, deny any knowledge of the money and there would be no DNA or fingerprint evidence that he had tampered with the door or handled the cash. The money would be confiscated, since he couldn't explain its origin and thus could assert no claim to it. The Durango might be impounded as well. His flawless military background, lack of criminal record and complete cooperation with the Canadian Border Services just might be enough to get him through. He would provide the Durango's bill of sale, the custom upgrades, the online Nebraska fishing license, gas receipts and anything else requested. Technically, it is not a crime to take cash into or out of Canada, but as Kiara advised, it must be disclosed to the border services by way of a Form E677 (Cross-Border Currency or Monetary Instruments Report) if the sum exceeds $10,000 CDN. Needless to say, if he didn't know the cash was there he couldn't report it. This was a back-up plan only, better than nothing—but not by much.

He had picked a Sunday night to return home, with its guarantee of several hundred vehicles ahead and behind him. Although rotated hourly, border guards are only human and they get bored and disinterested after asking the same questions thousands of times a day. Pearce was counting on that. A few times a year there is a big drug or weapons bust which makes the papers, but for the most part if CBS catches anything it's usually a motorist trying to smuggle in a few extra cartons of cigarettes or maybe his wife bought expensive shoes or clothing in Bellingham and is hoping to evade paying the duty.

Pearce was now nearing the crossing. He could take a right at Blaine and enter into the truck crossing (which also allowed regular motor vehicles) or he could stay put and take Peace Arch. Rafa had advised him that there were no reports of incidents at either crossing that day. That was good, as there would be no heightened security in place at either crossing. He decided to take Peace Arch. With about a hundred vehicles ahead of him in the outside lane, he settled in for over an hour-and-a-half wait. The Durango inched ahead as car after car was eventually waived through. His line moved fairly well, if you can call fifty cars an hour a decent pace.

Every once in a while, a border guard would ask a driver to roll down the back windows, pop the trunk or get out of the vehicle. The guard would make a big production of searching the vehicle for the benefit of the waiting motorists. "Make sure you declare everything or you could be next" was the clear message. With a line-up of a thousand cars and trucks behind a suspicious motorist, the guard could easily waive the vehicle over to the search area where other border officers would conduct the search and question the driver. However, by conducting the cursory search at the crossing gate, the guard also conveyed the clear impression to the idling motorists that he was the man in charge. They could damned well wait until the guard was finished with his due diligence, as their time was of zero importance to him. This was after all, a matter of national security.

Peace Arch Park, which straddles the Canada-U.S. border is picturesque, bounded by Semiahmoo Bay on the west side where gorgeous sunsets over the water dazzle the eye and scenic south Surrey on the east. The roads to and from the border cut through the perfectly manicured lush green grass and myriad flowerbeds of pansies, violets, buttercups, roses and anything that met the gardeners' fancies. On the U.S. side, local artists are allowed to display their cutting-edge stone, metal and wooden artwork. The gigantic concrete Peach Arch looms over the borderline some one hundred feet high, and is an absolute favorite for photographers of all skill levels. On the U.S. side, it's inscribed with "May these Gates Never be Closed" and on the Canadian side with "Brothers of a Common Mother." Floodlights illuminate the Arch as dusk approaches making it a sight worth seeing. In short, it's not the worst place in the world to idle whilst you wait to be passed through the border gates.

Pearce mentally counted over twenty-five vehicles directly ahead of him, but not a one had been signaled out for any search or observation procedure in his line. That was not good, as sooner or later one of the next vehicles would get the treatment. Sure as shit, it was his.

CHAPTER 49

Crashing the Party

Even though she had a rigorous litigation schedule, Kiara found the time to dig out every detail about the grand opening festivities of the Grizzly Bear Hunt. The government had decided to get some mileage out of the enormous amount of free publicity surrounding the otherwise low-key event. With local, Canadian and worldwide media on hand, why not showcase the place and let everyone know that British Columbia, Canada was open for business?

Trip Sullivan, the minister of commerce, would be there to make a speech about the many opportunities available to those who may have an interest in opening a business in the Pacific Province. Margie Pannabaker, tourism minister, would explain why supernatural British Columbia was the best place in the world to visit. For security, there would be fifty members of the Royal Canadian Mounted Police on hand, about a dozen wearing their red serge formal uniforms and riding horses. The international press would definitely eat this up. There would be photo ops a plenty. Though not mentioned in any public government document, about a half a dozen undercover CSIS agents would be milling about and at least that number of FBI operatives, as U.S. assets were potentially at risk.

Normally, grizzly bear hunting season got underway without fanfare, but this year, at the insistence of FLNRO, everyone involved was encouraged to meet up at noon on the opening day at the southern entrance of the Great Bear Rainforest. As a strictly "cover-your-ass" liability precaution, in addition to the waiver which all the hunting parties signed, FLNRO deputy minister Praveen Sandhu would warn the participants on national TV that the B.C. government was not offering protection nor providing security for the hunting parties. FLNRO's official position, contrary to that of virtually every U.S. security expert and media pundit, was that the individual who managed to post the threat on its website was likely just a hacker or other malcontent looking to cause trouble or stir up controversy.

When he read about FLNRO's position in the *Nanaimo Daily News*, Sergeant Provost mentally gave Praveen a thumbs-up for seeing through the flimsy hoax which was fooling so many people around the globe, even so-called experts. He just hoped that the Travis boys would not gum up the works too badly for Coburn's sake. Notwithstanding its position, FLNRO's ever cautious legal counsel felt it necessary to warn the hunters that there was still the possibility, however small, that a real terrorist made the threat and would try to cause them harm. Deputy Minister Sandhu would publicly commend the guide and outfitter companies for taking preventative measures like adding personal security details to the expeditions, on their own dime, no less. Local newspapers had already reported that many animals' rights and environmental groups planned on showing up. The Peregrine First Nations would be out in force opposing the hunt. In fact, they had filed a law suit in B.C. Supreme Court claiming aboriginal title to the entire twelve-thousand square-mile rainforest. In their view, everybody was trespassing and the hunt was therefore illegal from the outset as it was not sanctioned by the band. Naturally the hunting enthusiasts and gun lobby would be there in force to counter what they considered to be lies and misinformation spread by the animal rights groups.

Kiara estimated that with no less than fifteen news services covering the event, there would be upwards of a thousand people at the opening venue. It would be most interesting to see what KJ had up his sleeve to crash the party.

CHAPTER 50

Fall Out

The Burdennys did their level best to play down the destruction of their minkery, but the media and federal investigators were all over the story. Within a half hour of the many explosions that vaporized virtually every structure on the farm, hundreds of police and firemen had been dispatched to the scene. As soon as the Burdenny caravan was back within cell and internet coverage, the Dreaded D's discovered that something was up at the ranch—and it wasn't poison gas. When Boulder police chief Wexler told Burdenny on the phone that every single structure on the farm had been destroyed by explosions, Don's face turned purple with rage.

"Every building?" he sputtered. "Are you sure every building was razed?" He was thinking about the two sheds.

"Sorry to say, Don, absolutely every building has been leveled to the ground," an apologetic police chief answered, worried he would be blamed for not preventing the carnage. So much for the mink coat for his wife.

"How the fuck does something like that happen on your watch, Pete?" Don demanded. Dom grabbed his dad's arm and mouthed, "What happened?" Don flipped on the speaker function on his smart phone and said to his son so that Wexler could hear, "What happened, Dom, is that *apparently* our entire farm was blown to smithereens right under the noses of Denver, Colorado's finest!"

"Whoa, Don." Wexler knew that MMB Colorado was a big taxpayer in the state and a major contributor to all police causes. "That's not exactly a fair assessment. We are forty miles from the farm and there was NONE, NADA, ZERO warning that anything like this was coming down the pipe."

"No warning?" Don was clearly incredulous. "What about the explosion at the Fort Gary Army Base? Wouldn't that tip you off that maybe something was up in the area?"

"What explosion?"

An exasperated and fuming Don explained. "Jezuz, the explosion at Fort Gary. You know? The one that that released toxic gas all over the goddamned area, you know, that fuckin explosion!"

"Who on earth told you that?" Pete asked. "Because we would sure as hell would have heard about it long before you did, that is, if it actually happened."

"What do you mean *if* it actually happened?" Don shouted. Dom was starting to get a queasy feeling in the pit of his stomach, listening to this. "My wife called Excel Energy when we lost electricity earlier tonight." Don's fury was starting to mount. "Then when I got on the phone the power guy told me there was an explosion at the army base and that sarin gas was heading our way."

"What?"

"Yeah." Now Don was trembling with rage. "And to get the hell off the property before the gas reached us! So we did. Every damned one of us deserted the farm to avoid being gassed!" He gripped his phone so tightly, Dom thought he might just shatter it. "The power guy said we were next on his customer list to call but Rube beat him to the punch." He paused, recreating the scene in his mind. "I am positive it was Excel's number. Rube looked it up and made the call herself." Don sounded like he was trying to convince himself as much as the chief. No comment from Wexler. "Pete, I was at home, watching *Furious 7*, when the power went out." Still nothing from the Chief. "I am not fucking making this up!"

"You know, I think that's the best picture in the franchise," opined Pete, "especially with Jason Statham raining on Vin Diesel's parade at the tail end."

"Yeah, though it was too bad that they had to kill off the Chinese kid and his girlfriend. She was a peach." said Don, now the movie critic.

"You got that right," said the chief. Turning back to the business at hand, Wexler responded, "But, Don, I can tell you for damned sure there was no explosion at the army base and no poison gas was released."

You could have heard a pin drop. Seconds went by.

"Say again?" Dom said into the massive phone his dad was holding. He rocked back and forth on the balls of his feet, hoping somehow that he had misunderstood the police chief's statement.

"You were hoaxed," Pete said. There was no way to soft-peddle that kind of news. "I don't know who you talked to, but there was no explosion at the base, and as far as I know the army doesn't even store sarin gas any more. I think that they got rid of that shit in the nineties." Thoroughly baffled by Don's comments, the chief continued, his hand resting atop the police cruiser. "But there were multiple explosions at the farm. That I know. In fact, my boys and the feds are here now combing through the wreckage. I am looking at it as we speak and it looks like a goddamned war zone."

"Get the Audi," Don ordered. "Don't move an inch, Pete. We are on the way back!"

CHAPTER 51

Porous Borders

"Sir, would you pull your vehicle over to the left in the inspection area," said the junior border guard from her perch in the booth.

"Is there a problem?" KJ asked, keeping his voice steady.

"No problem," she responded. "Just pull your vehicle over where I told you to."

"You know I can pop the rear hatch and you can have a look through the Durango yourself right here." KJ's voice was friendly. "And save the boys the trouble back there."

He knew any inspection at the booth would not be nearly as invasive as one in the inspection area.

"Sir, do you have a hearing problem?" The guard was surly. She had been sitting in the booth for close to an hour and was in no mood for backtalk, even from a decent looking guy in a cool black SUV. "I said drive your vehicle to the inspection area on the left NOW!" she commanded. "Or I'll call security and they'll do it for you."

KJ maintained a neutral tone of voice while weighing his options. "Hey, I was just trying to be helpful," he said. He could pull through the gate and then rapidly accelerate down Highway 99, grabbing the first exit and head eastward. By the time the border patrol jumped into their waiting chase car, a tricked-out Dodge Charger, he would have rounded the traffic circle and could easily take the Durango off road into the bushes and lose the border patrol. The downside was that the border cameras would have already captured his plate number and probably his face, so he would have a tough time explaining why he drove off when the RCMP came knocking later that evening.

"That kind of help I don't need," the guard said. "Now move it!" She was mid-twenties and probably a rookie. She was definitely not going to take any guff. Her boss had told her that at that booth she was the law and anybody trying to drive through better damned well respect that. It was a privilege to enter Canada, not a right, he had maintained—and don't let anybody forget that. In point of fact, it was a legal right for any Canadian citizen to enter the country, but border guards are not lawyers and it is pointless to argue with them.

"Suit yourself," KJ said, putting the Durango into drive. He noticed she picked up the phone as he motored by. He drove the vehicle into the third stall on the left of the highway where he was immediately met by two customs officers who asked that he get out of the SUV and kindly have a seat inside the customs office. They also asked for his keys to the vehicle. The two customs inspectors would start searching the SUV, while their supervisor would conduct the interrogation. He willed his heart rate to remain 55 bpm and, in case he was being watched, casually sauntered.

In a short time, he was looking at the high-vaulted ceiling of probably the nicest looking customs offices anywhere on the planet. The building looked like a huge, modern-day Noah's Ark. It was specially designed that way for the 2010 Winter Olympic Games which were held in Whistler, B.C. Figuring that the news media would certainly report on this unusual, but striking structure to their millions of viewers, the government had spared no expense in its construction.

Pearce, however, was not thinking about the architecture of the building when he was summoned to the front counter by Sergeant Tommy Doroshenko, CBS, a grouchy-looking customs supervisor.

"Passport," stated Tommy matter-of-factly, without glancing up. Just another tourist who was probably trying to smuggle in some cigarettes or weed. Hardly even worth his time.

"Don't have one with me," KJ replied. "Will a Nexus Card do?" he asked, knowing in advance that it would.

"Hand it over." Still not looking up.

Pearce did so.

"Hmmmm," said Doroshenko, gingerly examining it as if it was radioactive. "How long you been gone?"

"Seven days," KJ responded.

"What was your business in the U.S.?"

"No business. Just some fishing and hiking," KJ said, keeping his answers short and to the point. He could imagine the two officers taking out his luggage and fishing gear and shining the strobe lights inside the Durango.

"Where?" Doroshenko was mildly interested.

"Box Butte Reservoir."

Doroshenko asked where that was and KJ told him it was in Nebraska. "Whatcha catch?" asked Tommy now looking up and staring him straight in the eye. He was watching for telltale signs of nervousness. Fidgeting and hesitancy were both sure giveaways that the perp was hiding something.

KJ returned his gaze, however, and stated, "About a half a dozen Jack Smelt. And a Blackfish or two, just before I left." He tried to keep the exchange conversational.

"How much?" the supervisor asked.

"What?"

"How much was the license?"

"What license?" asked KJ, somewhat perplexed.

"The fishing license. You can't fish anywhere without a license," explained Doroshenko. "Or were you fishing illegally in Nebraska?" Now he was certain he was going to catch this guy in a lie.

"Oh. That license. It was around twenty-five bucks, for two or three days," KJ said, scratching his head and closing one eye for effect. "Yeah, three days I think."

"You think? You don't know?" the supervisor's tone had become accusatory. "How did you pay for it, by credit card or cash?"

Fortunately, KJ was expecting this line of questioning. "Cash." He volunteered that he might still have the receipt.

"Well let's see it then."

After purposely fumbling around in his windbreaker and pants' pockets KJ pulled out his wallet. He slowly went through it section by section, knowing exactly where the license was, but making sure it was the last place he looked. "Damn, I was sure that I kept it…" he muttered, still searching.

Doroshenko's countenance remained skeptical, his thumbs hooked on his holster belt. A Colt .45 hung at his side—now standard issue for Canadian border personnel who were unarmed until just a few years ago.

Finally. "Ahhah!" KJ said, with feigned excitement. "Found it." He handed the license to Doroshenko, who thoroughly examined it.

"Date, April 16/15 check, place, Box Butte, NB, check, fish (Smelt and Black), check, fee, $27.00, check." Looking disappointed, the customs supervisor eventually decided it was legit and returned it. Undeterred, he ploughed on with the interrogation.

"Bring any fish back?"

"No."

Doroshenko's eyes narrowed. "Why not?"

"I ate them while I was camping."

"Makes sense." He followed that up by asking, "What else you got stashed in your car?" Now he was fishing.

"Just my camping gear and luggage," KJ said. "And a rod."

"You're sure about that?"

"Yeah, I'm sure," said KJ.

"Cause Rosie at the booth put in a Code 9 so we are going to take apart your vehicle piece by piece to see what you are hiding," the sergeant warned him sternly. "If you've got something else in there we should know about, you better come clean now."

"Why would she do that?" asked KJ, trying to sound like the uninformed tourist.

"Hey, I ask the questions bud, not you," was the curt reply.

"That's funny." KJ briefly smiled.

"What's funny?"

"That's exactly what my old C/O used to say." It was a calculated risk trying to extend the conversation. However, since the prick was going to have his vehicle trashed anyway, likely finding the cash in the process, he had nothing to lose.

"CAF or U.S. Army?" Doroshenko was mildly interested.

"CAF."

"What outfit?"

"JTF2. Master sergeant first class."

"Bullshit!" exclaimed Doroshenko. "Jesus Christ himself couldn't get into that outfit!" Pearce said nothing. "Who was your C/O?"

"Major John Connell."

"You gotta be shitting me," Doroshenko said, now grinning from ear to ear. He was a CAF vet himself who had tried on three separate occasions to get accepted into JTF2 before he retired a few years back to join Canadian Border Services. That fucking asshole Connell had personally turned him down each time. Now the supervisor was warming up a bit—just a couple of ex-military vets having a casual chinwag.

Pearce wondered if there was something to work with here.

"What was your specialty?" Doroshenko asked, as he started filling out the paperwork, his handwriting almost illegible.

Trying to sound as chummy as possible without being too obvious, KJ replied, "Two actually. Sniper and hand-to-hand combat."

Having had some long-range shooting experience himself, Doroshenko asked KJ what his best shot was.

"Let me think," said KJ trying to recall one of many long shots he had made while in JTF2. Doroshenko was definitely interested. "I'm pretty sure that my longest was near our base in Kandahar. Took out an Al Qaeda scout with an M107 at just over a mile, eighteen-hundred and eleven yards to be exact." Snipers always remember their best shots to the yard.

This resonated big time with Doroshenko who told KJ he had once made a nine-hundred and twenty-five yard shot on an outdoor army range in a field competition—and only two inches off the bullseye. Won him the contest.

"That's a pretty decent shot," KJ said, one professional to another. "What did you use?"

"Mac Tac 50" Doroshenko replied. "Hell of a beast though." His tone was no longer officious. At twenty-six pounds unloaded, the fifty caliber McMillan Tac-50 was indeed a beast. Its kill range was up to twenty-one hundred yards. To serious marksman, McMillan was more than a leading firearms brand—it was a philosophy.

"In shooting as in life, success is defined by whether you hit what you aim for. Always shoot to win," Pearce quoted. It was the company's tag line verbatim, well known to many shooting enthusiasts—including Doroshenko, who was thoroughly impressed, and now looking at KJ as a comrade in arms. Out of the blue he picked up the phone and punched in a number. "Bobby, cancel the Code 9," he said, "and put everything back into the guy's vehicle where you found it."

"But, Sarge, we've only just finished the compartment search. We haven't even pulled anything apart yet," Private Bobby Collins said.

"You find anything so far?"

"No, but..." The supervisor cut him off. "Then put everything back."

"You know sir, Rosie has been pretty good with her calls lately," Bobby Collins added.

"And?"

"Well, she will be some pissed off."

"Like I give a crap," snorted Doroshenko. "Just do it." His tone left zero room for further debate. "She doesn't like it, she can come and see me."

"Yes, sir."

Handing back the Nexus card, Doroshenko said, "Master Sergeant Pearce first class, you and your vehicle are free to go."

KJ made a crisp salute with his left hand as he turned to go. "Thank you Sergeant Doroshenko." The salute, a gesture of respect universally known to every soldier, originated in the eleventh century when knights of the realm fought jousting matches on horseback. The motion of raising and lowering the visor on the knight's helmet before engaging in the charge eventually became the military salute. As Pearce strode through the door, the supervisor called out, "Hey, remember the next time you come through here it's Tommy."

KJ gave him a thumbs-up. Almost without fail, KJ had that effect on people. Except of course Rosie at the booth.

CHAPTER 52

Aftermath

You would think 9-11 had happened again. The Colorado Chronicle carried a front page story, complete with pictures, of the devastation at the MBM minkery. News reports showed police, fire trucks, Homeland Security and the FBI all over the fifty-acre spread looking for clues. Mind you, there was not much to look at. Conspicuously absent were ambulances or paramedics, as there seemed to be no casualties—not even dead mink.

Reporters were camped out in front of where the huge house used to be, waiting to interview anyone within hailing distance. The FBI's bomb squad had determined that the blasts were caused by C-4, which raised all sorts of speculation in the media.

"Where the hell are all the mink?" Rick Stoner, the lead investigator with the FBI, asked. "I mean this was the biggest mink farm in the state, right? I don't see one body anywhere."

Checking his notes, his assistant Randy Tamlin explained that the owner, "a guy named Burdenny, big shot businessman it seems, let them all go with the click of a mouse before everything blew up."

"Why the heck would he do that?"

Randy shook his head. "There's something about a poison gas leak heading toward the farm…"

"What kind of bullshit is that?" queried Stoner. "There were no independent reports of a gas leak were there?"

"No sir."

"Is the owner here?"

"He is."

"Well then get him over here right now," Stoner ordered. "Gas leak my ass, there's got to be something more to this." A twenty-year veteran with the FBI, Stoner had a knack of getting to the truth with brutal efficiency and a most definite lack of tact. He was mid-forties, six-two and weighed in at two-ten, give or take a pound after a big dinner. He stiff-armed Homeland Security and the locals out of the way and pretty much took over the scene with his boys. That was his standard m.o. He felt the other investigation agencies were all basically incompetent.

"I'm Stoner, FBI," he announced, "You the owner of this farm?"

Don Burdenny tried to muster up some authority. "Yes sir, I am. You got any leads on the lunatics who blew up my farm?"

Ignoring the question, Stoner asked, 'Why did you let the mink go?"

Burdenny avoided making eye contact. "Well, I was told that there had been an explosion near Fort Gary and that toxic gas had been released, which was coming our way." Stoner was looking at him as if he was explaining that Martians had landed on the farm. Burdenny continued anyway. "And since the mink pens and barns are not airtight, I had to let the mink go or they would be gassed."

"Yeah, right," Stoner said. "Who told you this gas leak was coming?"

"The guy from Excel Energy that my wife called. I talked to him, too," Don said.

"This guy got a name?"

Don sounded defensive. "I didn't think to ask." This interview was not starting off as he had expected.

"That's handy," Stoner said, nodding at Tamlin, who was taking notes. "You didn't think to maybe call the cops to verify that outlandish a claim?" Burdenny said nothing. "I hear you are pretty chummy with the police chief in Denver."

"What the hell's that supposed to mean?" Don objected, not used to being interrogated, except by Ruby when she was pissed off.

"It means that I think that your story is bullshit," Stoner said. "Agent Tamlin, check the phone records from last night from the house number—what was your house number Burdenny?"

"720-309-1181."

"And your wife supposedly placed a call to Excel Energy at what time?"

"About 8:30 p.m.," Don said. "And it wasn't supposedly. I heard her make the call and I talked to the guy myself."

"The guy with no name, right?"

"I told you, I didn't ask for his name. Should I be calling my lawyer?"

"Why, you got something to hide?" Stoner shot back.

"No, but you're treating me like I blew up the damned farm myself!" Don said in an agitated voice.

"Well did you?" Stoner stared him straight in the eye.

Don looked aghast. "Look, I just spend twenty-five years building that farm up into a profitable enterprise. Why the hell would I destroy it now?"

"Oh, I don't know. How about for the insurance money?" asked the inspector rhetorically. "You been having any financial problems lately?"

"No way. We just had one of our best years ever," Don said. "You can check my financial records."

"Bank on it," Stoner replied, emphatically. "That's a given in every arson case."

"Arson! I can't think of anybody who would want to burn the place down," Don exclaimed.

"Really? How much does a mink pelt go for these days?" Stoner changed tack and caught Don off-guard.

"Um, let me think. I'm not exactly sure."

"Well who would be sure?"

"My son, Dom," answered Burdenny. "He handles the sales."

"Is he here?"

"Yes."

"Bring him over here," directed Stoner. Dom was watching the proceedings from a distance and came over upon seeing Don's hand motion. Asked the value of a mink pelt, he said, "Well, at the last auction just over a month ago in Denver, a top quality pelt was fetching between $50 and $60."

"And you had what, a couple thousand mink on the property?"

"A lot more than that. It was closer to five thousand," he replied.

"Yeah?" Mentally doing the math he said, "Then that's almost three million bucks your dad flushed down the toilet based on a call to some guy without a name. Have I got that right?"

"It was a call to Excel Energy," Don was close to shouting, "… right after our power went out."

Tamlin reappeared and put his cupped hand over his mouth as he said something into Stoner's ear. Stoner's eyebrows raised. Not a good sign, thought Don.

"The phone company has no record of receiving an outbound call from your number to Excel Energy last night."

"That's impossible!" exclaimed Don.

"And Excel doesn't either," Stoner added. "And as you know, most service providers now record all of their customer calls—and they don't have one from your phone. Furthermore," my agent reports that Excel has no record of a power outage at your farm yesterday. Care to explain that?"

Now Don looked totally stunned.

"You still got your cell phone handy, Burdenny?" asked Stoner.

"Why?"

"Maybe you should call your lawyer."

CHAPTER 53

Home Base

The two young inspectors showed KJ a considerable amount of deference when he arrived back at his vehicle from the customs office. They had never had an inspection quashed in midstride, and assumed that Rosie had inadvertently snagged some kind of VIP. Bobby held the door open like a valet would and handed the keys to KJ as he slid into the Durango. "Sorry for any inconvenience, sir," said Private Collins. "Everything's back where it was."

"No problem officer," said KJ evenly, "I know you are just doing your job." It never hurts to show some respect to the minions who were in fact, just doing their jobs. You never know when they might come in handy. He turned the ignition switch and woke up the three hundred and sixty ponies under the hood with a seriously loud rumble.

"Nice wheels," said Bobby's partner. "I'm sure glad we didn't have to rip this baby apart sir."

"You and me both." KJ gave them a curt nod and he drove off with a sigh of relief. He motored straight north on Highway 99 and took the Cloverdale exit on the right. Rounding a quarter of the traffic circle he continued east on 8th Avenue towards his home base. He hit the BBM messenger icon on his Blackberry Z-30. After the usual *"I told you so's"* Rafa's reaction was one of relief, but not total surprise. He was beginning to think that his friend, KJ, had something more than good luck on his side. Who knew, maybe Divine Providence was overseeing this campaign.

"I just have to know how you wrangled your way out of a Code 9 inspection order," Rafa said, amazed. "Are you Harry Houdini reincarnated?"

KJ didn't answer that right away, but asked him to set up a meeting with the next day after work. "Maybe at K's office?"

"Can do."

"I'll definitely fill you both in on all the harrowing details of escape from the confines of the Canadian customs office then. For now, I'm bagged. Over and out."

"Roger that."

Fifteen minutes later, KJ punched the remote on the visor over the passenger's seat and the steel gate quietly swung open. He was back at *Animal Farm* and happy for it. The gate closed behind him as the Durango eased along the dirt and gravel driveway toward the house. It was coming up on 8:30 p.m., and being late spring, darkness would overtake this part of the world in about a half hour. He pulled into the old double-attached garage and by habit, cautiously exited the vehicle looking for signs anything was amiss. As he closed the overhead door he was jumped from behind by two powerful Afghans. Tamu, a ninety-five-pound male and Paikea, his sixty-pound female companion almost knocked KJ to the ground. Both dogs acted as if he had been gone for a lifetime, rather than a week and required repeated pats, which he enjoyed as much as his dogs did.

He heard Floriana close the front door. She'd been babysitting the hounds while he was gone and was now off to her own apartment at UBC, where she attended law school.

"Everything go okay?" he asked.

"No hay problema, Senor," she replied, smiling as she tried out her newly learned Spanish on KJ.

"That's a surprise. These two can be devils at the best of times." Tamu ploughed into him looking for more attention. Paikea leaped onto the porch and settled in beside Floriana, like a sphinx.

"They were good as gold," Floriana, a dog owner since she was five, replied. She planted a kiss on the hound's cold nose as she picked up her small duffle bag and started descending the stairs.

"I'll just have to take your word for it," said KJ.

"I left a fresh pot of coffee on," she said as she opened the trunk of her 1984 Wolfsburg Edition Rabbit convertible, a gift from her dad for getting into law school. He had completely restored the vintage car which included a rebuilt, turbo-charged 220 h.p. engine, custom pearl white paint job, lowered chassis, Pirelli racing tires, Invictus-Z mags and black steel roll bar. Just the car for a sophisticated, twenty-something law student to tool around in.

KJ peeled two Ben Franklins from a wad of bills and handed them to her.

"Hey, that's too much by about sixty bucks with the current ex-

189

change rate." Floriana said, mentally doing the calculations in her head. "It's okay, I had a profitable trip," KJ said, an understatement by a country mile.

"You sure? I can give you a credit toward next time." She was earnest. Sixty bucks in the life of a university student is not peanuts.

"No credit needed. Have a safe drive home."

As she opened the door of the Rabbit, Tamu bolted in front of her and jumped on the passenger seat, obviously looking for a car ride. At ninety-five pounds, he was far too big to lie down on the seat, but somehow managed to sit upright. His large head appeared over the top of the front windshield, scanning the far distance as sight hounds are want to do.

"You sure they were good as gold?" asked KJ.

"Si, Senor Pearce," Floriana replied, winking at Tamu. "Los perros ... uh ... estaban bien como ... let me think ...el oro!"

KJ opened the Rabbit's passenger door and shooed out Tamu, while Floriana popped her *Spanish in 10 Minutes a Day* CD into the console, then sped off into the dusk.

"Buenos noches, Senorita," said KJ as he watched the Wolfsburg Edition's tail lights disappear around the bend. Tamu barked a farewell.

CHAPTER 54

Terrorist or Arsonist?

"**B**urdenny is a lying sack of shit!" Stoner stated emphatically to his boss, FBI Director Clinton George III. "He's hiding something, I can feel it."

The Director, a sixty-three-year-old veteran of several White House administrations and a Vietnam army vet himself, nodded. "Be that as it may Rick, it was C-4 that took out the farm, not gasoline. Where would Burdenny get that quantity of military grade explosives?"

Stoner paced back and forth in front of the Director's massive glass and steel desk on the top floor of 935 Pennsylvania Avenue. The Feds' headquarters had recently been remodeled offices and as one would expect, the Director's was the nicest one. Extraordinarily comfortable white Italian leather chairs were scattered about the nine-hundred-square-foot office, which could accommodate a staff meeting of over twenty people. Too stoked to sit, Stoner continued. "He kept asking if anything was recovered from the wreckage, but when Randy pressed him he wouldn't reveal exactly what he was interested in."

The Director sat back in his expansive executive chair and cracked his knuckles. "So he's got contraband of some kind stashed and he wants to know if any of it turned up. He wouldn't exactly be the first you know."

"Sure, but why the cock and bull story about a poison gas cloud coming over from the army base?"

"That one's a mystery I have to say," the Director replied. "He'd have to know that we could check out the phone records and power outage reports."

"And then there's the release of five-thousand mink worth an estimated three-million bucks on the fur market," added Stoner. "He claims it was to let the mink escape from the gas cloud—like he would give a shit since he was going to have them all skinned anyway."

"Yeah, releasing the mink sounds something more like an animals' rights group would do, mind you they don't usually level the place with C-4."

Rick dropped heavily into one of the chairs facing the Director. "Shit these are comfortable!"

"Right from the factory in Italy. The wife did the whole office interior and it's the most comfortable stuff I've ever sat in."

"Okay," said Stoner, switching gears, "if he was hiding some contraband I want to know what it was. Right now, Burdenny is trying to paint himself as the innocent victim which we both know is bullshit."

"I agree. Why don't you get a warrant for a wiretap on his phones—call Judge Laurence Atmore. He's a golfing buddy of mine and more likely to say yes to a warrant application rather than no."

"I'm on it." Stoner jumped up and the two men shook hands. "I can't wait to nail that prick."

CHAPTER 55

Debriefing

It was 5:05 p.m. and the receptionist was packing up to leave when KJ strolled in the front door of Sierra Legal Defense. He looked just like any other lawyer would with a crisp, white shirt, sharp red-patterned tie, midnight blue double-breasted suit and fashionable leather briefcase. "Can I help you sir?"

"I'm here to see Kiara Davies," he evenly replied.

"Is she expecting you? I don't have any appointments listed for Ms. Davies at this hour." Melinda Page was the guardian of every lawyer's calendar at Sierra Legal Defense.

"Oh, hi KJ," Kiara said, flashing a huge smile and giving him a quick hug. "It's alright Melinda, I forgot to mention KJ was coming in," she advised the receptionist, as she directed KJ down the long, hardwood hallway towards her corner office. Melinda gave her friend a wink plus an approving thumbs-up.

"Just friends," mouthed Kiara.

"*Sure*," whispered Melinda, with a twinkle in her eye. As a matter of passing interest, rather than having shelves of real books, the hallway was wallpapered with an incredibly realistic imprint of floor-to-ceiling shelves of case reports, law journals and legal tomes. A stack of law books is something every client expects to see, but in point of fact, most lawyers never pick up an actual case book anymore, as all legal decisions are available online.

After KJ stepped into the surprisingly spacious office, he noticed Rafa sitting at a round glass, client table, laptop open and typing away.

"Hi, Houdini," Rafa said, reminding him in advance of his promise to tell all.

"We're holding you to that promise, soldier," Kiara said.

"Okay, okay." KJ held his hands up. "But how about something to drink first."

Kiara grabbed three Perriers from the fridge in the coffee room and returned to find KJ emptying the contents of his briefcase over the large surface of her desk. He unloaded several documents and a topographical map of B.C. "Cool briefcase," she noted, ever the leading edge fashionista. "But leather?"

"Cork actually," KJ replied. "It looks like leather, but it's much more durable, waterproof and of, course, animal friendly—vegan in fact."

She snatched it off the desk and opened the flap. *Cork by Design, Nature's Leather* was on the label inside. Local shop no less. She made a mental note to buy one for court.

KJ spread the map and pointed to the area which would become the center of the grizzly bear campaign, namely the entrance to the Great Bear Rainforest. "This is where everyone is going to be in about a week and a half," he said. "If we're going to make a lasting impression it's here."

"What do you have in mind?" Rafa looked at the map.

KJ's response surprised both his friends. "An ambush."

Rafa plunked down in one of the comfy client chairs and gulped Perrier from the bottle. Kiara remained standing by her desk, sipping hers with a slice of lime and ice cubes. KJ held the stage and continued.

"I figure that no one will expect a strike with all the cops, security and media milling about, so tactically that is likely the best time to do it."

"You're not talking about a firefight, are you?" Kiara asked.

"No, we don't have the manpower for that counselor and even if we did, there would inevitably be casualties, which I am trying to avoid at all costs," he explained as he spread the map out. "So instead?" He looked side to side and spread his arms, waiting for suggestions.

"We maybe plant some C-4 strategically," ventured Rafa.

KJ had to smile. "Now you are cooking with gas Rafa." He pointed to a couple of areas where explosions would have a huge effect, but almost certainly not kill anyone. "Here, here and ... over there. When these massive explosions go off simultaneously, everyone there will think that WW III just started."

"How about in this area?" asked Kiara.

"That's a definite possibility too," said KJ.

"You still have some C-4 left over?"

"No. All used up at the mink farm, but there's no shortage on this side of the border."

"So, you plan to open the ceremonies with multiple explosions," summarized Kiara.

"Yeah."

"Anything else?"

"As a matter of fact, yes," KJ said. "A friend of mine at JTF2 can get his hands on a prototype RQ7 Shadow drone which can be armed with two missiles, for about a quarter of a million dollars."

"We can afford that?" asked Kiara, eyebrows raised.

"Courtesy of the MBM Colorado's political slush fund, yes we can," said KJ.

"Damn, that's cool," Rafa said. "I've never flown a drone before!"

"Well you better start practicing, because the hunting season is not far off. To start," KJ carried on, not missing a beat, "I have ordered a DJI Ronin from MultiDrone in Hawksberry, Ontario. It should be arriving tomorrow. Its three-axis, stabilized GIMBAL system is professional grade. I'm told that it's suitable for filming a Hollywood motion picture—it's that good. It has long-range, Bluetooth-controlled, full suite of software, multi-lens swivel cameras and about seven hours in the air…"

"Holy crap! What's *that* puppy going to set us back?" Rafa asked, interrupting KJ. "Surprisingly, under four grand," he answered. "We will need you to do an aerial recon of the Great Bear Rainforest entrance from all angles before we get there to make sure that no one else beats us to the punch with advanced security measures." He asked Kiara to get Rafa a license or permit to operate that bird as soon as possible.

"Consider it done," she said, catching the excitement of the moment. "I've got a classmate who works at Transport Canada. I'll call her first thing tomorrow morning."

KJ looked up at his two cohorts and said, "So I figure we detonate the C-4 during the opening speeches, you know, right around the time that the minister says that the government's pretty sure that *the guy* who made the threat is just a prankster."

"That will get their attention," said Kiara "and then some."

"Right you are." KJ motioned a laser pointer over the map. "And then over here, as the cops and other security forces try to make some kind of stand, Rafa will blast their vehicles to bits with a couple of

195

missile strikes from the Shadow over here."

"I like it," Rafa said, "as long as I don't take out half the security forces as well."

"You won't. We'll err on the side of caution. But the effect will still be devastating, particularly after I shoot out their windshields from a mile and a half away first..."

"Sounds like *shock and awe* to me," said Rafa.

"That's the whole point." KJ took a long swig of the cool, bubbly spring water from the pristine aquifers of France. "With any luck, everybody goes home with their proverbial tails between their legs, we get huge press coverage for the cause and the bears live to hunt another day."

"Amen to that," said Kiara.

"Ditto," added Rafa.

They clinked their bottles and glasses together—an advanced toast to success.

CHAPTER 56

War of Words

The Colorado Chronicle wasn't buying FBI innuendos that Burdenny was probably behind the whole thing and running an insurance fraud scheme. MBM Colorado Inc. was a high profile corporate citizen that had lined the pockets of many a politician and charity alike, so the denizens of the Centennial state did not easily cotton to the theory that its CEO was a fraudster and arsonist. MBM's income tax filings were current and, in fact, they showed that the company had made a healthy profit for the last five years running. Upon examining the company's tax returns at the FBI's request, the IRS was somewhat suspicious that MBM may have even been underreporting its taxable income by the use of cash transactions, and exaggerated farm expenses—although that was hardly a novelty in corporate America.

The Burdenny clan was holed up in the five-star Ritz-Carlton Denver while the house staff and foremen were staying at the local Holiday Inn. The farmworkers and housecleaners were housed in the Raven Woods Trailer Park on the outskirts of Denver. Furious at having to continue to pay everyone with no monies coming in, the Dreaded D's had instructed Seamor, Hobbs LLP to file an insurance claim post haste and back it up with a we'll-sue-your-ass letter. After conducting a conflicts-check, the firm's founder, Harry Seamor, instructed his litigation team to put a priority on this claim as MBM was a prime client and he was thinking that this one could definitely get the firm exposure in the press.

"Get the Writ ready," he instructed Tony Frakes, his most experienced litigator, "and drop it the second they deny coverage!"

"You got it, Harry," said Tony, an in-your-face litigation lawyer with a couple decades of courtroom warfare under his belt. "But what's the rush?"

"Firstly, we want to show those bastards at Multi-State Insurance that we mean business," Seamor evenly said.

"And?"

"We can probably triple-bill the extra time for drafting the pleadings and legal research even if they don't deny coverage!" exclaimed the boss. "Burdenny has made it clear he wants all the ducks in a row right *now.*"

"Totally makes sense to me," Tony said, "not to mention dollars. I'll get two juniors working on the pleadings and research right away." He exited the grandiose office of Harry Seamor and shouted out to two under-five-year calls to "drop everything and see me in my office this minute!"

Meanwhile, Dom Burdenny and family were not sitting idly by waiting for the insurance company or the lawyers to solve their problems. Dom had been on the phone all morning with contractors, looking for bids to start rebuilding the mink barns and equipment sheds. *Realtek* was ready to reinstall the security system on short notice. He instructed Johnny to make arrangements for the wetbacks to be driven back to the farm to start cleaning up the debris as soon as the Feds got the hell off the property—which better be damn soon by the way. Otherwise Seamore Hobbs LLP would be in court seeking a mandatory injunction to move their asses. He also had Johnny's assistant foreman raid the local unemployment office and hire twenty-five workers at minimum wage to go out and try to recapture as many mink as possible—although he was not holding his breath for great results on that front. Temporary barns could be constructed if any mink were found.

Ruby Burdenny had her favorite builder on speed dial and was chatting about which architect they should hire to draw up plans for a replacement home. The new one would be bigger than its predecessor, and with all the latest materials and finishings (including a ventilation system for those damned *Cubans)*. No expense would be spared—even if it topped the insurance coverage by a country mile. After all, Don could afford it and he damned well owed this to her after all that she had been put through lately.

Burdenny also asked Shem Appel, a senior columnist with the Denver Chronicle, to drop by the hotel for an exclusive interview so he could get his side of the story out for the local media. No way was he going to stand by and let some asshole at the FBI insinuate that he was an arsonist, and ruin his otherwise sterling reputation in the Blue Spruce state. Shem had suggested that he also call Barry Rivers, the local talk radio host on the city's Morning Line for an on air Q&A about MBM's situation. Ruby would set this up right away. At present the media didn't have a lot to go on other than the reports from the fire department and local police. Chief Pete Wexler had tried to put an MBM-friendly spin on it for the press:

"Yes, C-4 was responsible for the explosions."

"Yes, military grade."

"No clues as to where it came from."

"No, we don't have any suspects yet."

"Is Don Burdenny a suspect? No, he is not. Mr. Burdenny is a local pillar of the Denver community and he is not under suspicion at this time." Obviously, that could change if incriminating information came to light.

It was a slow news week and local reporters were sensing a story hiding somewhere between the chief's soft-soaping and the FBI's innuendos. From Burdenny's point of view, it was time to go on offence, and he was aiming to field a team that would make Tom Brady and the Patriots green with envy.

CHAPTER 57

Setting the Stage

The Ronin proved to be remarkably easy to fly once Rafa got the hang of it. The onboard camera was mounted on a swivel which could give him a 180-degree panoramic view or zoom in on a dime. The resolution was nothing short of astonishing. Kiara quickly determined that under Canadian law he did not need a permit to fly the drone, since it was under thirty-five kilograms. He simply had to follow Transport Canada's safety guidelines—piece of cake. Rafa conducted an aerial recon of the entrance of the Great Bear Rainforest inside of an hour, with HD footage of every likely entrance and exit, the most probable parking areas, the opening ceremonies site and the best places to plant the C-4. Combining this with satellite imagery *borrowed* from an orbiting weather satellite, he had a super detailed map of the whole area.

KJ was already on route, having secured Floriana's dog-sitting services for a day and a half. He was headed to a spot a few miles from Griesbaugh Barracks army base in Alberta to meet up with a JT2F contact and purchase a large amount of C-4.

Kiara was working on a press release for Rafa to anonymously post online after the opening ceremonies were reduced to rubble. At their meeting at Kiara's office the previous night, the three of them were ambivalent about the press coverage which the MBM matter was getting in the U.S. The FBI's unexpected stance on Burdenny's allegedly felonious involvement had pretty much sidelined any discussions about animal rights. In Pearce's view, there was virtually no chance that the incident would ever be traced back to him and he was certain that Burdenny would never utter a word about the missing coats nor the cash. The upshot was that the good guys had inherited a huge war chest, thousands of mink had a fighting chance to survive (as opposed to no chance in their cages), some ex-vets had warm coats for the upcoming winter and Burdenny's operation would be

200

out of commission for months if not years to come. Not exactly perfect, but not half bad either.

Still, it would have been nice if the Colorado public had more information about the actual farm operation and why it was necessary to disrupt it. Pearce figured his team would have to see how the story unfolded in the papers, then play it by ear. Or maybe they could stir the pot a bit. Perhaps a text to Inaara Burdenny was in order.

CHAPTER 58

Hunters Start your Engines

After five minutes of questioning, the RCMP constable at the makeshift entrance was satisfied that Abe LaFlamme had the proper permits and licenses to be allowed to enter. No way was any terrorist getting in to these proceedings, unless of course he had proper credentials. Abe pulled his Ford F-350 Super Duty crew cab into the ad hoc parking area near the entrance of the Great Bear Rainforest. In it he had his guide Tony Proudfoot and three American hunters, one from Washington and two from South Dakota. The back of the truck was chock full of provisions and camping gear. A heavy duty utility trailer was in tow to haul back three grizzly bear carcasses (at seven hundred to a thousand pounds apiece) and store the hunting rifles, accessories and ammo. More than once LaFlamme had experienced thefts and break-ins of his vehicles while on hunting expeditions. It was not unusual to be away from the truck for a couple of days and it was normally unattended during that period. This customized trailer had reinforced steel walls and triple-glazed security glass windows. The rear doors were secured with AASA High Security Locks which were designed to withstand any form of attack including drilling, prying, driving, pulling or pipe wrenching.

Abe and Tony jumped out of the front seat and the three hunters exited from the rear cab. Abe headed towards a large cluster of people, while Tony and the hunters grabbed a smoke. They were among the first to arrive, but already a huge number of semi-trailers, cargo vans and other vehicles were at the opposite end of the parking area where equipment was set up to broadcast the event to dozens of countries live. The sense of excitement and energy was like at the start of a Super Bowl game, and the scenery was spectacular. The sun was shining and the blue sky almost cloudless. To say the air was fresh was a gross understatement—the air pollution index was zero. The fourteen-degree Celsius temperature with a five-mile-per-hour breeze made the conditions for opening day near perfect.

"What the hell is going on," asked Abe, collaring one of the uniforms milling about.

"Kick off for the 2015 Grizzly Bear season, mister," answered the cop crisply.

LaFlamme gave him a look. "Yeah, I already know that, but why are you guys and half the press in the country here?"

"For security. There's going to be upwards of fifteen hundred people arriving by noon." "What?" Abe was more than a little surprised. "There's never been anybody at these openings in the last twenty years."

"This time is different," explained constable Roberts. "There's at least two B.C. Cabinet Ministers—Commerce and Tourism I think, a bunch of high-profile journalists and TV people—see over there, that's Geraldo Rivera from Fox News." He pointed to a man in sun glasses. "And there's also a bunch of activists of every stripe— pro-hunting and con, hunters and guides and of course, members of the public," the officer explained. Gesturing to his holstered Smith & Wesson he said, "And since some nut job posted a threat on FN-LRO's website a few weeks back, we're also here to catch his ass." The officer seemed confident. "That is if he has the balls to show up!" Leaning toward LaFlamme, his eyes peeled toward the podium, he confided, "I shouldn't be telling you this, but *since it's for your safety*, we've got some horses, a couple of Humvees, tracking dogs and even helicopter air support here today." A smug look followed. "If *the guy* surfaces, he's toast."

"He would have to be crazy to come here with a hundred cops in plain sight. Why would you think he would show up?" Abe looked around at the crowd.

"That information is classified, sir," said the cop tipping the bill of his hat as he left to attend to his duties.

LaFlamme was not impressed. "Must have cost a bloody fortune to have all these clowns here just to protect a few politicians and bigwigs," he fumed. "How about spending a few bucks to protect the guides and hunters from a public threat? No way Jose, the province is always *short of cash.*" He headed back towards his truck and spotted the 86' Le Baron convertible pulling into the parking area. His security detail had arrived. The doors swung open and Jessie Spooner and his son, Tanner, got out. The two big guys, side arms holstered at the hip, were sporting aviator shades, Jessie's dark and

Tanner's mirrored. Tanner was wearing camo pants and a hunting vest while Jessie was attired with a Scottevest Expedition Jacket and twenty-pocket cargo pants. Slowly and with deliberation they walked over to the trunk, their high-end Vasque hiking boots crunching the gravel just so. Jessie popped the trunk and carefully removed a Saiga 12 semi-automatic, the twelve-gauge shotgun version of the infamous AK-47. Saiga, which means Steppe antelope, is a line of firearms manufactured by Izhmash OJSC of Izhavsk, Russia. Created by Russian designer, Gennady Nikonov, the Saiga is a magazine-fed 12 gauge, semi-automatic shotgun—which means that reloading in a hurry—the bane of shotgun owners, is a breeze.

Tanner hauled out a SIG SG 550 military assault rifle, which is used by elite special forces units. It's a gas operated, selective fire weapon with an operating system also based on the AK-47. Adopted by the Swiss Army since 1990 as standard issue, it has proved to be as accurate and reliable as its country's watches. It is excellent in close quarter fire fights and surprisingly controllable even on full auto. LaFlamme, who knew a thing or two about firearms himself, was starting to feel better about his choice of security. These guys sure knew their guns.

"Hey, Abe, how's it goin?" shouted Jessie, noticing LaFlamme heading in his direction.

"Hi, Mr. LaFlamme," Tanner called out.

"Good to see you guys," replied Abe now reaching the LeBaron and shaking their outstretched hands. "I see you've come loaded for bear."

"That we have," Jessie said, cradling the Saiga, "but as you can see, not the animal variety."

Abe asked to have a look and Jessie carefully handed over the shotgun as if it were a precious artifact. "Damn, that's light for a shotgun. I've read about these box-fed babies but I've never actually held one," Abe said, marveling at the design.

"That Saiga's one mean motherfucker at point blank range," Tanner said. "But if we got to shoot it out at a longer distance, I've got the SIG. It's dead accurate up to four-hundred meters."

"Shit, where do I get one of those?" Shane Travis eagerly said.

"Who are you?" Tanner asked, turning toward the young man.

"He's the dim bulb who shot out the windows at my hunting lodge," LaFlamme said before Shane could open his mouth.

"Hey, like that was totally an accident man," Shane whined. "I got royal shit for that from Mr. Coburn! He told me that if anything like that ever happened again, my brothers and me would be back in the hoosegow before we could take a piss."

"And so you should be," stated LaFlamme. "Where's your boss now?" A brisk slap on the back answered that question as Rich Coburn appeared from behind him.

"Abe, damned good seeing you out here!" Rich said, smiling. The men shook hands and introductions were made, although Shane was ignored. The four men exchanged small talk about the fine weather and the large number of people arriving.

"It's a goddamned circus," Rich said.

"In twenty years, I've never seen anything like it either," Abe replied.

"You think *the guy* might actually show?" Rich asked the other three.

"Damned if I know," Abe replied, "but he'd have to be plum loco to try something with so many cops around."

"I reckon that there's undercover security here too as well," Tanner said. The other men nodded in agreement.

A brief hiatus followed. The Travis boy grabbed the opportunity to put in his two bits. "I agree," he said. "We'll definitely find the guy if he tries to sneak up on us in the forest."

"Who are you kidding, Shane," Rich replied. "I doubt you could find your own pecker with a roadmap." The three guys got a kick out of that and started snickering. Jessie was outright belly laughing. Peeved, Shane stomped off back to the truck to find his brothers.

Following Shane out of the corner of his eye, LaFlamme asked, "You sure that you got those three morons under wraps?"

"Yeah, I have personally reloaded all of their rifles, so there won't be another incident like the one at your lodge."

"Thank god for that." Tanner and his dad looked puzzled.

"Long story," explained Rich, "we'll tell you over a beer sometime."

"Sounds good to me," Jessie said, accepting the Saiga back from Abe as if it was a newborn.

Abe squinted into the sunlight and looked toward what was rapidly becoming loaded a podium and stage. "I guess we get started soon as those windbags run out of hot air!"

CHAPTER 59

Fanning the Flames in Colorado

Inaara Burdenny was thrilled to get the text message from KJ. "How R U? Still want to help out?" She had reluctantly gone home after a two-day stay with Jake and Marcy. When she got back she was berated for an hour by her stepmother and grounded indefinitely—school only, with no outings whatsoever, not even extracurricular school activities. One of the house staff would drive her from the hotel to the door of St. Thomas More private school for girls and pick her up the minute classes were over. Inaara was effectively a prisoner at the Denver Ritz Carleton. She told Ruby that her phone had been lost on the highway or it would have been confiscated.

"I'm 100% in. What do u need" she texted back. After a brief exchange of messages, Inaara set about formulating a plan to discover what was now going on at the mink farm. Since Ruby and Dom basically resented her existence, the next best option would be Don, her natural father, if you could even call him a parent. From the day his lawyers had gotten custody of her through the courts Don had fobbed her off on Ruby and Dom, as he was always too busy to spend time with her—not that the two of them fared much better in that department. When Inaara was about ten-years-old, in a rare moment of weakness Don had confided to her that he was her real father but insisted she never, ever reveal that to Ruby or Dom or it would bust up the family for good and she would probably wind up a ward of the government. That was enough to scare the pants off any ten-year-old kid, so she kept her mouth shut about it for the next six years.

She managed to corner Don when he was getting ready to drive over to radio station KGNU to be interviewed by Barry Rivers. It was early Saturday morning so no school. "Hey, Dad, can I come along?" she asked.

"No," he replied matter-of-factly. "You're grounded remember?"

"I'll stay in the car. Please, I'm going nuts in this hotel suite," she pleaded.

"You should have thought about that before you ran away from home," said Don. "As if we didn't have enough shit to worry about that night, what with the farm blowing up and all." Don was trying to get a tie on and it kept slipping up over the back of his collar. "God-damned cheap Chinese silk ties!" he cursed.

"Here, let me do it," Inaara offered, grabbing the tie and slipping it under his collar.

He let her. "You know, your mother was hysterical when we couldn't find you when we got away from the farm and arrived in Denver.

"Yeah, that'll be the day," she retorted. But she felt a small pull in her gut. Ruby cared?

Don brushed her hands away and finished the tie knot himself. "Okay, maybe not hysterical, but definitely concerned," he said.

"How about relieved that I might be out of her hair for good?" she suggested, her voice dripping with sarcasm.

"Don't be a smartass! Ruby has been a good mom to you, considering that she's not your natural mother."

"Bullshit, dad!" Inaara was having none of it. "She's been suspicious that I might be your daughter from day one!"

That hit a nerve like a dentist's drill. "Keep your friggin voice down! The last thing I need now is Ruby barging in here and accusing me of sleeping around sixteen years ago." "Well you did, didn't you? That's how I got here right?" she taunted.

"One more word and you go over my knee!" Don warned, a menacing look crossing his face.

Inaara was all too familiar with *the knee*. Both Don and Ruby had been liberally doling out corporal punishment to her since she was a kid, with Dom always happy to cheer them on from the sidelines. Her backside had tasted the leather belt, the braided rope and even a wooden spatula from time to time. But this time was different. She was on a mission to help animals. For reasons that she couldn't quite fathom, she summoned up the courage to speak her mind in no uncertain terms.

"Yeah, well the next time that I go over your knee, Ruby is going to hear the whole sordid story of you and my mom!"

"She'll never believe you!"

"You know better than that."

"You're trying to blackmail me now?"

"No, I'm just trying to get out of this fucking hotel room!" she yelled back.

"Hey, watch your tongue, Missy! Nobody talks to your dad that way!" Don didn't like being stood up to by anyone, except of course Ruby. But he sensed that this time the daughter wasn't bluffing, so he relented. "Ah crap. Get your school stuff and get ready," he commanded. "But you so much as set one foot out of the car and you will live to regret it."

"Deal," Inaara said, gleefully.

"Jesus Christ, you could have just asked to go along," sighed Don. He had plenty of other things on his mind this morning.

"I did."

"Just get your books and let's get going. The radio show starts in twenty-five minutes." As they headed out the door, Ruby was back from a meeting with the designer.

"Where do you think you're going, young lady?"

"With dad," Inaara said. "I am going to study in the car, while he does the radio interview."

Ruby raised her eyebrows and looked at Don with skepticism.

"It's okay, I cleared it," Don said, looking as if the train was just pulling out and he wasn't on it. He grabbed Inaara's hand and yanked her out the door.

"You're getting soft Don!" Ruby called out as they hurried toward the elevator.

Firing up the Audi diesel, Don told his daughter to buckle up as they had to get over to KGNU "five minutes ago." Slamming the SUV into gear, he roared out of the underground parkade past the doorman's post and hung a hard right on Arapahoe, narrowly missing an elderly cyclist. "Goddamn granny!" he cursed. "Why the hell do they let someone that old loose on a bike?"

"She's riding in the bike lane, Dad," Inaara pointed out.

"I hate bike lanes!" Don whined as he turned left on Champa Street accelerating up to fifty. "They're a nuisance to drivers and a waste of taxpayers' money."

"But they cut down on pollution."

Her father cut her off. "Old wives tales, brought to you by the same idiots who opposed Keystone."

She scratched her head. "The pipeline?"

"No, the *lifeline* from our northern neighbors that would have created thousands of jobs, not to mention long-term energy security for this great country of ours."

She replied, "But what if a big oil spill happened in the wilderness?"

He leaned hard on the brakes, abruptly stopping the car at Champa and Broadway, directly in front of KGNU. "Oil spills are a fact of life." He turned off the engine. "If you want oil that is—otherwise everybody is stuck riding a bike like granny good witch back there."

Inaara rolled her eyes. Don unbuckled his seat belt and grabbed his briefcase from the back seat. "Stay put," he warned her. "I mean it!"

"Sure dad." She'd work on him on the way back.

CHAPTER 60

Political Mileage

Governments in the western world are supposed to epitomize the very essence of democracy, but as soon as officials are elected they tend to abandon that quaint notion, citing the overriding concerns of privacy and national security to justify secrecy and opaqueness. For example, Teagan Connors' caucus was meeting behind private and totally closed doors. While not often the case, her personal assistant and strategist, Victoria Wang was sitting in on the meeting.

"The polls are not looking particularly good this week, Teagan," senior minister, Trip Sullivan, said. "Jobs are down, the LNG projects are stalled due to falling oil prices and Moody's is making noises about downgrading us to AA+ status again."

"Tell me about it," said Teagan swiveling in her chair from side to side like a kid. Ignoring the bigger picture issues for the moment she said, "I thought the Fallon show would be a dream-come-true, but it turned out to be a nightmare!"

"Hey, that was not your fault, Madame Premier," Victoria interjected. "I should have never let you appear on it."

"Well why did you then?" Margie Pannabaker asked. "I mean you're supposed to be the know-it-all, whiz-kid with the PhD in political science, right?"

Victoria felt like punching her in the face but she bit her tongue and replied, "You are absolutely right Madame Minister. I take full responsibility for that debacle."

"So, are you going to resign as the Premier's assistant then?" Fred Scambatti chimed in.

Victoria remained silent as a statue, staring down at her perfectly manicured finger nails, while visualizing Fred being suddenly taken out by a sniper. Teagan stood, strolled over to the window and looked out at the well-maintained grounds of the legislature. Soon the flower beds would create the appearance of a wonderful multi-colored quilt across the lush green grass. There had been no snow this winter to delay that inevitable, annual process.

"Well, the show was not *all* bad," she said, tossing her hair to one side. "I got a lot of calls and mail from constituents saying that I looked younger than I have in ages." Teagan turned from the window and looked at her caucus. "And that's not a small thing when you are staring down the big *five oh*."

The sartorially aware, junior minister for Women's Affairs, Jade Elizabeth Allan threw in her two cents. "I thought the hair cut was fabulous and you totally nailed it with that cream-colored outfit."

"You know it was Victoria who convinced the show to send me to Hershberger's," replied the Premier. "And she is definitely not quitting. I won't hear of it."

"Thanks boss," Victoria said. "I really appreciate that."

"Right on," cheered Darlene Smythe, the Minister of Municipal Urban Affairs, giving Victoria a big smile and a robust "thumbs up."

"Well before everybody starts hugging and singing kumbaya," groused Fred the Grinch Scambatti, "me and my staff are getting the angry voice messages and emails accusing the B.C. government of turning its back on the hunters, guides and outfitters in British Columbia." The Minister of FLNRO squirmed uneasily in his seat. It was not an enviable task to call out one's boss. "All due respect, Madame Premier, those comments about you opposing the Grizzly Bear Hunt on primetime TV were not helpful to the Ministry."

"But she made it perfectly clear that those were her own personal opinions," Victoria fired back, "not those of the B.C. government!" She glared at Scambatti, with the renewed confidence that the premier had her back. "You did catch that personal disclaimer on the program, didn't you?" she asked, "or was your hearing aid turned off?"

"Why does she get off talking like that?" Trip asked. "She's not even in the cabinet!"

"She's here because I asked her here, so she gets to voice her opinion—got it?" snapped Teagan. Trip feigned a wounded look. Frowning, the premier added, "Dial it down a notch, will you, Victoria. Remember we're all on the same side."

"Sorry, Madame Premier," Victoria said. However, the premier was starting to get testy herself. It had finally dawned on her that despite her political instinct to say nothing controversial on national TV the show, that smooth-talking charmer, Jimmy Fallon—friendly,

211

big smile, "you're too young to be a premier" and all that crap, had gotten her to actually provide a direct answer to a loaded question. That is a big no-no for any politician—much less a seasoned one, but she fell for it like humpty dumpty.

Still, the dinner with Jimmy and a couple of his guests (Mark Wahlberg, Christian Bale and Pamela Anderson—who was a lovely person) after the show was absolutely out of this world. She was momentarily lost in the memory.

"Madame Premier?"

Jolted her back to the present, she focused on what to do about the faux pas. "Do the polls still show that most British Columbians oppose the hunt?" she asked.

"Eighty-five point eight per cent," said Fred.

"What was the contribution from the guides and outfitters industry to our party last year?"

"Let me see," said Paul Wagner, the minister of B.C.'s finances. He looked up as if he would find the answer written somewhere on the ceiling. "I believe that it was about eighty thousand dollars. That was actually a bit over their average campaign contribution, if I recall correctly."

Teagan returned to her seat at the head of the boardroom table and said, "Look, there's going to be ton of exposure when the Grizzly Bear Hunt opens this year." All eyes locked on her. "And we've got to get some major political mileage out of it." Heads nodded in agreement. "But we can't come across as anti-hunting to the media. After all, it's supposed to be open season on the bears," she explained.

"All too true Madame Premier," offered Fred Scambatti. "But you know that every wacko animals' rights group on the continent will be there to protest the hunt and doubtless disrupt the proceedings."

"Who knows, maybe *the guy* will even show up!" Trip Sullivan said, trying to throw fuel on the proverbial fire.

"Not likely," Fred replied. "We've got over fifty RCMP officers with dogs, horses and Humvees, a police helicopter, a dozen CSIS agents and even a couple of FBI anti-terrorist specialists, at our request, ready to take him down if he comes within a mile of the proceedings." All five feet six of him stood up as he said with bravado, "Most of them will be in plain sight *to intimidate*, so I don't imagine that he would be dumb enough to show up."

"Okay, enough about *the guy*." The premier said. "Let's get back on point." She looked at her assistant. "Victoria, what's your take on who should go?"

Flipping open her MacBook Pro and eying her comprehensive twenty-page brief on the situation, Victoria said with assurance, "First off, Madame Premier, I don't think that you should be going."

"What?" Teagan was definitely taken aback. After all, this could turn out to be one of the biggest photo ops in her career—right up there with Fallon and then some.

Her assistant continued evenly. "The fact that you stated on TV that you *personally* oppose the hunt will only invite heckling and controversy. That tends to look particularly bad on live TV and it would definitely damage your own approval rating."

"I guess I can't really ignore that," said the premier reluctantly. She barely concealed her disappointment "Then who *should* we be sending?"

"First off, I would suggest Praveen Sandhu, the deputy minister for FLNRO." Victoria suggested, clearly prepared with an answer. "She's pretty and articulate. I've seen her being interviewed on C.B.C. and she comes across well on camera—and, she has three other things going for her." Making eye contact with each of them as she spoke, she said, "She is young—thirty-five-ish, an ethnic minority and a woman."

"Why is that important?" the premier asked.

"Yeah," Trip said, "that sounds ageist, racist and sexist all in one sentence!"

"Those factors will tend to slot the pro-hunting message into a more sympathetic envelope for the media to slice open," answered Victoria in her best communications jargon, ignoring the minister's barb. "The audience will assume that if a relatively young woman with an ethnic background no less, can support the hunt, then anyone can."

"Hey, what about me?" queried Fred, half jumping out of his seat again. "I'm the *minister* of FLNRO for god's sake! Since when does the deputy minister rank ahead of me?"

"Permission to speak freely Madame Premier?" Victoria said, as if she was a junior officer on the bridge deck. The premier nodded, and Victoria stood—all six feet of her. "Minister Scambatti, with all due respect, you are a smart and capable minister, but your media skills leave much to be desired."

"What the hell is that supposed to mean?" he demanded, eyes

bulging.

Her response was immediate. "If you recall, the last time you were interviewed on Global you almost got into a fist fight with the reporter. That was one year ago almost to the day."

"Yeah, well that young punk had it coming," snarled Fred. "He was insinuating that we were giving preferential treatment to the run-of-the-river power projects because they had been awarded directly by the premier's office."

"In retrospect, I should have popped him one," said the former junior *Golden Gloves* runner up.

"Thank you for just making my point, Minister." Victoria sat down, calm as a cucumber.

"Fred, you're not going," Teagan said, her tone firm. "Move on, Victoria."

Victoria suggested that Minister Pannabaker be there to promote *the supernatural British Columbia* angle. "Apart from the 2010 Olympic Games in Whistler," she explained, "I doubt that we'll ever see this much media coverage concentrated at one event in B.C. in any of our lifetimes."

"I agree," said the premier. "Are you up for that Margie?"

"For sure," replied the Minister for Tourism. "I've been to the Great Bear Rainforest once and it's absolutely breathtaking. Nothing could be a better advertisement for B.C.'s tourism industry than that."

"Finally," said Victoria, coming to the last page on her report, "I suggest that Minister Sullivan also attend to remind the audience— not so much those in attendance, but the TV audience, which will be worldwide, that B.C. is a good place to do business."

"I'm in for that," said Trip without waiting to be asked. "We've cut so much red tape out of the business process in B.C. it's not funny. That's what potential business startups want to hear—and I'd love to make that pitch on national—hell no, international TV." He could picture himself holding millions spellbound with his brilliant presentation on the best place in the world to do business.

"Done," said the premier emphatically. "Maybe *the guy* who posted the threatening message on FLNRO's website has inadvertently done us a favor."

"Quite possibly, Madame Premier," Victoria said. "No one can buy that kind of media exposure for love or money."

"Yeah, so why the hell are you leaving me out of the limelight?"

Scambatti was ever the pit-bull. "I say that we put it to a vote!"

"This isn't a democracy, Fred," the premier countered. An uncomfortable silence followed, while that Freudian slip percolated through the group. After a pregnant pause the premier said, "You know, maybe Fred's right. After all, we are all democratically elected representatives of the people, are we not?" Everyone nodded.

"Now you're talking turkey, Madame Premier," beamed the Minister for FLNRO, suddenly elated.

"Show of hands," commanded the premier. "Who is voting for Fred to go to the opening ceremonies?" Only one hand went up. It was Fred's. "I guess you're not going, Fred," said the premier.

CHAPTER 61

Hot Air Rises

"Welcome to Super Natural British Columbia!" Trip Sullivan was the most senior cabinet minister of the government of British Columbia. His voice, amplified by many loud speakers, boomed across the wilderness of the mouth of the magnificent Great Bear Rainforest. "Not only do we have the best hunting and fishing in the world," he continued, trying to look as photogenic as possible for the millions of TV viewers, doubtless hanging on his every word, "but we are the best place to do business in the world!" Wearing a new three-piece Hugo Boss suit with a brilliant red tie, he was doing his damnedest to look statesman-like. "I can personally assure every businessman and woman listening to this broadcast that the term "red tape" has been expunged from the vocabulary of the B.C. government," he guaranteed. His apparent sincerity prompted Victoria to consider buying a used car from him, but only briefly.

Fully two-thousand people were in attendance on this most memorable occasion. Media coverage from over twenty-seven countries worldwide was being provided by a myriad of TV cameras and reporters. While they were there ostensibly to cover the opening ceremonies, which had never been done even once in the past two decades, the fervent hope of every producer, TV camera man and commentator was that *the guy* would show up and try to make his point in public. A splashy confrontation and dramatic takedown would make front page news everywhere, sparking heated comment on both sides of the hunting debate for weeks—a journalist's wet dream.

It was now officially the start of the twenty-second annual B.C. Grizzly Bear Hunt. RCMP in their red serge ceremonial uniforms were everywhere, some on horses and some keeping the pro-hunting groups and the animal rights activists separated to avoid an out and out riot. Tempers were already running high. The hunters and their allies looked at the activists as if they were trespassers, barging in on their annual soiree. The animals' rights groups including PETA, Mercy for Animals, Animal Justice, the B.C. SPCA, the ASPCA, Animal Legal Defense Fund, the Association for the Protection of Furbearing Animals and many lesser known groups viewed the hunters as violating the rights of grizzly bears to live out their lives in the remote wilderness free from the idiocy and violence of mankind. There was no room for compromise on either side, so the cops had their hands full, from the get go. It would hardly be apropos for the host province to have a riot appearing on the evening news across the globe. Such an incident would dwarf the Stanley Cup riots in Vancouver in 2011, thus miring the Pacific province in shame.

The security forces were alert to the possibility that the crackpot who posted the threat could conceivably appear at some point, although they doubted it to a man. Despite their misgivings, however, plans had been meticulously laid out for his capture, or demise if need be, if he showed up on foot, dirt bike, ATV, jeep or even by air. Thus far, no news or security organization had connected the MBM incident in Colorado to this one, thanks to the FBI's take on the incident. Otherwise the security would have been tripled. Nonetheless, the security forces were still heavily armed and would protect the dignitaries on site at all costs should *the guy* somehow mount any serious resistance.

"We are as open as these magnificent skies for business in beautiful, British Columbia," the senior minister continued. Flash bulbs continued to go off and cameras of all shapes and sizes pointed in his direction. "And the business you are all here for today, the guiding of skilled and fearless hunters on the iconic Grizzly Bear Hunt, is just one of many which are available to companies the world over who want to locate in beautiful British Columbia." Trip and Margie had been told to make it short and to the point or they would lose the audience. After all, the real issue was the hunt and its legitimacy or lack thereof. Oblivious to that directive, the minister continued. "The government of B.C. is one hundred percent committed to protecting our existing businesses…"

"What bullshit!" LaFlamme snapped, still furious that the government wouldn't pick up a one red cent of his security costs.

"…and fostering new ones who want to locate in this great province," Trip promised, spreading his arms wide—now the business prophet. He was just dying to watch himself on the late-night news.

He had also made sure that his trophy wife, Brie, was taping the proceedings at on at least two channels. Hats off to TELUS, his cable company for providing him with a fancy PVR with his TV subscription that could do just that. Despite the time warning, he droned on for another fifteen minutes on the virtues of doing business in B.C.— less red tape (mentioned for the third time), faster start-up times and umpteen government-sponsored grants and subsidies. You'd think that libertarians had taken over the provincial government. Mercifully, he stopped and after sparse applause, mostly from his own staff, Margie Pannabaker stepped forward to pitch the tourist angle. She was painfully aware that Trip the ham, had overstayed his welcome on the airwaves by a mile, so she would have to cut her presentation to the bone. To her credit, she did it in ninety-seconds flat. Finally, Praveen Sandhu, the deputy minister of FLNRO, stepped to the podium. She was a photogenic, mid-thirties, East Indian woman dressed in a custom-tailored black linen *DKNY* suit. To the delight of the cameramen, she cut quite a figure as well, double C cups at least. As she began to address the large crowd, the plethora of cameras focused dead in on her and *voila,* the ratings went up on the spot. A pretty face with an articulate voice tends to do that, a fact that most news shows are keenly aware of.

"Ladies and gentlemen, the department of Fish, Lands and Natural Resource Operations of British Columbia oversees and regulates the annual Grizzly Bear Hunt in B.C." This was met with a vocal chorus of boos and jeers from members of the many anti-hunting and animal activist groups in the audience.

"How would you like to be hunted down and killed you bitch?" shouted one angry activist. He was quickly grabbed and pulled to the ground by police.

"Yeah, hunting is for dinosaurs, like your Jurassic-age government," yelled another twenty-something protester with pierced ears, nose and tongue. She was similarly subdued by security personnel. Praveen continued, unfazed. "We respect everyone's right to an opinion," she said smoothly. "But the Grizzly Bear Hunt is lawfully sanctioned by the British Columbia government." She looked squarely into the cameras, the gold pendant on her chest occasionally reflecting the dazzling sunlight back to the viewers when she shifted her weight just so. "It has been in existence for twenty-two years and it has been carried out in a safe and environmentally responsible manner since its inception."

"Yeah, by killing off over seven-hundred bears, including females and their cubs in the process!" screamed another protester.

"Hey kid!" shouted a fifty-something Ducks Unlimited supporter from other side of the crowd. "There's almost sixteen-thousand grizzlies in B.C. The hell's the big deal about killing seven or eight hundred over a span of twenty years?"

"Murder is murder!" replied a Mercy for Animals advocate. "Even killing one bear for sport is too many!" He too was grabbed and cuffed. The cameras were catching each of these incidents, causing the Twitter-sphere to light up.

"What did any bear ever do to you?" shouted a teenager wearing a black PETA t-shirt. "Not a damned thing, junior," replied the Ducks Unlimited guy. "That's not the point. Bears were put on the earth for us to hunt! It's as simple as that." Gratuitously he added, "It's even in the bible for Chrissake!"

"You are fucking retarded!" the teenager shot back. He was carted off by two RCMP officers.

Praveen soldiered on, adlibbing somewhat in response to the heated exchange. "For the record," she stated, "FLNRO takes bear conservation *very seriously* in this province." She paused for a few seconds, as if waiting for applause or acknowledgement. There was none. "Our environmental biologists are constantly monitoring the bear population with a view to preserving this magnificent species for generations of future guides and outfitters," she informed the audience. "These B.C. residents depend on the bears for a livelihood—not to mention the avid hunters who flock here from all parts of the world to have the once-in-a-lifetime experience of *bagging a B.C. grizzly.*"

Cheers and clapping ensued from the pro-hunting side. "Right on, babe!" shouted one of Coburn's American hunting party. "You can hunt with us anytime, girl!" Oddly, he was not silenced by the security forces.

Rather than ignoring the remark, Praveen, the would-be hunter, flashed a hundred megawatt smile in his general direction and continued. "Grizzly bears are among our greatest natural resources," she said like teacher talking to her elementary school students. "As long as we ensure that their population is stable and viable, there is no reason why they cannot contribute to the success and prosperity of all British Columbians by participating in the Annual Grizzly Bear Hunt."

"Yeah, like the Jews *participated* in the Holocaust, you fascist!" screamed another protestor, holding a megaphone. Jeers and more derogatory comments spewed from a great many protestors—far too many to all be silenced by security. When they finally simmered down, she took the opportunity to shift gears. "However, let me make something perfectly clear," her demeanor becoming serious and officious for the masses viewing around the globe. "The government of British Columbia will not, I repeat, will not be intimidated by the person or persons who illegally posted the ill-advised threats on our website." The huge audience went dead silent. This was the part they were all waiting for. "In fact, I say to this self-styled animal rights vigilante that whoever you are, we will catch you and prosecute you to the full extent of Canadian law for the..."

Then the roof fell in.

CHAPTER 62

World War III

Like millions of other viewers, Rafa watched the opening proceedings on TV, but he also had a bird's eye view from the RQ7 Shadow which was patrolling just above the tree line about a half a mile in the distance. Its twenty-one hundred megapixel HD camera could zoom in and read the time off Praveen's Victorinox wrist watch, which he noted read 12:47. The camera's 360-degree GIMBAL mount allowed Rafa to surveil the entire proceedings and determine who was in blast distance of the half dozen C-4 charges strategically placed throughout the area.

Pearce was positioned about two-thousand yards west of the gates under camouflage netting. He had secured a Canadian-crafted Mac-Tac 50 sniper rifle, just like the one his new friend, the border supervisor had used when he was in CAS. Through the Leupold scope, he could see the two yellow Humvees and a dozen police cruisers. Oddly enough the police helicopter was *sitting* in a field a hundred yards from the vehicles rather than circling the proceedings. He didn't know, but the copter had experienced a mechanical problem with its tail rotor a half hour after its arrival in the wee early hours of the morning. It was temporarily grounded and a mechanic from CCH Helicopters had been summoned from Prince Rupert. ETA was mid-afternoon. There was a gigantic state-of-the art, high-resolution TV monitor behind the speaker's podium which allowed the many spectators who were not up close to see the proceedings as if they were in their own living rooms. The specially designed, tempered, non-glare glass would permit the large audience to see crystal clear images from all angles, even on this gorgeous, sunny day like this one. That would be the opening target.

Kiara was stationed about fifteen-hundred yards east of the proceedings with an unobstructed view of the main logging road leading to the entrance of the forest. She had arrived two hours earlier to set-up shop. Even in the middle of nowhere, she was a sight for sore eyes. Her long blonde hair, fluttering in the gentle breeze contrasted starkly with the North Face all-weather jacket, MEC hydrofoil hiking pants and Asolo GV backpacking boots, all in jet black. She slid off her Ray-Ban Aviators and carefully unpacked her oversize backpack. It contained an ultra-portable Wildblue dish to receive the satellite signals through HughsNet, and would allow her to connect with the internet in this remote area of the world with no cell towers or ISP feeds in the vicinity. Rafa's detailed instructions were sufficient for her to calculate the elevation, azimuth, polarization and skew of the dish so that it would have a direct line of sight to the geosynchronous satellite parked in the sky some twenty-two thousand miles overhead.

Rafa had also equipped her with a pair of American Technologies Network HD Smart Optics binoculars with built-in wi-fi, so he and Pearce could see what she was observing with the flick of a switch. The satellite's bent pipe architecture would essentially connect her to the guys via the *bend* in the communications signals at the point of the satellite's orbit. She also had a Global Star GSP-1700 satellite phone (as there were no cell towers for the Priv to utilize) and a nine millimeter Beretta with a half-dozen clips *just in case*. Rafa was astounded to learn that she had a concealed carry permit for the restricted weapon, as he had never fired a gun, although come to think of it, he might actually pull the trigger on a *Hellfire* missile, a claim which few people could ever make. As a defender of many environmental causes vehemently opposed by multinational oil and mining giants, Kiara had not surprisingly, been threatened on more than one occasion by anonymous parties to *"stop these shenanigans in the courts—or else you won't live to tell the tale!"* And so, a member of the British Columbia bar, she had lobbied the Attorney General's department to make an exception to the ban on civilians carrying concealed firearms. In the end, her outstanding advocacy skills won out and she became the only female barrister in the province to pack a handgun in her purse.

Through the ATN Binocs, she was able to monitor the old, wooden bridge over Cascadia Creek which connected the rest of the mainland to the area where the opening proceedings were being held. It was not a large bridge, maybe only a hundred and fifty feet from end to end, but it was the only way in or out of the rain forest from this particular area for miles. Kiara had previously researched the bridge on FLNRO's website and discovered that it was a Class B bridge, built in 1999 using stressed timber cross ties, decking and running planks. Total cost at that time, as mandated by the government's Forest Service Bridge Design and Construction Manual was under $250,000. Fifteen years of harsh weather and logging trucks had put the bridge into less than ideal condition, which suited Pearce just fine. He had planted C-4 charges at each end of the bridge. If reinforcements were called in, they had better be good swimmers.

Before Praveen could finish her last sentence, the seven-hundred-inch TV monitor behind her literally exploded, raining down shards of tempered glass on her and all the dignitaries on stage. Screams and pandemonium ensued as the dozen or so men and women on the podium scrambled to and fro trying to avoid being cut by flying glass. The thunderous sounds of the .50 caliber bullets would not reach the proceedings for another few seconds, so initially no one knew what had happened to cause the monitor to suddenly shatter to bits. Police and undercover security ran towards the podium to help the dignitaries get down the stairs. The audience was motionless, witnessing a seemingly inexplicable event, until the KABOOMs from the Mac-Tac started rolling in. Instantly everyone knew that they were under attack.

"Holy shit!" Abe LaFlamme exclaimed. "*The guy* is here!" Like the phenomenon of entrainment that allows a flock of flying birds to all turn in one direction at the same time, the police and security forces to a man drew their weapons in unison and started craning their necks left and right trying to locate the enemy. The crowd panicked and ran every which way for cover. Some decided that they had seen enough and started to high-tail it toward the make-shift parking lot some two-hundred yards away. In the meantime, Rafa maneuvered the Shadow around the back of the proceedings and unleashed a Hellfire II missile from it which obliterated most of the vehicles before anyone got near them. The explosion was deafening and sent the crowd into a total frenzy as they turned and ran back towards the entrance. As yet no one had spotted the low flying drone so the explosion in the parking lot seemed to have come out of nowhere.

The police tried valiantly to herd the dignitaries and the crowd, but with no enemy in sight and everyone fleeing in all directions it was a virtually impossible task. The CSIS agents were on their short-wave radios requesting back-up, while two FBI agents raced toward their mobile command center to get their own drone into the air to see what the hell was going on.

"Where's that damned helicopter mechanic?" yelled constable Provost, on loan from the Nanaimo precinct. Several constables raced towards their Humvees without knowing exactly why, since no one had identified the source of the attack yet. Again, the RQ Shadow's formidable camera alerted Rafa to this so he remotely detonated charges one and two. The C-4 blasts lifted both Humvees skyward, and the gravity sent them crashing to the ground, in a burning mess of scrap metal and glass. The incredulous cops stopped in their tracks. They were damned glad they hadn't reached the vehicles as planned. This was a fucking war zone. A couple of kamikaze camera men from CNN and NBC had the balls to keep their cameras rolling. Pictures of this carnage were transmitting live to half the world. British Columbia, Canada was under attack.

Trip's PVR would pick up the whole show for posterity, on two channels no less. Later he would have the government's tech staff edit out the part where he was spotted hiding behind Marge Pannabaker for cover. Premier Teagan Connors, who was watching the proceedings live from her luxurious office the province's capital, was horrified. However, she made a mental note to give her personal assistant, Victoria, a sizable bonus for convincing her to stay at home.

LaFlamme's guys, Jessie and Tanner grabbed their guns and motioned their hunting party to scoot back to the rig and "get under it!" They got no argument from the hunters. The numerous vehicles owned by the guides and outfitters had been parked in a separate lot roped off for their convenience. As a result, they hadn't been blown up by the drone strike. "You see where any of that is coming from, Tanner?" Jessie asked, cradling the Saiga, itching to unload the sixteen-shot mag at someone or something, as he poked his head out from the side of the 4X4.

"Not a damned clue, dad!" Tanner responded, snapping the scope into the groove on the barrel of his Swiss-approved sniper rifle. He attempted to scan the horizon through the scope using the hood as a makeshift tripod, but the smoke from the explosions obscured his view, not to mention the multitude of bodies hurtling by. "This feels just like Afghanistan, only the other side seems to be way better armed!"

"I never seen anything like this in CAF in twenty-five years of service," Jessie said, grimacing. "Tanner, we gotta get LaFlamme and our party out of here in one piece. That's what he's paying us for."

"I'm with you on that." Tanner kept scanning for any movement or muzzle flash in the distance. From a mile and a quarter, however, no muzzle flash would ever be visible.

Kapow, kapow, kapow.

Shots rang out from about twenty feet east of the LaFlamme's rig and the sounds caused Tanner and Jessie to train their weapons in that direction, ready for a firefight. "At last," thought Jessie, slipping the safety off the Saiga, "let's see what this baby can do!" About twenty RCMP officers did likewise, also sorely itching to blast someone. Fortunately, the smoke cleared just in time to reveal the three stooges, Shane, Donovan and Eddie Travis, firing their rifles into the distance at nothing anyone could make out. No one but Coburn and LaFlamme knew that the boys' rifles were loaded with blanks.

"What the hell are you idiots shooting at?" yelled LaFlamme, holding his Colt .45 in a two-handed firing stance in the general direction they were firing.

"Don't know for sure," shouted Eddie. "But we gotta shoot back don't we?" Before he could utter another word, he and his brother, Donovan were tackled to the ground by a couple of stocky RCMP officers. Shane fared worse, having been hit in the chest by two flying paws connected to a hundred and twenty-five pound German shepherd police dog. He was deposited hard on his ass, but he didn't let go of the rifle until Rin Tin Tin clamped his teeth on his arm and bit down.

"Ouch!" he screamed, dropping the rifle as if it was on fire. "Get him off!" he shouted at the top of his lungs. "GET HIM OFF!"

"Release!" commanded the officer handling the dog and the shepherd dropped Shane's arm immediately. The boys' rifles were confiscated and they were thoroughly reamed out by the cops.

"Don't you imbeciles know that you could have gotten yourselves killed—BY US!" shouted Lucien Provost, shaking with anger, but hugely relieved at the same time. Before any of the beleaguered lads could answer the next C-4 charge detonated with an ear-shattering blast that shook the ground. This caused Shane to pee himself. Despite his throbbing arm, he kept still and hoped that no one would notice. He decided he'd rather be shoveling shit at Mason's farm after all.

"Jesus Christ, I've seen enough," Abe said. "Jessie, Tanner, get everybody in the truck NOW! We're getting the hell out of here!"

"Does this mean that we get a refund?" one of the hunters asked half-jokingly. "Your refund is that you get to keep your life—maybe!" countered the tracker Tony Proudfoot.

Tom Conroy, the senior FBI officer on the scene, finally reached his specially equipped van and immediately activated a twenty-eight-inch surveillance drone. Not nearly as sophisticated or expensive as the RQ7, it did have a passable camera and LAN wi-fi to transmit the pictures back to its operator. Up it went until finally it cleared the billowing smoke. Sure enough, it spotted the Shadow. Looking at the picture on his laptop, Conroy gasped. He recognized the state-of-the-art predator drone from his training sessions at Quantico. "Holy fuck!" he said to his field partner, Ben Goldberg. "That's U.S. military ordnance!"

Ben was shocked. "Where the hell is *the guy* getting his hands on this kind of shit?" As far as either of them knew, such high-end, weaponized drones were not for sale to anybody in the world. Unfortunately for the FBI duo, the Shadow's swivel-mounted camera had also spotted the smaller, slower surveillance drone. Rafa fired a small munitions burst from the Shadow in its general direction. Something like buckshot sped across the sky, expanding as it travelled. The tiny lead pellets shredded the drone's frame and sent it back to earth in a hurry. From a quarter mile high, there was not much left of it when it hit the dirt. Pearce pumped more rounds into police cruisers and the helicopter, so it would not be airborne any time soon, mechanic or not. He also shot out the windshield of Conroy's van, sending the FBI duo scurrying for cover.

Kiara's ATN Smart Optics binocs were picking up some reinforcements coming up on the logging road. It looked like an armored personnel carrier and a military jeep, maybe from CFB Esquimalt. She activated the wi-fi connection for the binocs and called Rafa via the Global Star sat phone. Comfortably ensconced in an easy chair in KJ's ops base in South Surrey, B.C., he took the call and flicked on his second laptop screen to pick up the images from Kiara's binoculars. He took a swig of steaming matcha green tea from one of KJ's Contigo mugs, then saw the reason for her concern, which was a troop carrier hauling maybe fifteen soldiers and a jeep with a commander and staff sergeant. "I hope you boys like water," Rafa said into the phone speaker as he detonated the C-4 charges at each end of the bridge. Given its compromised condition, the wooden bridge buckled like balsa wood and collapsed into the creek.

The twin blasts shook the road for blocks causing the military convoy to screech to a halt. The troops immediately debarked from the vehicles, assault rifles drawn and ready, but no enemy was in sight. They would stay put for now, until the general area was painstakingly secured. Only then would they attempt to ford the stream—no doubt suspecting an ambush while they were in the water.

On the other side of the stream, LaFlamme, Coburn and a half a dozen other guides and outfitters' parties were also stymied. Jessie and his son jumped out of the back of the crew cab, rifles drawn and ready to shoot at anything that moved. Similar actions were taken by the occupants of the other vehicles. The security guys, hunters and, hell, even the guides and outfitters were all waving guns. Everybody's nerves were on ultra, hair trigger alert. "Hey, can we get our guns back now?" Eddie asked, as he leaped out of Coleman's trailer.

"When pigs can fly," Coburn snarled, thoroughly exasperated by the troublesome threesome.

"But Mr. Coleman, sir," said Donovan Travis in earnest, "We want to do our part to protect your hunting party. It's why we were hired on."

"Yeah, I want to kick some ass too!" Shane chimed in, seemingly oblivious to the warzone around them. "Cause when the chicks back home hear about this, then I'll score some real ass!"

Coleman gave him a thoroughly disgusted look and said, "The only ass you are going to get is if your finger slips through the toilet paper!" That cracked up all of the hunting parties and lightened the tension just a notch. "Now shut the fuck up and get under the rig!"

"But ..."

"No buts," Sergeant Provost interjected. "One more word from any of you, and I mean even one, I lock your asses back up for three months—no credit for this whatsoever! Capice?" They nodded, not daring to utter a word.

Just then, Rafa detonated the last two C-4 charges for good measure causing everyone to hit the ground and cover their ears. A steady fusillade of .50 caliber bone crunchers from the Mac-Tac continued to slam into empty police vehicles—cars, jeeps and the helicopter, which was now permanently disabled. The thunderous KABOOMs were as scary as the damage caused by the fifty-caliber armor-piercing slugs. Everyone was effectively pinned down and it seemed that when anyone even thought of moving, another C-4 charge went off.

Emergency calls were made to CAF Comox for the base's only attack helicopter, which was an old Apache which had been re-furbished from the Vietnam war days. Also requested were a couple of CF-18 fighter jets, circa 1995, but still serviceable, and two dozen soldiers. They were at least a half an hour away at best.

"This is agent Tom Conroy, FBI, badge number 79141" Conroy said into his sat phone. "Patch me through to the Director and I mean *now! It's an emergency!"*

"What the hell is going on up there, Tom?" Clinton George III was watching the carnage on CNN like millions of other viewers. Like the O.J. police chase, these proceedings had pretty much commandeered every TV channel's coverage on both sides of the border.

"I don't exactly know, sir," Conroy replied, "but we are under attack from an unknown enemy and we need air support ten minutes ago!"

"From the pictures on TV it reminds me of my days in Nam," George III, a former combat pilot, said.

"Yes sir, I am sure it does." It's always good to agree with the boss even if you weren't in Nam yourself because that was twenty years before you were born.

"Tom, I've got our tactical guys here looking for back-up and..." He looked to the bank of monitors. "Hmmm, let's see, our satellite map shows Whidbey Island Air Naval Base in Washington to be the closest air support." The Director put his hand over the mouthpiece and motioned to his assistant. "I want the commander of that naval base on the line this instant." He asked his aide to get the Department of National Defense on the line as well. "Technically, we need permission to fly warplanes into Canadian airspace, though I doubt that they'll have any objection in this situation!" Within ten minutes two fully-armed F-18's were scrambled from Whidbey Island Air Naval base and on route to Canada. But even flying at Mach 1.8, the Hornets would not reach the area any sooner than the Canadian Armed Forces' planes.

With Rafa and Kiara on his laptop screen Pearce signaled with a fingers-across-the-throat gesture that it was time to cut and run. Kiara left her perch overlooking the logging road, shut the laptop, threw it and the binocs into her backpack and unplugged the dish. Jumping into her Land Rover, she would follow an abandoned dirt road in an extremely roundabout and somewhat perilous route back to civilization. The vehicle's impressive off-road capabilities, including terrain response, hill descent control and roll stability control would prove to be worth their weight in gold.

KJ disassembled the Mac-Tac and quietly retreated back into the Great Bear Rainforest. His Durango was parked five miles away. Rafa dropped the Shadow to tree top height, one Hellfire II missile still on board if needed. He flew a wide circle around the carnage observing, with some satisfaction, that there was lots of damage and no casualties that he could make out. As the Shadow silently disappeared into the rainforest, he transmitted a radio signal to a device to which a ten-foot helium filled balloon was tethered approximately two hundred yards south of the decimated podium area. The "UNLOCK" signal caused the device to release the balloon on its one hundred-fifty-foot nylon rope. The helium lifted the three-meter-wide, highly visible, bright orange balloon to its maximum height well above the tree tops. A huge, white banner with bold black lettering hung from the bottom of the balloon and was quickly spotted by one of the hunters. Word spread like wildfire as one by one, the beleaguered politicians, police, guides and hunters, cameramen and the audience strained to read the fluttering message.

"What's that say Abe?" asked Rich. "I can't quite make it out."

"I dunno," answered Abe squinting. "Maybe, it's *we'll tell*? No, it's WELCOME, I think."

"Yeah, I can see it now," said Shane, the eagle eye. "It says, **WELCOME TO OPEN SEASON—ON YOU!** That image went viral instantly.

CHAPTER 63

After Effect

Needless to say, the 2015 Grizzly Bear Hunt was immediately shut down and all hunting licenses revoked with full-money back refund—no questions asked. So badly was the government embarrassed, it took the unprecedented step of compensating the guides and outfitters for the economic loss of their hunting season. This move was sanctioned under the *Disaster Relief Act,* which in the province's one-hundred-forty-four-year history had been reserved solely for natural disasters. This cost the province of British Columbia some three and a half million dollars, a little less than one tenth of one percent of its annual budget, but they got a ton of good PR for that gesture. The hunters went home with a story to tell they would never forget. Being hunted wasn't so much fun, it seemed. After that demonstration of fire power, it was absolutely, unequivocally, categorically evident that *the guy* was real—a real fucking nightmare.

Given the flavor-of-the-week nature of global news reporting, the world media spotlight was focused on British Columbia. Thus, the Connors government was on its toes, trying to look as concerned and competent as possible under the circumstances. Teagan's marching orders, backed up by those of the new prime minister, were simple. "Get to the bottom of this now. Find out who did this and catch them!" Fully two-hundred-fifty-million viewers worldwide had witnessed the government's would-be photo op decimated. The police and security forces were holed up under vehicles and behind trees. Meanwhile a nonstop bombardment of fifty caliber rifle fire, C-4 explosions and armed drone strikes terrorized the dignitaries and audience alike for almost ten minutes non-stop. Maybe B.C. was the best place on the planet to do business, but it sure as hell didn't look like the safest to a whole lot of viewers.

By the time reinforcements had forded the creek and the F-18s arrived, the perpetrators were long gone—not that anyone saw them in the first place. SWAT teams from as far as Seattle, Vancouver and Victoria arrived about ninety-minutes later. Fighter jets from both sides of the border swept the skies for hours trying to spot movement in the forest, but the dense underbrush and towering trees made that next to impossible. FBI and CSIS agents quickly determined that the explosions were caused by military grade C-4, detonated by remote radio signal. Conroy's eight-second transmission from the bureau's surveillance drone captured on his laptop showed the RQ7 Shadow in action, but the picture was grainy and not completely in focus.

Techs at Quantico would begin analyzing the footage to enhance its clarity with a view to identifying the particular drone and tracing its manufacture and sales history. It should have had only one buyer, namely the United States government. However, as the veteran security agents knew all too well, high end military ordnance, no matter how proprietary, has a way of changing hands for large sums of money all around the globe. Tracking dog teams had been dispatched in the general direction where the sniper fire had thought to have originated. Since there was no guarantee that the sniper was not still there nor that he had not booby-trapped the area, this operation would proceed at a snail's pace. Homeland Security was asked to provide logistical and tactical assistance, so at least a dozen HLS operatives flew down on a U.S. army transport to liaise with the FBI and local law enforcement. One thing was certain. This was a military operation through and through. It was professionally planned and executed flawlessly. It had caught those present with their proverbial pants down. It was immediately clear to the investigators that the onsite security was designed more for show than to protect the assemblage.

To *the guy's* credit, there was not one casualty. Investigators figured that was no accident. The C-4 charges had been planted just so. The fifty-caliber slugs were fired into empty vehicles and the unmanned copter and the drone strike was on a parking lot full of unoccupied cars. If *the guy's* purpose was to raise public awareness about trophy hunting, it would have been imperative that nobody got killed or injured during the strike. Otherwise he would lose all public support. In that case, mission accomplished—in spades! He managed to get a quarter of a billion people watching the performance and they were now talking about the issue on every media channel on the planet. That, however, was damned well not the point. No one could be allowed to carry out such an operation in broad daylight in front of the whole world on North American soil—NO FUCKING ONE! *The guy* and his team, for it was certain that there were more than one perpetrator, would have to be found and brought to justice before they decided to end their no kill policy.

Conroy discussed this over his sat phone with Clinton George. "The full field reports will be on your desk at 0-800 tomorrow, sir," Conroy said.

"That's a given if you want to keep your job, Tom," the Director said matter-of-factly.

"I hear you sir," the agent responded.

"What else can you tell me right now, agent Conroy?" The Director used his speaker phone, as he paced back and forth in his office. The pacing always increased his anxiety level however. He grabbed the key to his credenza and unlocked the top drawer. There sat a *Drew Estate* bundle of twenty-five hand-made, Nicaraguan filler, Fat Robusto cigars just begging to be opened. Each individual cigar was painstakingly enclosed in an oily San Andreas Maduro wrapper encircled by a paper band which read "My Uzi Weighs a Ton." It was fitting for the Director of the Federal Bureau of Investigation, who owned one of these sub-compact Israeli-made machine guns. As he slit open the packaging, the irresistible flavor of Brazil nuts, cashews, white gravy and coffee wafted through his office. He lit up a big stick and took a heavy drag. "Aaaagh ...that's as good as sex on a honey moon," he opined. Shit, every time he even remotely thought about quitting the habit a new menace seemed to appear out of nowhere, sending his stress level skyrocketing. Running the FBI was in George III's view like playing *whack-a-mole* at the county fair. You knock down one threat and another one pops up to take its place.

"Sir, the operation just smacks of special ops," Conroy said. "It was just too damned good to be standard military."

"Okay." The Director agreed. "Then get me an up to date list of every one of our special forces operatives who retired within the last two years."

"Can do."

"Chances say he's got an axe to grind and he's probably made that known to fellow officers before he left," said George III thoughtfully, now sitting comfortably on his Aston executive office chair and swiveling from side to side. Taking another puff on the aromatic cigar, he continued, "Navy Seals, Green Berets, marines, Airborne, CIA Special Activities Division ... anybody else train at Ft. Bragg that you can think of, Agent Conroy?"

"Well there's British SAS, Israeli Mossad and once in a blue moon Canadian JTF2, sir," Tom replied. He had been invited once to the legendary training facility much earlier in his career. "Get me the British and Israeli lists. I'll put in a call to MI-5, but those bastards in the Mossad are more secretive than Putin's FSB, so I'm not certain that we'll get much out of them," complained Clinton George III as he blew out a couple of perfectly formed smoke rings.

"Don't forget to call the Canadian DND," volunteered the agent.

"What the hell for Conroy?" The Director was scornful. "Our northern neighbor's military, if you can even call it that, doesn't have a pot to piss in." He carried on, obviously a burr under his saddle on this issue. "You know Tom, they have a bunch of old WWII CF-18's that passed their *best before* date last century!" he explained testily. "Then to make matters worse, their new Liberal government just cancelled the mega contract to buy our new F-35's from Lockheed Martin."

"But sir, I thought those planes had had a ton of hardware malfunctions, engines that catch fire, software issues and massive cost overruns," Conroy said. He was a bit of an aviation buff himself. "And, I gather, it can't even win a simulated dogfight with an old F-16!"

"That's not the point agent Conroy," the Director countered. "Every new weapons system costs money and there are bound to be a few bugs on a fighter jet that has more than eight million lines of code programmed into its flight computer to keep it in the air." Clinton George III was not at all impressed with Canadian military or security operations. "Those cheap Canuck bastards have been piggybacking on our efforts since the end of the Second World War and it's hardly cost them a penny to do it!" He shook his head in disgust and added, "I don't think they would have *anybody* retired or not on their roster, who would be up to performing that little number we just witnessed on CNN."

Conroy reluctantly decided it best to share his information, even if it contradicted the Director's. "But sir, I heard that last year a Canadian special ops guy won the hand-to-hand at Ft. Bragg."

"Must have been a pretty weak field then I would think," offered the Director. "Don't waste your time on that dead-end agent Conroy."

"Yes sir."

CHAPTER 64

The Value of Life

If anyone thought that the original threat that Rafa posted on FL-NRO's website got a lot of traffic, it absolutely *paled* in comparison to this nonstop, front page story carried everywhere. Networks' news sites recorded a billion webpage hits from around the globe in less than twenty-four hours. Chatter at coffee shops, water coolers, schools, churches, universities—hell, even on playgrounds was ubiquitous. Everybody seemed to have an intractable opinion one way or the other.

"The guy is an out-and-out a terrorist."

"Not on your life, Jack! He is a champion of animals' rights!"

"Trophy hunting is wrong-headed and barbaric."

"Wake up, buddy! North America was built on hunting and trapping. It is both our right and our national heritage to kill animals for sport, food, fur or otherwise."

"The cops and security forces completely bungled their security assignment at the Great Bear Rainforest."

"Are you nuts? No one could have predicted a military strike of that magnitude on the opening ceremonies."

"Vegetarianism should be practiced by all."

"Bears are not vegetarian, so why the hell should we be?"

Back and forth, on and on it went—an intense debate about animals by people with polar opposite viewpoints. Facebook, LinkedIn, Pinterest, Instagram, Snapchat, Twitter, tens of thousands of blogs and of course, every conventional media channel were, en masse, boiling over with comments, opinions and articles on this issue. KJ smiled with some satisfaction. That was exactly *the dialogue* he wanted to start. Ditto for Rafa and Kiara. To change the status quo, one has to start a conversation, which might go something like this:

"Time for a change everyone."

"Why is that? What is wrong with the current situation?"

234

"Here are a few things for starters. We kill thirty million animals a day, experiment on millions more and imprison hundreds of thousands in zoos and game farms. The wildlife population in the world has declined by almost 40% since 1970 and that trend is *accelerating*."

"Well, I agree that some of those things are bad, but they don't justify wholesale change."

"Yes, they do and here's why—no animals, no people. If the trend continues we will eventually wipe out all the wildlife on the planet by destroying their habitat and then we'll be next."

"I never thought about it that way before…"

"Well, now's a good time get your head out of your ass and start thinking!"

In KJ's humble opinion the best recipe for change was to mix up a batch of spirited discussion, add a pinch of awareness, then toss in a good measure of brute force and stir well. Discussion is a necessary first step to awareness. Awareness shines the light of day on the darkness of evil, unfairness, discrimination, oppression, brutality and enslavement. However, mere awareness has never by itself precipitated even one significant social or political change by itself. Knowing about something is one thing, but doing something about it is another matter altogether. In the entire history of mankind, rights have never been willingly ceded to anyone, no matter how enlightened or aware were the rulers of the day.

It was axiomatic in KJ's mind that rights must *always be taken by force*. The political masters of society have invariably had to be dragged to the table kicking and screaming before they would even consider relinquishing rights to their citizens or other subordinates. That feat has never been accomplished solely by talking, pleading, petitioning, reasoning or educating. Ending slavery, bringing about women's suffrage, organizing trade unions, even passing the UN Charter of Human Rights all had one thing in common, namely that they had to be earned the hard way. Blood, sweat and tears were the norm, not the exception.

The fight for animals' rights would be no different. However, unlike in Orwell's *Animal Farm*, the animals of planet Earth could not fight that battle themselves. KJ could however, with a little help from his friends, and maybe some of the millions of animal lovers and activists who were publicly expressing their support for his campaign on social media worldwide. With the strategic application of force he could get the conversation going and maybe people could come to appreciate that *other forms of life are valuable*, not just the lives of the denizens of **The Invisible Reich**.

CHAPTER 65

Lending a Hand

One of those millions was Inaara Burdenny. Once she saw the Great Bear Rainforest scene on TV she put two and two together. Cool guy driving a black Durango SUV just picks her up out of nowhere and *whammo!* the mink farm blows up and not even a single one of them is killed. His buddy owns a gun shop with more weapons than most army bases. Now someone decimates the Grizzly Bear Hunt up in Canada. Coincidentally, not a single person is killed, despite the massive carnage. It just had to be him! He was so, so…, she was at a total loss for words to describe *the guy she only knew as KJ.* And now he had actually asked for her help! She was literally beside herself with anticipation.

Before he arrived on the scene, she was just another pissed off, moody teenager with a shitty family. Now she had something to believe in, a cause of monumental magnitude. It was far more important than anything she could have imagined just a few short weeks ago. She desperately wanted to be a part of his campaign for the welfare of animals, however small that part might be. So she had to redouble her efforts with Dad. What the hell had he been up to on the farm other than knocking off thousands of mink for profit? She decided that whatever her father had up his sleeve, her dickhead stepbrother, Dom, would likely be in on it. He fancied himself as the next CEO of MBM Colorado when Pops kicked the bucket.

"Hey Dom," she said in a chatty tone as he entered the expansive hotel suite at the Ritz Carleton.

"Since when do you even acknowledge my existence?" asked Dom sarcastically.

"Since I want to be a part of rebuilding MBM," she said with feigned enthusiasm.

"Yeah right," he scoffed. "You've been bitching about the mink' conditions and treatment since you got here."

"Yeah, well we all gotta grow up some time," she said. "Don't we?"

"You serious?" Dom squinted as if he wasn't seeing right.

"Dead serious," she said looking him in the eye. "I want to learn the business so I can help out."

Dom settled in the suite's commodious couch. "Inaara, Dad's been waiting to hear you say that for as long as I can remember," he said. "I kept telling him you don't need her when you got me. But he kept saying two kids are better than one, even if one's adopted." Inaara winced. Dom got up and strolled into the huge kitchen to get a Bud. "But of course, I would be the boss of the two of us," he added.

"Of course," she agreed, "since you are older."

"And a damned size smarter," said Dom glaring at her. "And don't ever forget it!"

"I'm sure you'll remind me if I do," she said, ever so politely. "Now can I start on lesson one."

Dom doffed his black suede blazer, dropped back onto the couch, took a pull on the long neck and smacked his lips. "Make me a ham and Swiss and I'll think about it."

CHAPTER 66

Sitting Still

One of the hardest things for a bank robber to do after a successful heist is *nothing*. Usually after a short while the typical thief can't wait any longer and goes out on a spending spree which tips off the cops every time.

"Hey, Sarge, you know Howie Bostik's driving a new F-type Jaguar convertible, bright red! How's he do that on a bus driver's salary? You think maybe he was in on the First Federal job last month?"

"I don't know, corporal," his CO would say. "Could be he was just been putting in a lot of OT, but probably not. Let's get a warrant to be on the safe side."

The search would turn up the stolen loot in Howie's basement or garage or bank account and he'd end up doing a dime in a for-profit, maximum security prison. KJ et al would not make that mistake. For now, the three of them would disappear off every radar screen known to man. Kiara would return to her long-running case against Trans Mountain Pipeline Company. Rafa would cover everyone's digital tracks and go back to his computer law practice. KJ would return to his base in South Surrey and lay lower than a snake's belly. They had landed some hard blows to the open the match and the authorities would be looking for payback. Sooner than later they would connect the dots and figure out that the MBM and Great Bear Rainforest incidents were related and then it would become an all-out, manhunt for KJ and his team on both sides of the border. No stone would be left unturned and of course, in the meantime every police department and security agency was on red alert waiting for the next strike. The authorities would surely be expecting someone to claim *responsibility* for the attacks and then to threaten further action unless their *demands* were met. At the moment, KJ et al didn't have any demands, at least none that would be complied with. As far as responsibility, the government knew that *the guy* who posted the threat on FLN-

239

RO's website was behind the strike. It was enough that worldwide attention had been focused on the idiocy of the Grizzly Bear Hunt and, soon enough, the cruel captivity of furbearing animals, courtesy of MBM Colorado.

KJ had a hunch that most people would prefer to do the right thing once they knew the facts. Truth be told, however, up until now the average person had just remained blissfully ignorant of the appalling relationship of homo sapiens with all other species on the planet.

"You know, now that I think about it, I don't really want to know how the bacon got onto my plate. My wife went to the supermarket and bought it—on sale no less."

"Fur trim looks just fine on my winter parka, but I've never thought to ask how it got from the animal to my coat."

"Hey, I'm just the consumer! It's not my job to police the garment industry."

"Thank God for that new cancer drug. Without it I would be dead and gone. You know, I have never considered the welfare of the many thousands of mice, rats, cats, dogs, chimpanzees and other lab animals the drug was tested on before it got to me. I am just thankful to be alive."

Twenty years ago, people had that same infuriating indifference about where their clothes were manufactured, until a building collapsed on a group of women in Bangladesh. Hundreds of them were killed. The indentured women were working for the companies of billionaire fashion moguls in horrible, unsafe sweat shops for pennies a day. Publicity of this event enraged North American consumers who demanded better working conditions and wages for the seamstresses. Pearce was hoping that the same sort of thing might occur for the billions of animals on the planet that were exploited to a far greater extent than even those Indian and Asian women. For now, he would remain quiet and still until he saw how the aftermath of the two events unfolded. Further action would be taken when the time was right.

KJ leaned back on his chair in the war room at *Animal Farm*, the thirty-one-inch computer monitor staring blankly back at him. One can sit still and wait in a number of different ways. Instead of sinking into a deep, meditative state, which he would normally do, he unlaced his combat boots and dove onto his black microfiber couch, flicking on the movie channel. For a few hours he would kick back and relax after what had to be considered a hell of a good start to his longshot campaign. He would take it one day at a time from here on in. Tamu and Paikea immediately leaped onto the couch, avid TV fans themselves. Although they preferred *the Nature Channel,* anything would do if the owner was also watching. Tamu always maneuvered himself on one side with his huge head on KJ's lap. Paikea curled up on his other side apparently asleep, but like a cat, she was always imminently ready to spring into action.

"Let's see what tomorrow brings," he said aloud. Little did he know.

CHAPTER 67

Meeting in the Park

K J had arranged to meet Kiara for lunch the following Monday. She had received a notice of motion requesting a two-day adjournment in her Supreme Court case against Trans Mountain due to illness of one of their key witnesses. Since the adjournment would be routinely granted in those circumstances, she gladly agreed to meet. After taking the hounds for a run and completing an hour-and-a-half workout at the Steve Nash Club at Morgan Crossing, KJ was motoring along the TransCanada highway by nine a.m., heading to Vancouver, the second most desirable city on the planet. Kiara's office at Sierra Legal Defense was in the historic Marine Building on Burrard Street in the business district of the city's core. In the bright daylight, it was simply stunning. Built in 1929, the twenty-one-story tower is one of the great art deco buildings in the world. The lobby is a virtual masterpiece. The five elevators have doors of solid, polished brass and intricately inlaid interiors made of twelve kinds of different hardwoods. Sea horses and puffer fish, boats and ships, even biplanes and a zeppelin are carved into the sides of the building to dazzle the eye. From the upper floors, the one-hundred-eighty-degree water view over the Burrard Inlet is unsurpassed by any of the much larger buildings which have gone up since.

Pearce would meet Kiara at her office at 11:45 a.m. The fickle traffic patterns of the highway and downtown core had chosen not to hamper his progress this day, and he arrived downtown at twenty minutes past ten. With almost an hour to spare, he decided to stop off in Stanley Park to clear his mind and strategize. He pulled the Durango into one of the many pay parking lots and placed a couple of toonies into the parking meter. He had to shake his head at the uber, politically correct "No smoking in the park - By-Law 7801" sign posted near the lot. Camp fires were ok, but perish the thought if some second-hand smoke blew your way from a cigarette thirty-feet away. He sighed. Politicians were the same the world over—nitwits.

Before he moved away from the vehicle, force of habit required him to complete a cursory reconnaissance of the surroundings. He removed his Aviators and pulled out his 35 MM Nikon pretending to survey the surrounding landscape for a good shot. This took fully five minutes. When he was satisfied nothing was out of the ordinary, he started strolling toward the duck pond. The thousand-and-one-acre Stanley Park, surrounded by the waters of Vancouver Harbor and English Bay, is one of the most beautiful parks in the world. Ponds, bike and walking trails, art and cultural exhibits, a world class aquarium, complete with vigorous public debate over maintaining sea mammals in captivity, a miniature train, public tennis courts with a water view to die for, restaurants and concessions a plenty, public beaches, a fantastic seawall and a half million or so trees towering up to two-hundred-fifty-feet high made this *Trip Advisor's* pick for "top park in the world in 2014."

KJ was dressed in attire suitable for a casual business lunch, but fully functional for anything else which might come up. First was a loose fitting ScotteVest sport coat with twenty-three concealed pockets which allowed him to carry a wide variety of items other than the usual cell phone, ear buds, writing pen, sunglasses and wallet. A couple of spare clips for the Glock 20 and the K-Bar combat knife fit perfectly into pockets 21 and 24 (there was actually a pull out "pocket map" on a cord in pocket 12 to help the wearer locate all of the pockets). His charcoal Lululemon *abc* (anti-ball crushing) athletic pants made of Warpstreme, four-way stretchable fabric were suitable for a business trip, the golf course or a hike in the park. Super comfortable ECO walking shoes were waterproof, breathable and good for any terrain imaginable.

As always, the Glock 20 was tucked securely in his shoulder holster beneath the sport coat. Being retired CAS he had no problem obtaining a concealed carry permit for the handgun. In fact, once the permit supervisor learned that he was a former member of the ultra-elite JTF2, he had tried to persuade KJ to teach a fire arms course for the department. "Sorry, no time for that," was KJ's reply. He took the guy's card and promised to call if his calendar ever cleared up.

The day was cool, but clear and sunny like a day on the prairies. This was unusual for springtime in Vancouver, but it did happen from time to time. KJ sat on a park bench facing the duck pond in the "lost lagoon" area of the park and without thinking, pulled out his Blackberry to check for messages from Rafa or Kiara. Nothing. He then surfed the Web looking for news updates on the Great Bear Rainforest campaign as well as the strike at the MBM minkery. Sixty-two thousand search results appeared on his first try—which could keep him reading for a decade. Only a handful of articles appeared on the MBM matter.

He started to read a NY Times article, "Why Any Form of Terrorism is Toxic to Democracy," when something moved into his peripheral field of vision. He reached for the Glock, but relaxed. It was a Jack Russell puppy, sans owner. The energetic pup, maybe six pounds soaking wet, was dragging a short nylon leash, but no one was in sight. It looked like she had something in her mouth, maybe a glove or sock. Pearce got up to grab the leash, but the dog was too fast and bolted into a thicket of red osier dogwood shrubs. Pearce had half a mind to sit back down and wait for the owner to show, but he couldn't resist a challenge. He snuck around the bushes and waited. A minute went by. Then two minutes. After a full one-hundred-ninety seconds the dog sniffed him out and gingerly approached. KJ located a couple of dog biscuits in pocket seventeen and dropped them on the ground in front of his shoes. Floriana had a habit of packing biscuits and poop bags in his jacket pockets so that he could grab the hounds and head out on the spur of the moment.

The terrier dropped the glove and grabbed the biscuit, ready to make off with it, but KJ stepped on the leash. Now where the hell was the owner? He walked the dog back to the park bench in plain view, hoping someone would spot him and claim the pooch. Sure enough, a young kid, maybe eight or nine, came running into sight yelling, "Hey Mister, that's my dog!"

"Good for you," said KJ. "Here's the leash. And you can take a few biscuits for good measure," he said, as that sense of something about to go wrong intruded on his consciousness.

"Thanks, Mister," the kid said, taking the biscuits and handing one to the pup.

"Is this your dad's?" KJ held out the expensive black, deer skin leather driving glove.

"No, my dog stole it from some guy who was having a beer, way over there," pointing toward the North Shore mountains. "I tried to get Jacki to drop it, but I let go of her leash when the guy came at us with a club. She ran off and I chased her." The young boy was excited to find his dog, but still visibly upset over that incident.

Pearce asked where the boy's parents were.

"Dad's at work. My mom was getting us hot dogs, but I didn't want to lose Jacki so I just ran after her, but she was way too fast."

"Gimme that fuckin glove!" said an odious, aggressive voice out of nowhere. Pearce turned to see an angry, late-twenty-something man approaching with a menacing gait. He was dressed in black—leather pants, tee shirt and leather vest. A single black driving glove was on his left hand. Pearce, it would seem, was holding the other one. Secured to his wrist by a short lanyard was a baton, the type used by riot police.

"Looks like this belongs to you," said KJ, tossing the glove to the man who snatched it out of the air. KJ spoke in a casual, but reassuring voice, designed to put the guy back on an even keel. It didn't work.

The guy looked at the glove. "It's got dog spit on it." He had a cockney accent. Inspecting the glove he added, "Oh shit, look at this, bloody puncture marks!" By then his girlfriend, similarly attired, and two other guys arrived. If you looked up the term "juvenile delinquent," the second guy's picture would surely appear under the caption, while the third guy, Asian, was maybe thirty-five, much heavier and definitely stronger.

KJ wondered if he was a bodyguard. But then who would need a bodyguard in Stanley Park? There was a tattoo of the Red Scorpion gang on the guy's thick neck. What the hell were these clowns doing in the park, sightseeing? KJ's instincts initiated a state of *combat readiness*, automatically defaulting to the option of fight rather than flight.

"These gloves cost me over ninety quid!"

KJ could barely understand the heavy, cockney accent.

"And now they are bloody ruined by that filthy, little vermin!" He glared at the kid's dog.

"Hey, they're driving gloves," KJ pointed out. "No one will ever even notice."

"Who asked you, fuckhead?"

"Just saying," offered KJ, still trying to keep a lid on the situation.

"Well you can just shut your fucking mouth and mind your own damned business!"

"Hey, Alex, he's cute," said the girlfriend. "Give him a break."

"Break my ass," said the boyfriend, "you'll fuck anything standing on two legs and breathing, you whore!"

"Up yours, you piece of shit!" She gave him the finger.

This area of the park was relatively deserted. No police patrol on horseback happened by, confirming the old adage, *there is never a cop around when you need one.* Alex told the kid in no uncertain terms to hand over the motherfucking leash. He graphically explained how he was going to string *the Jack* up by the neck until she croaked. Some people would say this just to scare the kid, but Pearce's sixth sense was telling him that this psycho was probably not joking. Making a final effort to avoid an altercation Pearce said, "Hey, how about if I buy you a new pair of those gloves." He took a step towards Alex and continued. "Let's see ninety quid, that's about $180.00 Canadian?" He fished two crisp hundred-dollar bills from his wallet and said, "Make it an even $200 for your trouble."

Alex ignored the bills. "You are going to give me a plane ticket to London too, 'cause that's where I bought them man—*Dents on Brook Street* as a matter of fact."

KJ cocked his head to one side, somewhat bemused. "You ever hear of FedEx? The extra twenty should cover shipping. In fact, Dents offered free shipping to Canada, but that was beside the point."

"Now aren't you the smart ass," said Alex, spinning the baton on the lanyard, an obvious warning gesture. The bodyguard produced a switchblade which he flicked open with a snapping gesture. Guy number three didn't appear to be armed but he also seemed to be getting ready to fight. "Here's the deal," he said to KJ. "Gimme the two C-notes right now!" He snatched the bills out of KJ's hand. "And we might just let you walk out of here in one piece!"

KJ, now completely in combat mode, scanned the area. Shit, still no cops and scant few people, except for a pretty brunette woman who appeared to be running toward them. She arrived out of breath.

"Johnny, where the heck have you been? I've been looking everywhere for you!" she yelled, panting. Kneeling, she gently scolded the pup. "Jacki—you little rascal you! Did you guys find him?"

"We did after the thieving little mutt stole my boyfriend's glove right off his hand," said the girlfriend. "And then chewed it up!"

"I'm terribly sorry, she does that at home too," said the mom. "If it's ruined I'll pay for a new pair," she offered right away, sensing that these likely weren't the nicest folks in the park. She didn't know where KJ fit in, because he didn't seem to be anything like the others.

"I already told asswipe here," pointing to KJ "that I'd need ninety quid and a plane ticket to Wiltshire, England to replace the gloves," said Timmie, not mentioning that he had taken KJ's money.

"Hey, I already gave you two hundred," Pearce said.

"That just gets you off the hook, matey, not her," replied Alex, somewhat surprised at his own cleverness.

The mom was getting nervous. "Ninety quid, is that like ninety pounds sterling?" she asked.

"Now aren't you the smart tart! Fucking right it is," answered Alex, showing her the baton and slapping it in his free palm.

"That's a lot of money for me, but I can get the cash out of the ATM over there," she said. "I can't afford a plane ticket to England for you. Can't you just Fed Ex the gloves?"

He scowled menacingly. "Now listen up, bitch! I want the ninety-fucking quid and cash for a first-class plane ticket to England or I'm stringing up the dog by its neck right now!"

The mom was literally frozen on the spot. She held onto the leash and her son as tightly she could. She silently prayed to the heavens that they would all get out of this mess alive.

KJ had seen enough. "I think I'll be on my way now. I've got an appointment downtown. You can keep the cash by the way."

"Bank on it, chickenshit," quipped Alex, baiting him to just try something.

Starting to turn away, he stopped briefly and said to the mom, "Hey, I'm sorry that I couldn't be of more help ma'am." She almost died on the spot when she heard those words. She shut her eyes tight, forcing a couple of tears down her cheeks. It seemed that her prayers were not going to be answered on this terribly inauspicious day.

"Now fuck off, tosser, before we decide to kick your ass too," said the guy who looked like the juvy, also with a strong, cockney accent.

"Yeah, go home to your mommy while you still can!" said Alex in an aggravating tone, still doing his best to provoke a response. He grabbed the kid by the collar and his girlfriend took the leash away from the boy's mom, yanking Jacki off the ground. The terrier yelped as she dangled briefly in the air. The bodyguard grabbed the mom by the arm and started pushing her toward the forested area. She was too scared to resist or even scream, but she held on to her son for dear life.

"This is going to be a party the mom, the kid and the pooch will remember for a long time," said Alex. "Well, maybe not the pooch so much," correcting himself. A *clockwork-orange* type grin crossed his face. "What the hell, might as well have some fun while we are in Vancouver. All work and no play makes Alex a dull boy!" he said jubilantly to the group.

"I'm with you there, mate," said the juvy. As they started toward the wooded area of the park, the group forgot about Pearce. They assumed that he was doubtless slinking away, thanking his lucky stars that he was being allowed to leave without being beaten up. That was a mistake they would live to regret, or maybe not.

With blinding speed Pearce turned and grabbed Alex's right shoulder, spinning him around. Before the English thug could raise the baton, KJ hit him in the throat with an elbow strike. Unlike the one delivered to Master Ishikawa, this one did not stop short. Timmie collapsed like a sack of potatoes, clutching his throat and gasping for air. His windpipe was almost crushed. It was fifty-fifty whether he would live out the day. KJ backhanded the startled girlfriend across the face, knocking her senseless on the grass. She let go of the leash sending Jacki scurrying. The bodyguard flicked out his switchblade again and came at KJ, waiving the blade menacingly. In a split-second Pearce extracted the K-bar from pocket sixteen of his sport coat and threw it right into the upper thigh of the bodyguard, burying it almost to the hilt. The enforcer screamed in pure agony, dropping his blade and clutching his thigh. This was the most excruciating pain he had ever experienced in his life. KJ leapt toward him, kicking him full on in the groin and then kneeing him in the face as he bent over. Nose broken in a half a dozen places, blood gushing out of his upper thigh, his chances of survival weren't much better than Alex's. Rather than turn and run, stupidity took over and the juvy jumped on KJ's back trying to gouge his eyes from behind. With a deft aikido maneuver, Pearce flipped him over his head. The guy landed hard on his tailbone. As the searing pain shot up the juvy's spine, Pearce drove a knee into his back breaking several ribs and knocking the wind out of him. This was followed by a lightning fist strike to the side of his neck, rendering him senseless. He was still breathing. KJ walked over and extracted the K-bar from the Asian's prone form, slowly wiping off the blood from the blade on the guy's shirt. For the briefest instant, the thought of slitting all of their throats crossed his mind, but it quickly passed. This wasn't Afghanistan and they weren't Al Qaeda.

The fight lasted all of twenty-two seconds. The mom hadn't moved an inch but the kid was mesmerized. He'd seen that kind of stuff before on *"Into the Badlands"* (when his mom was not watching TV of course). KJ told him to go retrieve the dog. He gently shook the mom's shoulder and told her, "It's okay. You and your son can go home. These assholes aren't going anywhere soon." He checked the Cobra. It was 11:30 a.m., just enough time to get to his lunch meeting with Kiara. A few patrons of the park were now approaching and someone was making a call on their cell phone. That was good. Given that no one had been around right when the gang tried to escort the mom to the woods, he was pretty sure the scene hadn't made it to YouTube. He turned and jogged back towards the Durango.

CHAPTER 68

Manhunt

KJ knew that the authorities would link the MBM and Great Bear Rain Forest incidents sooner than later. The next day turned out to be the sooner. Front page headlines splashed across major newspapers in both countries and around the globe, proclaimed a terrorist was on the loose. He was armed to the teeth and dangerous beyond description. *The guy* was taking on legendary characteristics every time the stories were retold, now being described as a combination of Rambo, the Terminator and Chuck Norris in his heyday. The stories claimed that the C-4 from both explosions at MBM and the Great Bear Rain Forest was identical military grade, likely from the same manufacturing batch. Unfortunately, since so much of the explosive was sold to not only the U.S. military, but pretty much to every other army and para-military organization around the world it would prove next to impossible to determine its first point of sale, let alone trace its history thereafter.

Reporting also focused on the military precision of the MBM strike, which not only resulted in no human casualties, but, amazingly, no dead mink either. The latter observation was somewhat muted in the press. Despite this, the public was reminded that both strikes were unlawful. They were considered terrorist activities under the Uniting and Strengthening America by Providing Appropriate Tools Required to Intercept and Obstruct Terrorism Act (more commonly known as "The USA PATRIOT Act") and its Canuck equivalent, the Canadian Anti-Terrorism Act. Both the U.S. Attorney General and the Canadian Minister of Justice stated unequivocally that *the guy and his band of terrorists* would be hunted down and prosecuted to the full extent of the law in both countries. In Canada that could mean a jail sentence of ten to fifteen years. But in the U.S., once a *terrorist* label got attached to an accused, the sentence could be an indefinite term in a supermax prison—and that might even be without a trial.[3]

The perpetrators were painted as ex-military animal rights zealots who had no regard for the rule of law or the sanctity of private property. All citizens were urged to report anything that they found suspicious at either location before or after the incidents. Director Clinton George III and his counterpart at Homeland Security, Janice Ralston, had immediately ordered a U.S. Customs review of surveillance footage of all personal and vehicular traffic coming into the U.S. for the forty-eight hour periods before and after the MBM and Great Bear Rainforest incidents. However, the nine-thousand kilometer Canada-U.S. border contained over one-hundred-nineteen crossings. On average over three-hundred-thousand people in one-hundred-seventy-thousand cars and nearly thirty-thousand trucks per day go back and forth between the two countries.

Hence, that footage could take weeks, if not months, to analyze. In the spirit of cooperation, Canada Border Services ("CBS") agreed to do likewise, even though everyone assumed that *the guy* was ex-U.S., not Canadian, special forces. He would have had to come into Canada to execute the Great Bear Rainforest strike, so CBS was promising to analyze footage from up two days before the incident and the same span of time afterwards, presumably when he left to go back to the States. With their archaic technology and limited resources, a year might not be too far off in terms of an even a preliminary report from CBS.

A dozen Homeland Security agents were pouring over special forces' *Cessation of Active Duty Reports*—honorable discharges and otherwise, from 2013 onwards to see if anything was amiss. That was a huge job, as the U.S. had many such forces both in the U.S. and abroad, *and* that didn't include SAS or Mossad. So far, neither of these agencies had cooperated in releasing any details about their recently retired special forces operatives. A synopsis of the full report to the Director read:

---

3   Corporal Bradley Manning, now Chelsea Manning, who leaked the classified documents to WikiLeaks spent years in solitary confinement in a U.S. supermax prison without charges or a trial and eventually copped a plea to a thirty-five-year sentence to avoid going insane.

CLASSIFIED REPORT to Director C. George III
April 2, 2015
Colleen Page: Profiler Level III, Quantico, Badge No. 89461
RE: Terrorist suspect, MBM Colorado Minkery, Colorado, U.S.A (6th of March
2015), Great Bear Rainforest, B.C., Canada (18th of March, 2015)

EXECUTIVE SUMMARY "Male suspect is likely in his late twenties or early thirties, definitely special forces, disciplined, probably used to following orders to a tee and completing every mission assigned to him meticulously. Doubtless has an outstanding service record. He is capable of operating independently as well as working with his special ops team. Obviously, he is highly trained. He is certainly capable of killing, but making a point of not doing so thus far. The animals' rights angle just doesn't add up. In studying the military and security forces personnel for over twenty years I have never come across an animals' rights sympathizer in any unit or cohort. However, from the two strikes and the messages on the B.C. government's website and on the floating balloon concluding the Great Bear Rainforest strike, the suspect's motivation is completely apparent—lay off the animals or else. I anticipate that his no-kill policy will evaporate if he or his team is cornered, so *shoot to kill* would be my recommendation, as I don't believe that he or his team are likely to be captured alive. Expect to take casualties." -C. Page

The Director rubbed his temples, but resisted the urge to break out another cigar. "Expect casualties? How many bloody casualties we supposed to expect?" he muttered. "Get Ralston on the line and set up a meeting with her tomorrow morning at her office in Chicago," he ordered. A curt nod from his efficient, not to mention shapely assistant, Jenna followed. "And don't take no for an answer. It's important. And one more thing, Jenna, get my pilot, Roger down here now. I want the jet ready to go in sixty minutes." No way that the Director of the Federal Bureau of Investigation ever flew commercial. Now he had an hour to kill. He smacked his forehead with the palm of his hand. Better phone the new wife and let her know I'm flying to Chi this afternoon. Of course, she'll be devastated that there will be no stud in the bedroom tonight but, hey, everyone's got to take one now and then for national security, right?

Truth be told, after the initial two-week honeymoon in the Maldives, the Director had been away more than he had been at home. He paced, now preoccupied with the wife. He realized that she was bound to start wondering where the hell that mink coat that he promised her was. She had done such a bang-up job decorating his office, it was the least he could do. But now, that fucking Burdenny was out of stock! He made a voice note on his Blackberry to jump on his fat ass to get a fur coat over here pronto even if he had to go to Saks and to buy it retail! He rang his thirty-six-year-old wife and got voice mail. She must be at the spa he thought. "Hey, Corinne baby, how's your day going? Look, I got to fly to Chicago right now on urgent FBI business, so don't wait up tonight. I should be back tomorrow. I'll text you when I'm in. Love you, sweetie!" He paused before hanging up and added, "Hey, by the way, that fur coat I ordered for you is only a couple of short weeks away. I am sure it will bring back your fondest memories of being on the cat walk! You will look absolutely sensational in it, especially if you aren't wearing anything else underneath! I can't wait to get back home, Clinton." He dropped his behind into the thirty-six-hundred-dollar Aston executive chair, one of Corrine's picks of course.

"Fuck it, I'll have another goddamned cigar," he said, as he reached for the box of *Drew Estates*.

CHAPTER 69

Undercover at MBM

Inaara was aghast at the number of mink that had been snuffed out by MBM Colorado over the past ten years—almost ninety thousand! Gross profit, on average, of the cost of a pelt was fifty-two dollars. This equated to just over four point five million dollars. However, she noted from the financial summaries that were explained to her by Dom that MBM had received more than double that amount in government farm subsidies from state and federal agencies. That put the gross at closer to twelve million! How was that even possible? They only paid the farmworkers half of the state minimum wage, mandated by Colorado minimum wage order #31. That came to the princely sum of $5.11 per hour (actually $5.115, but MBM rounded it down). As a part of the Division of Labor Department, the Farm Workers Protection Bureau allowed Colorado farmers to pay less than minimum wage as a way to keep them competitive. The maximum discount was half, which was what MBM paid. It wasn't immediately clear to Inaara why it was called Farm Workers *Protection,* when it allowed their wages to be cut in half. However, the state Farm Assistance Bureau also compensated certain select types of farms with a further subsidy up to $5.00 per hour for every worker employed. It just happened that mink farming was on that select list. Was that just a coincidence?

The Department of Labor would also chip in an additional $3.50 per hour per migrant worker. Then there was the farm property tax relief bill which cut the MBM's five-hundred-acre property tax down to pennies a year. It seemed that the farm lobby, or at least the MBM farm lobby, had some pretty good clout with the powers that be.

"You see, Inaara," said her dad, delighted that his only daughter was finally starting to see the light. "Mink ranching is just like any other business. The key is money in versus money out."

"And the money out had better be the smaller number," Dom

chimed in. "And to sweeten the pot, you've got to get your hands on every subsidy out there and when that's not enough, you've got to get busy and persuade the government to create some."

"How do you do that?" She was definitely interested.

Dom flipped open the "coat list" and showed it to Inaara. "See these two hundred people? Every one of them gets a mink coat," he didn't mention the possible two or three coats, "for their wife, girl-friend or whatever *gratis*."

She raised her eyebrows, quizzically.

"That means free, Inaara," said Don.

"Oh, wow," she replied. "A free mink coat!" What would one cost at a store?"

Dom, the valuation expert, swiveled around on the kitchen bar-stool and said, "Around $20,000 retail for a top-quality coat—which of course would come from MBM pelts."

"Holy smoke!"

Don carried on from the sofa, pleased she was impressed. "Which means that Senator so-and-so or Congressman what's-his-face or Colonel Joe Blow has got a real happy partner on his hands so he is liable to look with favor on MBM when we need something."

The tag team duo continued. Dom added, "Mind you he's under no legal obligation to do so. We simply wouldn't hear of it." Apart from the fact that would be an illegal bribe, which Dom, the always ethical businessman, neglected to mention. "In addition, we contrib-ute to every fundraiser and go to every political function across the country that even remotely affects the fur business."

Inaara was soaking this all in. At one point, she inadvertently re-verted to type and blurted out, "But, Dad, couldn't we just treat the mink just a bit better on the farm?" then quickly bit her lip and wait-ed for a verbal lambasting. It didn't come.

She was on the team now, so Dom, the guardian of animals, looked directly at her and said, "Look, Inaara, Dad and me care about the mink just as much as you do, don't we Dad?"

"Damned right we do, son," said Don earnestly. "We got the crates specially made ten percent bigger than law requires and we feed the mink better quality hash than most other farmers feed their workers," which actually didn't say much. "You see, that allows us to get more money for their pelts at the fur auctions—which keeps us in business and the mink get better food and more space to live in the bargain."

That's what's called a "win-win" explained Dom, tagging in. She didn't seem convinced, even though she was trying her best to look like she was. Dom sensed this and said, "Look Inaara, lemme ask you a question."

"Okay."

"Why do you think that mink have fur?"

"I don't know, maybe to keep warm in the winter and swim in the water to catch fish and stuff," she offered.

"Wrong!" he exclaimed.

"They have fur so we can make coats out of it for the special women in our lives," explained Don.

"Does mom own a mink coat?"

"Sure, three or four at last count," Don said. "And you know, she was always ragging on us about better conditions for the mink just like you, only not as much after she got the first coat. Then she kept asking for more."

Dom, now the theological scholar, carried on. "The Holy Bible tells us that man was made in the image and likeness of God. So God looks like a man, not a mink or a horse or a turtle. That puts us above everything else—way above." He went and plucked a King James Bible from the kitchen drawer of the hotel and read out the passage about mankind having *dominion* over all the other creatures on the planet. "See it says that right in the holy book that we run the show for all the animals, birds, reptiles and fish, so we are right to use them for our sole benefit!" Dom looked like the cat that swallowed the canary.

"Can't argue with God now can you, Inaara?"

"I guess not," she replied meekly.

CHAPTER 70

Are You In?

"Hi, KJ," Kiara said, her smile dazzling as always. They shared a warm hug in the reception area. "Where are we off to?"

"The Heirloom restaurant," he said. "Our reservation is for 12:15 so we should be off." Kiara rushed back to her office and grabbed her coat. On the way out she told the receptionist she would be back "at around two-ish."

As they sped along Burrard Street south, KJ asked for her evaluation of the Great Bear Rainforest strike.

She didn't pause. "I thought that it couldn't have gone better if we had written the script," she said, shooting a quick glance his way. His profile reminded her of *Captain America, the First Avenger* which she had seen at the Scotia Theatres with him and Rafa a few months back. Under that calm, cool exterior he was probably one of the deadliest guys alive. The Serengeti Aviators concealed his deep, hazel eyes which missed nothing on the battlefield—which was as of now, the planet Earth.

"We did," he said. "Don't you remember how many hours we spent planning that operation K?"

"Lots," she said. "But what I meant to say was that the press coverage and the response on social media was unbelievable." She grabbed her phone out of her handbag for a quick browse of the net. Seconds later she reported that there were over twenty-million positive comments from around the world on the incident.

"I guess that's not bad out of two-hundred-and-fifty million views," he replied. His eyes darted to her phone. "Still like the real keyboard I see."

"Wow, you don't miss much," she said. As they pulled up to the front door of the white brick, restaurant on West 12th, he told her that he didn't have to look at her to see what she was doing.

"Hmm…because of some kind of ninjitsu training or something?"

she was half teasing.

He almost smiled. "No, it's the small convex mirror concealed in the dash just below the CD player, see there," pointing. Sure enough, there was a small convex mirror embedded into the dash which allowed him to see the passenger's actions without having to turn his head to look.

"That's pretty cool, but what's it for?"

The SUV came to a stop at the parking meter. "If someone's got a gun pointed at me in the front seat, it gives me a split-second advantage if they turn away or get distracted."

"That ever happened?"

"Not yet, but with the field of operations expanding every day, you never know," he replied as he slid out of the driver's side. He insisted on opening the passenger door for her, old school for sure, but she sure didn't mind. Chivalry in the male species never goes out of style. As they were being seated at the corner table near the window, KJ caught a glimpse of the nine millimeter Beretta in her handbag. She had noticed the slight bulge under his armpit where his Glock was holstered. Doubtless they were the only armed couple in this high-class vegan establishment.

When the waitress came, Kiara ordered the House Caesar—mixed kale and romaine lettuce, cornbread croutons, cashew parmesan, beet bacon and signature Caesar dressing. KJ opted for the Heirloom Gomae, a huge plate of spinach, daikon, cucumbers, carrots, braised Shitake mushrooms, ginger beer tofu, toasted sesame seeds and wasabi lime dressing.

"Wow, that's a huge salad!" Kiara said.

"Skipped breakfast this morning so I have to make up for it. And I got in a little exercise in the park, while I was waiting," Pearce said. He asked the waitress to bring a bottle of The Prisoner Napa Valley Red Blend U.S. 2012 V (vegan-friendly of course) which he thought fitting for the occasion, given that at least four-thousand prisoners had been sprung from the MBM Colorado ranch!

Sans Aviators, he looked into Kiara's clear blue eyes. "I really appreciated your help on this mission. Rafa's too, I might add."

She looked back into those unfathomable, eyes of brown, green and amber and replied that it was an honor to be chosen to be a part of his campaign to end massive injustice to animals. He gave her a little Clint Eastwood type squint. "You know it's going to get dangerous pretty fast. The B.C. government has been thoroughly embarrassed and now the Americans are on the bandwagon, so they are going to leave no stone unturned."

She tossed her silky blonde hair. "So what?"

The salads and *The Prisoner* arrived at the same time and the ancient wine steward poured each of them a half a glass. They toasted to "success to all other species!" She reached into her stylish, new *Cork by Design* handbag and quickly banged out a short text, then deposited her phone back in its pocket.

"So, I think that for the time being you and Rafa are virtually invisible and untraceable no matter what."

"How about you?" she asked, a little apprehensive.

"Well, I had to procure the Shadow and the ordnance from my ex-JTF2 contacts. I trust them implicitly."

"Okay." She took a sip of her wine.

"There are also a couple of U.S. ex-special forces buddies I had to hook up with in Colorado and Utah on the MBM op."

"They're solid too, I would guess," she offered. "Beet bacon—zesty!"

"One-hundred per cent," he replied, biting into the Shitake. "Damned, that's good."

"Looks delicious, can I try a bite?"

"Help yourself."

The waitress reappeared and asked if they needed anything else. No everything was fine. She left.

"Remember the teenager at MBM, Inaara? She's spying on MBM for me."

Kiara speared a mushroom from his plate. "Yeah, you said your gut feeling was that she was totally on board."

"I did and I still do. But then there was the supervisor at the Peace Arch Border crossing," he added.

"But he called off the search of your vehicle, didn't he?" she said.

"He did, but it's just one more loose-end that could eventually unravel if someone keeps digging—which you have to assume that both the Canadian and U.S. governments will do."

A frown crossed her brow. "Where is this going?"

"Well," he said hesitantly. "You know, Kiara, if we get caught it'll be curtains for both you and Rafa's legal careers, not to mention some serious jail time."

"What about you?" she shot back. "Right now, JTF2 would take you back in a heartbeat and the sky's the limit for you there." She finished her wine and the waitress cleared her plate. No thanks on the dessert she advised the waitress, but it looked fabulous.

He nodded. "That's different. I am a soldier first and foremost." he said earnestly. "If I take on a mission and I get killed or captured, that's part of the job description, but I don't think that's what you or Rafa had in mind when we first talked." He paused and then added, "And frankly, I should have known better myself."

She looked him square in the eyes. "Look, KJ, Rafa and I are grown-ups. We are practicing lawyers, not kids. We knew the risks, but we also knew the rewards for the billions of animals on the planet, if this campaign is even partially successful. I can't speak for him, but I'm in and I'm staying in—understand?" She leaned slightly in his direction. Her palms were flat on the table, her long, slim fingers spread wide apart. She was firmly entrenched. The steel in her voice was the same steel that had persuaded judges and juries alike to come down hard on environmentally irresponsible logging and mining companies, forestry giants and multi-national oil corporations in supernatural British Columbia. She was dead serious, KJ knew, and there was no use trying to talk her out of it, high risk or not.

"Ok, counselor," he said. "I just thought that I might have gotten you into something you hadn't bargained for." Her gaze did not falter. "Not that you aren't extraordinarily capable of handling anything that life has to throw at you."

"You got that right, soldier. And don't ever forget it!" she said with exaggerated bravado as she curled her fingers into fists. The Priv in her bag rang. She put the phone to her ear and handed it to KJ. "It's for you."

"Me? Who would even know that I am here?" he asked suspiciously, taking the phone.

"Hey, I'm still in too!" Rafa said, on the secure line. "And don't try to talk me out of it either!"

"What? Rafa?"

"You heard me, KJ," Rafa boomed. "You know me and Kiara are grown-ups. Practicing lawyers, not kids. We know the risks, but we also know the rewards for the billions of animals on the planet if this campaign is even partially successful!" Kiara's words verbatim.

"All right you two, how did you manage this?" asked KJ incredulously, trying unsuccessfully to suppress a smile.

"No big deal," replied Kiara. "Rafa just remotely turned on the microphone in the Priv after I texted him that you might try something like this."

KJ's eyebrows raised. "Saves you the trouble of giving Rafa the same speech, right Rafa?" she said smiling her dazzling white smile.

"Right you are, madam attorney!" Rafa said on the speaker phone. "Now let's get a move on with the campaign!"

CHAPTER 71

Leverage

Inaara's encrypted email to KJ included a file with names, photos and detailed contact information including private email addresses, home, office and cell numbers of two-hundred politicians, judges, police chiefs, high ranking military officers, senior bureaucrats and top-level security officials including, but not limited to, the Director of the FBI. These officials were the recipients of mink coats, *gratis* from MBM, Inaara wrote, taking the opportunity to use her newly acquired word. Not exactly PETA supporters to begin with, the donees would be more likely to resist the relentless barrage of negative press that the disruptive, anti-business groups were always manufacturing. The stunning fur coats were, in effect, their own argument for MBM-style mink ranching. Sure, once in a while some animal rights dork would go undercover at MBM and film a mink getting its head bashed in for biting one of the workers. That biting part was conveniently edited out, of course. There was no shortage of YouTube clips showing mink being electrocuted. The gruesome process involved the insertion of a metal clamp in the mink's mouth and an electric prod shoved up its ass. When the power was tuned on the mink's body completed the circuit and voila, fried mink with the coat intact! If the prod slipped out the process had to be repeated a few more times. Sometimes, even after two or three zaps, one of the damned things would be still writhing and bouncing around like a fish out of water. It would be smashed in the head with a baseball bat by one of the workers to put it out of its misery.

One of those clips would go viral in about five seconds and immediately spark an investigation by the state attorney general into animal cruelty at the facility. There would be some critical newspaper articles. Talk of criminal charges would be bandied about. The workers in question would of course, be fired. MBM would claim that incidents like that were one-off, that a couple of nut cases slipped through the farm's rigorous practice of hiring only caring workers. New policies and procedures would be promised. The state AG's wife or girlfriend, mistress or whatever would have already been draped in one of MBM's gorgeous mink coats, which meant the AG would be inclined to accept the company's story at face value. Prosecutorial discretion would be exercised and charges dropped. That would be the end of the matter, as the decision to prosecute or not is not reviewable by any court of law.

That is how the "coat operation" worked, Inaara wrote.

And apparently another "slush fund" of several millions of dollars was used for "some kind of payoffs," but Inaara was not clear where the money was kept or who it went to, as it did not seem to show up on the books. Dom had promised to fill her in later. She signed off with, "that's it 4 now." Her email was routed through the TOR network so it bounced off of at least six anonymous nodes before reaching Rafa's inbox, where it would be triple scanned for viruses and then re-routed to KJ's Z-30. Her list could prove to be useful to Pearce, as he knew full well that any successful campaign in history always involved multiple levels of leverage from brute force to political, economic or diplomatic pressure.

"Rafa, can you collate the information and put it into a useful database."

Rafa responded he'd done that adding that his database was "as secure as Fort Knox, digitally speaking of course."

Pearce asked Kiara how many laws they would break by using that information to anonymously persuade the recipients of the coats to actually do their jobs and follow the law. She was a precise as possible. "That's hard to say. Many politicians have been co-opted into passing legislation that favors the farm and agribusiness, so technically they are *following the laws on the books*. And," she added, tapping a printout from Westlaw, "the police and other enforcement agencies are too."

Pearce rephrased his question. "In that case, what laws would we be breaking by persuading politicians to pass different legislation?"

"That depends on the type of persuasion you use," she replied. "If it is along the lines of *change the law or we'll expose you on the net*, that could be categorized as blackmail, extortion, tampering with a public official and probably more."

"The list is growing all the time," KJ dryly commented. "Maybe we'll make the top ten, someday."

She smiled. "I think we may already be there."

"In that case." He paused, reveling in the possible disruption. "Can you draft a letter to Congressman Al Waxman." Waxman chaired the House Committee on Agriculture. "Maybe suggest he might be favorably disposed toward taking a somewhat tougher stand against animal cruelty on factory farms."

"Can do," she said.

"What's his home state, KJ?" Rafa asked.

Pearce checked the list. "New Hampshire. Currently ranked in the bottom five states in the U.S. for farm productivity and output."

Kiara said Waxman was, "Perfect. He'll have the least amount of local pressure to back off on farm reforms."

"Didn't stop him from taking multiple mink coats," pointed out Rafa.

"Multiple coats?"

Rafa said he'd been given three mink coats. "That was the most any one person got."

"But why three?" queried Kiara.

"One for his dutiful wife, Kathleen, of twenty-four years," Rafa responded. "So obviously he's a caring husband." She'd campaigned with him every election since he got into office over two decades ago. She never missed even one.

"Okay, that's the first one," Kiara said. "How about number two?"

"He pays so his mistress can live in high style, in a forty-six-story high rise in the West D.C. She got a jet black fur coat—very rare I understand."

"Let me guess," Kiara said, "his executive secretary got the last one?"

"No."

"Administrative assistant?"

Rafa was having fun. "No."

"Daughter's soccer coach?"

"No."

"I give up."

"His personal trainer. Apparently, Waxman works out three times a week. He must need to stay fit to keep up with the ladies."

Kiara rolled her eyes. "Of course." Her look of disgust mirrored that of Ruby Burdenny's.

"Hey, you two," KJ gently chided. "We're not here to judge. We just want to *encourage* Waxman to adopt a more enlightened view on farmed animals from a legislative point of view."

Kiara got up and headed into the kitchen. "Anyone want a matcha?"

KJ and Rafa said yes, Rafa adding, "With raw organic sugar—shaken not stirred."

"Sure thing, Mr. Bond," Kiara said, turning on the stove. "Will *M* be joining us for high tea?" She placed matcha leaves into a strainer and lowered it into the hot water.

"I doubt it, but I'm sure KJ could use a few of *Q*'s gadgets."

"Sometimes the pen is mightier than the sword, Rafa," KJ observed, then moved on. "Kiara's demand letter to the good senator will mark the start of part two of our campaign." He thanked Kiara for the tea, served in a Contigo mug he'd given her. It would stay warm for hours.

"What's the general drift of Part II?" asked Rafa, gingerly taking the steaming mug of green tea from Kiara and blowing over the rim to cool it down.

"I'll let K fill you in, Rafa," said KJ, motioning to Kiara as if he were the magician and she the drop dead gorgeous assistant about to take the stage, so he could work his sleight of hand in the background. He reiterated that they wanted to appeal to the base instincts of the donees of the mink coats, starting with Senator Waxman.

"Fear and greed," Rafa said.

Kiara agreed. "Precisely."

"These guys can afford to buy the mink coats, but why should they when they can get them for free?" Pearce said.

"Okay, that's the element of greed," said Rafa, sipping his tea. "And I can guess the fear part, but can you elaborate?"

Kiara did. "The one thing every politician and senior official fears most is not getting reelected." She started pacing two steps to one side then two steps back, unconsciously reverting to type—now more like a litigator trying to turn the jury than a magical assistant attempting to distract an audience. "Just the thought of the unsavory publicity, not to mention the potential for a messy divorce, should throw the fear of God into most of them," she explained. "So rather than come clean, we are hoping they just do what they normally do and slant the legislation in a different direction."

"Just like they do with every lobby group," Pearce added, "which is holding their purse strings."

"Ever see *Charlie's Wilson's War* with Tom Hanks and Julia Roberts?" she asked. "Great movie!" he replied. "Politics on *the Hill* is all about horse trading, to use a fittingly derogatory term. These guys are basically amoral. They sponsor and vote for legislation because they are catering to their own lobby group or paying back a favor to someone else's."

"We're the lobby group for good," Rafa said. "Advocating on the side of animals instead of agribusiness."

"That's a perfect way of framing it." KJ raised his tea for a toast.

"To putting animal welfare ahead of corporate greed!" Kiara said as the three friends clinked their Contigo mugs.

CHAPTER 72

Doing the Right Thing

The letter was like any of the hundreds of letters the House Committee on Agriculture received every business day. Established in 1820, the powerful committee had by way of the Legislative Reorganization Act of 1946, jurisdiction over "matters related to agriculture," specifically including:

"2. Agriculture generally; 3. Agricultural production and marketing and stabilization of prices of agricultural products and commodities (not including distribution outside of the United States); 4. Animal industry and diseases of animals; 5. Dairy industry; 6. Inspection of livestock, poultry, meat products, and seafood and seafood products; 7. Human nutrition and home economics."

Unfortunately, like many committees and other so-called *governing bodies,* the House Committee on Agriculture was little more than a shill for the U.S. agribusiness lobby, a powerful lobby indeed. Most bills introduced by HCA were essentially written by the lawyers for the farm and dairy lobbies, under the pretense of being "in the national interest of food security."

The junior secretary charged with sorting the mail was paying attention and placed the "Personal and Confidential" letter in the confidential stack, to be reviewed by her supervisor.

"Only one confidential today, Cassiday?" Steven Weathers was the Committee's senior administrative supervisor.

"That's it," said Cass Leyland, a bright-twenty-something black woman who had worked her ass off on the congressman's last election campaign and was rewarded with this reasonably well-paying job.

"Anything suspicious about it?"

"Nope. I ran it through the scanner for foreign substances and it came back NIL, same on the x-ray, so as far as I can tell, it's just a plain, old letter."

He nodded and said he'd drop it on Congressman Waxman's desk over the lunch hour.

When Al Waxman returned at 2:15 p.m. after an exhilarating romp in the hay with his twenty-six-year-old mistress, he sat at his desk, pleasantly tired but enormously pleased with himself. His performance was definitely an A-plus. Damned if he couldn't still keep a filly like Eugenie satisfied even though he was more than twice her age. He absently reached for the gold embossed letter opener on his desk to slit open the single, white envelope addressed to him as:

"Chairman of the Agriculture Committee, Personal & Confidential, For the Eyes Only of the Chairman."

He thought that might be overkill, but began reading.

July 27, 2015
"Dear Congressman Waxman: We certainly hope that your wife and your two girlfriends are enjoying the mink coats."

His blood froze. But his eyes remained involuntarily glued to the letter.

"Mink is such a gorgeous fur, don't you think? I am sure that most mink would agree, but we suspect that they would far prefer to keep it on their own backs. However, what is done is done. Those hundred-and-twenty-odd mink that were cruelly raised and then brutally slaughtered to provide the three coats for your wife and lady friends are now dead and gone. Nothing we can say or do can bring them back nor retroactively eradicate the suffering they endured during their short, miserable lives. The next best thing is to try to alleviate the suffering that other mink and farmed animals are currently experiencing and will continue to experience for the foreseeable future. In that regard, there is a Bill in the preliminary stages in the House called HR-279, A Bill to Amend the Farm Practices Act, sponsored by Congressman Hank McCoy of Wyoming. That bill would see the plight of farm animals across the U.S. worsened by a large measure.

"The changes would include allowing smaller pens and crates, easing of restrictions on the usage of antibiotics in cattle and chicken feed, removal of any type of health or safety conditions for the transport of live farm animals to the slaughter house and finally, repeal of the somewhat humane slaughter methods now in use in favor of less expensive methods such as bludgeoning, stabbing, hacking, spearing or crushing. It would shave off a few cents a pound at the supermarket to be sure, but at what cost to the millions of farm animals? We feel that this is a step in the wrong direction, so we want you to call in some markers and make sure that this Bill never sees the light of day. In addition, we want you to sponsor your own Bill, to be called The Best Farm Practices Amendment Act, a copy of which is attached to this letter. We think that the BFPA Act will be a small step in the right direction, namely recognizing that farmed animals are living, sentient beings who experience fear, pain and suffering just as your dog Monty does."

"How the hell do they know my dog's name?" Waxman demanded, unaware he was talking to a letter.

"Congressman, we feel that you are a skilled and able politician, so we are confident that you can have this Bill passed without significant amendments, whereby its effect would be watered down. Once these two things are accomplished, you will never see nor hear from us again. Honest, you have our word, sworn on the backs of those hundred-and-twenty dead mink. However, if you fail to deliver, your name will be mud, not only with your wife, mistress and personal trainer, but in the media. Doubtless you will be ousted from office and likely prosecuted for taking bribes. That would not be a pretty sight."

The Chairman hunched over the desk, necktie undone, the back of his Kingsman & Turner, double cuff, cotton-twill white shirt drenched with sweat. His long-time staff assistant, Petra, knocked on his door and gingerly stepped in to ask if he wanted a freshly brewed coffee. This was a time-honored after-lunch ritual between them to which he always agreed. To her utter disbelief, he shook his head no and asked her to shut the door behind her. With a herculean effort, he turned to page two.

"Now, Congressman, by this point you are probably sweating bullets."

"What are you watching me you prick?" he muttered, quickly glancing around his office, then forcing his eyes back on the page.

"You might even be thinking about picking up the phone and calling your friend, John Hancock at the Bureau or maybe the D.C. police."

"How the fuck could they possibly know about his brother-in-law, John?"

"Rest assured, Mr. Chairman, that this course of action is a complete waste of time and will only precipitate your political and personal demise sooner than later. This letter is written on paper that can be purchased in any of a hundred thousand stores in the country. There is no fingerprint or scintilla of DNA on it or the envelope. The typeset is universal and the printer a name brand which sells in the seven figures a year. The postmark is from Oregon, a letter anonymously dropped into a mailbox just like millions every day. In short there is nothing for the authorities to investigate or trace, so your plea for assistance will be in vain. On the other hand, you can do the right thing and for once in your unremarkable political career sponsor a piece of legislation that will do some good for hundreds of millions of your fellow creatures on the planet. Who knows, maybe other countries will be inspired and follow suit! The choice is yours, Congressman. We sincerely hope that you make the right one.

Yours truly,
Friends of Farmed Animals Everywhere

PS: To indicate your acceptance of our proposition, just visit your Facebook page and post a message which contains the words 'right choice' somewhere in the text. If that doesn't appear by this Friday, we'll assume you have made the wrong choice and the chips will fall where they may."

Waxman was overcome by exhaustion. He felt like he'd run a marathon—no, not even a marathon, a goddamned Iron Man triathlon. He rubbed his temples and rocked back in his chair. "How the fuck does a day start off so good, hit the zenith over the lunch hour and then turn to pure shit by 2:30?"

Life can turn on a dime, congressman, for better *or worse.*

CHAPTER 73

You've Got Mail

And speaking of *worse*, sixty-three similarly worded letters were simultaneously mailed to other U.S. senators and congressmen across the country. Like Waxman, these mink coat donees were not the meek and mild types. They had been carefully selected by the *Dreaded D's* because they were powerful, influential men who knew how to win friends and influence people. They had definitely come through for MBM on more than one occasion, delaying or outright quashing investigations and keeping farm-restrictive legislation off the books. Now, courtesy of Pearce and company, their savvy and political clout could be put to good use. To his surprise, Chairman Waxman would find a lot more cooperation and understanding than he would have otherwise expected among his peers.

"Who do you think will spill the beans first?" asked Rafa as he catalogued the last letter in his encrypted flash drive.

"Don't think any will," KJ said.

"Ditto," said Kiara. "After all, they have nothing to lose, when you think about it. If they play ball and we disappear from their lives they will have managed to dodge a bullet.

"If we renege on our promise and come back for more concessions, it's no skin off their hides because they should have all gone down in the first place," KJ said. "I'm sure that they're used to being double-crossed. I would imagine that it's a way of life on *the Hill*."

"So," Rafa continued as he shut down the *Alien*. "We're making it easy for them to cooperate and virtually disastrous for them to go public so to speak."

"That's about it," Kiara said, somewhat cheerfully. "Take the carrot or get whacked with the stick. It's a no-brainer, really."

"Now let's get cracking on those Facebook pages."

While the three of them divided up the fifty-two other Facebook pages to search, Senator Marvin Zodd was on the phone to his lawyer in Austin, Texas. The good ole boy was noticeably shaken by the anonymous letter and while he would not consider calling the cops (their internal security leaked like a sieve—he knew first-hand as his cousin was the Austin police commissioner), his long-time attorney, Charlie Penner, had gotten him out of a good many jams—this kind and even worse, throughout his political career. It was why he was still in office.

"Yeah Charlie, I know it's late, but it's an emergency. You gotta come over here right away, please!"

"But Marv, it's the wife's birthday and I promised…"

"This can't wait, Charlie," insisted the senator, cutting him off.

"I absolutely hear you Marv, but …"

"Are you actually hearing me, Penner?" Zodd shouted. "Goddamned it, I said it's a fucking emergency!"

The anger, not to mention panic, in the senator's voice caused Charlie to capitulate—consequences with the missus be damned. "Okay, okay I'm on my way Marv." The line went dead on Zodd's side. No "thanks for doing this off hours." No acknowledgement, not even a "good bye."

"Hey Olivia." Charlie looked forlornly as his wife. "Come sit here for a minute will you."

"What is it, hon? You look worried." Clad in super-faded *Pilcro* jeans and her favorite *Frame* linen t-shirt, she padded over in her bare feet. He had to think fast. A few seconds of silence passed. Olivia took his hands and threaded her fingers through his. "What's wrong?" No answer. "Come on, spill it," she prodded. Inexplicably, she still loved the conniving, amoral, heartless shyster after eighteen years of marriage and two kids. He really couldn't believe his good luck. That she hadn't seen through his "good provider and father" façade after all this time was truly a miracle for which he would be eternally grateful. Suddenly it came to him.

"I've got good news and bad news," he said, their hands firmly entwined.

She was looking apprehensive. "What's the bad news?"

"I've got to go over to Marv's house right now."

"Marv Zodd? The senator?" she queried.

"Yeah," he replied, "the one and only." "But right now? It's almost nine p.m."

"I told Marv that, Olivia, but he says it's literally life and death," he explained earnestly, embellishing as much as possible.

She looked at him, her features forming into a frown. "But what can you really do for him at this hour of night, Charles?" She always called him Charles when she was pissed off or thoroughly disappointed. The former condition seemed more likely of the two with every passing second.

"Not much," he reluctantly conceded. "Then just cancel and tell him you'll see him first thing tomorrow!" she said encouragingly.

"No can do, hon," he retorted. "He's a major client and his political ties are probably keeping six or seven of our intermediate attorneys busy full time and billing the government like crazy," he explained, this time truthfully. He was a senior Partner at Penner Jackson Foley LLP.

"But it's my birthday," she pleaded. "You know, it's traumatic for a girl to no longer be a *thirty-something.*"

"Hey babe, don't I know the feeling," Charlie said. "When I hit the big five oh last year I was devastated!"

She looked at him, her full, Botoxed lips pouting. "But if I recall correctly your then thirty-nine-year-old wife gave you the night of your life to ease your transition into becoming ancient." She looked him pleading *and* teasing. "Am I right or am I right?"

"Well, fifty is not exactly *ancient.*" He remembered that night in the sack, the silk lingerie, the champagne—she had even gotten a *Brazilian* for him. She really outdid herself and then some. "As usual, you are *right as rain,* Olivia. That's why I've got some good news too!" He hoped like hell this would work.

"I'm listening." This had better be good.

"You know that spanking brand new, white Audi A-4 convertible you've been eyeing on the lot at CWL Auto?"

"The one with the black leather interior and rear spoiler?" She was all ears. "And the cool mag wheels?"

"The very one," he said. A pregnant pause ensued.

"Well?"

"I've bought it for your birthday!"

"No way!" she shouted, eyes wide as saucers. "Really?"

"Way and really!" he replied matching her excitement level. She had been subtly dropping hints about the fifty-five-thousand-dollar snow-white beauty for the past several weeks. She hugged him and roughly threw him on the couch imminently ready to go down on him, but he had to restrain her. "When I get back, I promise, we'll continue," he said re-zipping his pants.

"Well you better make it fast," she said. "You know, a girl of my advanced age can't stay horny forever!"

"Just call me *the Flash,*" he said, grabbing his briefcase and heading out the front door of their expensive suburban West Austin home. As he got into his Mercedes 450 SEL and hit the pushbutton starter, he dictated a memo into his Samsung.

"Call CWL Auto first thing in the morning." He was hoping like hell the dealership hadn't already sold the damned thing, as he sped into the night toward the senator's mansion in Tarrytown.

CHAPTER 74

When Hell Freezes Over

Like many young boys, KJ idolized his dad. In addition to more or less nonstop Aikido training, Pearce and Commander Leonard Joseph Ares Pearce were inseparable when the commander was home. With no mom in the house, his father made his only son priority one, planning hiking, camping, fishing and hunting trips aplenty across the vast expanse of Canada and the U.S., whenever possible. Len occasionally brought along his military buddies, who added a learning dimension to the outings. A ranger scout showed KJ the secrets of finding a trail in a rainstorm. A decorated marksman revealed the tricks of long-distance shooting. Len's special forces survivalist pal demonstrated how they could "live off the land" when they had little to no supplies. Sometimes the guys brought their sons and daughters along, which made it extra fun for the younger Pearce.

However, one day when he was eleven, father and son were on a long hike in Banff National Park when Len decided that it was time to show his son how to trap and skin a rabbit. He carefully explained how to make the snare and then had KJ build it. The two took off for a hike and would check the trap when they returned to their camp. Sure enough, a few hours later, a beautiful white and grey cottontail rabbit had been caught in the snare. KJ was amazed at its boundless energy and vitality, as it scurried to and fro in the makeshift trap, a simple crate with wooden slats held up by a stick. A piece of apple had been tied to the stick and when the rabbit tried to make off with the apple, the string pulled the stick out and the crate fell down, imprisoning the rabbit. For a split second, KJ and the rabbit made eye contact—the connection was fleeting but extraordinary. It was as if he could feel, or maybe sense would be the better term, the rabbit's *chi*, its life force, and probably vice versa, but that part he would never know for certain.

"Now watch and learn," said his dad, as he pulled his gloves

276

on and reached under the trap to grab the rabbit by its hind legs. With practiced precision, the elder Pearce pulled the rabbit out and swung it by its hind legs smashing its head into a tree, immediately rendering it unconscious. KJ gasped. His father set the limp creature on its stomach and pressed down on its back while placing his other hand around the rabbit's neck. He pressed his thumb into the back of the rabbit's neck and wrapped his fingers around its *chin* area. In one swift motion, he pulled up hard while pressing on its back. A sharp cracking sound ensued signaling that the creature's neck was broken.

Chinning, as this method is called, is fast and silent. It doesn't need any equipment or special conditions. It is the most discrete and 'clean' method. It is also the fastest, once mastered—and Leonard had mastered it cold. KJ, however, was in a state of shock. One-minute this beautiful, vital creature was in existence as part of this intricate eco-system that was spread over six-thousand square kilometers of Banff National Park and the next, it was a dead heap. Oblivious to KJ's emotions, Leonard proceeded to skin the rabbit before his son's eyes, a necessary survival skill, in his mind, now being venerably passed on from father to son as it had been done for eons. His dad pulled out his K-Bar knife and cut a notch into the rabbit's hide. He peeled the rabbit's fur towards its rear. The bottom three-quarters came off intact like a fur sock. He pulled it over the rabbit's hind feet and then pulled the remaining fur from the top side of the cut over the rabbit's head. This left the rabbit without its fur, except for its feet. He cracked the joints in each leg and cut the legs off with the K-Bar, slipping the remaining fur off. Next, he gutted the rabbit, slitting it at the pelvis and sliding the K-Bar up its belly to its throat. He gingerly pulled out the kidneys and heart. Finally, he sliced off the two back legs, shoulders and saddle and gathered them up into a plastic container to be cooked over an open fire later that night—*a rare delicacy* for the hunters.

"That's going to make a tasty stew tonight, Ken," his dad promised, still not looking up as he gathered the pieces of meat which were a rabbit a few short minutes ago. Engrossed in the process, he didn't notice KJ was frozen stiff on his knees, tears streaming down his cheeks, speechless.

"Whoa what's wrong?" He'd finally noticed his son's dramatic reaction and that no words could escape his mouth. Leonard was, of course, concerned, but as men are accustomed to doing, he downplayed the situation. He explained to KJ that it was the rabbit's time to die and they, or rather he, had been chosen to accomplish the task. That didn't seem to register, so Leonard went on to point out that the rabbit's death was *humane* (KJ would come to utterly despise that word), in that it was both quick and painless. Still nothing. Tears continued to stream down KJ's cheeks. The father put his arm around his son's shoulders and hugged him, trying to figure out what the hell the problem was. He had learned this skill from *his* dad when he was only ten and he didn't think anything of it. Animals are there to be hunted and killed for the benefit of humans. That was the food chain, like it or lump it. He didn't set it up.

"Son, that's just the way the world works," he said, trying to be as calm and soothing as possible, without turning his son into a sissy. After all, real men hunt and his son was damned well going to become a real man someday. He would personally see to it. Finally, after what seemed like an eternity a sobbing KJ said, "But, Dad, why did you have to kill it? You could have let it go. We have plenty of food."

"I had to show you how it's done, son," Leonard responded, still not understanding his son's reaction. "You can't learn that just out of book or a video. You know, someday that skill might just save your life."

KJ was thoroughly conflicted. His dad was absolutely everything to him—strong, kind, infallible and up till this minute, could do no wrong. Now, inexplicably, he had senselessly, in KJ's mind, killed a beautiful rabbit just to show him a hunting lesson. How could his dad do such a thing, and actually be proud of it—like it was some kind of accomplishment? His eleven-year-old mind simply could not reconcile the *cognitive dissonance*, as psychologists would call it, so he unconsciously compartmentalized the experience, locked the door and threw away the virtual key. The world was no longer as it seemed. People, even really good people like his dad, were, in the last analysis, just predators, not guardians as he had once believed. This just could not be—but it was. His blood ran cold. His eyes turned to ice.

"It's okay Ken, you'll get over it," said Leonard sympathetically, hugging his son, not noticing his frightful gaze. He got up and added a few more branches to the fire. "Now I am going to make you the best damned rabbit stew on the planet. I'm sure you'll want seconds after you try it," said Commander Pearce.

When hell freezes over, thought the eleven-year-old. He never touched the stew.

CHAPTER 75

Push Back

"What the fuck have you been smoking, Al?" asked Bud Abrams, CEO of Consolidated Agricultural Products Inc. ("CAP"), one of the biggest meat producers in the world. The anger in his voice was palpable even across two thousand miles and umpteen cell towers.

"Good morning to you too, Bud," said the chairman, trying to sound as cheerful as possible. This was the fourth such call he had received this morning and his ears were still burning. First it was Hover Cohen, the president of TMN Foods. He literally tore a strip off Waxman's hide and expressly threatened to use every ounce of the food giant's clout to personally turf him out of office if the Humane Farm Practices Amendment Bill was ever passed.

"You will be lucky if you can get elected as a dog catcher after I'm through with you, Al!" he promised.

"Well, fortunately I happen to like dogs, Hover," quipped the chairman, trying his best to appear jovial. "And at least I wouldn't have to put up with assholes like you," he added under his breath.

"What was that, Al?"

"Nothing, Hover, just mumbling to myself," said Waxman.

George Constopolous of the Associated Chicken Farmers of America hammered him mercilessly about the major layoffs and other economic hardships the farmers of this great country would suffer due to the increased production costs associated with larger chicken crates and less antibiotics in the feed. Constopolous grilled him mercilessly.

"Do you want to be personally responsible for putting thousands of small farmers out of business?"

Jesus, you'd swear that the bill was going to start World War Three. Not ten minutes after that call his receptionist put Randy Ewing of the Texas Cattlemen's Association through. He went ballistic over the "overly stringent, not to mention ridiculous" proposed regulations to make cattle transport safer and more humane for the millions of cows moved from ranches to slaughter houses every day. "They're going to be killed anyway! What possible difference would it make to them, you stupid moron?"

The chairman had felt it necessary to put Ewing in his place by firmly reminding him that "stupid moron" was a tautology. "Bud, it's not *that* bad," he said as he unclenched his jaw and stared out over the Potomac. "Times are changing and the industry's got to get on board before the train leaves the station."

"How the hell is that, Al?"

"Take a look at one of your biggest customers, Bud. None other than the ubiquitous symbol of America, the Golden Arches."

"Well what about them?" queried the CEO testily. "It's no secret that they are closing restaurants left and right, profits are down and they are getting lambasted on social media over the crap they serve. Look up "junk food" on WIKI and there is a picture of *The Arches.*"

"What's your point?"

"The point is that consumers want the animals that become their food treated right and if that doesn't happen, the food industry is going to take one hell of a shellacking!" Waxman said. "I've got report after report to prove that. Public opinions are being swayed, nope, manipulated by the animal rights nuts on a daily basis."

"Funny I haven't heard of any of those reports in Tennessee, Al," Abrams said.

"Well no offence, but your home state, indispensable as it may be to U.S. national food security, is not exactly on the cutting edge of public opinion," explained Waxman.

Abrams, a sixty-something, Harvard graduate with a Ph.D. in farm economics reluctantly conceded that point. But he assured Waxman that the animal rights movement was a passing fad, "just like hula-hoops and eight track stereos."

"I damned well hope that you are right, Bud." Waxman's tone was conciliatory. "But for now, this *fad* as you put it, is in full swing and we on the Committee are feeling the heat from the consumers." The "consumers" included *The Friends of Farmed Animals Everywhere*—something he neglected to mention. "Pressure's on to do something."

Bud dismissed that as "bullshit." He swore on his mother's grave that another passing fad would be the political careers of every fucking person on the Committee who voted in favor of that bill—and then he hung up.

"Son of a bitch," Waxman muttered not quite under his breath. "You'd think those dipshits own me the way they are mouthing off!" He was up for re-election in another year. At sixty-two, he wanted two more terms under his belt and then he could comfortably retire with about twenty-million dollars in surplus Political Action Committee funds, not to mention his fully indexed government pension which included Cadillac medical coverage. No fucking Obamacare for the Congress! Now those meddling asshole billionaires were making a point of interfering with his sworn duty to introduce and support fair and effective legislation for all Americans. He almost felt violated. Usually, the lobbyists just hinted or circuitously promised that good things *might just happen* if such-and-such legislation was looked upon favorably. All of a sudden someone's daughter with less than stellar grades would get accepted into Princeton or senator what's-his-name's son would be awarded that plum internship at Facebook ahead of fifteen better qualified candidates.

Occasionally, when that didn't work, the lobby boys would make indirect reference to someone who "didn't want to play ball" and by pure coincidence met with misfortune. "Remember Peter Bryer, that promising kid from upstate NY?" the fixer would ask. "Junior senator for … what was it, a year and a half before he forgot who buttered his bread." Pause. "What's he doing now? Running a sanitation truck in Jersey."

These guys outright threatened, promised, *even guaranteed* to bring him down—and hard, if he supported the HFPA Bill. Shit, he should have had his phone voice recorder on—maybe he could have blackmailed them into backing off. Yeah, blackmailing four billionaires—that's got a snowball's chance in hell of succeeding!

Better get the thinking cap on, Al, or your year is going to start looking worse than world oil prices, he instructed himself.

CHAPTER 76

Clash of the Titans

The thought of confronting his wife of twenty-four years, his mistress of two, and his personal trainer all at once and in the harsh glare of the media, no less, would be paralyzing to many, but to Al Waxman, chairman of the powerful Agricultural Committee it was just another challenge. And Alistair George Thomas Waxman *never* backed down from a challenge. After all, he was a resourceful and powerful man in his own right. He wouldn't be on the *Dreaded D's* coat list if he wasn't. Although not in the same financial league as his blustering callers, he was about as well connected as anyone on *the Hill* and, come to think of it, he had a bushel full of markers which he could call in at will. His first call was to his old buddy, Herb Gerstein, on the powerful Appropriations Committee, which regulated all of the expenditures of money by the government of the United States. After the appropriate amount of small talk, Al got down to business.

"Herb, I need to ask you for a favor."

"Name it," Gerstein said, knowing full well that this was not a request but the calling in of an outstanding marker. In politics, markers are sacrosanct. You don't honor them, you don't stay in office. It's that simple.

"My committee's been getting some serious heat over a proposed farm bill, which is gaining some traction with the U.S. consumer." To Gerstein's request for specificity he responded, "HR 291, the Humane Farm Practices Amendment Act."

"Yeah, I heard about that one," Herb said.

"You have?"

"Well that is one controversial piece of legislation, my friend. Why the hell did you sponsor it?"

"It's complicated."

"It usually is," Gerstein responded. "What can I do about it?"

"Well, you know the Agricultural Workers Wage Subsidy Act which is up for review next month?"

"Do I ever, my friend. That piece of garbage costs the taxpayers of our fair country a small fortune," he observed. "The agri-farmers pay the spics and wetbacks next to nothing and then they pick up close to twenty billion to *subsidize* their labor costs. I think only about five per cent of that ever trickles down to the workers."

"That part of the Act doesn't really trouble me Herb," said Waxman. "As far as I'm concerned, those *undocumented workers* are damned lucky to have any job in this country, regardless of the wage."

"You've got a good point there," conceded Gerstein readily.

"After all, nobody put a gun to their heads to come here, did they?"

Gerstein didn't bother to answer the senator's rhetorical question.

"So," said Waxman, "what I need is an amendment reducing the subsidy for meat producers—cattle, pigs and chickens. Then move the cost savings over to the crop farmers."

"Makes a certain amount of sense," Gerstein observed. "They've been getting killed with the severe droughts plaguing the south and California over the past four or five years."

"Exactly," replied Waxman.

"But you know, that's going to start a war between the growers and the meat producers, don't you?"

"I'm banking on it," said the senator.

"I assume somebody on the meat producing side has put that burr under your saddle? Couldn't be over the HFPA Bill, could it?" Herb asked. It didn't take a rocket scientist to put two and two together and Herb Gerstein was as smart as they had on *the Hill*.

"Maybe," said Waxman. "Can you manage that amendment?"

Herb took a minute to make some mental calculations. "Can't promise anything but let me see what I can do for you." Coming from Herb, that was a virtual lock.

"I owe you one Herb."

"No, I still owe you two," corrected the Vice-Chair. "But who's counting, right?"

CHAPTER 77

Lending a Helping Hand

"They're going to do what?" shouted Bud Abrams, incredulous. "Cut the worker subsidy to zilch!" said his operations manager, Conrad Zitko, a hard-nosed fifty-two-year-old plugger who had worked his way up the company ladder over twenty-seven years. "The Ag Workers Subsidy Bill is being overhauled to pass almost all of *our* subsidies over to the crop growers."

"Lemmee see that," said Abrams snatching the fax out of Zitko's hand. The Chief Executive Officer of CAP was apoplectic with rage upon reading the missive. With over twenty-six thousand employees on staff, that wage subsidy was damned near a guarantee that the huge company would be profitable. Without it, making a buck year-in-year-out, as the company had done since the subsidy bill was passed, would become a crap shoot. As every CEO knows, the 'competition mantra' sounds good until you actually have to compete. "Where the hell did you get this from?"

"It says here that it is addressed to Harley Vanes of the Ways & Means Committee, from Herb Gerstein of Appropriations. And it says Private and Confidential, too."

"Yeah, I know that, boss, but look closely at the fax number that it was sent to," Conrad said pointing to the header. "See, 202-225-2161—that's the fax number of Springfield Rose LLP, our registered lobbyist in D.C. The W & M's Committee's own fax number on the header is 202-225-2171, just one keystroke off."

"So some clerk mistyped the fax cover sheet and sent our guys the memo?"

"Looks like it, boss," Zitko replied "Soon as Springfield got it, the head honcho there, Jonathan Rose I think, called me up and sent it over here, rather than returning it to the Ag Committee."

"Remind me to send those boys a bonus, Conrad," said the CEO. "Now get my Rolodex, I need to call a meeting of the meat producers and processors pronto! We're sure as hell not going to take this double-cross bent over!"

In point of fact, the Appropriations Committee had sent out no such memo. Pearce had Waxman's office bugged so he was well aware of his request to Gerstein. Rafa copied the Appropriations Committee's government logo and letterhead with a simple *cut and paste* from their website, signed the memo and sent it out to Springfield Rose LLP via computer fax on a proxy server which mimicked the Committee's fax number. Thus, to the recipient, it *appeared* to have originated from the Appropriations Committee's office. Pearce was counting on the ethics (or rather lack thereof) of the lobby firm to send the memo to their client rather than return it to the Appropriations Committee, as being received in error. If questioned, the principals of Springfield Rose LLP would of course claim to never have seen the memo.

Forewarned is forearmed, as the old saying goes, so the meat producers would be getting ready to throw everything but the kitchen sink into fighting the wage subsidy re-distribution amendment to the Agricultural Farm Workers Subsidy Act, rather than wasting their time with the HFPA Bill. The former bill would have at least ten times more negative impact on the meat producers, as the wage subsidy was money out of their pockets which simply could not be recovered. The much smaller hit that would result from the passage of the Humane Farm Practices Amendment Bill could be passed along to the consumers at the retail level as "increased cost due to more government red tape."

To stir the pot further, Rafa leaked a copy of the proposed redistribution memo to several corn, soybean and wheat grower organizations, to make sure that they would be getting prepared to do battle to keep the increased subsidies. While all of these groups were technically part of the agricultural production system under auspices of the federal department known as the U.S.D.A., driving a wedge between the relatively "animal friendly" growers and the "animal unfriendly" meat producers would put some powerful interests on the side of animals, albeit not for any ethical reasons. However, oftentimes economic or political self-interest of powerful people or groups creates changes in society which can result in unexpected social or political benefit to the disadvantaged.

Ending slavery in the U.S. was a classic example. Arguably the North used the issue of slavery to vilify and eventually to go to war with the South with the ultimate goal of preserving the Union. As Abraham Lincoln famously stated in his 1862 letter to Horace Greeley, the editor of the New York Tribune: "I would save the Union. I would save it the shortest way under the Constitution. .... *My paramount object in this struggle is to save the Union, and is not either to save or to destroy slavery*. If I could save the Union without freeing *any* slave I would do it, and if I could save it by freeing *all* the slaves I would do it; and if I could save it by freeing some and leaving others alone I would also do that. What I do about slavery, and the colored race, I do because I believe it helps to save the Union; (emphasis mine)"

The positive spinoff *was* the abolition of slavery in America formalized in law by the Thirteenth Amendment to the U.S. Constitution of 1865.[4]

For his part, Pearce was simply following the time-honored practice known as *divide and conquer.* The U.S. government has used this strategy successfully in the Middle East and other parts of the world for many years, fueling long-standing rivalries between local factions and ethnic groups to prevent them from uniting against U.S. interests. If he could get the meat producers and the crop growers at each other's throats, the Humane Farm Practices Amendment Act might just slide into law without further ado.

---

4   Slavery was abolished *except* as punishment for a crime. This turned out to be a loophole you could drive a truck through. Since many of the impoverished state governments of the South could not afford penitentiaries, they leased out tens of thousands of prisoners to work in coal mines, lumber camps, railroads, quarries and farm plantations. The governments maximized their profits by foisting the responsibility for food, clothing, shelter and medical care on the lessee companies, with little or no oversight. This resulted in possibly the most inhumane labor system that existed in the U.S. until 1927 when the last state, Alabama, abolished this practice. In keeping with the legislated bigotry, most of those "leased convicts" were black.

CHAPTER 78

The Last Piece

Soon the proverbial fur would be flying in the media about the huge squabble within the agricultural sector in the U.S. The press was still having a field day with the hunting fiasco in Canada and the FBI publicly linked it to the *terrorist strike* on MMB Colorado. The mainstream media couldn't believe their good luck. This stuff was manna from heaven to cash-strapped news outlets whose circulation was in continuous freefall courtesy of the World Wide Web—a service that the vast majority of its billions of users had come to regard as a free utility.

Pearce asked Kiara and Rafa out to *Animal Farm* for a strategy session. Kiara's big trial was still in recess and Rafa always managed to juggle his computer law practice with the demands of KJ's campaign. Pearce felt that he owed them both big-time.

Kiara punched the code into the gate at the entrance of Pearce's leased acreage and the black Land Rover coasted through as the gate closed behind her. Paikea and Tamu appeared, to escort Kiara's vehicle to the residence. Looking at Paikea in full coat, hair perfectly quaffed and parted naturally between her huge brown eyes, Kiara marveled at how elegant she looked, prancing along beside the Rover. Like many women, and some men, come to think of it, Ms. Davies would die for that kind of hair—gorgeous cream color with no-tint, wash and wear and seemingly self-parting. Wow, she could save a bundle on hair salons—if only. Tamu, on the other side of the vehicle, was equally striking. A blue black at ninety-five pounds and thirty-one inches at the shoulders, he was way bigger than the breed standard.

Rafa arrived in his utilitarian, 2012 Honda Element and was also escorted by the hounds.

Floriana had ordered a giant pizza from Ocean Park Pizza but it was out of delivery range so she picked it up and pulled in behind the Element in her tricked-out Rabbit Wolfsburg. Floriana doubled as a dog groomer for Pearce for extra cash and was pleased to see her "clients" admired by Kiara and Rafa. She couldn't stay for dinner, as law school exams were looming. She wasn't privy to the campaign, so it was just as well. She evaded Tamu's usual attempts to get into her car for a ride and waived adieu, and set off down the driveway, with the Rabbit's top down, her strawberry blonde hair blowing in the wind. Once she was out of sight the three went inside. Rafa grabbed plates and cutlery from the kitchen cupboard, while KJ pulled out a bottle of Township VII "Black Dog 2013." It was a classic Bordeaux-style blend full of aromas of rich, ripe blackberries, black plums, cassis, brown sugar, leather and tobacco. Part of the gorgeous Fraser Valley, Langley was full of splendid wineries such as Township VII. Kiara carried in the three wine glasses in one hand and the twenty-four-inch, veggie-supreme in the other. As the three friends dug in, KJ provided his analysis of the campaign so far.

"First strike at the mink farm was nine out of ten," he said, setting down his wine glass.

"Why only nine?" Kiara asked. "Mink were sprung, no casualties taken and the place blown to smithereens. What am I missing?"

"The girl," Rafa said. "Inaara was a loose end."

"I remember you mentioning that at the restaurant, Kiara said, "but she's worked out unexpectedly well. You said so yourself." She finished her first slice of pizza.

"Rafa isn't wrong. We got lucky," KJ said. "It happens once and a while on a mission."

"Yeah, but there was no way we could have known that she was on the outs with her adopted family and that she was planning to run away," Rafa said.

"I agree, but to answer Kiara's question, that's why I said nine out of ten, not ten," KJ replied.

"How about the Great Bear Rainforest mission?" Kiara asked. "That one went off without a hitch."

Peace nodded agreement. "So far, close to a ten. No one's tracked back Rafa's messages on FLNRO's website and no one's got a clue where the RQ Shadow drone came from—or where it went." The partially dissembled drone was in the barn. It would take a lot more than a casual look inside the door to find it. "Needless to say, both governments are scouring their books to try to find recent large sales of the C-4, but there's so much of that stuff floating around, it's like looking for a needle in a haystack."

Kiara was direct. "Won't the profilers and security agencies conclude that these were special ops missions and eventually figure out that you were behind them?"

"That's very *unlikely*, but I suppose it is possible."

Rafa jumped in, naming numerous special forces units operating in the U.S., Canada, Israel, Britain and the rest of Europe, not to mention umpteen dozens of mercenary groups. Thousands of soldiers fell into that category.

"But you'd have to assume that any special forces operatives would not be still on active duty, right?" Kiara said.

Pearce wasn't sure. "I suppose that the authorities would search the recently retired or discharged lists and see what turns up."

"Still, that must be a pretty big list," Rafa said, "and even then, how far back do you look?"

"That's why I said *unlikely,* not impossible," KJ said. "Which is why I suggested that maybe you two should consider…"

"Don't even go there," they exclaimed in unison, cutting him off.

"That's already been settled and the appeal period has run out."

"Okay, okay," said KJ, "motion to reconsider is withdrawn."

"Good riddance to that motion for once and for all," said Rafa. "You got any more wine? That dog brand was damned fine vino!"

"There's a second bottle on the top cupboard above the sink on the left side," KJ said, then announced he was going to have another slice of pizza.

"I'll get it." Kiara scooted to the kitchen and looked around. "I could have sworn that there were two big pieces left."

KJ slapped his forehead. The hounds were no longer under the table looking for handouts. As any owner of this independent, headstrong breed knows, their proud motto is "lie, cheat and steal." Sure as hell, he spotted a perfectly curved, thick black tail excitedly wagging side to side in the far hallway. The rest of the dog was not visible. Around the other corner a cream-colored tail doing the same. The last two pieces of pizza had been expertly removed from the box without so much as a sound. KJ rounded the corner to see Tamu licking his chops in the hallway, no pizza to be seen, but a few olives on the floor. Ditto for Paikea, who was lying down with a half slice of tomato stuck to her front paw. Both dogs maintained a "who me?" expression, implying that the evidence must have been planted.

KJ threw up his hands and asked if anybody wanted dessert, hoping it was safely tucked away. They had apple pie and coffee without discussing business, then he continued his assessment which included engaging outsiders like Pearce's suppliers of military ordnance. This was an unavoidable necessity as he did not have direct access to such weaponry, no longer being a part of JTF2. Then, of course, there were the events such as the near search at Peace Arch Crossing and the appearance of Inaara Burdenny—both unplanned and unexpected. Both turned out well, but in any mission there was always the possibility that they wouldn't.

"How do you deal with that on a military mission?" asked Kiara.

KJ reflected for a minute, then replied that often times "loose ends" were terminated with extreme prejudice.

Kiara raised her eyebrows.

"Knocked off," explained Rafa.

"Oh," she said.

Other times they could be captured and held until the mission was over. In every case in which he was personally involved, JTF2 was operating in another country so they would invariably pick up and leave at the end of the mission. However, as the three of them lived in the Lower Mainland of British Columbia and were operating *inside* of North America, that was not an option. This part of the discussion prompted Rafa to suggest a further security measure for the three of them which he believed was achievable.

"I think that I can program apps for everyone's communications devices—computers, tablets and phones that will erase every trace of information which connects us to each other if they ever fall into the wrong hands."

"Can't the FBI or the NSA still retrieve information from devices after it's been erased?" Kiara asked.

"Not after I'm through with it," he said proudly. "I'll program something like CCleaner's 35 pass (Gutmann) overwrite so *no one* will be able to unscramble that mess of data, once the trigger is tripped."

Pearce asked how that happened.

"If there are more than three tries," answered Rafa, "*poof!* The trigger's tripped and everything on the phone is toast. Once the cops or security agencies get their hands on a communications device or computer their techs invariably start trying to get by the password by various standard means such as a dictionary, rainbow table, brute force or hybrid attack. Or," he continued, "if they know whose it is, they might try to hack into the owner's insecure storage, replay a cookie, session ID, Kerberos ticket or other resource that authenticates the user after the password authentication process."

Kiara rolled her eyes. "You lost me somewhere after rainbow table."

"Ditto," said Pearce, not exactly a computer slouch himself, but realizing that he was not on the same planet as Rafa when it came to such things.

"Sorry for the jargon, guys," Rafa apologized. "I meant to say that I'll clean up your devices and the peripheral items like storage and cookie saving and once someone tries to crack the password with more than three attempts, it's bye-bye to everything on the device for good."

"That way, if one of us is captured, the authorities will have to resort to beating the password out of that person, assuming that they were captured along with the device," said KJ.

"That's illegal though," Kiara pointed out, "under at least a dozen statutes."

"Tell that to the prisoners at GITMO," sighed Pearce. "Laws go out the window when the issue involves terrorism or other so-called threats to national security."

"Plenty of prisoners in supermax prisons in the U.S. can attest to that," Rafa added. "In any event, the extra security can't hurt."

"If you have the time to do it..." KJ said, to which Rafa said he'd make the time.

Kiara refilled everyone's coffee and mixed Baileys into hers, dropping onto the couch between the two hounds, who immediately checked her out for additional food items.

"I think we need to stir the pot a bit more," continued KJ. "We have a fierce internet discussion going over trophy hunting around the globe, and the MBM incident should shed some light on the factory farming practices—for furbearing animals at least."

"And now the meat producers and crop growers will be mixing it up in the public spotlight," added Rafa, sipping his coffee.

"What's next, an uprising on the nation's campuses?" Kiara asked, rhetorically.

"Absolutely brilliant suggestion K!" exclaimed Pearce. "We need to get a grass roots movement going in the schools—colleges and universities for starters." Students are generally idealistic and always looking for a reason to take on the establishment for sure, they all knew. "But how do we get them engaged on the side of animals," Kiara asked.

Rafa agreed. "Most aren't vegans or even vegetarians."

"But…" Pearce interjected. "A hell of a lot of them or their families are pet owners."

"We're listening," his co-conspirators said.

"How would you like it if your dog or cat was kidnapped off the street and sold to a university medical facility for experimentation?"

"I'd go ballistic." Rafa was thinking of his orange tabby, Madison.

"I'd haul the university into court and sue their ass off," K declared.

"Most pet owners agree, but in point of fact, they don't know where their pets have disappeared to," KJ said. "I've researched this. There are Class A and Class B animals used in medical experiments in North America. Class A are raised in labs for specific purposes, like being infected with hepatitis, HIV, cancer or other diseases, and Class B can come from pretty much anywhere, backyards or animal shelters, and can be used for anything. Unscrupulous individuals have been known to troll neighborhoods, kidnapping dogs and cats to sell to medical facilities as well. With cutbacks on grants and other funding, some universities and colleges are happy to turn a blind eye and buy the animals on the QT for peanuts—usually less than ten bucks a pop," Pearce said. "According to PETA, over one-hundred-million animals suffer and die in the U.S. every year."

"Holy shit! That many?" Rafa was aghast.

"That many. And in cruel chemical, drug, food and cosmetic tests, medical training exercises and experiments. Some include forcing mice to inhale toxic fumes, force-feeding pesticides to dogs and dripping corrosive chemicals into rabbit's eyes to see how long it take them to go blind."

"We're quoting PETA now, are we?" Kiara asked.

"Well, you have to get with the times right counselor?" replied KJ, the guy who had never heard of People for the Ethical Treatment of Animals just a short while back.

Rafa grabbed the report and skimmed it. "The animal the university infects with HIV, hepatitis C, polio, swine flu or other dangerous or deadly viruses could be yours or your neighbor's very own pet."

"Yes, it could be," agreed KJ, "but we're going to have to come up with a dramatic way to prove it to the students."

CHAPTER 79

George Regis University

The surgeon was cutting into the shepherd's gum with a scalpel when she noticed the black-clad apparition out of the corner of her eye. Her hand slipped and the scalpel sliced through her left surgical glove.

"Fu-uck!" she screamed at the top of her lungs, the scalpel clanking off the metal instruments tray. The male nurse, Mark, rushed over, still oblivious to the intruder. Blood poured out of a severed vein in the surgeon's left hand. The other nurse, Dannie, held her hands up to her mouth to stifle a scream. Pearce stood in a combat shooting crouch on the balls of his feet, knees slightly bent, the Glock pointed menacingly. He was poised to shoot. Wearing a balaclava, combat fatigues, flak jacket, boots, knapsack, gun—all black, only his ice-cold eyes were visible. Calmly, almost impassively, he surveyed the situation. The surgeon had almost passed out and was helped into a chair by the male nurse, who finally saw the intruder.

"Who the hell are you?"

Ignoring the question, Pearce demanded, "Where did the dogs come from?"

"What?" asked the male nurse.

"You heard me. Don't make me ask again!" Pearce warned. The male nurse shook his head indicating he didn't know.

"You," Pearce swung the Glock in the direction of Dannie. "Take your mask off! Hers too," pointing at the surgeon. Both complied.

"Where did the dogs come from?" The nurse stammered she didn't know, she only worked here and was "not in procurement."

Meanwhile the surgeon was coming out of shock. She asked the intruder why on earth it mattered where the dogs came from. "They're only three worthless mutts, out of the thousands the university medical faculty purchases every year for scientific testing and medical experimentation," she said. Kiara had read the university's animal procurement policies on its website and pursuant to the institution's own bylaws, Class B animals were to be purchased from a list of "approved breeders" at a specified price depending upon the type of animal. The bylaws mirrored the State's *Animal Testing and Medical Experimentation Act* which specifically prohibited the acquisition of any animals for such purposes from animal shelters, puppy mills, private individuals or anyone else.

Pearce continued, his voice implacable. "Well then, where did these three worthless mutts come from?" The surgeon shook her head. She didn't know and didn't care.

"Not a good enough answer," Pearce replied, "if you want to live out the remainder of the night," the Glock still pointing menacingly. That got Dannie's attention and she volunteered to look up the origin of the dogs on the medical department's system.

"Go ahead," Pearce said, waving her over to the computer terminal with the Glock. Under his cold stare, she fumbled with the computer keys and had to try the password several times, finally getting it right. Up came the "Animal Procurement Manifest" dated July 15, 2015 for George Regis University.

"Read it out loud," said Pearce, although he could plainly see it over her shoulder.

"The following animals are procured for scientific testing and medical experimentation:

Species	Breed	Price	Authorized Vendor
Canine	mixed	$35.00	Ronson's Kennels
Canine	Bassett	$50.00	Remington Farm
Feline	mixed	$25.00	Karnack's Cattery
Canine	Doberman	$50.00	Ronson's Kennels.
Feline	Tabby	$40.00	Murph's Cats R Us
Feline	Forest Cat	$35.00	Karnack's Cattery.
Cottontail	Rabbit	$20.00	Murph's Cats R Us

Mountain Cottontail	Rabbit	$20.00	Murph's Cats R Us
Canine	Chihuahua	$35.00	Ronson's Kennels
Feline	Dom. Shorthair	$25.00	Cats Rule

The list went on for several pages—and that was just for the month of July. "Why aren't these three dogs on that list?" Pearce recalled no mention of a German shepherd being called out.

"I don't know," replied Dannie, "but that's not possible. All animals are supposed to be listed as medical inventory."

Pearce stared at the surgeon. "I'm not going to ask this again. Where did these dogs come from?"

Arrogant by occupation, the forty-something surgeon told him that it was not her job to know such trivial details. She was here for important dental experimental work which would prove to be of immeasurable value to implant technology. Furthermore, if he didn't like her answers he could shove them up his ass. Pearce shot her in the thigh. She shrieked, causing the female nurse Dannie to jump to her feet, upsetting the keyboard and sending it crashing to the ground. In a moment of insanity, Mark rushed Pearce, who deftly side-stepped him, grabbed his right arm and swung him into a wall of glass shelves containing drugs and medical paraphernalia. The glass shattered and flew. Mark wound up on his behind, stunned and covered with cuts.

"The next stunt like that will be your last," Pearce warned. He swung the Glock back toward the surgeon. Dannie was applying a tourniquet to her thigh. Tears streamed down her face.

"As for you, the next one goes into your knee," Pearce warned. "The 180 grain, 10mm bullet from this gun will impact your knee at thirteen-hundred and fifty feet per second leaving nothing for your colleagues to operate on." He aimed the Glock.

"Stop! STOP! For God's sake don't shoot me again!" screamed the surgeon. "The drawer, the drawer," she pointed. "There's a paper manifest to account for the dogs in there."

"Get it," he ordered Dannie, who quickly retrieved the manifest from the drawer and handed it to Pearce. The black shepherd, the Wheaton mix and the Bassett were the first three on the document along with forty-seven more. The purchase price for the lot was $500 and it was marked "paid in cash." The vendor's name was "Generic Seller."

"Explain this!" commanded Pearce, "or you can kiss both knees good-bye right now."

The now highly compliant surgeon quickly explained that the one hundred animals allocated by law for experiments and research per month was not nearly enough. Too often animals unexpectedly died before a procedure was finished or an experiment was concluded. The research team had stumbled across Jack La Van, a retired dog catcher who had agreed to sell the university cats and dogs for ten bucks a piece, "no questions asked." He picked these up by trolling residential neighborhoods looking for strays and raiding people's yards when no one was home. Sometimes he would steal animals from the local Humane Society when they were left outside for fresh air. His skill as a dog catcher enabled him to easily fulfill the fifty-per-month quota the university researchers set. The extra $500 cash, which he of course did not declare as income, was a nice supplement to his retirement pension, not to mention that the dognapping gave him something to do during the day.

"This guy is not an "authorized vendor," right?" queried Pearce.

"Right," replied the surgeon.

"Did the university sanction these purchases?"

"Not officially, but they allow us to use the *petty cash* fund to make the buys." She added, "At the end of the year the paper manifests are shredded, so there's no evidence of the purchases and by then the animals are dead and have been incinerated."

"So, let me get this straight for the record," Pearce said. "You are breaking the law by using too many animals and you are also buying them illegally from someone who is probably stealing them from people's yards."

"Well, *yes* to your first point. We don't actually know where he gets the fifty animals a month and frankly, we don't ask and he doesn't tell," said the surgeon.

"He'll tell me," Pearce said. "Back up against the wall, all of you! Move it!" Complying, the two nurses moved the surgeon's chair, with her in it. The three were terrified.

"Are you going to kill us?"

"That depends," Pearce replied. He said into his mike, "Meet me in the alley in ten."

"Roger that," came the reply in his ear buds. Pearce checked the dogs. The Bassett hound was dead. The Wheaton terrier mix was literally on its last legs, but the black Shepherd was still mostly alive. Pearce walked over to the Wheaton, put the Glock to its head and pulled the trigger. The soft "phut" of the silenced gun put the dog out of its misery in a split second. Pearce said a silent prayer. The three gasped, thinking that the jig was up for them as well.

"State your names and employment positions with this university," commanded Pearce as he faced them.

"Dr. Marsha Cline," groaned the surgeon, "chief research surgeon, George Regis U." The pain was now getting to her.

"Nurse Dannie Smith," said the woman. "O.R. research nurse, George Regis University."

"Nurse Mark Cochrane. Senior O.R. nurse, George Regis." Cochrane looked like he had just jumped through a plate glass window.

"You," Pearce said, pointing to Cochrane, "help Cline into that wheel chair and get her to the elevator and when you get there *stay put.* "Smith, you wheel the shepherd out the door to the elevator." He slipped off his knapsack and pulled out two C-4 charges and stuck in the remote-controlled detonators. As the four of them rode down the elevator, Pearce obtained contact information for La Van, whom he would be visiting soon. When they got to the ground floor, they left the building via the same back door by which Pearce had entered. Strapped to the gurney, the shepherd was wheeled into the alley. Pearce escorted the *surgical team* onto the side lawn, in an area partially concealed by the huge Virginia creepers. He pulled out a small tranquilizer dart from his flak jacket and jammed it into the arm of Cochrane. When Smith tried to hold him up, he did the same to her. Both collapsed. Cline wasn't going anywhere soon on that leg so he just wedged a large branch into the spoke of her wheel chair to make sure she didn't get any ideas. He would be long gone before the cops showed up.

"So, you're not going to kill us?" Dr. Cline was hopeful.

"Consider it your lucky day," he replied. "But if you keep carrying out experiments on animals, the next time you run into me you won't live to regret it." As he headed back into the alley he turned and said, "What if one of those animals up there had been *your* pet?"

"I've never owned a pet," Dr. Cline replied.

"No shit." When Pearce reached the alley, Rafa had loaded the shepherd into the back of a nondescript cargo van. "Punch it," he said as they drove away. Rafa punched the remote and the top floor of the old medical building vaporized.

"Good riddance to bad rubbish," he said. The explosion would bring the cops and firemen running—the medical trio would be soon spotted. Twenty minutes later, a semi-conscious, jet black German shepherd strapped to a gurney was found at the door of a 24-hour animal hospital. A message was pinned to his collar along with an envelope containing three of his teeth and twenty-five-hundred dollars in cash. The note read, "Please help me. I was a victim of nonconsensual medical experimentation at George Regis University, carried out by Dr. Marsha Cline."

Rafa placed an anonymous call to a reporter, advising that he might want to get down to Central City Animal Hospital pronto to "get a jump on a really big story that's just *exploded* at George Regis U."

CHAPTER 80

Blow Back

The tiny button camera concealed in Pearce's flak jacket recorded the whole incident from the time he stepped into the lab. With the help of sophisticated audio/video editing software, Rafa would alter Pearce's voice before uploading the footage onto YouTube. A visit to Jack La Van's apartment on Marietta produced equally compelling video footage. Pearce wore his Serengeti Aviators and a Navy Seals baseball cap which he had acquired at Ft. Bragg and knocked on the door of the old wood frame house on Powder Springs Street, just west of the Confederate Cemetery. La Van answered in his t-shirt and sweat pants.

"Who are you?"

"I'm the guy you better talk to if you want to go on living," Pearce said in an assertive and direct tone. After deciding he wasn't ready just yet to check out, La Van invited him in. With some arm twisting, he admitted to kidnapping dogs from back yards, animal shelters and pet stores for George Regis U. He even swiped the occasional pooch tied up in front of a store while its owner went in for groceries. And of course, he did catch the odd loose dog or stray cat on the streets as well. His thirty-odd years of dog catching for the city of Atlanta had given him good tracking and capture skills and he had kept most of his equipment (nets, nooses and other devices) which assisted him in collaring the creatures.

Did he know what the animals were going to be used for?

Didn't know and didn't care. Ten bucks a pop was easy money for him. He could do this till the proverbial cows came home.

Was George Regis U aware of how he acquired the animals?

"Sure as hell they were," said La Van. "They knew I didn't have a kennel or cattery. Where the hell would an ex-dogcatcher come up with fifty animals a month?" He continued, "As far as they were concerned I was doing a public service by getting rid of a stray of animals on the streets." He offered Pearce a soda (which was refused) and plunked down on his old chesterfield. "They hooked me in the first place by telling me that these animals would be *a benefit to all of mankind* so I thought, what the fuck, kill two birds with one stone you know—do some good and get a couple of bucks for it." He stared forlornly at Pearce. "I've never done a thing in my life for the benefit of anybody but me."

Pearce stared back, unimpressed. "You didn't figure that maybe the kid whose dog was stolen out of his back yard would be heart-broken? Or that the shopper who left his dog tied up in front of the store could be guilt-ridden for years?"

La Van's reply was quick. "Well they should have had better security, right? That's like inviting someone to steal your pet," he said, the kid caught with his hand in the cookie jar trying to come up with a reason. "Besides, they could always get a replacement, right?"

Pearce shook his head in disgust. *Moron.* He informed La Van that his contract with George Regis U was officially over *as of now.* It went up in smoke along with the university's medical facility which he could read about in the papers tomorrow assuming he could read. "But if you *ever* even think about getting back into this business again, I'll come back and cap you—no questions asked." He made sure that La Van got a good look at the silenced Glock for effect. It worked.

The next day Rafa uploaded a highly edited version of the incident at the lab and the "interview" with the dog catcher on YouTube. It immediately went viral and caused a shit storm with the students, some of whom had pets mysteriously disappear over the past couple of years. The graphic footage of the animals captured by way of Pearce's body camera provoked outrage among students and nonmedical faculty as well. Dr. Cline's callus attitude toward the dogs and other lab animals went over like a lead balloon with viewers. Who the fuck authorized this? Why are we paying tuition to the Gestapo? The torrent of vehement protest in person and online was unprecedented. Dr. Cline and the two nurses were immediately sacked, as was the Director of medical research.

And, as luck would have it, Glen Riley, the owner of the jet black shepherd who had been kidnapped from his backyard was a senior editor at the biggest newspaper in town, the Atlanta Journal-Constitution. The story hit the front page the following day and the paper was literally screaming for blood. Fire the board of governors! Cut

301

funding for useless medical research! Bring criminal charges against all those involved! The first three pages were devoted to the scandal at the university and of course, the demolition of the ancient medical arts facility. Although in Glen's mind the perpetrator was a hero for saving his dog, and actually had the class to leave money for the vet bill, his paper had to condemn the wanton destruction of public property by an obvious terrorist.

It didn't take the FBI twenty minutes to come to the conclusion that this was the work of the same pain in the ass that blew up the mink farm in Colorado and terrorized the hunters in British Columbia.

Jesus, did *the guy* have an unlimited supply of C-4? Conroy wondered. And again, not one bloody casualty to pin on him! Although Cline got shot in the thigh, she would recover, probably with no or minimal after effects. *The guy* was drawing a lot of public sympathy for exposing the egregious behavior of university officials and then, the icing on the cake—rescuing the newspaper's editor's dog from a gruesome fate, the reward including a front page picture in the AJC with Riley's pre-school kids each cradling a big, black paw! Tens of thousands of letters and emails were pouring in daily from pissed off dog and cat owners who were furious that this could happen to anyone's pet in a free, democratic country. What kind of institution of higher learning didn't respect citizen's property rights? Pets are of course legally considered *chattels* and thus are *owned,* so taking them without consent was theft of property, a criminal offence.

Eight of ten were supportive of the perpetrator and some were even calling for him to run for mayor of Atlanta. The collective political and economic clout of an estimated one hundred and forty million dog and cat owners in the U.S. was mind boggling.

"Shit," said agent Conroy. "We'd better get this guy before he gets elected for office!"

CHAPTER 81

Sooner or Later

When Rafa and KJ deplaned at YVR, the international airport in Richmond, just south of Vancouver, both of them were more than satisfied with the outcome of the George Regis mission. KJ looked at the orange glow of the setting sun over the tarmac, glad to be back on home turf. The photo-chromatic lenses of his Serengeti Aviators lightened as the sunlight faded into the western sky. Rafa, in his white jeans, army jacket and Ray Bans, came up beside KJ, the large black duffle bag slung over his shoulder filled with tech gear from the mission. Thirty years earlier they could have been mistaken for Crockett and Tubbs on *Miami Vice.*

Again, untold publicity, no casualties and now another couple of *big* issues for the authorities on both sides of the border to chew on—a student uprising in the making at campuses in the U.S. and Canada as well as a potential tidal wave of incensed pet owners who had no idea that medical research could *adversely* affect their lives. Thus far, medical research and experimentation had been given a free pass by the general public. After all, who could argue with *cancer research?* How could it be bad to find a *cure for heart disease?* "Not with my fucking dog you won't!" was the stinging reply of millions. Student protests were one thing. They went all the way back to the Vietnam war. Sure, they are a pain in the butt, but eventually the kids grow up and they blow over. Pissing off over a hundred million pet owners is a whole other matter. It is sheer political suicide. These people vote and they have money—definitely not a good group to alienate.

As one would expect the always-opportunistic mainstream media, trying to cash in on the issue, started running other stories about needless medical experimentation on animals for trivial reasons. Until now, few outside the animal rights activists had ever heard of the *Draize Test,* an archaic procedure invented in 1944 by Dr. John

Henry Draize, a toxicologist at the FDA. This test involved among other things, the application of toxic substances to the eyes of captive rabbits to find out how long it took them to go blind. Modern applications for cosmetics testing involve jamming a tube of lipstick into the rabbit's eyes, which are held open by clamps—presumably in case a woman misses her mouth with the stick. There are many far superior tests available today, but incredibly the *Draize Test* is still alive and well in America.

As they climbed into the Durango in the airport parkade, Pearce had an uneasy feeling he could not explain. Out of an abundance of caution, he and Rafa checked the vehicle for signs of tampering. No bomb had been planted on the undercarriage. KJ rang Floriana at the farm. The animals were good and she was too. Still, he could not shake the feeling. They had rolled *sevens* on each of the three missions so far, which in itself was unusual. Like coin tosses, campaigns don't keep coming up heads over and over. Sooner or later, something has to give. But what the hell was it? As they drove toward Vancouver, KJ hit the call button on the dashboard's screen and the onboard Bluetooth application connected his Blackberry Z30 to the SUV's speakers. The line rang several times and then, "This is Kiara Davies. Please leave a message and I'll call you back as soon as I can."

"We're back. Call me when you get this," said KJ into the speaker. The team never left detailed messages on voice mail, notwithstanding the military grade encryption software Rafa had installed on every communications device they used. It was unusual for Kiara not to answer. But she could be in a meeting, at a work out, swimming or in the steam room or sauna. No court at this hour though. Still, like many people these days, she was a phone junkie and her *Priv* rarely left her side.

"Why don't we swing by K's apartment on the way to yours?" KJ suggested.

"Sounds like a plan," said Rafa. The drive from YVR was uneventful—over the Arthur Lang Bridge, down Granville Street and across the Burrard Inlet over the Granville Street Bridge. They took the right stem off the bridge to Seymour and then another right on Robson Street. A few blocks over brought them to 1560 Homer Mews, where Kiara occupied the smallest unit in the luxury building, designed by the distinguished local architect, Arthur Erickson, now deceased. The Durango rumbled into K's second stall in the underground parkade at "the Erickson" in Yaletown. Rafa had a second fob from Kiara, this one to open the security gate. It also allowed them to ascend the elevator to the eighteenth floor. The coded security lock on the nine-foot hardwood door of her apartment would not have presented a problem for Rafa, but Pearce had the code. Kiara had given it to him as back-up.

The two men entered the suite cautiously, not sure what to expect. Pearce drew his Glock and stepped forward. He signed Rafa to hit the light switch. Suddenly the whole place was illuminated. Nothing seemed amiss at first. The fireplace was still on. There was a fresh pot of coffee on the stove. "Maybe she just stepped out for some groceries," Rafa said. Her sixty-five-inch LED TV which almost covered one wall was on and tuned to CNN at low volume. There was no sign of forced entry or any struggle. After a room by room recon of the one-thousand-one-hundred-square-foot condominium and the deck, they turned up nothing suspicious. "Let's wait for her," said Pearce, still uneasy despite no objective information to support that feeling. After twenty years of martial arts and meditation practice, he had learned to trust his gut feeling, intuition, or sixth sense some would call it.

"Okay, then I'm going to grab a coffee," said Rafa. "It still smells pretty fresh." As he walked into the kitchen he had an idea. "Hey KJ, why don't we find her phone? Experience tells me that she'll probably be near it."

Pearce gave a thumbs-up as Rafa grabbed the *Alien* out of his knapsack and powered it up. It picked up Kiara's local wi-fi link. Rafa punched in the password, typed in "Rogers Wireless" on his browser and when the phone carrier's site appeared he clicked on the *"locate my phone"* tab. Within seconds a map appeared on the *Alien's* screen which showed a fifty-foot circle within which the phone was located. Shit, it was in the apartment. After a few minutes of hunting they found it between the couch and a large armchair.

"Hey, KJ, I've found her back-up cell." He snatched it off the floor and swiped the touch screen upwards to get it up and running. "HeLLC@Tx2" unlocked the Smartphone and he quickly went to her phone messages. KJ's was the last one and nothing outbound.

"Anything?" asked KJ anxiously.

"Looking," said Rafa as his practiced fingers danced over the keyboard. As a concession to diehard Blackberry users, the *Priv* had a pull out QWERTY keyboard as well as the virtual one which all other smart phones possessed. "Emails—nada, texts—nada, BBM

305

messages—nada …so far nothing out of the ordinary, KJ. I'm looking in her voice memos… I'll put this one through the microphone."

"Two guys with guns … can't tell where …" then Kiara's voice cut off. She had dropped the phone in between the furniture when the first intruder poked his head back into the room from the kitchen.

"When was that made?" KJ asked.

Rafa determined it was thirty-one minutes prior, just about the time when KJ and Rafa were getting into the Durango at the airport parkade in Richmond.

"Now what do we do, call the cops?" Rafa asked.

"That depends on who took her. If it was a couple of burglars or thieves, then for sure we do."

"Gottcha," Rafa said. "If it's connected to our campaign, they're the last guys we want involved."

KJ went into the kitchen and took out two Contigo coffee mugs from the cupboard. He poured a coffee for each of them and sat down at the kitchen nook. Rafa followed him in and grabbed a bottle of cream from the fridge, *organic, free range, cruelty-free of course.*

"Maybe you should put on another pot, Rafa. This could take a while."

CHAPTER 82

Finding a Trail

Despite his cool exterior, Pearce's heart was racing like a greyhound's at the finish line. He couldn't believe it. His law school friend and staunch ally in this massive campaign was gone—snatched by persons unknown. It could be a random event, maybe some assholes bent on robbing her or worse. More likely though it was the government, Canadian or U.S. or both, which had somehow twigged to her involvement—although how was anybody's guess. Their communications had been airtight. No one, but no one got even a glimpse of her or Rafa for that matter. Pearce sat dead still willing his heart back to its normal 55 bpm. He had to think clearly and strategically, so anxiety or outright panic had no place at the table. His friend's life depended on it. Rafa set the pot to brew and opened the *Alien* on the kitchen table.

"Where do we start?" he asked hopefully.

Pearce unconsciously slipped into command mode and asked Rafa if he could hack into the building's security cameras.

"Probably, but I'd need a website or something to start with." He googled "the Erickson" but all he got was realtor's listings and rentals. He tried the deceased architect's site. No go. "While you are trying that, I'll go talk to the concierge," Pearce said. Ten minutes later he returned with the building management's website information. "Nobody saw her leave with anybody in the last hour," he advised. "They must have taken her down the parking elevator directly."

Hacking is an art as much as a skill, and once Rafa set his mind to it, he was both single-minded and relentless. A half hour later they were looking at the video footage in the lobby of the building on the *Alien*. No one could get in or out of the lobby without being seen, unless they deliberately covered their faces, a move that would raise suspicion at the front desk and with the concierge. A kid on a skateboard appeared and was intercepted by the deskman and escorted to the elevator *sans board.* An elderly couple toting a couple bags of groceries was assisted by the bellhop. Evidently the high strata fees of *The Erickson* warranted a deskman, bellhop and concierge twenty-four/seven. Then nothing seemed to be happening for a while.

"Hey, look there!" Rafa pointed to two suits, maybe late thirties, briskly walk into the building and approach the front desk. Appearing to show a badge of some kind one of them began questioning the desk jockey. He tried to pick up the phone, but the other one grabbed his hand and put the phone back in its cradle, shaking his head "no." They kept grilling the guy for a while and then seemed to direct him to make a call, which he did. It was likely to Kiara's unit. The suits then walked to the elevator and punched in the security code for the eighteenth floor which they doubtless got from the front desk. They had that swagger that cops and members of the military develop from being able to intimidate people into getting what they want. Okay, that explained why Kiara let them in. Once they were in the elevator the desk jock picked up the phone again and started punching in numbers, but changed his mind and put it back down.

"Looks like the random asshole theory is down the drain," said Pearce. "These guys are definitely feds."

"Which ones do you think? Canadian or U.S.?"

"Can't tell yet, but we've got to find out PDQ." Pearce speed-dialed *Animal Farm* on his Z30. When Floriana picked up he directed her to a small, built-in vault in his home office and gave her the combination. She fished out the small, burgundy binder he had in mind and found the page to his JTF2 contacts.

"Siv Hansen, that's the one, Floriana. Can you give me her number?" She did and returned the binder to the vault and re-set the electronic lock. "Any chance you can stay over," asked KJ. "I don't think that I'll be back tonight."

She could. "I'm on a break for the next few days, studying for midterms."

KJ was relieved. "That's great. I might need you there for your whole break. Double time of course!"

She said regular pay was okay, to which he replied, "No it's not."

"Hasta la vista senora!"

She smiled. Technically that should have been "senorita" as she was a young, unmarried woman, but she appreciated KJ trying.

Siv was the senior logistics support officer for JT2F at Dwyer Hill in Ottawa. She had a serious crush on Pearce when he joined

JTF2 and it was sort of mutual for a while. However, since he was rarely at the base, things really never got off the ground. When he left the force, they parted on pretty good terms with an unspoken promise of *maybe someday*. She had complete access to the most confidential DND data. If the Canadian feds, RCMP, CSIS or CSEC were involved in capturing Kiara, she could find out. Despite their history, this was going to be a *big ask*, not to mention a risk for both of them. But finding Kiara—and fast, was priority one and he would do whatever it would take it to get it done.

In the meantime, Rafa was going to work on the herculean, even for him, task of hacking into the FBI's website. One or both governments were in on this and the sooner they found out the better. KJ knew that Kiara was strong, resilient and headstrong, although little did he know how strong. However, the enhanced interrogation, read *torture*, techniques which could be brought to bear if she did not cooperate would be devastating to anyone. The fact that she was a practicing lawyer in Canada might buy her a little time, but not more than a couple of days. Then the heavyweights would be brought in. He had to act fast.

After a few awkward pleasantries KJ asked Siv if she could find out anything about a recently captured terrorist suspect named Kiara Davies, a practicing lawyer at Sierra Legal Defense in Vancouver. It was literally a matter of life and death he explained. "She was apprehended about an hour ago from her apartment in Vancouver," he said, adding they were, "Feds for sure, but not sure whether Canadian or U.S."

"What kind of terrorist activity?" Siv asked.

Not wanting to give away more information that absolutely necessary, KJ was careful with his response. "Not exactly sure, but the government would definitely categorize it as terrorism." When Siv asked why he cared, he said Kiara was a classmate from law school and they had the wrong person. "I'm one hundred per cent certain of that." "How do you know that she wasn't just kidnapped?" Siv asked.

"I watched the video footage from her building's security cameras. It was definitely the feds." The line, a secure line, went silent on her end for a while. Pearce could hear tapping sounds, keystrokes most likely. "Hey, Siv," he said, "I know this is a colossal favor to ask. Can you do it without getting caught?"

"Maybe... no... probably." She told him it would take her about an hour to route the inquiries through the standard com channels. "Otherwise it will definitely raise questions." His thanks were sincere and included an ironclad IOU.

"I'll make a note!" she said.

Pearce downed his third cup of java and set about brewing another pot. Rafa was transfixed on the *Alien's* screen, employing some of the most sophisticated hacking techniques known to computer geeks anywhere. He would keep at it until he dropped. Pearce brought him a steady stream of coffee, donuts and pizza to keep him going.

A little before midnight, Siv called. "No luck, KJ," she said. "This was not a Canadian government operation."

"Shit!"

Now it was all on Rafa's shoulders. Those bastards in the States had snatched her on Canadian soil without so much as a nod to their Northern allies. Pearce figured it was no big surprise, as the Canadian military and its security agencies were virtually beneath the Americans' notice. Doubtless she was in a military transport plane—hopefully it was to the U.S. and not to some fucking secret prison in Abu Dhabi or Yemen. He dialed the twenty-four-hour Flight Center number and booked a first-class ticket to Washington, D.C. on the first flight out, which would be a red-eye leaving at 2:45 a.m.

"Yeah, vegan meal," he told the operator. Hopefully, by the time he arrived, Rafa would have solid intel. It was a long shot for sure, but if the FBI had taken her, he was guessing she was in lock up at their headquarters on Pennsylvania Avenue. How he was going to get in there and spring her was a mystery at the moment, but he would have four or five hours to figure it out. Flying by the seat of his pants was definitely not his style of mission, but in the circumstances, he had no choice. Time was much of the essence to Kiara's wellbeing, if not her life.

CHAPTER 83

Locating the Package

There was no time to go back to *Animal Farm*. Pearce grabbed a cab to the Canada Line station on Pender and Granville. This would take him to the door of YVR. He would just have to pick up whatever ordnance he needed south of the border. Boarding the largely empty Sky Train compartment, he grabbed a window seat by force of habit. It didn't matter as most of the trip would be underground anyway. The automatic doors closed and the sleek, Mark II ART four car train constructed by Canadian engineering giant, Bombardier whooshed toward Yaletown Roundhouse, the next stop. Travelling at speeds up to ninety kilometers per hour, the train would arrive at the Vancouver International Airport in Richmond in thirty minutes flat, travelling through the tony Yaletown district, across the water and down the Cambie Street corridor, finally crossing Marine Drive East into Richmond. Its *Thales Seltrac* signaling technology ran Advanced Rapid Transit trains automatically without so much as a single human operator onboard.

In order to effectively deal with life or death combat missions Pearce had developed the ability to compartmentalize problems, putting individual ones away into separate mental shelves, to be brought out, analyzed and solved at a later time. How Kiara might be holding up under whatever kind of nasty treatment the Feds would resort to was one of those problems. For the moment though, that was beyond his control so he shelved it. How they twigged to her involvement was another nagging problem which could compromise the whole campaign if not resolved. This was a high priority issue but again, at this moment he had no way to discover the answer so it too was shelved. The most pressing concern was how to locate Kiara and extract her from the FBI's clutches—that is if they had her in the United States. If she was not in D.C., then he was up the proverbial shit creek without a paddle.

Just then the Z-30 came to life. It was Rafa. "I'm listening."

"Some good news to report," Rafa whispered guardedly. "I'm partially into the FIBBIES' site and it appears that somebody has been rendered from Canada in the last couple of hours. No names. It's totally hush-hush, as it seems that no one bothered to inform the Canadian government."

"It's got to be Kiara," KJ said.

"I agree," Rafa replied. "No location yet either, but I think that your D.C. guess is as good as any." They both knew Pearce would be in D.C. in about ten hours. Rafa said he would keep working and, "I'll keep you posted."

"Roger that."

"One last thing," Rafa said. "If we pinpoint her there, how are you planning on getting her out?"

"That's the sixty-four-thousand-dollar question." It was a question Pearce dedicated most of his flight to. Even though he was fairly sure that he could procure pretty heavy-duty ordnance if need be, it was a suicide mission to try to shoot his way into the facility, somehow find Kiara and then get out alive. That kind of operation would take weeks if not months of careful planning to have any chance of success and he had less than twenty-four hours. The wheels just kept spinning in his mind, but not getting any traction. Hours went by and thoroughly exhausted, frustrated and for one of the few times in his life, totally stymied, he decided enough was enough. He would have to get some shut eye. It would be a long day. He sunk into a shallow restless sleep, haunted by a recurring dream which saw him vainly trying to swim to a beautiful, white sandy beach. The closer he got to the shore the thicker and blacker the water became. Soon it was viscous, like heavy oil. Try as he might, he could make no headway. He started to tire as the shore seemed to be getting farther and farther away, when a gorgeous blonde woman on the beach got up and left ... he was sinking, drowning.

Pearce awoke at 8:00 a.m. tired, groggy and thoroughly dispirited from that fitful sleep. He pulled the comfortable, business class, seatback to a sitting position and was unexpectedly greeted by a brilliant morning sun peeking through the window shade and the smell of a tasty vegan breakfast—soy sausage links with multi-grain toast smothered with Olivina olive oil spread, kiwi, strawberry and blueberry fruit plate and strong, black coffee. Not half bad for a commercial airline. As the pretty Asian stewardess who was serving him leaned over to pour his coffee he couldn't help but notice the silver talisman hanging from her neck on a long, fine curb chain.

"May I," he asked. "That's an unusual piece."

"Sure," she replied as she filled the cup. The chain was long enough that she was able to place the delicate, handcrafted pendent in Pearce's hand without taking it off. It was a high end, sterling silver piece made by *Pyrrha*, which featured a bold lion on its hind legs atop a shield with a Latin phrase engraved beneath it in old English lettering. *Dum Spiro Spero*. His heart stopped. "While I breathe, I hope," he said softly, translating the dictum. In some mysterious way, the talisman breathed a torrent of *chi* in to his exhausted body. When he opened his eyes the stewardess was looking at him with a friendly, quizzical expression, her head cocked to one side.

"Not one in a million people would recognize that phrase."

"Lucky guess," KJ replied, a faint smile crossing his lips as he released his grip on the pendant. His body relaxed, the chi force manifesting itself as pure, raw confidence which radiated outwards like the bright rays of sunlight outside the jet. A golden sun, a delicious meal and now this auspicious omen—all in sync. Perhaps the gods of war were in a good mood today.

CHAPTER 84

Guantanamo, D.C.

"**W**here the hell do you get off kidnapping me at gunpoint?" Kiara shouted. The concrete room she was in was small and spartan, with a table and four chairs. She was seated opposite a tall, impassive man. A one-way window allowed the people on the other side to view the interview without being seen. Two small video cameras were positioned in the ceiling from either side. She was not shackled nor restrained, but she was definitely not free to get up and leave. The man did not speak right away, but simply stared at her, sizing her up and at the same time, trying to intimidate her. However, Kiara had been in many a courtroom battle with hardened litigation counsel so this tactic had little effect. Yet she was not in a courtroom dressed in her black gown with *Madame Justice Whoever* maintaining order and decorum in the proceedings, which required opposing counsel to politely refer to each other as "my learned friend."

Receiving no answer, she demanded, "Where is this place?" Still no answer. "Hey Jack, are you deaf? Do you even speak English?" she asked, as if she were the interrogator. She abruptly got up and walked to the door, grabbing its handle—locked of course. The man remained motionless, his back to her. The thought crossed her mind to jump the guy and maybe get a hold of his gun, she assumed he was armed, but that wouldn't get her out of the place, so she returned to her seat at the table and stared back. Ten minutes passed, then fifteen, and still no talk or movement from either side. So far this was better than she had expected. It certainly beat being water boarded.

Finally, Clinton George III walked in. "Ms. Davies, please accept our apologies for bringing you here in this unorthodox manner."

"You mean illegal manner, don't you?" Kiara taunted.

"Legal, illegal it doesn't much matter. You are here, that is what counts," he said.

"And where exactly is here?" she demanded.

"Federal Bureau of Investigation Headquarters, Washington, D.C."

"And who the hell are you, the Director of the FBI, I suppose?" Sarcasm.

"As a matter of fact, I am," George III said.

Kiara realized they were bringing out the big guns, but forced herself to maintain a neutral expression. "Am I supposed to be impressed?" she asked, looking him straight in the eyes. "That's up to you counselor," he said. "For what it's worth, most people are."

"Kidnapping and unlawful detention don't impress me much, Mr. Director," she said coolly.

He took no notice of the barb. "Let's get to the point. We've intercepted a communication between you and someone we believe to be involved with a notorious animal justice vigilante who has been causing mayhem of late in our country and yours."

"You have a warrant or a court order authorizing that?" demanded Kiara reflexively, as any defense counsel would.

"Not yet, but we still have five days to apply for it to the FISA Court," he explained. The U.S. Foreign Intelligence Surveillance Court was established under the Foreign Intelligence Surveillance Act of 1978. At Clinton's request, the U.S. Attorney General had made a determination that an emergency situation existed and therefore authorized the employment of electronic surveillance before obtaining the necessary authorization from the FISA court. The Attorney General's designee had followed protocol by notifying a judge of the court at the time of authorization a few days ago and he would apply for the warrant as soon as practicable but not more than 7 days after authorization of such surveillance, as required by the law (50 U.S.C. § 1805).

"You mean the *rubber stamp* court," scoffed Kiara. "Has it ever turned down a request for a warrant since its inception?" she asked in a mocking tone.

The Director replied, "Not that I know of." He went on to explain it was not his mandate to evaluate the efficacy or practices of the FISA Court. The FBI would comply with the law and the warrant after the fact and before the seven-day deadline was up. "In the meantime, I will play you the portion of the intercepted message and you will tell me the identity of the party with whom you were speaking. If you don't do so, you will be here for a long time. Do I make myself clear?"

To Kiara it was suddenly clear as a bell. Relief flooded through her tense muscles as she realized that these jokers didn't have anything solid to go on without her cooperation.

Clinton nodded toward the guy standing at the door. The guy stepped out. There was a pitcher of water on the table with two crystal glasses. Clinton offered Kiara a glass of water.

"Are you going to get after-the-fact authorization for kidnapping me too?" She ignored his offer.

"The provisions of the U.S. Patriot Act already allow for that," he bluffed. "We can hold you here indefinitely."

"Bullshit!" Kiara retorted. "I've read the entire Patriot Act and it doesn't sanction the illegal rendition of a citizen of a U.S. ally."

"Smart ass," the Director thought as he calmly replied. "Be that as it may counselor, you are here now and the Act does permit us to hold you if we believe that you, and I quote, *may cause a terrorist threat or are aiding or supporting terrorism.*" The tension was creeping back into her muscles, but she willed herself to maintain a face of stone. "That partial phone call, which you will soon hear, gives us that reasonable belief." The Director leaned back, pausing with raised eyebrows, for maximum effect. "And as you seem to be so knowledgeable about U.S. laws and customs, then you know that we have a habit of holding suspects in supermax prisons in segregated administrative detention for extended periods of time."

"You mean solitary confinement, don't you?" she replied.

"Didn't I just say that?" The Director was smug.

"You ever hear of *habeas corpus?*" When no immediate reply was forthcoming she said, "In case you haven't, it means *bring the body* before the court."

"I know what it means, Ms. Davies," said the Director. "But in matters of national security, which includes anything related to terrorism, that legal right no longer applies."

"How about *due process*? Or is that just a quaint, historical artifact in this country too?" she asked, her voice dripping with sarcasm. She was starting to get worried. It was dawning on her that when it came to matters of national security, the U.S. was not a country governed by *the rule of law.*

"To quote our esteemed former U.S. Attorney General, Eric Holder," answered the Director, "due process and judicial process are not one and the same, particularly when it comes to national security. The Constitution guarantees due process, not judicial process."

"Sure, if you're living in Nazi Germany," she shot back. The guy returned with a digital recorder. He put it on the table and with a nod from Clinton George III was about to press the play button.

"Stop!" Kiara ordered. "I am a practicing member of the British Columbia bar in Canada and if that is a recording of a conversation with a client of mine, it is protected by solicitor-client privilege which my client declines to waive."

"Duly noted, Ms. Davies," said the Director. "Play it, Agent."

They heard Rafa's voice. ".…… George Rejones was an …. easy barget counselor. One dog shaved … two left …… animal hospital..… No casu … and ……. blown up… C4." No more of the sentence was audible, but Kiara's reply was somewhat. " .…. What are you doing about ..… medical stoff? .… (long pause with garbled words) How does the ..… fit in?"

"Does that female voice sound like anyone you know Ms. Davies?" said the Director. It was definitely hers, but she did not acknowledge it.

"Could be anybody's," she commented.

The male voice continued. "We will be ..… through ..… on internat.… next time …… Canada" She replied, "You and Kge okay? Wh… is… scatus of…… local ..… response?" His answer was again mangled, "Too soon .… leaving Atlanta on ..… next flight 2… to .… ada." The conversation went on for another thirty seconds with bits and pieces audible sound and other parts rendered incomprehensible by Rafa's high level encryption technology.

Good luck cracking that, she thought. The FBI wasn't exactly short on resources, however, so she couldn't totally rule out that possibility. The silent agent stood right beside and slightly behind Kiara, to rattle her. Was he going to hit her? Put a plastic bag over her head? Break a few of her fingers? She had to try with all her might to quell those thoughts.

"Now, who was the person that you were talking to?" asked the Director.

Kiara forced herself to remain silent thinking over her options. Obviously, anything she said would be used to incriminate her and justify, in their minds, her indefinite detainment until she spilled the beans. There was little to no chance the cavalry would be arriving anytime soon. She doubted that KJ and Rafa could even find her, much less spring her out of this concrete fortress, so she would have to figure a way out of this mess on her own.

"Do you need some help remembering?" asked the tall man, speaking for the first time.

CHAPTER 85

Leverage

The Boeing 767 jet landed at Ronald Reagan Washington National airport on schedule and without incident. Pearce gave the stewardess a smile and a thumbs-up as he left the plane and headed toward the terminal. Having only a small carry-on bag, he proceeded directly to the cab stand to hail a taxi to a hotel downtown, as close to FBI headquarters as possible. The Willard Intercontinental would do the trick. The old luxury hotel was only a hop, skip and a jump from the FBI building on Pennsylvania Avenue. He told the young woman at the front desk his luggage would be arriving later and went directly to his suite on the nineteenth floor facing west.

Rafa had been up all night trying to crack into the FBI's mainframe, with *some*, albeit limited, success. Pearce had run mental scenarios of getting into the FBI's headquarters every which way—faking credentials, taking an employee hostage to gain entrance, posing as a delivery man, janitor or other service provider—they all came up short. He could only hope that Kiara could keep it together while they figured something out. He assumed that she would know that they were tracking her. While he waited for Rafa, he called the concierge.

"Type of vehicle sir?"

"Cayenne Turbo, black."

"Needed when?"

"Ten minutes ago."

"I'm on it, sir."

The concierge was waiting with the car keys. Pearce donned his Aviators and gunned the sleek SUV down Pennsylvania Avenue making his way out of downtown Washington. The onboard GPS directed him to Scott Cir NW, next to 16th and then a sharp right on K Street put him on U.S.-29 South/Whitehurst Freeway NW. Finally Canal Road NW took him directly to Rockville in exactly thirty-one minutes. Rockville is a city located in the central region of Montgomery County and forms part of metro Baltimore-Washington. A population of 65,000 or so, makes it the third largest incorporated city in Maryland, behind Baltimore and Frederick. Pearce's interest in the town, however, was limited to one address, 5455 Randolph Road, the location of the Union Gun Shop. He parked the Cayenne at the back.

Hailey, the twenty-four-year-old daughter of Jeff Parker, the owner, greeted him from behind the counter. "Can I help you find the weapon of your choice, sir?" she asked with a big smile, spreading her arms apart gesturing to the wide assortment of guns lining the walls—handguns, rifles, shotguns and semiautomatics. It sure wasn't Watts Guns & Ammo, but it would do. KJ asked her if Jeff was in. "Sure," she said, picking up the phone. Her father was in the basement repair shop. Union Gun Shop was a certified armorer for Glock and Jeff was downstairs refining the trigger-pull on a Glock 20 handgun just like KJ's. Jeff and KJ shook hands and after chatting for a few minutes, Jeff invited KJ downstairs. Hailey thought that somewhat unusual, since as a general rule, *no one* but staff, close friends and the occasional long-term customer was allowed into the repair facility in the basement—and she had never seen this guy before. However, she was distracted by a couple of customers who were interested in a handgun for their nineteen-year-old daughter. The husband asked how she could get a concealed carry permit as well.

Twenty-five minutes later KJ left Union with a fair bit of fire power. Sixty-five Ben Franklins changed hands—no paperwork, no receipts and no questions. Jeff was a part of an unofficial network of former soldiers who owned and operated gun shops and shooting ranges throughout the U.S. and Canada. For the most part, they were law-abiding citizens who had done more than their fair share for king and country. However, they knew that other vets who had served may have come upon hard times after leaving the military. Many had debilitating physical and psychological injuries which required major therapeutic intervention. Spending cuts affected both sides of the border. Politicians loved to spout the *let's support the troops* mantra before the soldiers shipped out, but were not so keen on spending tax money on the broken pieces when they came back. As a result, many vets had criminal records for property and violent offences committed upon their return to civilian life. This would usually mean that they were unable to legally acquire a firearm for self-defense, so cash transactions without paperwork were offered without questions. KJ didn't exactly fall into this category, but as an ex-vet with a vote of confidence from Jake Watts, Parker was happy to do business with a former comrade-in-arms.

With lighter than usual traffic, the Cayenne made the trip back to the Willard in twenty-four minutes flat. The ordnance was stored in two large duffle bags, not unlike the ones used by hockey players to haul their gear, except these were equipped with heavy-duty locks on the connecting zippers. The instant the Porsche rolled to a halt under the hotel's huge *Porte Cochere*, the valet opened the driver's door for Pearce. The service at the Willard Intercontinental was ten out of ten. Two bellboys loaded the heavy bags onto a trolley and the vehicle was parked nearby for instant retrieval. A twenty-spot found its way into the valet's hand to guarantee a repeat performance on demand. KJ grabbed a take-out espresso at the hotel restaurant and by the time he reached his room the bags were on the floor, waiting to be opened. A tiny cloth bag cinched with a gold tassel containing three Jacques Torres chocolates sat on his night table with a card embossed with the Willard's distinctive logo: *"Thanks for permitting your valet service to be of assistance."* Pearce thought, *"My valet service,"* had a nice ring to it. As he crouched down to unlock the canvass bags, he mused, "Not too damned much these guys at the Willard don't think of."

Being a meticulous planner himself he appreciated that unusual attention to detail. His Z-30 rang and he punched the receive call icon on the nearly indestructible, Gorilla glass screen. It was Rafa.

"Good news and bad."

"Let's hear the good," replied KJ, sitting down on the edge of the bed, taking a sip of the hot espresso.

"I've hacked into their system and they have K in D.C. at their headquarters a couple of blocks from your present location." Relief washed over Pearce, but only for an instant. They had guessed right, which was a good first step, but there was way more to do to resolve this situation. He still had no idea how they were going to liberate Kiara.

"It seems like the Director himself has taken an interest in the matter," Rafa said. "His five-year appointment is up at the end of this year and he may be looking to score some political points if he can bag the high-profile animal rights vigilante who is grabbing all the headlines as of late."

"What do we know about this guy?" Pearce sensed that he might turn out to be an important piece of the puzzle.

"He's a lifer at the Bureau. Graduated top ten at West Point in 1990 and landed at Quantico in 91' and has been at the Bureau ever since." Rafa continued to scroll down the Director's dossier. "He's a control freak. He's centralized all command and operations functions to pass through his three immediate subordinates, a Jack Harney, Tony Plath and Deputy Director, Anna Shallal—all long timers as well, and they sit right outside of his office."

"Looks like he's another J. Edgar—one-hundred per cent control centered in his seat," commented KJ.

Rafa kept reading. "He's known for being smart, ruthless and re-sults-oriented. He'll deal, but always from a position of strength and only if he comes out ahead in the end."

"Keep going," said KJ, not missing a word.

Rafa said that in his last five years as Director, his team had cracked some big cases. "The Jonas serial murder in New York, the shoe bomber airline case, the plot to blow up the port at the LA docks and the human smuggling operation in Miami involving the Medel-lin drug cartel."

KJ rubbed his eyes and said, "Okay, it sounds like he knows what he is doing. Does the guy have any weaknesses or foibles?"

"Yup, heavy smoker—cigars mostly, even *Cubans* it seems be-fore the embargo was lifted," reported Rafa. "And, he's no slouch when it comes to the booze either. He's been charged on three sepa-rate occasions with impaired driving over the last fifteen years."

"Ever convicted?"

"No. The charges were all withdrawn."

"It figures."

"Looks like he's a bit of a ladies' man though," continued Rafa. "Divorced twice and just recently married to a former runway model about half his age."

Pearce pounced like a hungry Cheetah. "That's it!"

"What's it?" asked Rafa.

"That's our way in!" he exclaimed triumphantly. "Dig up George's home address. I'm going to pay her a visit."

CHAPTER 86

Revolt

Pet owners across the continent were livid upon discovering their beloved dogs or cats could conceivably wind up in a medical experiment or research project at a university or college funded by *their* tax dollars. Thousands of pets go missing every day across both countries for many reasons. After reading the expose of the George Regis University, however, many distraught owners jumped to the conclusion that some asshole like La Van had kidnapped their cherished pets and sold them to an unscrupulous institution of so-called, *higher learning*. The George Regis incident had been splashed across papers nationwide due to the fact that the medical building had been blown up by the same guy who was wreaking havoc on both sides of the border. More than a few tweets and posts expressed sympathy, if not outright support for *the guy*.

Uncannily, he seemed to be dancing back and forth between Canada and the U.S. with impunity while making asses out of the governments of both countries for their egregious treatment of animals. Now the politicians and the research establishment were about to learn the hard way that *you don't mess with peoples' pets*. Poison the environment, invade another country under false pretenses, nearly bring down the world economy—big deal, that's life in America. Fuck with my dog or cat however and you will live to regret it! When the former dictator, Muammar Gaddafi was deposed in 2011, mega-recording artists like Nellie Furtado, Beyoncé, Mariah Carey, Usher and Fifty Cent found themselves under tremendous public pressure to return the huge fees that they had received to give private performances for the dictator and his family. Suddenly, receiving *blood money* from a scumbag was not so savvy.

After the George Regis episode, major research universities like Harvard, Yale, Princeton, Columbia and MIT as well as top drawer hospitals, including Johns Hopkins, Sloan Kettering, University of

Texas MD Anderson, Massachusetts General and the Mayo Clinic had hints their research funding would dwindle. Private donors started feeling like those recording artists. Chit chat around the dinner tables of the *'one percent'* was rife with now politically correct comments. "I've had the board pull our company's funding for animal torture. It's just ridiculous that my daughter's Yorkie could wind up in a medical experiment!" (unlikely as that was since the family lived in Brentwood.) It was not uncommon for the high society debs to hold fund raisers for the ASPCA, American Humane Society and World Wildlife Fund (although the likes of PETA, Mercy for Animals and the Sea Shepherd Society were still a bit too far left for their delicate sensibilities) and now there was even more interest. College and even high school kids across the continent, ever ripe for an excuse to oppose the establishment had jumped on the bandwagon and were holding demonstrations on campuses and in school yards everywhere.

And in the middle of the most media-grabbing events was a doozy initiated by Inaara Burdenny at St. Thomas More, an exclusive girls school in Englewood, Colorado. Inaara had organized a group of seniors in her biology class to stage a protest against fur. Reliance on animal skins and fur-bearing animals was an integral part of Colorado's history, dating back to the bone needles found at the thirteen-thousand-year-old Linden Meier Site and progressing all the way up to the modern factory farm operations like MBM. Undaunted by history, Inaara and "her posse," as she referred to them, tried to make fur an historical artifact in the Centennial State, because *it was the right thing to do.* Consequently, a dozen seventeen-year-old naked female students were presently being arrested, clothed and taken to the Englewood police station amidst a plethora of cameras and news people from multiple TV stations and news outlets.

The teens had resurrected PETA's 1991 ad campaign, *"We'd rather go naked than wear fur,"* which featured the punk-rock, all-female band, The Go-Go's, who posed nude behind a huge poster with that slogan. The original ad campaign was quickly picked up by national TV and replicated worldwide, the historical equivalent of going viral, and resulted in fur sales dropping to an all-time low everywhere on the planet. Unfortunately, as one generation passes, the Madison Avenue crowd is always on the lookout for a new group of suckers who missed out on the life lessons of the last one. Since then, fur experienced a resurgence of sorts, especially with the economic rise of China and other Asian countries, whose farms and businesses are notorious for their ill treatment of all animals, furbearing and otherwise.

When their teacher was out of the classroom on a bathroom break, the teens locked the door. Then they stripped and Inaara brought out the huge banner behind which they would pose. "Jessie, Kelly and Megan, get a hold of the TV stations, stat!" said Inaara, borrowing a term from her dad's vernacular. The trio grabbed their designer handbags and purses and out came the ubiquitous IPhone 6's and within seconds there was an excited chatter in progress with Colorado TV stations KOAA, KWGN and KMGH. Soon, Sister Pomeroy would be pounding on the door so they had to get organized fast.

"Who's got a really good camera in their phone?" asked Inaara.

"Me," chirped Pippa Smythe. "My Galaxy S6 Edge got top billing in *Tech Advisor*, which is why I got it for photography class."

"Yeah, she's taken some really cool photos around the school grounds for us," volunteered Samantha Penn, editor of the school paper.

"Not to mention at least ten thousand selfies!" laughed Cameron Thompson, who, at six-foot-one, was captain of the basketball team.

"You should talk, goddess of the self-portrait!" chimed in point guard, Connie Adams, giggling like a fiend.

"Enough already!" said Inaara, cutting in. "Pippa, set it up over there," pointing to the teacher's desk.

"Open the door!" shouted Sister Pomeroy, knocking briskly.

Samantha hunted down several placards which the girls had made on the sly in their art classes and passed them around to the others. The placards were plastered with majorly enlarged photos of captive mink being electrocuted, bludgeoned and one being skinned alive— all courtesy of ring leader Inaara Burdenny. Bold captions underscored the horrific pictures: "Animals need their coats a hell of a lot more that you do!" "Wear faux fur not cruelty!" "You look like shit in a fur coat, animals don't!"

"Come on, come on!" Inaara was stark naked and holding on to the huge banner in front of her. A half a dozen of the female students had joined her, each grabbing the top edge of the banner. Three others were fiddling with their hair and make-up.

"Jesus, it's not a beauty pageant!" complained Candace Bronwyn, who had already gotten a full makeover the previous day in anticipation of this event.

"Yeah, yeah, it's going to be everywhere by tonight, so get your reporters down here pronto!" Megan Underwood told the manager at KGWN. Kelly was pulling her by the arm towards the girls with the banner, but she kept talking on her phone. "That's what I said—no clothes, probably they'll call the cops and arrest us for good measure. Yeah, you heard right, St. Thomas More *private school.*"

"Young ladies, if you don't open this door right now, I'm calling the principal!" shrieked Sister Pomeroy, pounding on the door. The stern nun was not used to such defiant behavior by her students.

Word that something big was going on in classroom 9B rippled throughout the school. The cafeteria had emptied, and the gym, the schoolyard and now even the parking lot was draining. It was as if everyone was being pulled over by a gigantic magnet. Sister Pomeroy tried to shoo them away, but to no avail, as more and more students appeared in the hall. The overflow of about a hundred teens assembled outside and some began banging on 9B's window to have someone pull up the blinds. Several teachers appeared, curious to see what the heck all the racket was about.

"Is it a fucking hostage-taking or what?" shouted one freshman trying to be a smart alec, but unfortunately with recent events in the U.S., that was akin to yelling "fire" in a crowded movie theatre. Hostages! Holy shit, maybe that's why the classroom door was locked and the blinds drawn! Immediately everyone started backing up. Panic gripped the crowd as the devastating *"H word"* ricocheted from student to student like a pinball in an ancient arcade game. Just as the kids were disbursing, KGWN TV's news van pulled into the school parking lot, followed closely by KOAA's and KMGH's vehicles. Cameramen and reporters jumped out of the vehicles, reinforcing the students' fears that something really big was going down. Thinking they were coming to report on some high jinx at a well-heeled private school, the reporters were surprised to see scared kids running in all directions.

Grabbing a young girl by the arm, Joe Kemp, a veteran KOAA cameraman asked, "What the hell is going on here?" Panting, the tenth grader told him that the whole twelfth-grade biology class was being held hostage in classroom 9B—"probably by *ISIS!"* Joe couldn't believe his ears, but that did make some sense of the pandemonium he was witnessing, which was definitely not consistent with a prank photo shoot. Kemp and reporters from the two other TV stations immediately placed 911 calls to the Englewood Police

Department. Englewood is part of the Denver-Aurora Metropolitan Area, in the South Platte River Valley immediately south of central Denver.

Police Chief Eldon Sharp ordered four cruisers to the scene. "Tell them to secure the area but DO NOT, I repeat, DO NOT engage the terrorists! Back up is on the way!" With a population of only thirty thousand, the Englewood police force had no Special Weapons and Tactics Team of its own, so his next call was to Chief Pete Wexler at Denver PD.

"You sure about this Eldon?" asked Wexler, incredulous. "I mean ISIS for Chrissake? What the fuck are they doing in *Colorado*?"

"Not so sure about the *ISIS* part Pete, but I just got calls from no less than three local TV stations who have reporters and cameras already on the scene telling me there's a hostage incident at the school!"

"Well how the hell is it that they are already on the scene and we're just hearing about it?"

"Shit if I know," offered Sharp, "but they are!"

Within five minutes, an armored response and rescue vehicle with a heavily armed S.W.A.T. team was on route. A cavalcade of six black-and-whites, sirens blaring and lights flashing accompanied the Denver PD's Lenco BearCat 3 which would have looked at home on any battlefield in Afghanistan or Iraq. The BearCat was outfitted with .50 caliber armor and high ground clearance so there was virtually no location that it could not go—on road or off. By now a police helicopter was circling the school and the students and staff had been cordoned off from the main building. Frantic calls had gone out from the school secretary to most of the parents including all of those of the students in the biology class.

Inside classroom 9B, however, the teens were oblivious to the commotion outside. Sister Pomeroy had stopped yelling and pounding on the door, but for the time being the girls were too busy to wonder why. Eleven of the twelve were behind the banner, some holding up signs and others the banner itself. Pippa took a quick look through the viewfinder at the back of her phone, satisfied that it would capture the whole group in the classroom venue. She set the timer and joined the group. The high-end Samsung took a half a dozen HD photos at fifteen second intervals with the girls posing this way and that.

"Switch it to video," Samantha suggested.

"Good idea," Inaara said, "that way we can get in some commentary too."

Pippa scampered to the teacher's desk to toggle the camera phone to HD video when all hell broke loose. The classroom door flew off of its hinges crashing to the floor, courtesy of the battering ram wielded by four burly police officers from the Denver PD. A half-a-dozen heavily armed members of the S.W.A.T. team poured into the room wearing Kevlar vests and toting M-16 assault rifles. The red dots from their laser sights quickly found the banner and the terrified girls behind it. They screamed and held their hands up, dropping the signs and the banner in the process. It was nothing short of a miracle that no one got shot to death at that instant. Maybe for the S.W.A.T. team members it was the unexpected sight of eleven naked, defenseless teenagers that registered a millisecond before their collective instinct to pull the trigger.

Frozen behind Sister Pomeroy's desk was Pippa Smythe, still holding the Samsung which had just captured the whole thing on crystal clear 1080 HD video. Figuring that the cops would likely confiscate her phone she hit the "upload to YouTube" icon and off it went, scoring over twenty-five million hits in the first half hour. Once it was discovered there was no terrorist, relief washed over the school campus. Parents who were thoroughly distraught just minutes ago were allowed into the classroom—now elated as they hugged their daughters. Of course, there would be supreme shit to pay later on, but for the moment all that mattered was that the girls were safe. Like the other frantic parents, Don and Ruby Burdenny had dropped everything and raced to the school. After a few minutes, the twelve now fully clothed female students were separated from their parents and taken into police custody for questioning and possible criminal charges. Multiple TV cameras rolling, the teens were lead out of the school in hand cuffs by police amidst cheers from fellow students. "Don't say a goddamned thing," shouted Don Burdenny as Inaara was ushered into the back seat of a police cruiser. "Our lawyer is on his way to the station!" Ditto for most of the other well-to-do parents who had not the slightest intention of seeing their daughters wind up with a criminal record of any kind. In the meantime, the hunt was on for the idiot freshman who touched off the whole mess.

CHAPTER 87

Let's Talk

"No, I don't need any goddamned help in remembering," Kiara told the tall man. "And you'll keep your hands off of me if you know what's good for you," she hissed—a cobra ready to strike. From her seat on the chair she considered a quick elbow strike to his privates, but knew the repercussions would not be good.

"Ms. Davies, I am a pretty patient man on occasion," the Director said. Kiara did her best to look impassive. "Like now for instance." He sat back and spread his hands, palms upwards and raised his eyebrows in a gesture of mock reasonableness.

"What is that supposed to mean?"

"It means that you can think it over in one of our holding facilities until you want to talk," he answered calmly.

"You mean a jail cell?"

"That's a bit harsh. I prefer to call it a holding facility."

"What am I being charged with?" demanded Kiara.

"Nothing yet, Ms. Davies, and if you fully cooperate, probably nothing at all," assured Clinton George III.

"Well, if I am not being charged I want to leave now," she said unequivocally.

"Not until you identify the other person on that phone call."

"Then I want a lawyer."

"I am afraid that is not possible," he replied. "Lawyers just gum up the works, no offence intended to your honorable profession."

Kiara was furious. "First you kidnap me in my own country at gunpoint and now you are unlawfully imprisoning me! What kind of banana republic is this?"

"I told you that this is FBI headquarters in Washington, D.C. in the United States of America," answered the Director. "This is the home of the brave and the land of the free and we in the Bureau are determined to keep it that way regardless of your trivial legal arguments."

"Since when is the *rule of law* a trivial argument?" she shouted. "Your whole goddamned country is supposed to be built on it!"

The Director remained calm despite her obstreperous demeanor. "I agree that the rule of law is paramount in any democracy and ours is no exception," he said. "But sometimes it has to be suspended, particularly in exigent circumstances like the terrorist strikes that we believe that the person on the other end of that call is involved in." He put his palms flat on the table as he said, "And once the terrorist threats have been removed, then the rule of law can be re-activated."

"Funny how that never seems to happen in real life though," she snapped.

"Why do you say that?"

"The former Egyptian dictator, Hosni Mubarak declared a 'state of emergency' when he took power," she responded. "He suspended all legal and political rights of the citizenry."

"Doubtless for good reason," commented George III.

"It was still there forty years later!"

"That would never happen here, Ms. Davies."

"Yeah, Hitler said the same thing after he dissolved the German parliament," she retorted. "It's just short term just until we get things fixed up!"

The Director rose and motioned to the tall man to open the door for him. As he walked out he said, "I really do appreciate your legal arguments, but you will have to come up with something a lot better than that if you plan on getting out of here any time soon. He leaned his head back into the room and said, "Think about it, Ms. Davies. No one knows that you are here." The tall man closed the door behind them.

"Shit!" she said aloud, with only herself there to hear. "What the hell am I going to come up with to get some leverage on this asshole?"

CHAPTER 88

Two Can Play at that Game

When Kiara awoke, everything was pitch black and she was lying on her back on a cot or a small single bed. She sat up and blinked a few times. A wave of panic engulfed her. Had she gone blind? It was no different with her eyes open or shut! She rubbed her eyes gingerly and tried again. Still no difference. Bile welled up in her throat but she held it down. She was shaking. This couldn't be. Did they do something to her? How the hell did she get here, wherever here was?

"Get a grip, counsellor," she admonished herself, aloud. "They want you to panic, to lose your nerve." She wondered how long had she been here. Her Nighthawk quartz chronograph watch had permanent, high-resolution, luminous numbers, but it was gone as well as her shoes and socks. She rolled off the bed and shivered as her bare feet touched the cold concrete floor. She felt into the darkness. Nothing. Letting go of the bed she stepped forwards, hands outstretched. After two steps her hand pressed up against vertical metal bars. She inched sideways clasping the bars as she went, and ran into the cell wall. A couple of steps backward she touched the bed again and to its right was a small sink, with a toilet adjacent. She paced off the perimeter of the cell and estimated it to be about ninety square feet—just about the size of a supermax prison cell. Kiara was not sure how she got here—where ever that was, nor for how long she had been unconscious. She had no idea what day it was or if it was day or night. Panic threatened to overcome her again. She couldn't see her hands or feet or anything else and to make matters worse, it was dead silent. She could hear her heart racing.

Think dammit, think! she instructed herself. You've been in tight spots before and you've somehow always managed to come through. She took deep breaths to calm down as KJ had taught her on camping expeditions to the high plateaus of the Alberta Rockies. Sometimes on a cloudy night on a ten-thousand-foot peak the sky was almost as black as this cell and just as unnerving. She closed her eyes (not that it made a difference) and remembered his powerful, reassuring words: "Breathe from your diaphragm and focus on your *chi*. It's always there. It connects you to everything in the universe, including this pure blackness which is part of the Void."

She dropped to the ground in a lotus position and commenced the slow breathing ritual. After a few minutes she felt more centered. Suddenly, a bucket of ice water landed square in her face, drenching her to the bone. She screamed. When the shock wore off and the cold started setting in she collapsed, sobbing uncontrollably. The tall man cracked a smile. He'd been watching on the night-feed camera.

A few miles away KJ reconned the Landmark Lofts building in the prestigious Capitol Hill neighborhood in Washington, where FBI Director, Clinton George III and Corinne, his lovely wife of three months lived. When he parked the Cayenne Turbo S a few blocks away he snapped a couple of fake plastic license plate covers over its D.C. plates. Printed for pennies on a 3D printer, the plastic covers looked real enough from a distance so if any traffic or surveillance camera spotted the vehicle in the area, the Maryland license plates would make it appear that it belonged to a Ronald King, senior district attorney who also drove a black Cayenne. According to the FBI's records, the Director and his wife resided in the penthouse on the twenty-seventh floor of the Lofts in a three-thousand-square-foot luxury condominium. The state assessment office had it valued for tax purposes at one point eight million dollars. Pearce figured George III would have a security detail on his wife, whether she knew it or not. It would serve the dual purpose of protecting her from potential threats due to his pre-eminent position with the Bureau, and just as importantly he could keep an eye on her comings and goings. After all, a knockout of a wife some twenty-five years his junior might just get a roving eye from time to time.

KJ had only a short time to ascertain the number and location of the security agents watching her. He assumed Kiara was in a precarious position. Extricating her as soon as possible was of the utmost priority. Still, it wouldn't do for him to get apprehended or to have to take out the whole security detail in the process. He had to grit his teeth and play it by the book, however excruciatingly long it took. Positioning himself at a window table in an upscale java bar across the street from the entrance of the Lofts he pretended to read the Washington Post. He drank a grande latte with a double shot of espresso to ensure that he kept wide awake. He had a clear view of the doorman at the front entrance of the building as well as the parking entrance.

Corinne George III, formerly Corinne Cleary or "CC" as she was known on the modeling circuit, was never in the super model club, but she had managed to carve out a reasonably successful, fifteen-year career in the business. That was no small task in the cutthroat world of haute couture. Even when she was on the wrong side of thirty, she had averaged over six figures a year until she pulled the plug for good. When she retired from the catwalk at age thirty-five, she took a course in interior design she used a good chunk of her savings to start up her own business, *CChic Interiors.* She scored the contract to decorate Clinton's new office digs, and swept the recently divorced FBI Director off his feet and into the chapel in record time. KJ studied the photo he had of her.

He folded the newspaper and sipped his latte, wondering how many hours it would take to spot CC. He checked the Cobra—4:02 p.m. "Are you finished with that by any chance?" asked a silky female voice from behind him. He turned to look straight into the face of Corinne George III.

"Be my guest," he replied, stifling his surprise and handing her the Post.

"Thanks," she said, taking a seat across the room. She was still pretty damned attractive. Several male patrons were surreptitiously ogling her from the stand-up bar. KJ pretended to check his phone messages as he scanned the room for FBI agents. His training at Ft. Bragg had included a course on *role camouflage* which involved taking on the qualities and characteristics of another persona during the course of a mission. That could be a delivery man, cop, store clerk, waiter, tourist, customer or anyone else who just blended into the scenery. It was akin to training as an actor but for bit parts only. Sometimes the easiest way to obtain information or access was to pose as an unobtrusive person just doing his mundane day job. However, most security agents did not have sufficient patience to stay in character for more than a few minutes, after which they invariably gave themselves away. Sure enough, not five minutes after he sat down the coffee bar, the chubby Irish-looking guy in the plaid sports jacket double checked his arm pit holster as if his gun might have fallen out between the car and the coffee shop. Satisfied the Colt .45

was still there, he resumed his job of eyeballing Mrs. George III.

KJ figured two agents in the coffee shop and at least one trailer outside, maybe parked in a vehicle or loitering around on foot. Two minutes later he noticed the Irish guy making eye contact with another man seated two tables away from his. It was a subtle glance which would go unnoticed to anyone who wasn't looking for it. The other guy, dressed in a black suit, black tie and white shirt acknowledged it by touching his left middle finger to his earpiece mike. KJ left a tip at the table and then got up, strolled by black suit and out the door. Corinne was still at her table reading the Post. Once outside he donned the Aviators and did a quick scan of parked vehicles. Nothing and no one popped out. Most of the cars were empty and no stereotypical surveillance van was in sight. He ambled up the street toward McBride and Caldwell, glancing at the cars as he went. Still nothing. He crossed the street at the light and walked back towards the java shop. He came up from behind on a black Chevy Malibu parked a quarter of a block from the front entrance. Behind the wheel was a female, twenty-five-ish, smartly dressed in a dark suit, her gaze squarely focused on the café. She had to be the trailer. The passenger side window was partially rolled down so KJ gave it a tap and leaned down.

"Excuse me, do you know the area at all?" he inquired. FBI agent Maria Raines peered over at him as if he was dirt, but she replied with a feigned politeness. "Some, what are you looking for?" Figuring that she probably spotted him coming out of the espresso bar he said, "Union Station. The guy in the café told me to go up a block and that I would see a street sign showing the way." He pointed. "I went up there to the corner over there, but I didn't see anything, so I headed back in this direction."

"Wrong way," she said. "Keep going past my car to the first lights and then turn right. You'll see it."

"Hey thanks," he replied and started walking past her car. Still not totally convinced, he returned and tapped on the window again.

"Now what do you want?" she said in an exasperated tone.

"I was wondering if you were doing anything tonight. My buddy told me that Union Station has got some good bars and ..."

"Beat it!" She opened the flap on her purse revealing inside a standard police issue Smith & Wesson .38 snub nose revolver. "Or I'll arrest you for obstruction!"

"Wow, you're an undercover cop!" he blurted. "Are you on a

stakeout or something?" his eyes wide.

"Just babysitting," she said wistfully. And quickly added, "not that it's any of your damned business. Now get lost or I will personally make you wish you did."

KJ held up his hands in mock surrender. "I give up." He started to walk away and then whirled and came back to the car window and said, "But only if you give me your phone number!"

Agent Raines was not in a playful mood and snatched the handgun out of her purse. As the driver's door started to open KJ quickly retreated. "Okay, okay I can take a hint!" He flashed her a peace sign and set off towards Union Station.

Dickhead, she thought, placing the Smith back in her purse. But he did have a cute ass.

Rounding the corner, Pearce doubled back to the coffee shop through the alley. Short-term objective—take out three armed FBI agents and then grab Corinne George without being seen by anyone, including her. Piece of cake, right? Pearce had to make a command decision to take her hostage now or later. Under normal circumstances the answer would be obvious—later, after he had painstakingly planned the whole operation. But these were not normal circumstances. He entered the java shop and noticed she was still reading the Post, plaid jacket was watching her and black suit was watching them both.

Pearce slipped into the men's washroom and waited. It was quite large considering the size of the java shop. There were three urinals and three enclosed toilets with ornate wooden swing doors on each of them. Fortunately, it was deserted, so Pearce could peek out from time to time to make sure Corinne was still there. Okay, here comes plaid jacket for a pee after downing his third cup of Joe. Pearce entered one of the toilet stalls and stood rock still. Plaid jacket entered and headed to the nearest urinal where he whipped out his Johnson and let go. The agent uttered a huge sigh as his bulging bladder emptied like a water hose. Pearce left the toilet stall and snuck up behind the guy, who was now in the process of zipping up. A hammer fist strike to the side of plaid jacket's neck knocked him out cold. Pearce grabbed him before he could hit the floor and dragged him into one of the stalls. He sat the guy down on the toilet and closed the door.

This time Pearce waited behind the washroom door, anticipating that the second agent would come looking. The door opened and a teen age kid entered followed by black suit. Shit! Pearce had to think fast. The kid headed into one of the toilet stalls. Black suit spotted the other agent's shoes.

"That fat prick's probably got diarrhea—half a dozen cinnamon rolls and three coffees inside half an hour! Heart attack's a waiting bub," black suit said to no one in particular.

Pearce drew the Glock and shoved it into the guy's ribs from behind. "Make a sound and you're dead," he whispered. He grabbed black suit's collar and pushed the agent into the far toilet stall where he cracked the guy on the back of the head with the barrel of the Glock and then sat him down on the john as well. Pearce locked the door of the stall from the inside and slid under the opening between the stalls to do the same with Plaid jacket's door. That should buy him a bit of time. He had taken both agents' phones, badges and handguns. He dropped the phones into the toilet and slipped out under the middle stall door. Removing the clips, he dropped the empty handguns in the garbage can and left the washroom. Not a second too soon either, as Corrine was just exiting the front door.

He waited ten seconds and left through the front door, figuring the agent he'd chatted up would have eyes on Mrs. George and not notice him. He was right. Corinne was heading up the street and when neither agent appeared behind her, Agent Raines got on her cell phone calling plaid jacket. Pearce sprinted toward the Malibu, but on the opposite side of the street.

"What the hell, voice mail?" the agent cussed. "I wonder if that jerk off is on the phone with his ex, again!" As she dialed the second agent's number an FBI shield appeared outside her window on the driver's side. It was black suit's. She immediately rolled down the window and said, "Why the hell isn't agent Palmer answering his ..." Pearce's gloved fist caught her square on the jaw. He opened the driver's door and shoved her unconscious body into the passenger seat. Starting the engine, he put the Malibu in gear and left the parking stall in pursuit of Corinne. He voice-dialed Rafa on the Z30 as he drove.

"Anything new?"

"Yeah, but it's not good," answered Rafa.

"Spill it."

"Looks like J. Edgar Jr.'s had the unidentified suspect transferred to a supermax holding cell somewhere in the bowels of the Bureau's HQ."

"Goddamn it!" was KJ's reaction. "How long?"

"About eight hours as far as I can tell."

KJ told Rafa to keep him posted if anything else came up and clicked *end call*. He spotted Corinne at McBride, as she was about to go into a designer dress shop.

"Thank you, DKNY," Pearce said. He made a quick u-ey with the Malibu and hung a right into the alley near the shop. Pulling over into one of four "Customers of Capitol Hill Designers Only" parking stalls he killed the engine and popped the trunk. Confirming the coast was clear, he hauled agent Raines out of the passenger seat and slung her over his shoulder. Relieving her of gun and cell phone, he dropped her into the trunk and slammed it shut. Now he had maybe ten minutes to get Corinne into the Porsche and out of the vicinity. Pearce entered the dress shop through the rear door. It was a shop for women only, so he adopted the roll of thoughtful boyfriend seeking something for *that special girl*. He strolled down an isle stocked with dress blazers and white blouses, careful to remain unseen by Mrs. George. He noted that there were no security cameras in the store, no doubt because the merchandise was RFID- tagged. A cute, tall brunette sales assistant, twenty-ish, noticed him and strolled over.

"May I help you find something, sir?" she asked pleasantly.

"I'm looking for a dark blue blazer for my girlfriend's birthday," he said. "She's about your size I think. Would you mind picking out one of these and try it on for me?"

"Sure, I'll be happy to," she smiled. "Which label do you prefer? We have a pretty good selection at this time of the year." She pointed–DKNY, Missoni, De La Renta, Wijnants, Dolce & Gabbana, Armani….

"I don't know," he said honestly, peering at the row of expensive jackets. "You look to have pretty good taste in clothing," sizing her up with an admiring glance which she didn't seem to mind. "Whatever you would buy for yourself would probably be okay—black or really dark blue preferably."

She took that as a compliment and grabbed a twenty-one hundred dollar Missoni blazer with the four-button front-spread and sewn-in pocket kerchief. The ultra-fine midnight blue wool was so dark it looked to be black. "That is what I would buy," she announced, slipping into the blazer, "if I could afford it that is."

"Hey, that is nice," he commented as she spun around in the jacket for effect. He half thought of getting it for Kiara as a small offering for the hell she was probably going through this minute. He spotted

Corinne coming down the aisle and bent down, pretending to re-tie his shoe lace as she walked toward the dressing room with a couple pairs of super faded Calvins in hand. "Could you hold that blazer at the front counter for me," he asked the salesgirl. "And while you're at it, pick out the best white blouse in the store to go with it." Turning he pretended to search his pockets. "I think that I've left my wallet in the car but I'll be back in a jiff." For a twenty-five-hundred-dollar sale the employee was happy to oblige, with a big smile to boot. Pearce headed toward the back where the changing rooms were located and noted only one was in use. It had to be Corinne's. The clock was ticking way too fast. Someone was bound to find those two jokers in the toilet stalls and any minute Agent Raines could awake in the trunk of the Malibu and start screaming blue murder. He had to make his move now.

CHAPTER 89

Rise and Shine

When Kiara awoke again she was back in the original interrogation room at the table, unbound, but sans shoes, socks and watch. Her clothes were damp and she was shivering uncontrollably. She was sure they had purposely turned down the heat in the room. The tall man was again seated at the opposite end of the table staring at her, but saying nothing. He wore a cheap black suit, white shirt and black tie. What was it with these morons, dressing like *Men in Black*, she thought.

"Where's that asshole George?" she demanded.

The tall man stared at her impassively for a while. Then he replied, "The Director will come down to see you if you are ready to talk. Are you?"

"About what? Kidnapping, illegal confinement or torture?" she sneered, as she sat straight up.

"About who you were talking to on the phone call we intercepted," he stated. "The Director can't waste his time with your petty legal concerns."

"Then tell the Director that he can go straight to hell!" She folded her arms across her chest and stared back at the tall man—her eyes just daring him to come over. He made no observable response. "There will be a lot of people looking for me by Monday when I don't show up as lead counsel for the Plaintiff in B.C. Supreme Court," she declared. "And when it comes out that I was kidnapped and unlawfully detained by the FBI that's going to cause a shit storm of trouble for your boss!" She figured that would get him thinking.

He looked back at her completely unworried. "You're entitled to your opinion Ms. Davies," he said in a neutral tone. "Get ready for a long stay."

He left the room.

"Hey, where's my shoes and socks?" she yelled after him. No

answer. "And my Nighthawk watch!" The door clicked shut she heard the bolt slide into place. "Mother fucker!" Obviously, the room was monitored so she kept up a defiant demeanor although she was scared. How the hell long was a *long stay?* she wondered. Her B.C. Supreme Court trial would resume in a few days and obviously she would be reported missing. The Director and his goons of course already knew this. How were they planning on dealing with it when she was eventually released?

"Mr. Prime Minister, she came in voluntarily."

"Really, it was all just a big misunderstanding, as she was free to leave at any time but she mistakenly assumed otherwise."

Or maybe just make a bald assertion that U.S. national security trumps the rights of any citizen of any country? As she pondered this, a sinking feeling settled uncomfortably in the pit of her stomach— *what if she wasn't eventually released?* As resourceful and relentless as were KJ and Rafa, did they have any real chance of finding her, much less getting her out? She had to hope. *Dum Spiro Spero.* She was living it.

Not a dozen miles away, Kenneth Joseph Ares Pearce was doing his level best to give life to that aphorism. As he passed the change rooms he noticed only one door was closed. That had to be Corinne's. He slipped into the adjoining room and waited. When Corinne came out of her change room and started walking back into the main area of the store, Pearce stepped out behind her and landed a hard karate chop on the side of her neck. She collapsed without a sound. He caught her and slung her over his shoulder. Once outside, he popped the Malibu's trunk with his key fob, dumped her in with Agent Raines and shut it. He then sprinted back into the store, grabbed the faded Calvins and threw them back into her change room. He sauntered up to the front register, as if he suddenly had all the time in the world. The tall brunette asked him how he would like to pay and he said "cash," and peeled off twenty-five Ben Franklins. She already had the blazer and pure white, soft cotton Victoria Beckham blouse packed in a fancy La Monde box, which had its own carry strap.

"Would you like to be put on our mailing list?" she asked hopefully.

"Maybe next time," he replied.

"Lucky girl," said the brunette, as Pearce was turning to leave.

"What?" he asked, pausing.

"She's a lucky girl to have someone like you," she said, not knowing quite why she blurted that out. Her cheeks were blushing a bit.

"Let's hope so," he said flashing a big smile and wishing like hell that proved to be true.

CHAPTER 90

Fur History

Don Burdenny's high-powered lawyer from Seamor Hobbes LLP in Denver had Inaara out of police custody in no time flat. Truth be told, the teens were facing nothing more than mischief charges in the worst case scenario. Karyn Saunders, the local DA, had been called for advice before any charges were laid. She told the police chief in no uncertain terms that the city of Englewood's legal department had no stomach for a dozen misdemeanor trials with the grade twelve biology class of St. Thomas More. She figured that the parents would doubtless engage high level defense counsel who would turn the whole thing into a media circus and probably bankrupt the small city in the process.

"Here's the spin to put on it, Chief Sharp," advised Saunders. "Since the girls could not have reasonably foreseen that some dumb freshman would turn their anti-fur protest into a major police incident, you will tell the dozen odd lawyers at the precinct the students will be released with a stern warning only."

That didn't stop Tony Frakes Esq. from taking full credit for securing Inaara's release and thus, rendering a hefty fee to Burdenny. "Hey, they saw me coming and just handed over the keys!" he told a jubilant Don and Ruth Burdenny when they arrived at the station. "And they didn't get a peep out of her either! Bonus!" That's just the way lawyers work. Doubtless, this would be a nice billing day for the legal profession of Englewood and surrounding municipalities.

With the unprecedented media coverage generated by the incident, Father Stefan Pasic, the normally autocratic, anal retentive principal of St. Thomas More decided to take the high road and read a prepared statement to the reporters from the three local stations: "Our students are taught to be independent and critical thinkers—always within the law of course," he added carefully. "Sometimes that ruffles feathers or in this case fur—that's a little joke, haha …

but that is the price of independence! Freedom of expression is a constitutionally guaranteed right of all Americans—including our students." Pasic was definitely hamming it up for the cameras, suddenly the modern-day Thomas Jefferson. He adjusted his bow tie and round spectacles and in a stern voice solemnly continued.

"For the record, we at St. Thomas More completely support the fur industry of our fine state. We do not agree with nor condone the behavior of our grade twelve biology class, but the students who graduate from this sixty-year-old institution—yes this is our sixtieth anniversary this year and we are proud of it, must all be able to think for themselves and to articulate and defend their positions when called upon to do so. I cannot stress enough that those views must always be within the boundaries of civility and law however." Most of that self-serving drivel would be edited out before it hit the six o'clock news, but it made Pasic feel important for the moment—his sixty seconds of fame forever immortalized on the tube.

Inaara's ride home to the hotel was anxious. As expected, once the niceties with the lawyer were over and she was escorted to the front passenger's seat things would change fast. Dom had the wheel and he was livid, as was her dad, Don. "How the crap can you stage an anti-fur protest when you work for MBM Colorado?" shouted Dom, gunning the engine as they sped away from police headquarters.

"Well, for one thing..." Before she could finish her answer, the other half of the *Dreaded D's* jumped in.

"Have you totally lost your mind, Inaara? What the hell were you thinking?" scolded Don. "This is going to be an unbelievable PR mess for us!" The one-two tag teaming took over by habit. "Not to mention the bill I'll be getting from Seamor Hobbes! Jesus, they sent Tony Frakes over in the middle of the afternoon! Probably pulled him out of court to boot!" Don added for emphasis. A fifteen-thousand-dollar legal bill was hardly going to break Burdenny—he would doubtless write it off as company business, being the cost of damage control for MMB. Still, anybody with high-end legal talent loves to bitch about the fees. It's a sign of having *made it* when you can throw those numbers around at a cocktail party.

Dom sped north on I-25 at eighty-five miles per hour and took the turn off to west Colfax at close to that speed. This caused Ruby Burdenny to career into her husband's lap in the back seat. She was not wearing her seat belt and told Dom to slow down or else. He dropped the needle to sixty as the Audi crossed Speer Boulevard.

343

"Sorry, Mom."

Inaara had not said another word fearing that anything else she could say would only make matters worse.

That didn't stop Dom from voicing his opinion. "I think that Inaara should be permanently grounded. Home and school, that's it."

"She's already grounded or have you forgotten?" commented Don, "and this incident happened *at school!*"

"Damned, you're right, pops. She's getting into shit while she's grounded! Unbelievable!"

"Hey, watch your language, son! Mom's in the car," Don reminded him.

"Sorry again, Mom," said Dom again as he hung a hard left onto Broadway, which would take them directly to the Ritz-Carleton. "Maybe you should think of pulling her out of St. Thomas More," he suggested, Dom, himself a graduate of the prestigious Kent Denver School. "I mean that dick Pasic was just on the news blabbering about turning out independent thinkers and all that crap! It's just encouraging kids to be trouble makers like *someone we know.*" He nodded towards Inarra. She stuck her tongue out at him.

"That's enough out of you!" said Ruby, finally deciding to add her two bits. "I happen to support Inaara's decision!"

"What?" shouted *the D's* in unison. Inaara suddenly sat up straight. She couldn't believe her ears. "She showed some spunk in organizing her class to take a stand on a cause that she believes in," explained Ruby. "That's something I wish that I could have done when I was her age, but it wasn't permitted for a girl to express any opinion of consequence back then." The Audi was pulling under the portico of the hotel and Dom handed the keys to the valet.

Riding the elevator up to the penthouse floor, Dom, Don and Inaara were silent for the time being, dumbfounded by Ruby's remarks. This was going to be interesting.

CHAPTER 91

Prisoner Exchange

Not too familiar with the locale, Pearce located the Cayenne with the GPS in his Blackberry. He pulled the Malibu in behind it and turned off the ignition switch. It was close to dusk so there was not a great deal of light and the dinner crowds were not yet out. The coast looked to be clear. He was, however, well aware that the coast was never completely clear since it only took a couple seconds for anyone to pull out their smart phone and take an HD video of some guy moving an unconscious woman from one vehicle to another. Inside of thirty seconds it could be on YouTube and he would be the subject of a police manhunt within minutes. That simply wouldn't cut it. There was a stand of red maple trees between the Cayenne and the apartment buildings on one side, but the view from the other side of the street was less obstructed. He decided to fix that by double parking the Malibu beside and slightly behind the Cayenne, effectively blocking the view of the buildings across the street. Popping the hatch of the Cayenne and the trunk of the Malibu simultaneously, he pulled a car blanket out of the rear of the SUV, threw it over CC and rolled her into it. A quick scan showed no one in sight, and he hoped no one watching, so he picked up what appeared to be a rolled-up carpet out of the trunk of the Malibu and put it in the cargo section of the Porsche. Remote closing the Cayenne's hatch he checked on Agent Raines, who was still out cold—but for long? He closed the trunk of the Malibu, got into the driver's seat and pulled it into the alley.

Before abandoning the car he popped the trunk one last time. Removing the Glock from his shoulder holster he screwed on a silencer and examined agent Raines. Her breathing was okay, some bruising to be sure would follow but she'd live. He shot a couple of air holes in the bottom of the trunk. No point in letting her suffocate if no one happened along while she was still inside. He threw the keys into the bushes along with her badge, removed the battery from her cell phone and threw both into a trash receptacle near a bus stop. That would at least prevent the Fibbies from tracking her down via her phone. The Freetoo tactical gloves he wore would leave no prints. He sprinted back toward his vehicle only to find a couple strolling along hand in hand had stopped to admire the uber stylish Cayenne Turbo S. The guy was explaining to his girlfriend how the five-hundred-seventy horse power V8 power plant could rocket the heavy vehicle from zero to one sixty in four point one seconds, ultimately topping out at one-hundred-seventy-five miles per hour if the driver kept the pedal to the metal. Don't wake up yet! KJ mentally commanded CC as he got closer. Hitting the key fob, he unlocked the driver's door and jumped in.

"Hey, nice wheels," said the guy. "Must have set you back a pretty penny!"

"Yeah, don't remind me," complained Pearce not looking directly at him. He fired up the engine and pulled out giving the couple a quick salute that partially concealed his face. He disabled the Bluetooth in the vehicle to prevent it from storing his calls and phone messages and voice dialed Rafa.

"Got the package," he said.

"What's the exchange policy?"

"Working on it now," said Rafa from his office in Vancouver. "Will advise when it's finalized. Over and out."

"Roger that," answered Pearce. The sure-footed Porsche tracked along the narrow streets back toward the Willard Intercontinental Hotel. Dark clouds were gathering. A storm was imminent.

Prisoner exchange protocol—Kiara for Corinne, was at the top of Rafa's mind. He wondered how it could be done without the FBI double-crossing them in the process, given that they had the full resources of all the U.S. intelligence services at their disposal, with hundreds of agents available on a moment's notice. He had one ex-JTF2 lone ranger at his disposal, albeit a pretty damned formidable one.

Okay, let's run a few simulations on the computer …

CHAPTER 92

Unexpected Allies

The elevator stopped at the penthouse floor and the Burdennys all got out. Dom slid the magnetic key into the door and stepped in first. To break the ice, he said, "Who wants a drink?"

"Gimme a rum and coke," said Don immediately.

"Gin and tonic," said Ruby.

"I'll take a Corona," added Inaara.

"No, you won't!" said all three in unison. She sure as heck wasn't off the hook yet.

"Okay, okay, a rum and coke with no rum," she said timidly.

"That's more like it," said Ruby. "Now park your behind in that chair young lady."

"Oh, oh!" she thought. Maybe she misheard Mom in the car! The *double D's* collective ears suddenly perked up. Obviously, they must have also misunderstood Ruby's comment in the Audi. They could feel it coming. This was going to turn into a brutal triple-team pummeling of Inaara. Dom couldn't wait for his turn and tagged in first.

"I vote that we ground her in the hotel room period," he said. "And then we should …."

"Can it Dom!" said Ruby, firmly cutting him off.

"But, Mom…"

Don piped up. "Ruby's got the floor, Dom," sensing that she meant business.

"Damned right I do Don," said Ruby, "and don't interrupt me again either of you." She took a sip of her drink and then laid into Inaara like there was no tomorrow. "First off, Inaara, it is bloody well not alright to embarrass the whole family in public" she shouted. "Second, you never, ever, ever bite the hand that has been feeding you for almost your whole life!" holding out her palm as if she was feeding a biscuit to a dog. She stared straight at Inaara, who would not dare to look up to meet her withering gaze. "And last but

347

not least, you could have gotten your whole class killed by a po-lice S.W.A.T. team!" She steam-rolled on, not pausing for a breath. "How many kids don't even have enough to eat? Hmmm?" she said. There was silence.

"Lots, I guess," said Inaara timidly, still not looking up.

"Hey, look around downtown Denver. Tons of people don't have proper clothes to wear, much less sending their kids to private school! No response was forthcoming. "You hearing me, Inaara?" Inaara nodded yes, not daring to utter another syllable. The com-ments kept coming fast and furious. She was lucky she didn't get expelled—good thing that the family had a high-powered lawyer. On and on it went for five minutes non-stop. Inaara looked straight ahead and took the tongue lashing. "Now have I made myself per-fectly clear?" said Ruby.

"Yes, Mom," she replied meekly.

"Are you ever going to pull a stunt like that again?"

"No, Mom." Dead silence followed.

"Now as I was saying," said Dom, chomping at the bit to start in on his younger half-sister.

"I'm not finished yet, Dom," said Ruby.

"Sorry."

"Despite what I just said, I am still proud of Inaara," she an-nounced, to everyone's surprise. "She showed a lot of guts to take a stand on behalf of our farm animals!"

Don jumped up from the couch, almost spilling his drink. "What the hell is that supposed to mean?"

"You know darn well what it means!" she snapped back. "We treat those mink like crap and you know it!"

Dom weighed in. "Mom, that's the way you're *supposed* to treat farm animals—if you want to make money that is! I mean, they are just a commodity, right? It's not like they have a bright future or anything."

"That's right, sweetie," Don said. "Dom goes to the fur auction every quarter to get the best market price—no different if he were selling timber or wheat," he explained.

"That's bullshit and you know it!" she shot back. The *D's* were shocked. They had never heard Ruby swear before. "The mink feel pain. I've walked by the barn when the farm workers are electrocut-ing them and when that doesn't work bashing their heads in. They make the most pitiful, agonizing sounds I've ever heard. I can't sleep for days after that."

"That didn't stop you taking a coat or two, did it?" said Don, feeling betrayed.

"Well it should have," she replied dejectedly, dropping down on to the couch. Tears were coming to her eyes. "You know, every woman is at least *supposed* to want a mink coat," she said. "It's a status symbol and of course, the fur is extraordinarily beautiful. When I got my first one I thought that I died and went to heaven."

"Exactly!" confirmed Dom, sympathetically.

"But I knew," she added with regret in her voice.

"Mom, we're fulfilling every woman's wish!" He believed what he was saying. "Why do you think that the *coat list* is so popular?"

"I'll tell you why. It's because every politician, bureaucrat and police chief wants to make their wife or significant other feel like you did when you got your first coat!" added her husband trying to console her.

Inaara jumped up from her *hot seat,* hopefully not into the fire, but she had to say her piece. "That's just plain wrong!" she stated. Utter defiance framed her youthful features. "If those wives, girlfriends or whatever knew what the mink were going through so that they could have a coat they would puke!" She made a gagging gesture.

"Hey, who says that you have a say?" demanded Dom, pointing a finger. "You're in deep shit already."

"She's part of the family and she gets to talk," Ruby replied forcefully. "And don't bring up that 'she doesn't get a say' line again!" She downed the rest of her gin and tonic and ordered Dom to make her another one. "It's true that she screwed up royally with the protest at school, but she would have never had to do that if we had been responsible farmers who properly cared for our animals," explained Ruby.

"Hon, now you're totally losing it," said Don, thoroughly exasperated. "Ranchers raise mink so they can harvest their pelts for fur coats. See, that's the gist of the operation," he explained, as if addressing a five-year-old. "Every single one of them gets killed in the process. There is no way to dress it up as being nice or kind to the animals."

"That's right, Mom, it is what it is," confirmed Dom, now the pragmatist.

"Well maybe it shouldn't be that way," said Inaara. "Those animals have a right to live just like we do!"

"Says Miss Private School who hasn't worked a single day in her whole life!" retorted Dom. "How do you think that we pay the bills, including your thirty-six grand a year tuition?"

"If it'll save some mink, I'll go to public school in a heartbeat," Inaara shot back.

"And I'll downsize my Escalade to a Pathfinder. That should save a few more mink," echoed Ruby.

"Whoa, before we all get too carried away on social justice bandwagon, let's think this through," said Don, suddenly the voice of reason. Inaara and Ruby looked at him skeptically; Dom, expectantly. "MBM has been damned good to us for twenty odd years now. We've built up a nice profitable business which put the kids in top notch schools. We've got nice cars and a fabulous house ..."

"You mean we *had* a fabulous house! Do you really think that the insurance company is going to cough up for the re-build?" queried Ruby.

"Oh, they'll cough up alright," said Don, "or Frakes will drive a bulldozer right up their ass in court!" clenching his fist and waving it to and fro. "Now as I was saying," he continued. "We've got some money put away and a nice insurance payout will put the farm back on its feet. You want us to get some bigger cages for the mink—done. You want more humane killing-done. Maybe we get lethal injections like the prisons."

"But no last-minute reprieves by the governor!" added Dom, trying to inject some levity into the discussion.

Ruby and Inaara glared at him, not exactly amused. "How about no killing PERIOD," said Ruby.

"Well how do you suppose that we get the pelts away from the mink then Ruby?" asked Don somewhat sarcastically.

"You don't," answered Inarra, "because you change the business model to something more socially responsible—*and way more profitable*."

"Oh yeah," asked Dom incredulously, "like what?"

"Marijuana!" answered Inaara emphatically.

"MBM. Marijuana by Minx!"

"I like the sound of that," said Ruby.

"We have already done the research, Dad," explained Inaara gleefully. "With marijuana now being legal in Colorado we could get the insurance company to pay for new greenhouses instead of barns. Given the amount of land we have MBM could easily become the biggest legal grow-op in the state!"

"And with new, state-of-the-art greenhouses, we could produce *the* highest quality, organic weed which would sell at a premium price—way bigger margins than mink pelts, not to mention a lot more environmentally friendly!" added Ruby.

"And socially acceptable too!"

Ruby got up and went to the kitchen counter and pulled out from the top drawer a comprehensive business plan prepared by KPMG accountants at a cost of thirty thousand dollars. She had put on the farm's line of credit with Bank of America with neither Don's knowledge nor permission. It outlined in detail the substantial profits to be had by taking the farm in this direction.

Dom was impressed. "Holy shit! Whoops, sorry, Mom, but what on earth have you two been up to?"

Don the businessman was definitely not opposed to the idea of making more money, so he quizzed the girls about the licensing process, while doing his utmost to appear neutral about the whole idea.

"As the business plan mentions on page fifty-two," said Ruby, who had read it cover-to-cover twice, "it's getting pretty tough to get a new growers license for sure, but someone with Don's pull would have a pretty good chance." Don's mouth curled up in a smile without showing any teeth. He did have to admit that part was true. There was nothing in the *Fresh Air and Fond Memories* state that Don Burdenny could not procure.

Jesus, the girls might just have come up with something, he thought, not letting on that his interest was piqued. He couldn't give a rat's ass about the welfare of the mink BUT if more dough could be made growing weed ... he'd give it a look. "Gimme that report would you, Ruby," he said, plunking himself down on the comfy leather couch and accepting the thick coil-bound report. "Dom, order in a couple of large pizzas and bring me a Dos Equis from the fridge."

"Coming right up, pop," said Dom, now also in a jovial mood. "How bout I get the mega-meat lovers for us and maybe a large *veggie delight* for the ladies?" he queried now playing the smart ass.

"Vegan delight," corrected Inaara definitively.

CHAPTER 93

You First

Rafa had tried every scenario he could come up with but it seemed obvious that any contemporaneous exchange of prisoners would almost surely be met with a double cross by the Fibbies. There was just no way Pearce could get her and then get them both out of the country after Corinne had been returned. Once Clinton George III regained his wife, the gloves would definitely come off and he would have all the advantages.

"What have you come up with?" asked KJ, by way of the Z-30.

"Zip so far," Rafa replied. "I've run twenty plans and we get screwed at the end of each one if that dickhead George III reneges after he gets the package."

KJ considered that. "I think that we have to assume that's pretty much a given." He looked over his shoulder to make sure Corinne was still out cold on the bed. She was. "Then we don't do a simultaneous exchange at all. The Feds will just have to release our package first."

"How do you figure that they'll go for that?" Rafa asked. "Well, they snatched her out of her apartment to start with, so surely they could do it again as soon as she resumes her normal life as a lawyer—that is if *their* package is not returned in due course."

"Okay, I get it. We welsh out on our end, the Fibbies would just go back to Canada and grab her again," Rafa advised.

"Right you are, only we don't have that same option if we release our package first."

"Okay, it's worth a shot," said Rafa. "I'll get an encrypted message to the Director right away."

"His profile says that he's a pretty good chess player," commented Rafa.

"Well let's see how he copes with the *Stonewall Attack*," said Pearce, a bit of a chess buff himself.

CHAPTER 94

You've Got Mail—Again

Clinton George III was only partially satisfied with his catch. The intercepted call was definitely suspicious but since most of it was still undecipherable it wouldn't stand up in court without the Canadian lawyer's cooperation.

"Fucking asshole judiciary," he muttered. "Why couldn't they be all like the *FISA* court judges?" Calling out to his assistant, he said, "Jenna, would you get Agent Conroy in here right now please." The prisoner was going to break—of that he was certain, but it couldn't come too soon. In short order her disappearance as lead counsel in an important environmental case in the B.C. court system would become a big deal and a messy police investigation would ensue. He didn't want this to turn into a diplomatic row with the Canadian government. Although he was confident that Kiara Davies' disappearance could never be traced back to the Bureau, he wanted the information out of her sooner than later. Once she talked she could then be safely returned to Canada without further worries. Having breached solicitor/client privilege by informing on her client (if the guy on the other end of the call was in fact a client), she could be disbarred or at least disgraced in the profession if that fact became publicly known. After all, nobody likes a rat, even if the rat was forced to squeal—so there goes her legal career if we spill the beans on her. We agree not to and she agrees not to go public. It's a double victory as they say! Naturally we'll continue to spy on her, tap her phones, monitor her internet usage and all that, but she'll be none the wiser. Big brother at the NSA has the best technology to keep tabs on the wayward.

Clinton felt like patting himself on the back. The buzzer rang and agent Conroy was shown in.

"What do you have for me, Tom," quizzed the Director, now in a reasonable mood, for him.

"On *the guy* or the lawyer in lock up, sir?" replied Conroy, fashionably attired in his black Hugo Boss suit. As an FBI agent, even a senior one, Conroy was still required to stick to the *Men in Black* motif, but no one said that it had to be done in the Moore's Menswear style. His black silk tie was Armani and the classic white Thom Browne Oxford shirt was an impeccable fit, even on a guy somewhat past his best before date.

"Both," said the Director retaking his seat. "I need a cup of java. You want one?"

"Sure," said Conroy, not used to any niceties from the Director. He hit the phone intercom and asked Jenna to get two coffees, "black as usual," and looking at Conroy and reading his lips, "and one with cream and two sugars."

"Let's have it," said the Director.

"May I?" asked agent Conroy starting to remove his suit jacket, so as not to wrinkle it by sitting.

"Of course," responded George III, who also appreciated sartorial elegance himself. Conroy carefully hung the two-thousand-dollar jacket over the back of the chair and then got down to business.

"First off, we have got nothing whatsoever on *the guy*. Day and night, ten agents have been sifting through every special forces' discharge since 2013—honorable and otherwise, and there is not a thing-zilch that suggests that any one of these guys has one iota of sympathy for any animal rights or welfare cause."

"Tell me something that I don't already know," said the Director dryly. "There are no witnesses, no video footage and no tips worth shit so far. This *guy* is like a ghost."

"Do you have any good news?" asked the Director, getting up and starting to pace.

"Yes, I think our esteemed legal guest downstairs is going to crack anytime now. Gladys is going to douse her with a bucket of ice cold water again tonight when she least expects it. Wow, did that ever get a rise out of her on her first night!" boasted Conroy.

"Tom, we don't have a lot of time," the Director said. "She's got some kind of big environmental trial starting next week and if she doesn't show, a lot of people will be looking for her."

"That's why I've got a little surprise for her tonight as well," said Conroy.

"Do tell."

"I was talking to agent Nikki Patel in forensics this morning and by pure coincidence she happens to be working on a new, improved truth serum which she says is—and I quote, 'pretty much guaranteed to dissolve even the most stubborn perp's mental defenses,' unquote." The Director cracked open the box of *Drew Estates* and offered one to Conroy.

"Don't mind if I do," he said examining the fine cigar. "But isn't this a nonsmoking building?"

"Not for me," answered George III, holding out a flashy Bugatti B-1 torch. The sleek gunmetal lighter produced a blazing hot single flame which readily started the *Fat Robusto* in Conroy's hand and then the Director's as well.

"Apparently it's some kind of combination of ethanol, scopolamine and 3-quinuclidinyl benzilate which is similar to FP-117, the truth serum used by the FSB in Russia," explained Agent Conroy as he took a drag on the big stick. "According to Patel, the best part is that this new 'remedy' as she calls it, not only rapidly loosens the tongue, but it has no taste, no smell, no color, and no immediate side effects.

"Hmmm." The Director's tone was approving.

"And, get this," Conroy added with a sly smile. "A person doped up with this stuff has no recollection of having a chat and feels afterwards as if they just suddenly fell asleep."

"Sounds just like what the doctor ordered," quipped the Director. "How are you going to administer it?"

"After Gladys soaks her again tonight, we'll let her freeze for an hour or two and then we'll turn up the heat in her cell *a lot* and leave a nice glass of water laced with the stuff on the small sink by the bed. As soon as she drinks it we'll turn on the lights and have a little heart-to-heart," said Conroy, also quite pleased with himself.

As soon as the words, "Best plan I've heard all day," left the Director's lips, the emergency light on his Verizon Networx Enterprise phone system started blinking. The call was ultra-high priority and not to be ignored. "Jesus fucking Christ, now what?" he said, annoyed that his rare moment of well-being was being interrupted. Punching the intercom button, he warned, "This better be good Jenna."

"Sir, please check your email inbox," she said nervously. He glanced toward the monitor on his desk, swiveled in the Aston chair and hit the secure email icon. The new email immediately popped up.

"Attn: FBI Director Clinton George III. If your lawyer guest isn't released from her supermax prison cell in FBI headquarters and put on a plane out of Dulles to Vancouver inside of sixty minutes, you can kiss Corinne Cleary George III goodbye."

"Holy shit!" exclaimed the Director. "Tom, look at this!" The color rapidly drained from his face.

"Once the plane touches down at YVR, your wife will be returned to you safe and sound, assuming of course that the lawyer arrives in the same condition. If we renege, I am sure that you will find a way to illegally recapture your guest, as you did in the first place. For that reason, I can assure you that we will unequivocally honor our part of the bargain. When the lawyer is back in Canada you will agree not to surveil or spy on her in any manner, failing which we will re-acquire your wife and she will disappear without a trace *permanently*. Don't bother trying to trace this email. It's a technological dead end. Sixty minutes. The clock is running."

It was signed "*The guy.*"

"The nerve of that mother fucker threatening my wife!" George III was thoroughly pissed.

"How the hell did he know that we have the lawyer here?" asked Conroy.

"Obviously there's a hole in our security system big enough to drive a goddamned Mac truck through! Find it and I mean now, Conroy! And get it plugged!"

"Yes sir!" Conroy said, hopping to his feet. He grabbed his unwrinkled Boss jacket, then stopped. "Sir, you've got a security detail on your wife, right?" asked Conroy. "That's standard protocol for the Director of the FBI, is it not?"

"Of course!" stated the Director firmly. "I've got three experienced agents following her every move twenty-four-seven—even though she hasn't got a clue."

"Good, it's probably a bluff then," said Conroy as he grasped the door knob and left the room.

The Director immediately grabbed his Blackberry Priv and speed-dialed Corinne's cell number. "Hi this is CC. Please leave me a message and I'll call you back as soon as I can," said his wife's silky voice.

"Shit! Shit! Shit!" Clinton George III crushed out the *Fat Robusto* in his fancy Merlot ashtray—the damn thing was made of solid brass and could likely double as a boat anchor. He wished he could smash it over *the guy's* head. Hitting the intercom button again he shouted,

"Jenna get me one of those goddamned agents on CC's security detail on the phone stat!"

"Right away sir," his assistant answered anxiously. Holy smoke, what was up with the Director? He was normally very polite with her.

CHAPTER 95

Tit for Tat

When there was no reply from any of the agents guarding CC, the Director knew *the guy* had him by the balls. How that bastard managed to grab his wife right from under the noses of three experienced FBI agents was a mystery. Heads would roll when he got to the bottom of this, but for now he had to assume that she was being held hostage—probably somewhere in D.C. He summoned agents Conroy and Wyatt as well as deputy Director Anna Shallal to his office and sat them down at the front of his massive steel and glass desk (another CC special order no less). No pleasantries this time. He was all business and sober as a judge. After explaining the situation and shrugging off the "I can't believe its" from Wyatt and Shallal he ordered Wyatt to "go fetch Kiara Davies and put her on my jet to Vancouver, British Columbia—fucking stat!"

"Jenna, get my pilot on standby right now," he ordered his secretary through the intercom.

"Sir, you can't be serious!" said Wyatt. "Negotiating with a terrorist is to be discouraged. It says so right in the Bureau's Handbook. There's a whole chapter on it." Norman Wyatt was the tall man who sat in the holding room with Kiara on the two occasions she was brought there for interrogation. If he hadn't been a long-term, trusted agent who had actually saved George III's proverbial bacon on a mission gone wrong several decades ago, he would have been sacked on the spot for making a remark like that. No one openly questions the Director to his face.

"I'll put that comment down to a brain cramp just this once Norm, but don't *ever* question my orders again. Got it?"

"Yes, sir," said Agent Wyatt, completely put back in his place. The Deputy Director asked if she should have an agent or two at the airport to see who picks her up and then maybe follow them.

"That would be a good suggestion, Anna, in normal circumstances," said George. "This *guy* however is anything but normal. Sure as shit he spots the agents and my wife disappears for good."

"I couldn't agree with you more, sir," said Conroy, now the yes man. He leaned forward, his elbows on the desk, sleeves on his crisp white shirt rolled up and looking dead earnest. The black MTM Air Stryke II diver's watch that hung on his left wrist matched his black silk tie to a tee. "How *the guy* tracks your wife down, figures out who is watching her, takes all three of them out and grabs her in broad daylight—well, that's not a fucking normal operative. Pardon my language, ma'am."

"No need, agent Conroy," the deputy Director replied. "I was in the field for fifteen years before getting this desk job."

"Is this the same guy who got a hold of one of our RQ7 Shadows?" asked Wyatt, venturing back into the conversation.

"None other," replied Conroy.

"Same guy who blew up the mink farm in Colorado with a ton of military grade C-4?"

"Yeah, that's him," sighed Conroy.

"Same guy who hacked a government's website, posted threats to hell and back and nobody can still trace them?"

"Ditto," Conroy replied with grudging admiration in his voice.

"Blew up the medical building at George Regis U?"

"You got it. And the galling thing is there was not even one casualty in any of the campaigns, despite the substantial amount of destruction to property!" stated Conroy, thoroughly flummoxed.

"I know," replied Anna. "The newspapers are making *the guy* out as some kind of Robin Hood for animals," she said, a tinge of envy also permeating her tone.

"Maybe the FBI should try to recruit him!" offered Wyatt trying for a bit of levity, but the result went over like a lead balloon.

The Director slammed his fists down on his desk with a thundering sound, jolting everyone to attention. "Enough!" he shouted. "This bastard is nothing but a terrorist and kidnapper! The last thing I need is for my own goddamned agents signing up to join his fan club!" The emergency light on the Verizon started blinking again. "Arrrgghh!" He grabbed the receiver and motioned the three to remain sitting. "Okay, okay go ahead," he said into the receiver. "You're shitting me!" he said into the phone sarcastically. He listened for another minute, added "No fucking way," and then put the caller on hold. If you looked up the word *exasperated* in Wikipedia, a picture of the Director at his desk this minute would appear above the definition. He clenched his fists and inhaled a huge breath like he was going to explode. Instead he reached for the *Drew Estates* again, snatched out the last remaining cigar and lit it. Then he put the phone on speaker and said, "Repeat that again, agent Fowler. You are on speaker with the deputy Director and two other FBI agents, Conroy and Wyatt."

"Hello all," said Rand Fowler. "As I was telling the Director, agents Palmer and Dawson were both found unconscious in adjoining toilet stalls in the bathroom at the Starbucks Café across from the Landmark Lofts, where the Director and his wife reside. Agent Palmer had no recollection of what happened. One minute he was taking a pee and the next he was out cold." A short pause ensued as the three exchanged glances. Fowler continued his narrative. "Agent Dawson however, recalls going into the bathroom to look for agent Palmer and before he knew it a gun was shoved into his back and he was forced into a toilet stall and cracked on the head with a gun barrel."

He had a rapt audience.

"Both agents will be okay but neither of them has any description of the guy who took them out nor do the restaurant staff, as the café was quite busy at that time."

"Okay, what about agent Raines?"

"She turned up in the trunk of her Malibu near a clothing store where your wife was shopping before she disappeared," said Fowler. "A passerby heard kicking and screaming sounds from her car and called the cops who pried the trunk open and found her," reported Fowler. "She had a sore jaw, but that was about it. *The guy* left a bottle of Perrier sparkling water and a couple of aspirin in the trunk for her."

"Son of a bitch!" cursed the Director. "No wonder the bastard's got everybody eating out of his hand!"

The three almost smiled, but thought better of it.

CHAPTER 96

Free to Go

The lights came on out of the blue, or rather out of the black, temporarily blinding Kiara. Of course, she had no way of knowing it was only 2:00 p.m. Eastern Standard Time. The iron bars on the front of her tiny cell quietly slid open and the tall man stood there, accompanied by FBI agent Gladys Frost, whom Kiara had never seen before. Gladys was a twenty-year veteran of the force and looked every year of it. She had been working the *dungeons,* as the super-max cells were called, for the last thirty-six months—a demotion of sorts for botching an assignment to pick up a high school student and bring her home after school. It had seemed simple enough. The high school student was however, none other than Marianna Peloski, daughter of the Speaker of the House of Representatives. She was not only a spoiled brat, but on the verge of being kicked out of school for breaking pretty much every rule in the book—and a few which were not even in there.

Recent threats directed towards the U.S. government had caused the "terror alert" in the country to be ratcheted up to orange, so it was determined from above that the sons and daughters of the highest-level politicians should get an escort home from school for the remainder of the week, as a precautionary measure. No use in having one of the kids of a high-ranking politician snatched by a terrorist outfit on their way home. This took up the time of some four hundred FBI agents, who mostly saw this exercise as a waste of time, not to mention, tax payers' money. The powers that be did not care what they thought however. Due to a communications glitch, no one told Marianna that the feds would be picking her up. So when Frost and her partner showed up at the school in the standard black Crown Vic, she naturally assumed that she was being busted for something— maybe the large stash of drugs in her locker. Her and her boyfriend jumped in his Audi TT and sped off. The agents pursued them in a high-speed chase around the school grounds which in addition to scattering students to and fro, resulted in the Audi being wrapped around the goal post on the school's football field.

Thankfully, there were no serious injuries, but about sixty thousand dollars in property damage generated a lot of bad press for the Fibbies. Frost caught the flak as it was her team that messed up. So much for being considered for regional Director after her sixteen exemplary years on the force. Rather than a bucket of ice water, this time Gladys was armed with a stylish black women's business suit, new shoes and Kiara's watch and (uncharged) cell phone. These were placed on her small cot. The tall man spoke.

"You are being released, Ms. Davies." She was still rubbing her eyes, not entirely sure that she heard right.

"What did you say?"

"As soon as you are dressed you will be put on the Director's private Lear jet out of Dulles and flown directly to British Columbia."

"And why the hell is that?" she asked angrily. "The Director suddenly got an attack of conscience, did he?"

As usual the tall man ignored her remark and simply said, "You will be fully de-briefed before the plane takes off Ms. Davies." He motioned Gladys to come over and said, "If you need anything in the meantime, agent Frost will see to it." Agent Wyatt abruptly left without saying another word.

Kiara was ecstatic to be leaving this hell hole, but she willed herself to present a stern exterior. "For one thing, I'd like a shower before getting into these," she said to Gladys. "Somehow," raising her eyebrows, "accidently I am sure, a bucket of cold water got thrown in my face and ruined all of my clothes—and I'm still wet. I guess the heat in this place is not too reliable either."

True to FBI form, Gladys ignored Kiara's remark and said, "The shower is through there and to your right Ms. Davies," pointing the way. "There are fresh towels and toiletries in the stall," she added, now suddenly the amiable guest host.

Kiara grabbed her clothes and watch and headed toward the showers, passing by Gladys as if she did not exist. The suit was a basic Boss jacket and trousers probably from Nordstrom's, but they would do. Meanwhile, KJ was already making arrangements for a direct, non-stop flight out of out of Ronald Reagan International to Vancouver. As soon as he had word from Rafa that Kiara had landed safely, he would release CC into the streets of nation's capital no worse for wear, as she had been unconscious since he grabbed her in the DKNY store. A tranquilizer dart would keep her that way for a while longer. Still, KJ had serious doubts about the trustworthiness of Fibbies despite his major, albeit temporary leverage.

From now on Kiara would doubtless be the subject of surreptitious surveillance by the U.S. authorities, however remote or discreet. Clinton George III would triple the security detail on his wife and figure that *the guy* would be unable to pull off his snatch-and-grab trick a second time. He could live with that however. His main concern for the time being was making sure that Kiara got home in one piece. He could sort out the other issues later.

Meanwhile, Kiara tried to relax in the luxury cabin seat of the Director's private Lear jet on route to British Columbia. One stewardess was on board to see to her needs, so she ordered a gin and tonic and closed her eyes, recalling the debriefing with the Director before she was chauffeured to Dulles in his personal bullet-proof, IED-proof limo. Clinton George III was sitting behind his massive steel and glass desk and she was seated opposite him in one of the uber comfortable designer guest chairs.

"Ms. Davies," said the Director in a neutral voice, "we have made a mistake, a grievous mistake in bringing you here."

"You think?"

"Our techs at Quantico have finally made some headway with that telephone intercept and found that there is nothing which would suggest that you have any involvement with the animal vigilante," he lied.

"Didn't I already tell you that?"

"You did indeed," replied Clinton George III, feigning regret. "But as you know in matters of national security the FBI can't just take the word of a suspect or person of interest at face value."

"Goddamned national security!" shouted Kiara. "If I hear that term one more time I'm going to throw up!" She shot out of the chair and placed her hands on the edge of the desk, leaning toward the Director menacingly. Wyatt started to move from his station near the door, as did Conroy from the other chair, but the Director waved them off. She addressed Clinton George III, as a hard-nosed litigator would a defendant on the witness stand. "Every time the State tramples on someone's rights it plays the *national security* card," she stated looking him square in the eyes and gripping the front edge of the desk. "Invade a country to locate weapons of mass destruction and find none—*in the name of national security!* Spy on everyone's emails, phone calls and internet searches—*in the name of national security!* Terminate terrorist *suspects (including American citizens)* by way of armed drone strikes anywhere in the world with no charges, no trial, no defense—*in the name of national security!* Render suspects to secret prisons in foreign countries to be interrogated under torture—*in the name of national security!* Just where does this process stop, Mr. Director?" she demanded.

"I'm afraid it doesn't, counselor," Clinton George III replied, shifting in his comfortable seat and forcing a sigh. "After 9-11 the free world changed. There are more threats to the security of this great country than ever before—cyber threats, bomb threats, threats from the Middle East, Russia, ISIS, Al Qaeda, Syria, North Korea, Libya—the list is endless."

"And why do you think that the U.S. is a target for all these groups?" she asked.

"Oh, that answer is obvious, Ms. Davies," answered the Director with absolute certainty in his voice. "Clearly they are resentful of our way of life!" he explained.

"Sure as ants at a picnic," added Agent Conroy. "Why do you think that so many people want to emigrate here?"

"To live the American Dream, that's why!" replied Wyatt throwing his two cents in. "The good ole U.S. of A is the best place in the world to live in—bar none. Naturally people who don't already live here are jealous and they just want to take us down a peg or two." Nationalistic pride stirred in his voice.

Kiara Davies Esq. didn't look convinced in the slightest. "You don't think maybe invading other countries, overthrowing governments and installing puppet dictators, funding your own terrorist groups when it suits you and generally medaling in everyone else's affairs around the world might have something to do with that?"

"Hardly," said the Director, brushing off her accusation with a wave of his hand. "Every country of influence does those things. Historically it was the Brits, the French and Spanish and more recently the Russians and the Chinese—we just do it better!"

"That doesn't make it right!" she shot back.

"Might *makes* right counselor! And don't you ever forget it!" Clinton George III sat bolt upright, unflinching. "No one could publicly say that in our current world of political correctness but when you get right down to it you either take what you want or someone else takes it," explained the Director as if lecturing a grad student. "It's human nature, survival of the fittest as Darwin said—and we are by far the fittest empire in the history of the world!"

"Sorry, I don't buy that crap," said Kiara, sitting down, but far from resigned. She continued resolutely, "Canadians respect the rights of others to live as they wish on their own terms—and we don't just go take what we want from someone else, we earn it!"

Agent Conroy got up and slowly strolled over, eyeballing the savvy, good looking litigator with a certain amount of admiration mixed with distain. "And why, pray tell Ms. Davies, do you think that the citizens of our northern neighbor have the luxury of holding such lofty beliefs?"

"I'm sure that you are going to enlighten me," she said sharply.

"Due to the fact that *your southern neighbor* has got your back! Do you honestly think that the United States of America would sit back and allow *any country in the world* to attack Canada?"

Now the discussion was wandering into one of the Director's pet peeves—the Canadian military, a standing joke for many in the U.S. "He's got you there cold, counselor," he said, the fox crouching down for the kill in the hen house. "Your country has the option of spending literally nothing on its military while enjoying the full protection of the most powerful nation on earth."

"Stick that in your Canuck pipe and smoke it!" added Wyatt.

Conroy chipped in. "We spend almost six-hundred-billion dollars a year on our military to protect the U.S. and its allies—including Canada. What do you cheapskates spend, maybe fifteen billion—and that's in a good year!"

"Well, we are not a war-mongering nation," countered Kiara somewhat defensively, "we value peace over conflict."

"Really?" asked the Director, pulling up some Canadian defense contract stats on his monitor. "Is that why your country is shipping fifteen billion dollars' worth of military ordnance to Saudi Arabia over the next few years?"

Kiara deadpanned him. "Well that contract was put in place by a previous government," she countered.

"But not cancelled by the new one, right?" countered Clinton.

"Right," she conceded. "I suppose they needed the jobs in Ontario, with the bulk of manufacturing positions having gone to China by default over the last decade or so."

"Wow, what a newsflash counselor. Military spending creates

good paying, stable jobs—even in a supposedly peace-loving nation like Canada!" exclaimed the Director, sticking the knife in *hard and turning it.*

"Touché," she said reluctantly, not liking being outmaneuvered in a war of words by anyone.

"National security is not a dirty word, counselor," Clinton went on, pressing his advantage. "It's what keeps the barbarians at the gates and not inside the castle!"

"Save it for the neo-cons," she retorted. "You want a police state, that's your business. Now are you going to let me out of here or not?" her feistiness rapidly returning.

"Here in D.C.? But you've never been here Ms. Davies," replied Agent Conroy. "This little incident never happened and when you are back in Canada in a few hours, it will be just a distant memory, a mere day dream."

"What the hell are you talking about?" Kiara demanded incredulously. "What he means, counselor," said Clinton smugly, "is that there is no record of you having ever left Canada nor landing in the U.S." He examined his perfectly manicured finger nails for a minute (the Bureau had Simon Wong, the best esthetician in D.C. on staff and the Director's nails were always top priority). He continued earnestly, saying, "and there will be no record of you arriving back at any Canadian airport either. This has been an entirely secret trip."

"The hell it was," shouted Kiara. "When I get back I'm going straight to the press, the Law Society and the federal government! We'll see how bloody secret it turns out to be!" She was livid.

"Calm down, Ms. Davies," said the Director.

"Don't fucking tell me to calm down!" she shouted, standing up again.

Both Conroy and Wyatt rose from their seats.

"Who is going to believe you? How will you prove that you were even here?" the Director sneered.

"There have to be flight logs." She was not entirely sure of this, but it seemed logical. "The FAA and Transport Canada require them for all flights."

"The FBI is exempt from that requirement under the provisions of NORAD," replied Conroy, joining the conversation again.

"NORAD?"

"Come on now Ms. Davies, you have never heard of the North American Aerospace Defense Command? That surprises me coming from someone who has actually read the U.S. Patriot Act!" the Director chided. He swiveled the thirty-two-inch monitor toward Kiara and pulled it up on Google:

"NORAD is a bi-national military organization formally established in 1958 by Canada and the United States to monitor and defend North American airspace. It plays a critical role in the defense and security of Canada and the United States. NORAD monitors and tracks man-made objects in space and detects, validates and warns of attack against North America by aircraft, missiles or space vehicles, and also provides surveillance and control of Canadian and U.S. airspace. Canadians and Americans under NORAD command were the first military responders to the September 11 attacks. NORAD is the longest-standing partnership in our collective histories, and the only agreement of its kind in the world. It remains a powerful symbol of trust and confidence between Canada and the United States in the common defense of our nations and our borders."

Conroy decided to explain. "Under this longstanding agreement, there will be no public record of this jet entering or leaving Canadian airspace, so you will have an uphill battle convincing anyone that you ever left the country counselor."

"My phone's GPS will have a ..." and then she bit her tongue.

"Already taken care of," answered Conroy, a step ahead of her. "Although we couldn't hack the phone in such a short period of time, we managed to convince Blackberry to remotely disable the location function on your phone when we first picked you up. You can turn it on any time after you get home and re-charge the battery."

The Director explained that the U.S. government is the biggest single customer of Blackberry and while the Canadian originator of the iconic smart phone did not have the encryption codes, nor a *back door* into the phones, it has been known to cooperate on non-privacy related matters from time to time in matters of national security.

"Shit, that's discouraging." Kiara grudgingly acknowledged the FBI's ultra-long reach. The buzzer rang and Jenna entered the room with a tray of coffee and tea, which she carefully placed on the Director's desk.

He offered Kiara some freshly brewed Kicking Horse coffee directly from Indonesia. "Fair trade, organic, Kosher and brewed, I might add in your own country Ms. Davies," he said. "Or you can have steaming matcha green tea flown in directly from Japan— plain or with organic coconut sugar and/or organic dairy or coconut cream." The Director and his two agents accepted a coffee from Jenna and Kiara reluctantly allowed a green tea to be poured into her cup, plain.

"It's not drugged, is it?" she asked sarcastically.

Jenna quietly left the room. Apparently not hearing her question, the Director set his cup down and forcefully laid down the law. "Now here's how this is going to go down," he instructed. "You are going to get on my private jet and be flown directly to a small airport in Delta, British Columbia, called *Boundary Bay*. You will not mention this incident to anyone, as it never happened."

Kiara remained expressionless and said nothing.

"We will deposit the sum of $1M USD into your Canadian bank account, or any bank account you may designate, or to any charity of your choice, if you don't want to take our offering. This is as you lawyers would say, *a without prejudice* proposition which takes into account the inconvenience and mental distress which you may have experienced, but it does not constitute any admission of guilt or culpability on our part. No written documents will be signed or exchanged."

"So, I just take the money, shut up and forget the whole thing happened?" asked Kiara incredulously.

"Succinctly put, counselor," replied the Director.

"And if I don't?"

"Naturally we will deny everything and stonewall any investigation the Canadian authorities launch. Then we will do our level best to thoroughly discredit you and destroy your legal career," said the Director calmly, as if he was discussing the day's weather report. After a brief pause he took a swig of the sweet, smoky brew and continued. "As you can imagine, we are quite good at these sorts of things. For example, Agent Wyatt could…" he left the sentence hanging as Wyatt continued it for him.

"Plant some cocaine in your car or apartment and tip off the VPD drug squad," said the tall man whom she had only heard speak twice.

"Or maybe we could circulate some intel that one of the clients that you are so vigorously defending is a secret front for ISIS, of which you as his lawyer are fully aware," added Conroy. "That sics CSIS and CSEC on your ass for a long time."

"How about we …"

"Okay, okay I get it," said Kiara cutting him off. "If I play ball, how do I know that you won't do these things anyway?"

"You don't," replied Clinton George III. "But I can assure you that when the Director of the FBI makes a deal, he never breaks it. That goes back all the way to J. Edgar I might add."

Kiara was skeptical, but in the circumstances, what else could she really do but accept their deal? She sipped her tea and tried to analyze the pros and cons. Firstly, it would be next to impossible to prove that she was illegally rendered from Canada by the FBI and returned safely a few days later—no scars, bruises or other evidence of captivity. Secondly, if there were no flight records and no phone GPS data it would indeed be her word against that of the Federal Bureau of Investigation, the staunch ally of Canadian security agencies and senior partner in *NORAD*. Still, something just didn't add up. If the Feds did de-encrypt the phone call, they would have known that she was talking to someone who was involved in the George Regis incident. Likely she would now be facing felony charges as an accessory to an act of terrorism and be facing a grand jury indictment. If they hadn't cracked Rafa's phone cipher, then why the hell were they releasing her, with a cash bribe no less? The FBI wasn't exactly known as a benevolent outfit.

"I want your guarantee, Mr. Director, that if I take you up on your offer that as a *quid pro quo* the Bureau will also forget that this incident ever happened, erase me from its database and agree not to spy on or surveil me in the future."

"To reiterate, Ms. Davies, this incident never happened and therefore it cannot exist in our records either," the George III assured her obliquely.

She sat sraight up in the luxury chair. "That's not what I asked you," ever the litigator. "Are you or are you not going to erase my name and profile from your records and refrain from spying on me in the future?" she repeated. "Yes or no?"

"Yes," answered the Director, "of course."

"And I'll just have to take your word on that, too?"

"Yes, you will counselor, but when the Director of the FBI makes an agreement..."

"Yeah, yeah, I know," she said interrupting his routine.

"How would you like to receive the $1M USD payment?" asked the Director, preparing to end the meeting.

"I'll get back to you on that with wire transfer instructions," she answered, assuming that Rafa could figure out a way to receive and re-route the money anonymously. It would definitely replenish their depleted war chest.

"Fine," said Clinton George III, turning his attention elsewhere. "Agent Wyatt will escort you to my car." He hit the button on his intercom summoning his executive assistant, Jenna. "Now if you will excuse me, I have quite a few more moles to whack!"

CHAPTER 97

Return to the True North

The call to Rafa came in at 11:42 p.m. Kiara used a pay phone from the tiny airport in Boundary Bay, Delta. The pistol-packing, female trial attorney extraordinaire was back in one piece! "Halle-fucking-lu-jah!" Rafa said over the line, absolutely ecstatic. "It worked!"

"What worked?" asked Kiara puzzled, but as happy as a clam at high tide to be on Canadian terra firma.

"Grab a cab right away. Will fill you when you get to my place—not yours," he replied excitedly. "I've got to let KJ know, pronto."

"Where is he?" she queried holding the receiver closely to her mouth, while peering around the airport unconsciously scanning for Fibbies. As it was late at night and the Lear was the only plane that had recently landed in the small airport, it would be difficult for anybody to be watching her without being spotted. However, she couldn't tell if anybody else had deplaned from the jet after she had entered the airport—or maybe was already here waiting. A quick glance outside revealed that the Lear was no longer on the tarmac. "His phone went directly to voicemail when I called," she reported to Rafa.

"When you get here K, all things will be known to you" said Rafa, the omniscient one. "But make sure those contemptible federales don't follow your cab though!"

"How did you …?"

"Magic," he quipped. "Now I gotta make this call ASAP. See you soon."

"Wait," she said. "Before you go, the Director is prepared to pay $1M USD in hush money to me to be deposited anywhere I choose."

"Wow, is that ever an unexpected bonus!" he exclaimed.

"Can you handle that without it being traced back to us?" she asked.

"I'll see what I can do," he said.

Having no luggage Kiara skipped the small baggage carousel and headed straight out to the curb. A lone Yellow Cab was parked outside, the Boundary Bay airport being more or less deserted at this late hour. The youngish East Indian driver opened the back door of his Prius hybrid for her and asked "Weer tu Madom?"

"Vancouver," she answered. "And there's an extra fifty bucks in it for you if you make sure that there is no tail on us."

"No tail, Madom?" he asked unsure of the idiomatic expression. "What meaning is this?"

"That no one is following us," she explained.

"Ah ha," he said, a light bulb going on. "Like the movies?"

"You got it."

"I bill be 'berry expert at that, Madom!" he assured Kiara as he punched the meter on the dash and the electrically powered vehicle silently sped off into the night.

"The package has arrived safely," said Rafa, his Blackberry on speaker. KJ was relieved beyond measure, but said only, "Roger that."

"Over and out," countered Rafa.

Pearce stowed the Z-30 in his jacket and immediately began gathering his things. He had only a few clothes, but the ordnance and of course, CC would be the big ticket items to dispose of. The weaponry that he had picked up at Union Gun Shop upon his arrival in Washington was still stowed in the two huge, black canvass duffle bags. As it turned out it was not needed—and that was a damned good thing. He would dump CC in another large canvass bag and load the three bags on to a large trolley which he called for from the lobby.

"No, just have the bell boy leave it at the door. I'll wheel it down into the elevator myself," explained to the front desk. "And have the Cayenne Turbo ready to roll in ten minutes. I'll be leaving it at Ronald Reagan International later tonight." In fifteen minutes he had checked out of the hotel and the Cayenne was heading west on Pennsylvania Avenue. Two blocks later he hung a left on 15th and then four blocks later a right on Constitution Avenue. Twenty meters later he hung a diagonal right putting him onto Ellipse Road NW. The Ellipse, officially known as *The President's Park South* is a fifty-two-acre park immediately south of the White House grounds. Planned in 1791, the now public park had a colorful history. It was originally

372

used as a corral for horses, mules and cattle as well as a camp site for Union troops during the Civil War. In the mid-1800s it became a baseball field for the Washington Senators, as well as several other local teams. In the 1890s, Congress authorized the use of the Ellipse grounds to special groups, including religious gatherings and military encampments. Sporting events and demonstrations are still to this day held on the Ellipse, which came under the jurisdiction of the National Park Service in 1933.

Pulling the SUV off the road and in the shade of a thicket of trees, he killed the engine and turned off the headlights. Going EVA, Pearce re-conned the area extensively and when he was sure that no one was in the vicinity, he popped the Cayenne's trunk and removed the large canvass bag containing CC. Unzipping the bag, he gently removed her for the moment, unconscious body and placed her in a sitting position against a towering spruce. The park was getting dark and was mostly deserted by this hour. Noticing that CC was starting to come to, he stuffed her cell phone in her front pocket and then returned to the vehicle. He emailed Rafa from the Blackberry that the drop had been made. Rafa would pinpoint his location via her phone's GPS and email the coordinates to the FBI Director as soon as Pearce was gone. Pearce pulled out slowly, making one last visual sweep of the surroundings. Satisfied that the area was still deserted, he left the Ellipse without incident and headed toward the airport. Within minutes the place would be swarming with Fibbies who would find Mrs. Clinton George III no worse for wear and wondering what the hell all the fuss was about.

CHAPTER 98

They're Called "Fibbies" for a Reason

Just three miles south, Pearce reached Ronald Reagan Washington National Airport quickly and without incident. The local radio station made no mention of the kidnapping of the FBI Director's wife as Clinton George III had decided that embarrassing detail need not be released to the media. Upon entering the airport he maneuvered the Cayenne into the rental vehicle line and pulled it to a stop. The parking attendant gave it a whistle of appreciation and took the keys from Pearce. The high-end vehicle would be back under the portico of the Willard Intercontinental by morning. "I've got the luggage," Pearce advised hauling the big black canvas duffle bags and a small carry on satchel onto a parked luggage trolley which he rented for two dollars. Once inside the building he headed for the public lockers where he would store the ordnance for pick up by the owner of Union Gun Shop the following day. It would probably take three oversize lockers, so he checked his pocket for change. He had plenty.

"Shit!" exclaimed Pearce. To his dismay he discovered that there were no luggage lockers at Ronald Reagan Washington National Airport! Goddamn it! How the hell could he have overlooked that? With a huge sigh, he wheeled the trolley over to the food court and ordered a grande latte from the Starbucks's kiosk. Sitting down he mentally catalogued his options.

One: Check the bags and hope that they weren't x-rayed before boarding. A couple of hundred thirty-five pound, oversized duffle bags -fat chance! After 9-11 that was not going to happen. Dollars to donuts that was one of the main reasons that there were no storage lockers in the airport. Two: Stash the bag outside the airport somewhere and call Jeff Parker to pick it up. That was a no-go. He simply couldn't risk of the weapons being found by the wrong people before Jeff got there. Even if the bags were found by an innocent by-stander doubtless they would be turned into the airport authorities or the police. Conceivably the ordnance could be traced back to Union Gun Shop. Strike that option. Three: Get some storage advice. Finishing his coffee, he dragged the trolley over to the information booth on the other side of the mezzanine and asked the girl at the counter where he could store the bags. She advised him that the closest option would be Union Square. It had short term rental facilities starting at about three bucks a day. Checking the Cobra, he decided there was an outside chance that he might have enough time to make it there and back before his flight departed. Taking down the address, he wheeled the trolley out of the airport and hailed a taxi from the long line of waiting cabs. Out of habit the cabbie popped the hatch on his Ford Escape and before Pearce could stop him, he attempted to grab one of the large bags off of the trolley. It did not move, catching the Cockney cabbie off guard. "What cha' got in their mate, lead?" he asked Pearce.

"Close," replied KJ thinking quickly. "Just some fitness equipment for my kid brother. He's trying to make the football team."

"Oh," replied the cabbie. "I got me a bit of a bad back. I dunno if …."

"Here, I'll give you a hand," said KJ easily hoisting each bag and depositing them into the back of the hybrid. The good-natured cabbie knew the area like the back of his hand and quickly maneuvered the small SUV onto George Washington Memorial Parkway, turned onto I-395 and was cruising at highway speed inside of two minutes. As he slowed down to take exit 9 to Louisiana Avenue, Pearce got a ping on the Z-30 indicating an incoming email. "URGENT! K's in trouble. Her cab's being pursued by Feds on Highway 99 north!" KJ's heart skipped a beat and then another, as he realized he was completely powerless to help his friend. It figured that those bastards would renege on their promise the minute that George III had his wife back. They weren't called *fibbies* for nothing. But he wasn't expecting a double cross this soon! KJ speed-dialed Rafa. "What's going on?"

Rafa, trying to stay as calm and rational as possible explained he had gotten a call from K about ten minutes after her cab left the airport. "She spotted a tail—black SUV Suburban, and evidently told the cabbie to shake them."

"And did he?"

"Not exactly. The cab was a Prius hybrid, not a Jag—hold on, I think that's K on the other line!" said Rafa, switching lines. Pearce

375

literally stopped breathing, his heart still beating at 55 bpm, but that could change fast. Seconds ticked by as the cab rounded Columbus Circle and continued on Columbus Monument Drive North East. They were only a few minutes from Union Station Drive. After what seemed like an eternity, Rafa came back on the line and shouted, "Those lousy motherfuckers!"

"What happened?" Pearce forced his voice to remain steady and calm.

"The Delta police spotted the chase and got in on the act with two black and whites," he stammered. "As they were pursuing both vehicles the cabbie took the River Road exit and tried to ditch them by heading toward the River house marina and … and …" His voice was trembling uncontrollably. The pause was excruciating for both men. Pearce pursed his lips and continued to stare straight ahead. They were almost at Union Station now. "… and the cab flipped and landed in the water and then K's line went dead a few seconds later…." Pearce closed his eyes. The smallest tear trickled out of the corner of his left eye. He was dead silent.

"Hey mate, we're here," said the cabbie turning around to see his passenger, eyes shut and holding the phone to his ear straining to hear any scintilla of positive news. "Hey guy, sorry to disturb you but…" Suddenly, it was as if an unseen switch was thrown. In the blink of an eye Pearce was into *combat ready* mode. He commanded the driver to turn the cab around and immediately head to the Willard Intercontinental.

"I'm on it gov!" replied the cabbie, speeding back into traffic.

"Monitor the radio frequencies and news feeds," Pearce said into the Z-30. "Keep me posted. I am going back to pay K's former host a surprise visit! Over and out!" His command was crisp, his voice as cold as ice. A quick call to the Willard confirmed that his room had not been re-rented yet and therefore would be ready upon his arrival, as would be another identical Cayenne—it was no trouble at all, the night manager assured him.

"That's why you leave a $200 tip with the concierge when you check out," he reminded himself.

As the cab pulled up under the portico of the Willard, the bellhop opened Pearce's door. A second hop was about to try to lift the bag out of the hatch when Pearce told him to "leave it to me." His tone of voice was such that the bell hop stood still at attention.

"Yes, sir," the young man answered.

"Just bring the Porsche around," ordered Pearce. Before the words had left his lips, a black Cayenne Turbo S rounded the corner and came to a stop smartly beside the cab. Pearce grabbed the huge canvass duffle bags and deposited them into the hatch back of the Cayenne. He gave the Cockney cab driver a Ben Franklin and told him to keep the change.

"Hey, thanks mate!" exclaimed the good-natured cabbie, as the fare was less than half of the C-note he just pocketed.

"No luggage for now," he informed the bell boy. "Have the room key available at the front desk when I get back."

"Yes, sir," said the young man smartly, almost saluting. Pearce jumped into the driver's seat of the Cayenne and burned rubber out of the hotel lot, heading toward the Landmark Lofts in Capitol Hill like a guided missile. He punched the address into the Z30's GPS and did a quick mental rundown on the contents of the duffle bags: one AT-4 Anti-Tank Weapon, M-16 automatic rifle with 240 rounds of ammo, Glock 20 handgun (with silencer), Leupold night scope, two flash-bang-, and three explosive-grenades, a couple of smoke canisters and a Fostech Origin 12 automatic shotgun with three twenty round clips. He speed-dialed Rafa.

"Update?"

"Cops and fire trucks and ambulances all over the Riverside Marina," reported Rafa. "They pulled two bodies out of the capsized Prius cab."

"Bodies?" asked Pearce, almost biting his tongue.

"Living bodies," added Rafa. "But apparently not by much."

"Jesus!" said Pearce. "Where did they take her?"

"Chopper just left. News reports say that both were airlifted to University of British Columbia hospital emergency department."

"She doesn't make it, the Director won't live out the night," stated Pearce as a given.

"They have the best medical staff in the province, so let's hope," replied Rafa.

Still in combat mode, Pearce shifted gears and asked Rafa if he could locate CC by the GPS in her phone. He had left the IPhone 6S in her front pocket at the Ellipse and he assumed that like most phone addicts, she had it with her 24/7.

"Can do," he said as he powered up the *Alien* and started the tracking software. The powerful Cayenne Turbo S began rapidly chewing up the Washington pavement. He hoped that the gods of war would grant him a clear path to his target. If they didn't, given his present frame of mind and the amount of firepower he had on board, heaven help anyone who got in the way!

CHAPTER 99

Close, but no Cigar

Rafa telephoned Kiara's parents and told them to high tail it over to the UBC emergency department. When they heard the news, they were devastated and tried unsuccessfully to interrogate Rafa.

"Hey, just get over there and I'll get there as soon as I can and I will fill you in," he explained. He desperately wanted to be at the hospital if—no, when, Kiara woke up, but he had to help KJ get the Director's wife in his sights right now. She would be their leverage. If Kiara didn't pull through tonight he had no doubt that KJ would take out Clinton George III as soon as the opportunity presented itself. And for his part, Rafa would damned well do everything in his power to help KJ make that happen. The *Alien* started pinging and a map of metro D.C. materialized on the screen. She was moving, obviously in a vehicle given the speed, along I-695 in an easterly direction. Abruptly the vehicle turned off the highway and headed north along 8th street where it would intersect with Pennsylvania Avenue in four blocks. It appeared that she was headed home. He advised Pearce of her present and anticipated locations.

"Got it," he replied as he viewed the most direct route to Director's home address on the Cayenne's onboard map screen. As the Willard Intercontinental was not far from the Capitol Hill residential area, he arrived at the Landmark Lofts complex ahead of CC. He pulled the vehicle into an alley, popped the hatch and unzipped the large canvas bags. His mini-maglite illuminated the area. Removing his windbreaker, he put on the shoulder harness and holstered the loaded Glock 20, stuffing a silencer into the pocket. Next, he snapped a twenty-shot clip into the automatic shotgun and laid it on the backseat. Removing the M-16 automatic assault rifle, he noticed that the clips were empty. Fortunately, Parker had the two hundred forty rounds of 5.56mm ammo already mounted on stripper clips so loading the thirty shot magazines would be quick and efficient. As he affixed the speed loader to each magazine, he slid the stripper clip into the rails and pushed ten rounds at a time into the mags. Inside of ninety seconds he had the eight magazines fully loaded and one snapped one into the assault rifle. The AT-4 was next.

He cradled the weapon, pulled the transport safety pin and un-snapped the shoulder stop. Then he popped up the front and rear sites and unfolded the cocking lever by placing his thumb under it, pushing it forward and rotating it downward and to the right. It then slid backwards on its own. He would leave the final cocking procedure to just before firing. Grenades were placed on the front passenger's seat. He pulled on his black windbreaker and slid back into the driver's seat of the Cayenne. Doubtless there were several agents in the vehicle which CC would be arriving in and possibly an additional Suburban or two tailing them. The Director would have to surmise that there would be some immediate retaliation and that as before, his trophy wife would be the obvious target. Little did he know how much retaliation there would be if Kiara Davies Esq. did not survive the FBI initiated car chase. Scorched earth? Shock and awe? That would not even begin to cover it. He would take out the convoy, the Director and his whole fucking team including the agents driving the pursuit vehicle in Delta. Then he would get back to his campaign. For now, however, those thoughts were in the far distance as immediate action may be required when CC's vehicle appeared.

The Z-30's ringer sounded. "This is home base."

"I'm listening," KJ said.

"The convoy CC is travelling in includes two vehicles, one leading and one following. It is obviously taking a circuitous route," explained Rafa.

"To make sure no one is tailing them."

"Right you are. ETA at your location is about twenty minutes unless they increase the zigzagging," stated Rafa.

"In which case, it could be longer."

"Anything else?"

"K's parents are at the hospital waiting on pins and needles," said Rafa. "They promised that they would call me the minute they heard anything."

"Roger that." KJ hit the end call icon and the phone went black. All weapons were ready for a quick, lethal strike. He settled back into Cayenne's ultra-comfortable adaptive, 18-way driver's seat and hit the *Fast Tube* icon on the phone screen. Scrolling into the "history" he located 'OM @ 432 Hz' and tapped the start icon, ear buds in. Time stood still.

CC's and the Director's lives hung in the balance.

CHAPTER 100

The Clock is Ticking

The emergency department at the UBC hospital was not particularly busy for a Saturday night. A convenience store stabbing, an assault on campus, two ODs from a frat party and a few other odds and ends were occupying only about a third of the medical staff on call at the ultra-modern, incredibly well-equipped facility. In the metro Vancouver area, University of British Columbia Hospital and Vancouver General Hospital split the lion's share of all public funding for medical institutions. That was more than enough to ensure that each facility was outfitted with state-of-the-art technology and top caliber doctors and nurses. Thus when Kiara and the cabbie were air lifted to the heli-pad at the top of the hospital there were already two ER doctors and full nursing staff on hand to meet them as they were wheeled in by the paramedics. Triage protocols had already sorted out the procedure before the copter touched down. Each patient was dispatched to an emergency theatre and surrounded by an ER physician and several nurses who efficiently and methodically went about their business carrying out standard medical procedures—resuscitation for the cabbie and acute care for Kiara—x-rays, CT scan, full blood work up…the whole enchilada. Outside in the waiting room, Mr. and Mrs. Davies were beside themselves with worry. Several of Kiara's colleagues at work had been contacted as well and were anxiously pacing.

A dozen turban-clad cabbies milled about the waiting room. They had been alerted by their dispatcher that Interjit Sidhu, their colleague, was being treated for severe, life threatening injuries as a result of what was thought to be a road rage incident. Although he was a rookie cabbie—this was his first week on the job, many more cabbies were on the way along with Interjit's fiancée who was being driven to the hospital in his parents' old Windstar minivan.

A few miles away, Rafa was in his apartment waiting for any

update, while fully engaged with KJ to turn the tables on Clinton George III. The second hand on the Cobra raced ahead. CC and company were fast approaching the Lofts. Pearce mentally synced with the heartbeat of the universe, patiently waited for the gods of war to reveal the next step in this cat and mouse drama. Suddenly out of the corner of his eye Pearce caught sight of the first black Suburban pulling up to the front of the Lofts. It was followed by two other identical SUVs. The side and back windows of each were tinted dark so they were opaque. All three came to a stop, but remained idling, doors closed and headlights now off. Only the vehicles' running lights were visible. Clearly they were waiting for something, but it was not clear what that was. Pearce took the opportunity to check the AT-4.

The recoilless antitank weapon was a joint effort of the Saab Bofors Dynamics AB (Sweden) and ATK Inc. (U.S.). At one hundred fifty yards, the single shot, anti-tank weapon could easily blow apart the middle vehicle instantly killing all occupants. It would severely damage the other two in the process. The shock wave from the blast would disorient the passengers of the end vehicles allowing Pearce to go EVA with the Fosteck shotgun. On full auto, it could lay down a non-stop barrage of steel projectiles which would shred anything in their path, effectively preventing any return fire from the occupants. Inside of twenty seconds everyone in the remaining two vehicles would be dead. In combat mode, Pearce was prepared to take out the entire convoy. He bore no malice toward any of the occupants of the vehicles and in particular the Director's wife, but if Kiara died this night, they would all be joining her on the other side. No quarter would be given. Clinton George III would be next.

The Fosteck was at the ready in the front seat. He clipped a couple of grenades to his belt. They could be hurled into the burning vehicles in conjunction with the shotgun attack if any resistance was encountered. The three vehicles sat idling. Pearce sat waiting for a call. Many miles away in Vancouver, Rafa Matus was busily trying to re-hack into the FBI computer system. He tried various protocols and novel combinations of protocols with no success. His Z-30 rang, distracting him from the maze of numbers on the Alien's screen. It was Pearce.

"Any news on K?"

"Nothing yet."

"Any luck on the hack?"

"Ditto."

"Shit."

"Ditto that too." Rafa swiveled in his chair and explained that his earlier success with the Fibbies' system related to a couple of security flaws which seem to have been patched of late.

"That figures," said KJ. "We can't assume that they wouldn't do a full security scan after you got in the first time."

"What's going on there?" asked Rafa.

"I'm about two hundred yards from the target's residence and she is in the middle vehicle in a string of three black Suburbans at the front curb," explained KJ.

"What are they doing now?"

"Nothing, just idling .... it's as if ....," his words trailed off in thought, "they are waiting for something."

"Or someone," offered Rafa.

"Someone?" KJ queried. "Like who?"

"How about you?" A light bulb went off in Pearce's head. Suddenly it made complete sense. The Director knew full well that there would be retaliation from *the guy* and he was setting the stage for it. "Jesus, he's using his own wife as bait!" exclaimed KJ.

"Well, we always knew that he was a prick," said Rafa.

"But just not how big a prick!" answered KJ. It suddenly dawned on him that the neighborhood was probably swarming with FBI agents in waiting. Had he launched the AT-4 and then moved in for a mop up operation he would have doubtless been killed or captured. CC would of course be dead as well. Doubtless the outwardly grieving Director would publicly insist that he was merely trying to get his beloved wife to safety when this lunatic blew up her vehicle and security detail. Pearce mentally kicked himself for not noticing this obvious ruse. He had violated the first rule of battle—don't ever engage the enemy in an emotional state. Major Connell, his hard-nosed CO at JTF2 had told him and his cohort over and over. "You must be calm, alert and totally focused on the mission before you take the first step. Otherwise it will probably be your last." In retrospect, since learning of Kiara's plight, he had been none of the above. If not for the conversation with Rafa, it may have cost him his life. He heaved a huge sigh of relief and gently shut his eyes. His mind gradually grew calm and as such, began to logically assess the landscape. There were probably a dozen or so Fibbies scattered around the neighborhood. He would go EVA and find them and take them out one by one if possible. That would permit him to carry out the strike on the convoy if bad news came in regarding Kiara. In the meantime, he offered Rafa a suggestion. "If you can't get into the Fed's system, maybe try hacking the Director's phone and see who he's been talking to."

Rafa slapped his palm to his forehead. "You are a total genius!" exclaimed Rafa. "I'm on it. Out!"

"Roger that, said KJ slightly perplexed at Rafa's sudden enthusiasm." He quietly exited the Cayenne, slung the AK over his shoulder and screwed the silencer on the Glock. He was in stealth mode.

Rafa on the other hand was literally jumping for joy. Trust a novice in the world of cyber warfare to notice the obvious, he thought, and a true master to miss it. He had CC's cell number which would give him the keys to the Director's calls, emails and texts. The hack which Rafa had in mind used the network interchange called Common Channel Signaling System No. 7. It acts as a middleman between most public, switched mobile phone networks in the U.S., handling details such as number translation, billing, local number portability, SMS transfer and many other back end operations that connect individual callers and/or their networks together. By exploiting a protocol vulnerability in the CCSS7 system well known to hackers, and oddly enough still available despite widespread publicity in 2014, Rafa could track CC's location based on mobile phone mast triangulation. He could also read her sent and received text messages, and log, record and listen into her phone calls, simply by using her phone number as an identifier. And guess who she made the most frequent calls to? Rafa smiled as he initiated the same snooping procedures on the Director's cell phone! Now let's see what you have been up to Clinton George Motherfucker the Third.

Despite the high level of encryption on the Director's Blackberry Priv there was nothing that he could have done to have guarded against this kind of spying, short of keeping his mobile phone turned off with the battery removed. This hack happens on the network side, so it makes no difference what kind of phone is used nor what security software is installed on it.

As he started reading logs of the Director's emails and phone calls he came across some internal FBI communications to agent Patel about the truth serum to be used on Kiara—*no particular safety concerns as long as it gets results.* An email to Deputy Director, Anna Shallal, dated before Kiara was put on his plane to Canada instructed her to have operatives at the Boundary Bay airport to "pick her up" as soon as CC was recovered. Clearly the Director's word was worth shit—not exactly a news flash though.

"Wow!" Rafa exclaimed aloud, as he came across some juicy phone logs which the Director had recently intercepted off of CC's cell phone calls....

"Hi Ricky, it's CC, how's it going?"

"CC! Hey, long time no talk babe," said Ricky Monaghan, the ne're-do-well son of billionaire, Richard Merrill Monaghan Sr. The dad happened to own, among other things, a controlling interest in *Dial "M"* modeling agency, a profitable business connected with his numerous clothing manufacturing businesses and brand labels across the globe. The good looking, young Ricky was the notional head of the company's U.S. operations, but his position was more of a figurehead than a real CEO. He frequently attended haute couture fashion shows as a company representative—where he made a point of bagging a model or two off the catwalk just for the fun of it. CC was one of those catches a couple of years back at a fashion event in L.A.

"I was hoping that maybe we could get together sometime," she ventured anxiously.

"Business or pleasure?"

"Business," she replied and then added, "maybe a bit of both."

"But I thought you got married a while ago," said Ricky, "to some honcho at Homeland Security or something."

"FBI actually," she replied in a saucy tone, "and he's the Director."

"Well, what's the deal then, his dick not big enough?" he chided her.

"His dick's actually pretty good for an old guy," she replied. "But no one I've ever met could match the infamous rod of Slick Rick, as you well know."

"Countless chicks can vouch for that," he replied grinning from ear to ear. "What's a good time to meet up?"

The phone logs revealed that a rendezvous was scheduled for the following weekend at the Washington Ritz Carleton when, coincidentally, the Director would be at a G-8 security conference in Geneva. Wow, that information would go over like a ton of bricks with Clinton George III.

CHAPTER 101

Sure Shot

Pearce returned to the Cayenne satisfied that he had spotted most of the FBI agents in the vicinity, but incapacitating them without alerting the rest was not in the cards. He had counted eight and he figured probably another three or four could be somewhere, probably already in the Lofts building in case trouble spilled inside. It would not be possible to take them all out in a fire fight, particularly since the D.C. police response in an upscale neighborhood like Capitol Hill would be relatively quick. Instead, he methodically packed most of the ordnance into one of the large duffle bags and lifted it out of the vehicle. He would carry it to the top of the four-story low rise across the street from the Lofts. It was an older building equipped with sliding metal stairs on the backside for emergency exit and in this case, entrance to the roof top. The stairs swung down easily with the pull of the release lever at the bottom of each story. Lugging the heavy bag up four flights of stairs without making any noise was a bit tricky.

When he got to the top he was definitely breathing hard. Quietly and efficiently he began assembling and laying out the weaponry. The M136 AT-4 rocket launcher was first. He completed the remainder of the eleven pre-fire checks, pulled the transport safety pin and flipped the cocking lever off the SAFE position. The sights popped up when he removed the sight covers. Well inside the weapon's three-hundred-yard effective range, hitting stationary SUV in the middle of the convoy would be a fairly easy shot. Placing the launcher gently on its side, he snapped a night scope on the M-16 and laid out a half-dozen clips. It was not a long-distance sniper rifle by any means, but its six hundred-yard effective kill range would be plenty for this encounter. Grenades were already clipped to his utility belt and the Glock holstered. He lifted the launcher off the ground and placed it over his right shoulder, finding the idling Suburban in the middle in the sights. At nine hundred fifty feet per second, the fin-stabilized projectile equipped with a HEAT warhead would reach the Suburban in less than a second and blast through its frame like it was papier mâché. He checked the big luminous numbers on the Cobra—11:15. His right index finger gently caressed the trigger. The Z-30 rang!

CHAPTER 102

Springing the Trap

"Everything's in place, sir," reported Tom Conroy from his post two blocks from the Lofts in the mobile FBI operations command center, a converted Mercedes Sprinter van.

"Any sign of *the guy*?" asked the Director.

"Not a whiff yet, but I'll give you two-to-one odds he shows," offered agent Conroy, taking a swig of hot coffee from his thermos as he sat at the small bank of monitors in the back of the Mercedes van. "If you want to bet that is." The Fibbies had recently upgraded their mobile command center in D.C. from the stereotypical oversized GM cargo van to the Sprinter series, figuring that criminals would not associate the high-end van with a surveillance vehicle. It did not fool Pearce for a second.

"I'm not sure what his connection is with the B.C. lawyer, but I'm sure he's pissed that we tried to double cross him," said Conroy. "I'm betting he shows up here with a pretty big hard on."

A couple of miles away at the top of FBI headquarters, George III took a drag on a *Fat Robusto* (Jenna had a standing order to make sure that a half a dozen boxes got flown in directly from the manufacturer the minute he finished the last one). "That's a bit harsh, Tom," he replied with pretended defensiveness. "I wouldn't say that we tried to double cross him."

"How do you figure that sir?" asked Conroy incredulous, but trying to be as respectful as possible. "I was in your office when you guaranteed her safe passage back to Canada and promised not to spy on or surveil her once she got there." He shifted in his seat uncomfortably, knowing that his job was on the line if he misspoke. "As soon as she landed there was a tail on her with orders to bring her back. I could see how *the guy* could conceivably construe that as a double cross, sir."

The Director sighed and said, "Look Tom, if you want to split hairs, she did in fact safely arrive in Canada and we did not spy on or surveil her once she was there—we just decided to escort her back."

"Oh."

"We kept our end of the bargain to a tee—no harm, no foul," said Clinton trying hard to convince himself that he was indeed, an honorable man. "It's not my fault that she didn't insist on a guarantee that we wouldn't immediately retrieve her," he said. "After all she's the lawyer, right?"

"Of course, sir," replied Tom Conroy. "But sir, if she had asked, would you have made that guarantee?"

"Of course, I would have Tom. *The guy* had kidnapped my wife for god's sake. I would have agreed to anything!" exclaimed the Director, "and then naturally reneged at the first opportunity!"

Tom wisely held his tongue.

"By the way, what's the lawyer's medical status? Is she going to make it?" asked the Director casually.

"Funny you should ask sir," said Tom. "I just got a text from our guy at the university hospital that she's out of the O.R. and expected to recover, but it's not certain to what extent."

"Too bad," said the Director, "I wouldn't have minded to see that snotty little bitch kick the bucket—even though she had a pretty decent ass if I do say so."

"Well we could still take her out at the hospital," offered Conroy.

"No, there's too much scrutiny at the moment for that. Besides, I still want to finish the interrogation with Patel's new truth serum once she's back on her feet." "Here's what you do Tom," said the Director. "If we don't bag *the guy* tonight, have Wyatt's contacts plant some dope in her apartment and tip off the cops. I want to see her disbarred and disgraced, so when we grab her again, no one will notice or even care."

"That's absolutely brilliant, sir. Either we finish this tonight or we pick up where we left off before *the guy*, kidnapped your wife," said Conroy.

"That's why I get paid the big bucks Tom," said Clinton George III as he stubbed out the remainder of the expensive cigar in the Merlot ashtray that could double as a boat anchor.

CHAPTER 103

Payback

Pearce heard the news not long after Conroy did. He was immeasurably relieved and thanked the gods of war that Kiara did not become the first casualty of their campaign for animals the world over. However, it was clear to him that the Director need some further persuasion. Rafa had briefed him on the intercepted phone messages including CC's proposed indiscretion—no wonder she's suddenly expendable, thought Pearce.

"But get this," declared Rafa, "she's a vegan!"

"What?"

"Yeah, apparently she thought that it was easier to starve herself, as models are wont to do, on a vegan diet."

"How long?"

"About three or four years," answered Rafa. "She told Ricky that the vegan diet kept her on the catwalk well past the industry's usual expiry date for models."

"I'll be damned," exclaimed KJ. "Another example of how economic necessity can result in positive social consequences, albeit for but a single person."

"But lots of animals," added Rafa.

"Right you are," said KJ.

"What's the plan now?"

"Well, K is going to live so they will also," said Pearce, "but it's time to show the Director that it's not a good idea to renege on a promise to us." He scanned the area with the night scope and noticed that the vehicles had turned off their engines. The doors on the front and rear vehicles opened and four agents debarked from each vehicle, cautiously scanning the area and gingerly moving about as if walking in a mine field. When it seemed to them that the coast was clear, they signaled the middle vehicle and CC was escorted out via the rear passenger door accompanied by two more agents. The street was basically deserted but several of the agents had their handguns drawn, although partially concealed. No movement was evident from the other agents that Pearce had earlier spotted. CC was shuffled into the expansive foyer of the building literally surrounded by ten FBI agents. The doorman was obviously aware that the residents on the penthouse floor were VIPs of some kind so he said nothing and simply ushered everyone in. Besides, ten serious looking guys with ear mikes waiving handguns had a way of intimidating the help.

Pearce squeezed the trigger on the M136 AT-4 and the empty Suburban in the middle of the convoy vaporized in a gigantic ball of fire. The front and rear vehicles were momentarily lifted off the ground by the blast, their windows blown out by the shock wave which went right through the front door of the Lofts, shattering the glass in the foyer. Everybody in the building hit the ground instinctively. The remains of the Suburban were engulfed in flames and smoke. Guns drawn the Fibbies in the woodwork began to cautiously creep forwards, not knowing from where the blast had originated. Two agents in the Lofts hustled CC up the elevator and the other eight attempted to ascertain the whereabouts of—well, it had to be *the guy.* But Pearce was already half way down the back of the building and moving quickly. His mission here was over and he was now on his way for a rendezvous with the Director. Sirens started wailing in the distance. Tossing the duffle bag in the back seat with the other, he jumped into the Cayenne and gunned the engine. The black wraith sped off into the night without a trace.

"Can you pinpoint the whereabouts of that prick?"

"Working on it now," replied Rafa. The Cayenne was rapidly putting distance between Pearce and the carnage he had just caused. More was to come however—a lot more. "Just about got it. A couple of more triangulations and …. Bingo! Got him. He's still at the FBI headquarters, trying to call Corinne."

"Doubtless playing the role of the concerned husband, seeing as her ride just got blown up," commented Pearce. He turned onto Pennsylvania Avenue heading North West towards the FBI building.

CHAPTER 104

Hunter or Hunted?

"Tell me what the hell just happened?" shouted the Director into the phone. When no immediate reply was forthcoming Clinton III slammed down the phone so hard he broke the Verizon's handset in half. "Jenna, get me another goddamned telephone!" he shouted out the door of his office. He grabbed his Blackberry Priv from his coat pocket and speed dialed Conroy. "Talk to me Conroy and I mean this fucking second!"

"Sorry I couldn't answer right away," exclaimed the senior FBI field agent. "The middle vehicle in the convoy just exploded!" He paused a second to catch his breath. "It's basically a ball of fire and smoke now and the other two vehicles are also damaged," he continued to report.

"Was CC in it?"

"No, thank God," replied Conroy.

"Are you certain?" queried the Director. "The windows are smoked so how do you know?"

"Sir, as usual *the guy*, at least we assume that it was him, waited until everyone piled out of all three vehicles and made it into the Lofts. Then he blew up the convoy, probably with an RPG or maybe an LAW."

"Fuck!" swore the Director. "Where in the name of Jesus, Mary and Joseph is he getting this shit from?" He was not sure if he was going to throw the Priv against the wall or tear his hair out—it was a coin toss. "Well, where in Christ is *the guy* now? Is anybody at least chasing him?"

"No one knows where the rocket came from sir," said Conroy. "Everybody is laying low waiting for the next one to hit which will likely happen as soon as the first agent makes a move." The Director grimaced at his end—déjà vu. "Sir, this feels just like the Great Bear Rainforest strike in Canada. Everybody's pinned down, afraid to move. Whatever he used packed one hell of a wallop!" said Conroy.

"Where is my wife now?" demanded the Director, changing the subject lest he explode with frustration.

"She's been taken up to your penthouse, sir, by several agents. Fortunately, she was not harmed in the blast."

"Secure the area. Back the local cops off!" he commanded. "Tell them it's FBI business and don't take any crap from them. I'm sending a dozen more agents now and I'm coming down there myself soon."

"But is that wise, sir?" stammered Tom Conroy. "I mean, *the guy* could still be here, maybe waiting for you to show!" "Not likely Tom. That chicken shit bastard is long gone." "Why would you assume that Mr. Director?" asked agent Conroy.

"*Hit and git!*" replied the Director.

"What?"

"*Hit* like a fucking sledgehammer and then *git* the hell out of there as fast as you can!" It's a maneuver of guerilla warfare used when one side is seriously out gunned and entirely over matched. We saw it all the time in Nam." The Vietnam war was before Conroy's time, but he remembered that the Director was a veteran of some stature—two tours of duty and two medals for bravery and a slight limp in his left leg to show for it. "I'll be there inside of thirty minutes," said the Director and then hung up. By force of habit, he slid on his shoulder holster and grabbed his Colt .45 out of his desk drawer—standard Bureau issue. He waived off the escort offered by the dozen or so agents assembling to leave for the Lofts, instead riding his private elevator down to the secured parking area four floors beneath the building. His black Maserati Ghibli S Q4 sedan was parked beside the elevator in his "Reserved for the Director" spot. The Ghibli sported vanity plates which read "Honcho." They might as well have said "big dick," but he didn't give a damn. He was the boss and he made damn certain that everyone knew it.

Punching the starter button, all four hundred ponies woke up at the same time with a low, silky, Euro growl that always invigorated him -none of that rumbling American V-8 garbage that sounded like some lowly pick-up truck on steroids. No, the Ghibli's turbo V-6 had that Jaguar *purr*, but with far superior Italian styling in his humble opinion. He blew out of the parkade like a bat out of hell and screeched to a stop at the security gate, as it quietly slid open. The guard tipped the bill of his hat as the Director briefly glanced his way. He punched the GPS which connected instantly via Bluetooth connection to his *Priv*. This time CC picked up on the first ring. "Hey baby, it's me," he said reassuringly. "How're you holding up?"

"Holy mother of God, Clinton, I'm so glad you called! I'm fucking scared to death! I can hardly believe that I was in the van just a few seconds before it blew up!" She was crying and her voice trembling almost uncontrollably.

"It's going to be okay now, CC, I'm on the way."

"Please hurry," she implored. "I need you here this minute!"

"You got it," he replied and hung up. She told the agent on scene to pour her another drink to calm her nerves.

"I'm going to fuck that bastard over good for terrorizing CC," thought Clinton. "I mean, how low can you get, going after another guy's wife for God's sake?" forgetting momentarily that he had used her to lure *the guy* out of hiding. Her potential infidelity was pushed to the back of his mind as he focused solely on nailing this vigilante menace, which by the way, would pretty much guarantee him a re-appointment for another five years, probably with a fat raise to boot. He could see the headline in the Washington Post: "Clinton George III, *the guy* who bagged *the guy!*" Maybe he would be Time magazine's *Man of the Year!* The possibilities for recognition were endless! In addition, he would draw the coveted assignment of keeping a distraught CC warm and cozy tonight. Mega bonus! Doubtless she would be so grateful for his manly, calming presence on the home front that there would be some serious pay back sex. That was the second-best kind available after honeymoon sex as every married stud knew for a fact. Even though he was still totally pissed at the thought of her planning a roll in the hay with that dildo Ricky Monaghan, he was still incredibly attracted to her still *eight out of ten* looks and that slim, tight ass was to die for. He made a mental note to have a few of his agents pay a visit to Ricky for little heart to heart. The night was appearing promising indeed—so promising in fact that Clinton George III also forgot his normal safety protocols. The ventilated disc brakes smoothly hauled the four thousand pound Ghibli down from almost seventy miles per hour to a dead stop at the red light at the intersection where Independence Avenue turned into Pennsylvania.

The traffic light was a full sixty seconds and before it turned green, the rear door of the car opened and *the guy* slid into the back seat. Oddly, the first thing that popped into the Director's mind was

"What kind of a dumb fuck drives around in D.C. late at night with the car doors unlocked?" The barrel of the silenced Glock found the back of the Director's neck followed by the crisp command to "turn the rearview mirror down and drive." Rafa had plotted George III's route toward the Lofts and found the intersection in question which had the longest stop lights. Pearce had parked the Cayenne on Second Street S.E. He then waited behind a bus shack at the lights on Independence and Second. Luck was with him as the Director had decided not to run the light despite the late hour and light traffic. Pearce had donned his Aviators and the black SEALS baseball cap, so if the Director happened to catch a glimpse of him it wouldn't do much good, especially at this time of night.

"Take a right here," directed Pearce and the Ghibli made the turn onto Second Street. "Pull in behind that Porsche." When the Ghibli came to a halt the Director slipped the silky-smooth transmission into park. "Keep both hands on the wheel," ordered Pearce as he reached over the Director's shoulder and extracted the Colt from under his left armpit and the Priv from his jacket pocket. "Now pull out," he told Clinton, settling back in the rear seat but the Glock still resting on the Director's shoulder pointing toward his head.

"Where are we going?"

"Arlington National," said Pearce.

"The cemetery?" queried the Director suspiciously.

"That's right."

"Why are we going there?"

"I'll ask the questions Clinton and you answer them or...." said Pearce authoritatively.

"Or what?"

"Or you won't leave this vehicle alive," stated Pearce factually. The Director swung the Ghibli back onto Independence heading west. Traffic was light and the car quickly zoomed passed by the Library of Congress and the U.S. Capitol. Pearce removed the battery from the Priv and then threw the phone out the back window. No need in allowing anyone else to track the Director via his cell phone. On the right, the Smithsonian National Air and Space Museum literally flew by.

"Slow down!" commanded Pearce. The Ghibli dropped from sixty-five to forty and continued unimpeded by traffic past the 9th, 12th and 14th street intersections and then the U.S. National Holocaust Museum on the left. D.C. had by far the best array of first rate museums anywhere, seventy-eight at last count, many of which would take full day or two to view, particularly the seventeen Smithsonian museums. Pearce however was in no mood for sightseeing tonight and kept his focus on the Director, alert for any sign of treachery or trickery from the cunning bastard. You don't get to be the head of the FBI by playing by the rules. They continued on Independence swinging around the Tidal Basin and onto Ohio Drive SW. The Director was profusely sweating and when he tried to reach for the AC on the dash he got a sharp rap in the temple with the barrel of the Glock.

"Keep your hands on the wheel," he was told in no uncertain terms.

"Just trying to turn on the air conditioning," the Director said.

"You're not going to need AC where you're going," replied Pearce.

"Oh fuck," thought Clinton, remembering their destination. The Ghibli swung past the Korean War Veterans Memorial and continued on Ohio Drive as it turned northwards. They passed under the Arlington Memorial Bridge and followed the traffic loop which would land them squarely on the historic bridge. The Arlington Memorial Bridge was constructed in 1932 and thereafter placed under the auspices of the National Parks Service. Due to systemic funding cuts over the years, the landmark bridge has become one of the nearly fifty-nine thousand bridges in the U.S. that are structurally deficient. With a quarter billion-dollar upgrade on hold, it was scheduled to close for good in 2021 and the sixty thousand odd vehicles a day which passed over it would just have to look for another crossing when that happened. The Ghibli looped past the Lincoln Memorial and then entered the six-lane bridge in the curb lane.

"Slow down and pull over," ordered Pearce at about the half way mark. "And put the safety flashers on." George III complied. "Why did you double cross the lawyer, Kiara Davies?"

"I didn't," he replied. "I simply agreed that …Aaaghhhh!" yelled the Director as he received another smack on the side of his head with the Glock.

"I know what you agreed," said Pearce. "The next time you even think of lying I'll blow your fucking head off!"

"Okay, okay," the Director said. He was not used to being interrogated.

"Answer my question!" demanded Pearce.

"Look, can I be frank?" asked the Director.

"Your life depends on being frank," answered Pearce coolly. A couple of vehicles whooshed passed by them on the bridge, none thinking to stop to provide a hand at this late hour.

"You kidnapped my goddamned wife for Christ's sake," he explained. "I'm not going to take that shit lying down."

"You got her back in one piece, didn't you?"

"Just barely," he replied. "You blew up the fucking convoy she was riding in!"

"That was after your agents nearly killed the lawyer by running her cab off a pier back in Canada," Pearce replied testily. His stone-cold eyes bored into the back of the Director's head. "Our part of the bargain was met when your wife was dropped off safe and sound at the Ellipse Circle where she was picked up by your men," Pearce continued. "Then you decided to renege on your so-called ironclad agreement with the lawyer, remember the one that *the Director of the FBI never breaks, going all the way back to J. Edgar.*"

"How the fuck do you even know about that?" asked Clinton somewhat defensively.

Pearce delivered a hammer fist strike to the right side of the Director's neck. Searing pain shot up through Clinton's neck and shoulder almost causing him to black out. "I ask the questions," Pearce reminded him. Pearce caught a sudden glimpse of the flashing red and blue lights in the side view mirror. The black and white Dodge Charger had pulled to a stop about ten feet behind the Ghibli and a police officer was opening the driver's side door of the cruiser. His partner was typing something on the car's dashboard mounted computer in the meantime. Pearce heard the heavy door of the cruiser close with a solid thunk and the officer's boots walking on the asphalt toward the Ghibli. His left hand held a flashlight pointing at the driver's door. His right hand was holding a service revolver.

"Stay in the vehicle!" the cop ordered. "And put both of your hands on the wheel where I can see them!" As the windows were tinted dark, the cop could not tell whether there were any other occupants in the low slung, Italian sports sedan.

"Get rid of him!" commanded Pearce from the back seat. "Or there will be three casualties in the next ten seconds—and you'll be the first." A seagull flew over the car and pooped on the windshield.

Hopefully not a sign of how this scene was going to play out, the Director mused.

CHAPTER 105

It's Not How Hard You Can Hit …

S he still looked like a cover girl, hospital gown, bruises and all. Long, golden locks covered the pillow. Kiara's clear blue eyes were fixed on Rafa Matus.

"Hey, the doc says you are going to be okay!" exclaimed Rafa, moving in to give her a gentle hug. Instead of reciprocating in kind, she sat up and grabbed Rafa in a bear hug, almost pulling him off of his feet. That did, however, cause her to seriously grimace in pain.

"Whoa," cautioned Dr. Matus, "you have to take it easy girl. You don't want to pull a stitch or something!"

"That's the least of my worries," she said as she gingerly laid her head back on the pillow to stop the room from spinning. "How's the third musketeer?"

"KJ's paying the Director a friendly visit as we speak," replied Rafa making sure that all the other visitors were well out of ear shot. "That reminds me, he should be checking in any minute now."

"I hope he's being careful," Kiara said. "The Director's a real snake in the grass."

"Careful's his middle name," Rafa responded, "except where you're concerned," he added. "When he heard what happened to you he temporarily lost it and almost got himself killed."

"Oh my God! What did he do?"

Rafa explained the near catastrophe at the Lofts and that his conversation with Pearce had changed the outcome of the evening for the better. With a little prompting he went on to elaborate about how KJ's offhanded suggestion to hack CC's phone had lead him to the whereabouts and eventual capture of the Director.

"It's a good thing that you're so smart, Rafa," she said squeezing his hand.

"Smart, maybe," he conceded, "but not brave in the field like you and KJ. I sit behind a computer screen in the safety of my office or apartment while you guys are out risking your necks. It just doesn't seem right."

"Hey, knock it off," she said. "You're just as brave as any of us. You know we're all up the proverbial shit creek without a paddle if we get caught—and that includes you Mr. Hacker behind the computer screen."

He felt his cheeks get hot.

"If anything happened to either of you, I'm sure that I'd lose it too."

"Ditto, counselor," Rafa replied and added, "One for all and all for one!"

"I'll drink to that." Kiara raised the ubiquitous glass of apple juice which every patient in the world is given during their hospital stay. As Rafa lifted his paper cup of water to join in the toast, his Z-30 rang. It was *the guy*!

"Just checking in," said Pearce. "How's K doing?"

"I'll let her tell you herself," answered a gleeful Rafa, handing the phone to Kiara. She was still pretty weak from the bear hug that she had dished out to Rafa, but she sat up and tried to sound as jubilant as possible for KJ's benefit.

"I'll be ready to report for duty before you can blink twice soldier!" she said.

He was beside himself with joy to hear her voice, but replied in a stern voice. "Not damned likely on my watch, counselor! You will rest for as long as it takes before you are cleared for active duty and then, you will provide legal, logistical and operational support from the sidelines—NOT the field of battle. Understood?"

"Yes boss," she replied, starting to lose a bit of steam again. "This *Jason Bourne* stuff definitely reads better than it lives."

"I couldn't agree with you more," said Pearce, relieved that she had not gotten hooked on the adrenaline rush that often accompanies dangerous fieldwork.

"But now that the Fibbies know who I am, won't they try to spy on me or bring me back for more interrogation even if I'm on the sidelines?" she asked anxiously.

"I'm working on that," he replied. "I've got the Director standing on the edge of the Arlington Memorial Bridge right now, pondering that question."

"Are you kidding?"

"I'm not kidding, but I've got to go before he decides to do something dumb," he said.

"I hear you," she replied.

"One last thing before I sign off," said Pearce. "You don't *have to* report back for duty, you know that, don't you?" From the passenger seat of the Ghibli, he kept one eye on the Director. He was shuffling from side to side near the bridge railing, not sure if he should stay put or try to make a run for it. Pearce continued. "You've made an immeasurable contribution to this campaign—far more than I could have ever asked for. So if you decide to choose not to …"

Kiara cut him off in mid-sentence. "Listen to me," she said firmly, "because we are *never, ever* going to have this conversation again." A sliver of steel returned to her voice. "It's not how hard you can hit," propping herself up on her elbow with one hand and clenching her other hand into a fist. "It's how hard you can *get hit* and still get up!" she added paraphrasing Rocky Balboa. "And believe me, I'm damned well getting up! Is *that* understood?"

Pearce swallowed to clear a lump in his throat and gruffly said, "Understood, *loud and clear!*" and then tapped *end call* icon.

CHAPTER 106

Is there a Director in the House?

"You want to take this?" he asked his partner.

"Nah, I'll run the plates, you take a look," said corporal Pete McManus from the passenger seat. He was a veteran policeman of eleven years and had stopped thousands of vehicles in that time span, so he didn't exactly need the practice. Officer Stevens on the other hand, was in his sophomore year as a cop and had maybe twenty stops under his belt. As Stevens was opening the driver's door McManus added, "It's probably just some rich asshole getting a blowjob from his intern. I mean, that's a hundred-thousand-dollar car and this is D.C. right?"

"Yeah, but does he have to stop in the middle of the bridge to get one?" The inexperienced cop cautiously approached the idling black Maserati with his flashlight in his left hand and his Sig Sauer P226 nine mil in his right hand both pointed at the window of the vehicle. Clinton had already rolled down the power window of the driver's door. His hands were on the burnished hardwood steering wheel. His white shirt was soaked with sweat under his arm pits and down his back. He knew that one wrong move and he would end up dead, not to mention the two cops. The policeman came up beside the window and shone the light in the Director's face and pointed the Sig right at his head. A quick flick of his wrist and the powerful beam jumped around the front seat. No mistress or girlfriend was under the steering wheel or anywhere else for that matter.

Okay, no broad. Then what's the story? "Now with your left hand you are going to take out your license and registration and hand them to me out the window. Do you understand?" said the cop slowly and deliberately.

"Look here, officer," said the Director in an exasperated tone, "I'm the..."

"Shut up!" commanded the cop. "I don't give a crap if you are J.

Edgar Hoover re-incarnated! You are going to give me your license and registration NOW!" Sensing that the cop was both inexperienced and a bit nervous, Clinton gritted his teeth and slowly and carefully reached into his suit jacket pocket and extracted his license from his breast pocket. No use spooking the kid and getting everyone killed. "Registration is in the glove box. Okay to open it?" said the Director.

"Just make sure that I can see your hand all the way," said the officer, "and take it out nice and slow."

Clinton gingerly removed the registration papers and handed them to the officer who took them with his left hand, still holding the flashlight. "Can you get that light out of my face?" said Clinton "and just listen to what I have to say for a second?"

The cop ignored his request and quickly scanned the license and registration. "Why is your vehicle stopped on the bridge?" the cop demanded, the mag-light still shining in the Director's face, nearly blinding him. Clinton took a deep breath and rubbed his forehead. He was having a hard enough time being ordered around by *the guy* lying on the floor in the back seat, but by a fucking traffic cop? He snapped. "It's none of your goddamned business why I'm stopped on this bridge asshole! I'm the fucking Director of the FBI and unless you want your ass busted down to meter maid duty you'd better get that fucking light out of my face and holster your weapon!"

Taken aback and not entirely convinced, the near-rookie cop replied, "Sorry, but I'm from Missouri, pops. I'll believe it when I see it. *Capice?*" He heard the door slam on the police cruiser and McManus came up from behind, with no gun drawn nor flashlight in sight. Not a good sign. He whispered something into the first cop's ear.

"Really?"

"Really."

"Holy fuck!" said the sophomore policeman. The flashlight went out and the Sig found its way into his holster instantly. He stepped back to the driver's door of the Ghibli and leaned down. "I am sorry to have disturbed you *sir!* We'll be on our way."

"No you won't dickhead!" snapped George III. "Give me your name and badge number *NOW!*"

The cop looked like he was going to shit himself. "Johnny Stevens, sir," he stammered, suddenly no longer in command. "I mean, officer Jonathan Edward Stevens, Metro D.C. police badge 11394."

"Can you read Stevens?" asked the Director sarcastically, his elbow now draped over the side of the car door.

"Sir?"

"I said can you fucking read?"

"Yes sir, I can read, sir!" He stood at attention as if he was addressing his C/O.

"Step to the front of the car and read what the license plate says," ordered George III.

"I remember what it says sir," replied the cop.

"And what does it say officer?"

"It says *HONCHO*, sir," he replied.

"And do you know what that word means, patrolman Stevens?" asked George III as if addressing a preschooler.

"Yes sir. It means the big boss, which would be you, sir."

"Fucking right, that would be me and don't ever forget it!" exclaimed the Director.

Stevens remained standing at attention, hands by his sides and said nothing. He wondered whose dumb idea it was to pull up behind the Maserati in the first place, and then remembered that it was his. McManus wanted no part in this scene and had done an *exit stage left* back to the cruiser as soon as he told Stevens who owned the Ghibli. A native Washingtonian, he was well aware of the Director's reputation as someone you never want to mess with.

"You got a handkerchief Stevens?" the Director asked.

"Ummm, let me see," replied the young cop, somewhat perplexed at the request, but checking his pockets diligently.

"Yes sir, I have one," fishing out a fresh, white kerchief out of the breast pocket of his uniform.

"Wipe the bird shit off my windshield and then get the fuck out of here!"

CHAPTER 107

The End of the Line

The black Maserati remained idling with its flashers blinking while the police cruiser pulled out from behind it, the two cops relieved to be still employed.

"Good job, Clinton," said Pearce. "If I didn't know better I'd think that you had some management experience."

"Fuck you, asshole," replied the Director, now feeling a bit cockier, although his neck and shoulder were still throbbing from the punch.

Continuing where he left off Pearce asked, "Now how are you going to convince me that you won't try to render the lawyer again or spy on her in Canada?"

"I'm not," replied the Director.

"Do you want to keep on living?" asked Pearce casually.

"Yeah."

"Then you better change your answer or you won't be much longer," answered Pearce.

Pondering his precarious predicament for couple of seconds, the Director decided to roll the dice and go for it. "You don't scare me Mr. hot shot Green Beret or whatever the fuck you are," Clinton replied, gaining some momentum. "I'm going to grab that smartass lawyer the first chance I get and interrogate the shit out of her at Quantico until she rats you out!"

"Really?" said Pearce.

"And once I know who you are I'm going to track you and your band of animal's rights vigilantes down and make sure that you spend the rest of your miserable lives in an eight by ten in a supermax prison."

"Do you have any Valium?" asked Pearce unexpectedly.

"What?"

"Valium. Do you have any?" asked Pearce again.

"What the hell do you want Valium for?"

"To calm my nerves, you are scaring me to death," replied Pearce.

"Hah, hah, big joke" replied the Director, still trying for a defiant tone but not quite pulling it off.

"Listen Jack, when I am through with you …" and then he felt the barrel of the Glock pressing into the back of his neck.

"Get out of the car," ordered Pearce. "And walk to the railing."

Clinton reluctantly opened the car door and eased himself out of the low slung sedan. The bravado was waning, but he still made the effort. "I know that you're not going to kill me because if you do …"

"Walk!" commanded Pearce.

Clinton walked over to the railing as if in slow motion, not sure if he should keep talking, but nerves got the better of him and he continued chattering non-stop. "You'll lose all public sympathy you prick. And then the people will turn on you like a pack of wolves! In fact, it wouldn't surprise me if your own band of miscreants turned you in. You know it's a *big goddamned deal* to off the Director of the FBI …" As he reached the railing he risked the tiniest glance back toward the blackness inside the Ghibli. The back window was rolled down and -Jesus, *the guy* was on his cell phone talking to someone, completely ignoring his dire warnings. The barrel of the Glock was resting on the bottom of the open window of the Ghibli, but pointing right at him.

"Make a run for it or jump?" wondered Clinton, moving side to side on the balls of his feet, trying to figure out his next move. It was slowly dawning on him that he was probably not going to make it off the bridge alive—no grandiose headlines, no renewal of his term as Director and last but not least, no CC in the sack tonight, *even if she was a conniving, gold digging bitch.* A combination of fear and despair washed over him. This could actually be *it* for Clinton George III, the Director of the Federal Bureau of Investigation. Finis, done, over—full stop! He had to make a serious effort not to shit his pants on the spot. Fuck me with a broom handle! That would be an embarrassing way for the head of the FBI to go out, straining to constrict his sphincter muscles. What in the hell should he do? Run and get shot in the back? Or jump and probably drown in the ice cold Potomac. Talk about being between a rock and a hard place.

The guy seemed to be done his call and suddenly the back door of the Maserati opened. Wearing dark shades and a black baseball cap, the son of a bitch seemed to move toward him like a cat. He wasn't sure why that observation came to mind with him having maybe ten seconds to live. "Turn around and face the water," commanded Pearce, the silenced Glock dangling menacingly from his right hand. The Director did as he was told, but dammit, one last try was in order. He had to keep *the guy* talking.

"You're bluffing, asshole!" he shouted. "You think I'm scared?"

"I don't care one way or the other," replied Pearce coolly.

Clinton realized there was no traffic noise on the bridge. Where the crap were those sixty-eight-thousand cars a day that passed over this dilapidated piece of shit when you needed them? "I'll tell you what I'm going to do," he said, still trying. "When you let me go— and trust me you will let me go, I'm going to make an executive order that all of the cafeterias in Bureau's fifty-six field offices across the country get rid of any vegetarian or salad entrées on the menu and stock up on meat dishes—hamburgers, hotdogs, Canadian back bacon and chicken wings!"

"Is that supposed to matter to me?" asked Pearce.

"Well you're so goddamned worried about a bunch of worthless animals—which for God's sake were put here solely for the benefit of yours truly along with about seven billion other people," he said, "I figure that I might as well load up your plate so to speak."

"CC is a vegan," replied Pearce. "How do you deal with that?"

"What the hell? Do you have my apartment bugged?" he demanded. "And don't call her CC, that name is reserved for her friends!"

"And old flames apparently," added Pearce for good measure.

"You bastard!" snarled the Director. "You got my friggin phone tapped too?" he said, now completely flummoxed.

"You know I could have let the rocket fly a few seconds sooner and Corinne Cleary George III would be history now," said Pearce.

"Is that supposed to matter to me?" asked the Director, now mimicking Pearce.

"Well, she is your wife," commented Pearce.

"Since you've been spying on my phone messages, you also know that she is a worthless, two-timing cunt!" he snarled, risking a glance back at Pearce.

"You let that rocket go earlier and you would have done me a big favor guy!" Pearce remained impassive and replied. "Now you are getting a taste of what it feels like to be double-crossed, Clinton. Doesn't feel so good, eh?" He unconsciously used the ubiquitous Canadian ending. Pearce continued to stare at the Director's back through the aviators.

"Touché to you, asshole!" replied George III. Looking at the black waters of the Potomac beneath him, the Director figured his slim chances of living out the night hinged on keeping the perp talking. Sooner or later somebody was going to happen along, even at this late hour. As if reading his mind Pearce told him that the conversation was over and shoved the barrel of the Glock into the small of the Director's back.

"Time for you to check out, Clinton," said Pearce matter-of-factly. "Unless you want to provide me with one of those *ironclad guarantees* about laying off the lawyer."

He left the sentence dangling, just like the Director's life.

CHAPTER 108

That's a Wrap

The neighborhood of Clearbrook, British Columbia has the best drinking water *in the world* according to the 26th annual Berkley Springs International Water Tasting event at Berkley Springs, West Virginia. It beat out water samples from eighteen U.S. states, seven Canadian provinces and five foreign countries. The H20 is pumped from the pristine ground water of the one hundred square kilometer Abbotsford-Sumas aquifer and it contains no chlorine, fluoride or other chemicals of any kind. Yet a gallon of the crystal-clear liquid from the two-hundred year-old underground cavern costs less than a tenth of a penny out of your tap, if you happen to live in Clearbrook. Since learning that fact a few years back, Kiara had made it a practice to order huge bottles of the stuff for her own personal consumption in the heart of downtown Vancouver, the second most livable city in the world.

Three tall glasses of the chilled elixir, filled with ice cubes and garnished with lime slices were set down on a silver serving tray in her living room amidst bowls of almonds, walnuts, hulled sunflower seeds and other assorted crunchies and munchies. The three musketeers each grabbed a glass to toast their incredible good fortune thus far in this immense campaign to change the world's view of the billions of other creatures who inhabit the earth in competition with the species *homo sapiens*. Looking somewhat worse for wear, the ever-gorgeous Kiara Davies sat in a Buddha pose on the soft, micro fiber couch, leaning just a bit to her left, but looking happy and content none the less. She was wearing her faded Lucky jeans, a Max Mara white cotton shirt and of course her gift from KJ, the sterling silver Pyrrha necklace, whose motto she now lived by. A long, jagged scar was still partially visible which ran from her neck to below the bold, dolman sleeve covering her left arm. Plastic surgery may or may not ultimately get rid of that. Her left ear would require an operation in the near future to restore her balance and hopefully her hearing in that ear. Time would tell. Still, she considered herself unbelievably fortunate to be alive and sharing a toast with her comrades in arms.

Rafa in his summer whites looked like he could have just stepped off of a lawn tennis court in the nineteen twenties. He also looked elated to be reunited with his friends. Like KJ, he felt immeasurably guilty that Kiara had taken the brunt of the fallout from the campaign so far, while they had both escaped unscathed.

"This is war," KJ had told him. "And you are a digital warrior." Digital warrior! Rafa liked the sound of that. It *resonated.* KJ continued, "*Transform your guilt* into iron—iron resolve to do what you must when the time comes—and sooner or later, regardless of our expertise, planning and skill *that time will come.*"

Rafa took his friend's advice to heart. In fact, he would follow it to his dying day.

Pearce sat in the faux leather armchair next to the glass coffee table, calm and composed on the outside but implacable as a hurricane within. For sure, his team had won the first few rounds. They had the element of surprise and that, combined with superior firepower and penultimate planning had won the day—so far. However, forewarned is forearmed, so the enemy would be much more formidable in the weeks and months ahead. It wasn't inconceivable that one or even all of the musketeers could be killed on this mission. In fact, the odds were stacked against them from the start. But JTF2 thrived on bucking the odds. His two friends had made it clear as the Clearbrook water that both of them were in for the duration. He respected that commitment (if not wisdom) immensely.

"Kiara and Rafa," said KJ, lifting his glass. "I am proud to have you as allies in this monumental campaign to end the reign of *The Invisible Reich.* I have been on the battlefield with valiant, committed soldiers over the years and you are the equal of any of them!"

"Here, here," replied Rafa clinking his glass with KJ's.

"I'll drink to that!" said Kiara. "You know," she continued, her voice trembling a bit, "when I was in that god-awful dungeon in FBI headquarters, just knowing that you guys were out there somewhere looking for me… well … that was the only thing that kept me going."

"Needless to say, I was worried sick," replied Rafa. "But Master Sergeant Kenneth Joseph Ares Pearce here kept us focused on finding you rather than being immobilized by emotion."

"Never forget that, Kiara," reminded KJ. "We will always find you no matter what," downing the balance of the cool liquid, "because we three are connected ...." He left the sentence hanging. Kiara smiled.

Suddenly there was a ping on his Z-30. It was a text from Floriana.

"Passed second year!!! Yeah!!! (smiley face)

"Congrats!" KJ texted back, happy for his friend and dog sitter extraordinaire. He added, "R U up for another year of babysitting the hounds?" (question mark, smiley face) "Wouldn't miss it for the world!" (two smiley faces) KJ texted her back a "thumbs up" symbol.

"Those divas just worship her," commented Kiara.

"Well that's because she spoils them rotten!"

"Like you don't?" asked Rafa incredulously.

"Hey, come on, I try to maintain a firm hand with the dogs," said KJ defensively. Rafa and Kiara burst out laughing hysterically at that absurd statement. The intercom buzzed indicating that the extra-large, oven baked, vegetarian pizza had arrived.

"Grab the beer glasses, Rafa," said KJ as he headed for the door.

CHAPTER 109

Sink or Swim

He hit the frigid waters of the Potomac. The two-point-four-second fall from the bridge allowed the Director's one-hundred-eighty-pound body to reach a speed of 55 mph and generate 23,500 joules of energy upon impact. His legs were spread slightly apart when his groin contacted the water. At that speed, it felt like someone had hit him in the balls with a sledgehammer. Such was the pain that he immediately blacked out. Clinton George III refused to assure Pearce that Kiara Davies would be safe from the clutches of the FBI. In fact, he guaranteed the opposite. Pearce gave the Director the option of being shot or jumping off the Arlington Memorial Bridge.

"You have two seconds to make up your mind," Pearce threatened. "Or I'll do it for you!"

"You'll live to regret this, asshole!" warned the Director.

"One second," Pearce said, raising the Glock. Clinton George III scrambled onto the four-foot concrete railing at the edge of the pedestrian sidewalk. He turned towards Pearce and gave him the finger as he stepped off the railing.

"Fuck off and die you bastard!" were the last words Pearce heard as the Director disappeared from view. Not bothering to watch, Pearce returned to the idling Ghibli, hung a u-ey and headed back into D.C. He didn't much care whether the Director made it or not. If he did live, then he would have to figure that *the guy* would be back to take him out for good if Kiara was rendered again. If he didn't make it, well then, the Director would be the first human casualty in his campaign. Thirty million animals will have perished at the hands of humans this day. If one scumbag died on the other side it wouldn't exactly even the score—but it would be a start.

As it turned out, however, it was Clinton's lucky day (or night, actually). Ron Pyrch and his new bride, Jenny Wong were taking a late-night cruise on the Potomac in Ron's new Bayliner when they heard the splash. It sounded like someone threw a sack of potatoes off the bridge except that there was a sharp scream when the sack hit the water, then dead silence. Ron powered up the boat. Jenny worked the spotlight.

"Jeez," Ron exclaimed, "a body!"

"Probably a suicide attempt," Jenny suggested.

Ron pulled the Bayliner closer and Jenny got hold of the floating body with a long pole fitted with a hook. Together they hauled the nearly lifeless Director out of the water. Jenny, an O.R. nurse, performed CPR while Ron grabbed his cell and called 911 to request an ambulance. He was directed to head to the eastern side of the Arlington Memorial Bridge where paramedics would be arriving soon. A few short minutes later two paramedics waded into the freezing water with a handheld stretcher and Ron and Jenny slowly lowered the Director overboard. As the siren and flashing lights retreated down Ohio Drive, Jenny texted the details of their heroic rescue of a distraught man to her mom.

"First night out on the boat and we saved a guy's life!" she texted as Ron eased the Bayliner back into the river. They would never know that they had saved the Director of the Federal Bureau of Investigation. The ambulance and follow-up emergency room visit would be erased from all public records on orders from the deputy Director, Anna Shallal. It would not be in the interest of national security to reveal that the Director of the Federal Bureau of Investigation had been kidnapped in his own car and forced at gunpoint to jump off the Arlington Memorial Bridge by *the guy*.

CHAPTER 110

Marijuana by Minx

Inaara was ecstatic. No more mink to be electrocuted, bludgeoned to death, skinned alive or imprisoned in tiny cages! Reluctantly, Don Burdenny had been persuaded by his wife to turn the farm into a massive, legalized grow-op to replace the mink farming operation. Although it was almost a toss-up (Don arguing that they had made good money for over twenty years with the business that they had, so why change course?), surprisingly it was Inaara's oafish stepbrother, Dom who tipped the scales.

"Dad, you've got to get with the times," he explained. "Marijuana is the next big thing, so if we get in on the ground floor we'll have a major competitive advantage!" Neither of the *Dreaded D's* had ever smoked a joint, both being way too conservative—and besides that would have been against the law, at least until recently.

Ruby's comprehensive business plan prepared by KPMG indicated that within one to two years, MBM could be making profits in excess of five times that of the mink farm.

"Forget the new house design," Ruby told Don. "I'm going for something way more lavish!"

Don sighed. The profits hadn't even started rolling in and they were already being gobbled up! The home that Ruby and her architect had recently designed was over ten-thousand-square-feet with a six-car garage to boot. The estimated building cost was three hundred a square foot, putting it in the two-point-five-mile range. The newest version would be at least twelve-thousand-square-feet with an Olympic-sized pool, to entertain business contacts and hold fund raisers. Ruby thought it was time that she got into public office—maybe make a difference for animals on the political stage! Inaara was behind her mom one hundred per cent and texted KJ the good news.

"MBM is officially CLOSED FOR BUSINESS!! (smiley face)

414

Marijuana by Minx is coming soon to a theatre near you!! (smiley face)

"That's GREAT!! (smiley face X 2)" Pearce texted back. "Score another one for animals! Good job Inarra!!" he texted (thumbs up sign X 3)

"Thanks!! Will I ever see you again?" (question mark emoticon)

"Bank on it!" Pearce texted back.

She smiled and exited text mode, erasing all prior messages. She was learning.

Don Burdenny however was anything but smiling as he slammed the phone down into its cradle. "Fucking bastards!" he yelled.

"What's up?" asked Ruby.

"I'm going to put a contract out on that piece of shit insurance adjuster from Multi-State!" he replied seething.

"Okay pops, spill it," said Dom, perplexed at the sudden change of atmosphere. Don explained to the family that Multi-State had just finished its investigation concluding that the destruction of their former (in his opinion) palatial home and state-of-the-art minkery were not covered by their insurance policy as "acts of war, insurrection or domestic terrorism were expressly exempted from coverage."

"Who the hell says that it was an act of terrorism?" Dom asked.

"Some rumors put out by those incompetent nitwits at the FBI were trying to link the hunting fiasco up in B.C., Canada to our incident here," Don explained. He searched frantically for Tony Frakes' number on the contacts list in his phone. "I swear to God those asshole insurance companies exist to never pay a claim and yet their premiums just keep going up and up," opined Don gratuitously. "It was arson—plain and simple!" he said as if it was a foregone conclusion, ignoring the fact that most arsonists don't use C-4.

"Just like you said before, pops," said Dom, "that's why everybody hates them!"

"Well, fortunately, Seamor Hobbes LLP has a pretty good record of trashing the likes of Multi-State in court!" said Don, now connecting with Tony's private cell phone. Twenty minutes later, a calmed-down Don explained that Tony thought that the insurer had only a so-so case and that they would likely have a tough time proving that it was a terrorist who destroyed the farm, seeing as no one could definitively say that *the guy* did it.

"The other thing" added Tony, "is that he didn't claim responsibility for the destruction of MBM, as he did in the Great Bear Rainforest. Had he done so, that would have sunk us for sure under the standard policy exclusions."

Feeling a bit better, Don asked Ruby to get out the *coat list* from the wall safe in their hotel suite. He then placed a call to the home phone number U.S. Senator Rostyk Sadownick of the fine state of Nebraska, which was home to Warren Buffett's Berkshire Hathaway Home State Insurance Companies. It was said that Rostyk was on a first-name basis with Buffett, but more importantly he sat on FACI (the Federal Advisory Committee on Insurance) which advised the Federal Insurance Office of the United States. The FIO, established by the Dodd-Frank Act as a division of the Federal Treasury Department, has the authority to monitor all aspects of the insurance sector in the U.S. Rostyk was one of only a handful of people on the *coat list* who received three mink coats—one for his dutiful wife, one for his mistress and one for his senate aide who could handle double-duty when the mistress was indisposed. Even the faintest hint of a possible investigation by FIO into the MBM insurance claim would send those rats at Multi-State scurrying. Combine that with the aggressive offence that Tony Frakes would mount in court and it was a lead pipe cinch that a decent out-of-court settlement could be worked out with those crooks.

"Jesus, but those coats pay dividends," Don said, plunking himself down into the comfy leather couch in the executive, penthouse suite. "But I guess now we'll have to start sending out packages of premium, organic weed instead."

CHAPTER 111

The Director Strikes Back

Even from his hospital bed at the Quantico medical facility, Clinton George III didn't waste a minute ordering that Kiara Davies Esq. be rendered back to the U.S. for further interrogation. No calls to DND or the Canadian government would be made. This was a black ops caper, just like the first one—totally off the books and completely illegal under Canadian and international law. Three experienced FBI agents would break into her apartment, kidnap her again and fly her back to the Bureau's headquarters, where the experimental truth serum would be used on her until she broke. His current thought was: Fuck the consequences if she didn't show up in court. No one could pin this on the Bureau and besides, he was mad as hell for being bullied by *the guy,* not to mention almost being drowned. And to make matters worse, his balls still hurt like hell despite the morphine drip. The gloves were off and he would spare no expense to track this animal rights whacko down and incarcerate him for life!

Agent Jim Palmer was an ex-navy SEAL who had been with the Bureau for just under five years. He would be the muscle of the operation. Norm Wyatt, the silent tall man who first interrogated Kiara was the second agent. He was a big guy and no slouch in the physicality department either. Gladys Frost was along to redeem herself and just *maybe* get back on track for that long-awaited promotion. The trio gained entrance to Kiara's building in a brutally, efficient manner. Gladys walked up to the pizza delivery guy as he got out of his Echo, asking if she could purchase a slice.

"No can do, ma'am," said the teenager. "I got just the full pizzas that were ordered."

"Okay, how about I buy a full one of those you're holding?"

"Not a chance. They were ordered by other customers."

"I'll pay extra," she said, momentarily blocking his path. "You sure you don't want to make an extra twenty bucks?"

"Yeah, I'm sure, now if you could get out of my..." He never finished his sentence as Palmer kicked him in the groin from behind and then spun him around and smashed his face into the bus bench in front of the building. He was out cold. Gladys caught the insulated pizza bag in midair. She donned the shirt and Domino's hat and headed for the front door with the pizzas. Wyatt dragged the kid into the bushes where they took off his shirt and cap. He and Frost stayed in the shadows, waiting for their opportunity. The security guard at the desk noticed the pizza woman and came over to see why she wasn't being buzzed into the building. The damn intercom was probably acting up again. When he opened the door, she stepped forward, pretending to trip on the edge of the carpet. She lost her grip on the pizzas, dropping the bag. A true gentleman, the guard bent over to pick it up and she kneed him in the face, breaking his nose. Palmer leaped out of the woodwork and punched him hard in the mouth with a pair of brass knuckles, breaking the guard's jaw in several places. Wyatt dragged him behind the security desk and scribbled a note on the pad indicating that the guard had gone to the washroom.

The three of them rode the elevator to the 18th floor. Frost strolled to the door of Kiara's condominium and knocked. Palmer stood to the left side of the door out of view with his Smith & Wesson drawn as did Wyatt on the right side. As soon as Davies opened the door they would push their way in, bust her in the chops and haul her ass back to Washington—just like that. No one would be the wiser. They would all pick up some major brownie points with the Director in the process.

Pearce heard the knock and the words, "Domino's Pizza," through the door. Immediately his hackles went up. Nobody had buzzed the intercom and the guy at security desk hadn't called up. Also, he couldn't recall the pizza guy making an announcement like that at the door. He motioned to Kiara and Rafa to be silent and waved them toward the kitchen. Such was his expression, they immediately knew that danger was afoot. Instead of heading into the kitchen Kiara retreated into her bedroom and removed the Beretta Px4 Storm from her nightstand. She snapped in a ten-shot clip loaded with 9mm hollow points. No fucking way she was going to be captured, robbed or assaulted this time. It was uncanny. Pearce's surreally lethal presence somehow grounded her and made her inexplicably calm. She would shoot to kill. Rafa grabbed a wooden rolling pin off the kitchen counter. He was ready to jump into the fray if need be, although his

418

heart was in his mouth. Pearce tiptoed to the vestibule near the door where his Scottevest sports coat and shoulder holster were hanging.

As he slipped them on the door was kicked in by Palmer, catching everyone by surprise. He immediately spotted Kiara, Beretta in hand. Before she could sight it, he got off two shots. Rafa ran out of the kitchen, rolling pin in hand. Seeing Palmer's gun hand go up, he dove in front of Kiara and took both rounds in the chest. The .38 slugs knocked him backwards into the startled litigator. Pearce leapt out of the vestibule and grabbed Palmer's gun hand violently smashing it into the door frame. Palmer's forearm was fractured and the Smith went flying. Intense pain temporarily paralyzed Palmer. Wyatt and Frost barged into the room trying to get a bead on Pearce while scanning the premises for Kiara. Rather than letting go of Palmer's hand, Pearce grabbed his wrist and spun him into Wyatt and Frost bowling them both off their feet. With practiced ease, Pearce slipped the K-bar out of pocket number 23 of his sports jacket and drove it through Palmer's shoulder virtually pinning him to the carpet. Frost however had pulled herself up and was aiming her side arm at Pearce's back. Before she could pull the trigger, her head snapped backwards. A 9mm hollow point hit her square in the cheek blowing off half of her face. She was dead before she hit the floor. Kiara had regained her balance and in a target-shooting stance had squeezed off a single round with cold, calculating precision. Sorry, no promotion this go-round agent Frost.

Losing his side arm when he hit the carpet, Wyatt leapt to his feet. Shoulder first, he launched into Kiara's midriff, sending her flying backwards onto the coffee table. The crystal vase and the water glasses crashed to the floor sending broken glass everywhere. Wyatt landed on top of her, grabbing a shard of glass to stab her with. Watching with horror, Rafa gamely tried to get up but collapsed back into a heap. He could not budge. The feeling had gone out of his legs. His tennis whites were soaked with blood. Pearce drew the Glock but before he could raise the barrel he was tackled from behind by Palmer. By some superhuman effort he had forced himself off the floor, K-bar sticking right through his shoulder. With his right forearm broken and his left shoulder in burning pain, Palmer still managed to get his hand into Pearce's face, trying to gouge his eyes.

Special forces guys are trained to deal with pain and injury every day. The adrenaline rush of battle kept Palmer in the fray, as well. The two soldiers rolled on the floor, each trying to get an opening.

No holds barred, *Krav maga* rules prevailed, *Krav Maga* being the Israeli martial art developed by Imri Litchenfeld, which emphasized neutralization of the enemy by any means possible.

The combatants would bite, gouge, head-butt or anything else to incapacitate, permanently disable or kill the other. Pearce was spotting Palmer a good twenty-five pounds and an inch or two in height. The man was incredibly strong, despite his severe injuries. He shifted his weight, drawing Pearce's head near—he was trying to bite Pearce in the face. Pearce pulled his head back as far as he could and in a deft Aikido move, grabbed the small and ring fingers of Palmer's bad hand and snapped them backwards, breaking both, causing the agent to scream. Pearce elevated his torso, rolling Palmer onto his back. He punched him in the throat, crushing his windpipe. Palmer was dead on the spot. Half by instinct, half by design, Pearce pulled the K-bar out of Palmer's shoulder, yanked his head up by the hair and slit his throat from ear to ear. He dropped Palmer's head like it was garbage, his lifeless body crumpling to the ground.

Instantly Pearce trained his attention on Kiara and Wyatt. "Oh, no!" Wyatt was sitting on top of her, about to force a shard of glass into her eye! Kiara had her hand closed on his wrist trying to hold it away, but Wyatt was much bigger and stronger than her. She would come in second in that contest for sure. Suddenly a potted plant hit Wyatt in the side of the head, the clay shattering and dirt flying. Rafa had used up his last iota of strength to pull down a plant from the counter and hurl it at Wyatt. Dazed, Wyatt dropped the shard and fell sideways, allowing Kiara to scramble for the Beretta. Ear still ringing, Wyatt managed to shrug off the blow. He stumbled toward Rafa determined to finish him off.

"You fucking peon!" he snarled. "I'm going to send you back to whatever banana country you came from in a box!" He wobbled some, but kept on his feet. Eyes wide, looking maniacal he lurched toward Rafa. But before he could take another step Kiara fired the Beretta twice from a prone position, shattering his knee with a couple of hollow points. As he fell, a .40 caliber bone cruncher from the Glock hit Wyatt square in the temple killing him instantly. Pearce holstered his gun and raced over to Rafa. Kiara was already holding towels over the wounds to staunch the massive blood loss, but Rafa was not looking so good. He tried to half smile and said, "Good job amigos, we got em', …I think."

"We did," said Kiara. "Thanks to you!"

"Copy that," said KJ. "But we need some medical attention for you stat."

"Grab my phone KJ, it's over on the counter in my purse," said Kiara looking worried. Rafa's face continued to lose color and his eyes were closing.

"Stay with us buddy," said Pearce, "help is on the way!" Kiara took the phone from KJ while he held the blood-soaked towels in place on Rafa's chest. His breathing was slowing rapidly. "I'll make the call," she said, the 911 number already ringing.

"Police emergency line," was the crisp introduction. "How may we help you?"

"I need an ambulance immediately! My friend has been shot twice by intruders and he's bleeding to death, she said breathlessly. "I am at 1807—629 Pacific Boulevard."

"Are you safe? Have the intruders left?" asked the dispatcher.

"They are all dead!" she replied. "Please hurry, my friend is dying!"

"Paramedics are being dispatched from Vancouver Fire Hall no. 8 on Hamilton Street as we speak," said the dispatcher in a calm, efficient voice. Within seconds the twelve-ton Spartan Gladiator rolled out of the fire hall siren blaring and lights flashing. Two experienced paramedics with state-of-the-art emergency equipment would do their damnedest to see to it that Rafa would live to fight another day.

"EMTs will be at your building in approximately four minutes. Please make sure that they have access to the building entrance. VPD is on route as well."

"Thank God," said Kiara. "Do you want me to stay on the line with you?" asked the concerned dispatcher.

"No, I've got to try to stop the bleeding," and she hung up.

Pearce remembered that the security guy downstairs didn't call up. "I've got to make sure that the medics can get into the building K," he said.

"You're right, KJ," she said looking up at Pearce while holding Rafa in her arms, his blood now flowing over her jeans. "Once you've done that, get lost. You can't be found here!"

"But Kiara, what if you or Rafa needs …"

"I've got it KJ, now MOVE!" she said with urgency in her voice. He gave her and his friend an anguished look and then bolted out the door, grabbing the K-bar as he went. She was right of course. He couldn't be found at the scene. As soon as the Fibbies found out that

their three agents were dead it wouldn't take a rocket scientist to figure out that Pearce was *the guy,* once they ran a background check on
him. Leave it to Kiara to concoct some story to explain the presence
of a third player who took out two of the three intruders and then disappeared. He hoped with all his heart that Rafa would pull through.

CHAPTER 112

All's Well that Ends Well – Unless it Doesn't

Tamu's massive head resting on his lap, Pearce sat in an easy chair at *Animal Farm,* anxiously awaiting a call. Paikea was stretched full length and upside down on the couch, her head dangling over the edge. The 70" LED screen was playing *Dr. Strange,* the fall's blockbuster movie based on the Marvel Comic book. It was about a down-and-out surgeon who became the Sorcerer Supreme, defender of the planet Earth against all the dark forces in the Universe. Pearce sighed, feeling something like *Dr. Strange,* only there was no *Ancient One* in his life to offer him guidance and support. The war against animals continued unabated, another thirty million or so non-human souls biting the dust today, just like the day before and the day before that.

He unscrewed the cookie jar on the coffee table, removing a couple of dog biscuits and presto—they vanished instantly. No sorcerer's trick needed for that one. Still, there were a fair number of small victories to celebrate. Rafa had collected a million bucks from the Fibbies in *bitcoins* stored somewhere in a digital wallet, so the war chest was brimming. The B.C. government's grizzly bear trophy hunting season was cancelled, the program in tatters and likely to never return. The disruption of the opening ceremonies at the Great Bear Rainforest had picked up a quarter of a billion hits on YouTube sparking worldwide discussion about trophy hunting from Canada to Africa. Once the insurance litigation ended, MBM would become a massive marijuana grow-op, making people high with weed instead of coats from slaughtered mink.

Inaara had become a vegetarian and despite her young age, a strong ally south of the border. Her activism and determination had inspired her mom, Ruby, to seek political office as an animal's rights advocate in a state which was not exactly animal friendly.

The dental lab at George Regis U had been burned to the ground.

The likes of Jack LaVan had been taken off the streets, sparing a few neighborhood cats and dogs from the nightmare of medical experimentation.

And lastly, the *Humane Farm Practices Amendment Bill* stood a good possibility of being enacted into law, at least partially alleviating the suffering of many factory farmed animals across the U.S. A proverbial drop in the bucket? Maybe, but enough drops falling on a boulder can surely reduce it to sand over time.

Kenneth Joseph Ares Pearce didn't have *that much* time, but with some luck he could turn the drops into a stream and then a river and who knows, maybe someday Niagara Falls.

Suddenly the Z-30 rang, jolting him out of his musings. It was Kiara calling from the hospital. Pearce held his breath and steeled himself ......his heartbeat steady at 55 bpm.

THE END ... (for now)

Acknowledgements

Many thanks to my editor, Sarah Sarai, cover designer Carolyn T., interior formatter, Lin White, beta reader and pre-editor, Len Pazder, best-in-show ally, JE Allan, all my animals – past and present, as well as the many inspirational trailblazers who provided the motivation for me to put pen to paper including, but not limited to John Robbins (author of "Diet for a New America"), Ingrid Newkirk (founder of "PETA") and Nathan Runkle (founder of "Mercy for Animals").

About the Author

Kenneth Pazder is practicing lawyer in Vancouver, British Columbia who lives in White Rock, BC with his two Afghan hounds, Rafa & Spirit and two black cats, Tarot & Chi.

CPSIA information can be obtained
at www.ICGtesting.com
Printed in the USA
BVHW071940071118
532453BV00001B/2/P